She took another glance at the puppy thief holding her Yorkie mix and melted a little bit.

The two of them looked like they belonged on that Instagram account her dancer friends were always going on about—Hot Men and Mutts.

She swallowed. "Look, is there any way we could work this out ourselves before the shelter manager gets involved? The puppy is a gift. Couldn't you just pick out another one? I love that dog. What can I do to change your mind? Anything?"

Surely there was something he wanted, although Chloe couldn't imagine what it might be.

She lifted her chin and looked him directly in his eyes, so he'd know she meant business. No reindeer games.

Make me an offer.

His gaze narrowed and sharpened. For a second or two, he focused on her with such intensity that she forgot how to breathe.

So there is something he wants, after all.

When at last he gave her the answer she'd been waiting for, he didn't crack a smile.

"Marry me."

D1413221

Her Christmas Gift

Annie Claydon & Teri Wilson

Previously published as *Festive Fling with the Single Dad*
and *A Daddy by Christmas*

FEB 1 2 2021

HARLEQUIN MUST♥DOGS

MARTIN COUNTY LIBRARY

If you purchased this book without a cover you should be aware
that this book is stolen property. It was reported as "unsold and
destroyed" to the publisher, and neither the author nor the
publisher has received any payment for this "stripped book."

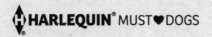

ISBN-13: 978-1-335-23081-2

Recycling programs
for this product may
not exist in your area.

Her Christmas Gift

Copyright © 2020 by Harlequin Books S.A.

Festive Fling with the Single Dad
First published in 2019. This edition published in 2020.
Copyright © 2019 by Annie Claydon

A Daddy by Christmas
First published in 2018. This edition published in 2020.
Copyright © 2018 by Teri Wilson

All rights reserved. No part of this book may be used or reproduced in
any manner whatsoever without written permission except in the case of
brief quotations embodied in critical articles and reviews.

This is a work of fiction. Names, characters, places and incidents
are either the product of the author's imagination or are used fictitiously.
Any resemblance to actual persons, living or dead, businesses,
companies, events or locales is entirely coincidental.

This edition published by arrangement with Harlequin Books S.A.

For questions and comments about the quality of this book,
please contact us at CustomerService@Harlequin.com.

Harlequin Enterprises ULC
22 Adelaide St. West, 40th Floor
Toronto, Ontario M5H 4E3, Canada
www.Harlequin.com

Printed in U.S.A.

Pups That Make miracles

CONTENTS

Cursed with a poor sense of direction and a propensity to read, **Annie Claydon** spent much of her childhood lost in books. A degree in English literature followed by a career in computing didn't lead directly to her perfect job—writing romance for Harlequin—but she has no regrets in taking the scenic route. She lives in London: a city where getting lost can be a joy.

Visit the Author Profile page
at Harlequin.com for more titles.

FESTIVE FLING
WITH THE SINGLE DAD

Annie Claydon

To Charlotte
With grateful thanks

Chapter 1

Up close, he looked even more…

More outdoorsy. Taller and blonder and… Just more.
A two-day beard covered a square jaw, and his mane
of shoulder-length hair was tied at the nape of his neck.
His casual shirt and worn jeans gave the impression of
an off-duty Norse god, and Flora McNeith resisted the
temptation to curtsey. It was slightly over the top as a
greeting for a new neighbour.

'Hi. I'm Flora. From next door.' She gestured towards her own cottage, tugging at Dougal's lead in a
fruitless attempt to get him to sit down for just one moment. 'Welcome to the village.'

He looked a little taken aback when she thrust the
food box, containing half a dozen home-made mince
pies into his hands. It might be more than three weeks
until Christmas, but the lights of the Christmas tree in
the village had already been turned on, and in Flora's
book any time after September was a good time for
mince pies.

'That's very kind.' His voice was very deep, the kind
of tone that befitted the very impressive chest that it

came from. And it appeared that whatever kind of deity Aksel Olson was, language and communication weren't part of his remit. He was regarding her silently.

'I work at the Heatherglen Castle Clinic. I hear that your daughter, Mette, is a patient there.' Maybe if she explained herself a little more, she might get a reaction.

Something flickered in his eyes at the mention of his daughter. Reflective and sparkling, like sunshine over a sheet of ice.

'Are you going to be part of Mette's therapy team?'

Right. That put Flora in her place. Apparently that was the only thing that interested Aksel about her.

'No, I'm a physiotherapist. I gather that your daughter is partially sighted…' Flora bit her tongue. That sounded as if everyone was gossiping about him, which was half-true. The whisper that Mette's father was single had gone around like wildfire amongst the female staff at the clinic. Now that Flora had met Aksel, she understood what the excitement was all about.

'You read the memo, then?' Something like humour flashed in his eyes, and Flora breathed a small sigh of relief. Lyle Sinclair must have told him about the memo.

'Yes. I did.' Every time a new patient was admitted a memo went round, introducing the newest member of the clinic's community and asking every member of staff to welcome them. It was just one of the little things that made the clinic very special.

'Would you like to come in for coffee?' Suddenly he stood back from the door.

'Oh!' Aksel's taciturn manner somehow made the words he did say seem more sincere. 'I shouldn't…

Dougal and I are just getting used to each other and I haven't dared take him anywhere for coffee yet. I'm afraid he'll get over-excited and do some damage.'

Aksel squatted down on his heels, in front of the ten-week-old brindle puppy, his face impassive.

'Hi, there, Dougal.'

Dougal was nosing around the porch, his tail wagging ferociously. At the sound of his name he looked up at Aksel, his odd ears twitching to attention. He circled the porch, to show off his new red fleece dog coat, and Flora stepped over the trailing lead, trying not to get snagged in it. Then Dougal trotted up to Aksel, nosing at his outstretched hand, and decided almost immediately he'd found a new best buddy. Finally, Aksel smiled, stroking the puppy's head.

'I'm sure we'll manage. Why don't you come in?'

Two whole sentences. And the sudden warmth in his eyes was very hard to resist.

'In that case… Thank you.' Flora stepped into the hallway and Dougal tugged on his lead in delight.

He took her coat, looking around the empty hallway as if it was the first time he'd seen it. There was nowhere to hang it and he walked into the kitchen, draping it neatly over the back of one of the chairs that stood around the table. Flipping open a series of empty cupboards, he found some packets of coffee and a small copper kettle, which seemed to be the only provisions he'd brought with him.

Dougal had recovered from his customary two seconds of shyness over being in a new environment and was tugging at the lead again, clearly having seen the young chocolate-coloured Labrador that was sitting watchfully in a dog basket in the far corner of the kitchen. Flora bent down, trying to calm him, and he started to nuzzle at her legs.

'Kari. *Gi labb.*' In response to Aksel's command, the Labrador rose from its bed, trotting towards them, then sitting down and offering her paw to Flora. Flora took it and Kari then started to go through her own *getting-to-know-you* routine with Dougal.

'She's beautiful.' The Labrador was gentle and impressively well trained. 'This is Mette's assistance dog?'

Aksel nodded. 'Kari's staying with me for a while, until Mette settles in. She's not used to having a dog.'

'Part of the programme, up at the clinic, will be getting Mette used to working with Kari. You'll be taking her there when you visit?'

'Yes. I find that the canine therapy centre has some use for me in the mornings, and I'll spend every afternoon with Mette.'

'It's great that you're here to give her all the support she needs.'

He nodded quietly. 'Mette's sight loss is due to an injury in a car accident. Her mother was driving, and she was killed.'

Flora caught her breath. The rumours hadn't included that tragic detail. 'I'm so sorry. It must be incredibly hard for you both.'

'It is for Mette. Lisle and I hadn't been close for some years.'

All the same, he must feel something... But from the finality in his tone and the hint of blue steel in his eyes,

Aksel clearly didn't want to talk about it. She should drop the subject.

Kari had somehow managed to calm Dougal's excitement, and Flora bent down to let him off the lead. But as soon as she did so, Dougal bounded over to Aksel, throwing himself at his ankles. Aksel smiled suddenly, bending towards the little dog, his quiet words and his touch calming him.

'Sorry… I've only had him a couple of days, I'm looking after him for Esme Ross-Wylde.' Aksel must know who Esme was if he was working at the canine therapy centre. Charles and Esme Ross-Wylde were a brother and sister team, Charles running the Heatherglen Castle Clinic, and Esme the canine therapy centre. 'He's a rescue dog and Esme's trying to find him a good home.'

'You can't take him?' Aksel's blue gaze swept up towards her, and Flora almost gasped at its intensity.

'No…no, I'd like to but…' Flora had fallen in love with the puppy almost as soon as she'd seen him. He'd been half-starved and frightened of his own shadow when he'd first been found, but as soon as he'd been given a little care his loving nature had emerged. The strange markings on his shaggy brindle coat and his odd ears had endeared him to Flora even more.

'It wouldn't be fair to leave him alone all day while you were at work.' Aksel's observation was exactly to the point.

'Yes, that's right. I drop him off at the canine therapy centre and they look after him during the day, but that's a temporary arrangement. Dougal's been abandoned once and at the moment he tends to panic whenever he's left alone.'

Aksel nodded. A few quiet words to Kari, that Flora didn't understand, and the Labrador fetched a play ball from her basket, dropping it in front of Dougal. Dougal got the hint and started to push it around the room excitedly, the older dog carefully containing him and helping him play.

Aksel went through the process of searching through the kitchen cupboards again, finding a baking sheet to put the mince pies on and putting them in the oven to warm. The water in the copper kettle had boiled and he took it off the stove, tipping a measure of coffee straight into it. That was new to Flora, and if it fitted exactly with Aksel's aura of a mountain man, it didn't bode too well for the taste of the coffee.

'I hear you're an explorer.' Someone had to do the getting-to-know-you small talk and Flora was pretty sure that wasn't part of Aksel's vocabulary. He raised his eyebrows in reply.

'It said so in the memo.'

'I *used* to be an explorer.' The distinction seemed important to him. 'I'm trained as a vet and that's what I do now.'

'I've never met anyone who *used* to be an explorer before. Where have you been?'

'Most of South America. The Pole….'

Flora shivered. 'The Pole? North or South?'

'Both.'

That explained why she'd seen him setting off from his cottage early this morning, striding across the road and into the snow-dappled countryside beyond, with the air of a man who was just going for a walk. And the way that Aksel seemed quite comfortable in an open-necked shirt when the temperature in the kitchen made Flora feel glad of the warm sweater she was wearing.

'So you're used to the cold.'

Aksel smiled suddenly. 'Let's go into the sitting room.'

He tipped the coffee from the kettle into two mugs, opening the oven to take the mince pies out and leading the way through the hallway to the sitting room. As he opened the door, Flora felt warmth envelop her, along with the scent of pine.

The room was just the same as the kitchen. Comfortable and yet it seemed that Aksel's presence here had made no impact on it. Apart from the mix of wood and pine cones burning in the hearth, it looked as if he'd added nothing of his own to the well-furnished rental cottage.

Kari had picked the dog toy up in her mouth, and Dougal followed her into the room. She lay down on the rug in front of the fire, and the puppy followed suit, his tail thumping on the floor as Kari dropped the toy in front of him.

'He'll be hot in here. I should take his coat off.' Flora couldn't help grimacing as she said the words. Dougal liked the warm dog coat she'd bought for him, and getting him out of it wasn't as easy as it sounded. Perhaps he'd realise that they were in company, and not make so much of a fuss this time.

Sadly not. As soon as he realised Flora's intent, the

little dog decided that this was the best of all times for a game of catch-me-if-you-can. When she knelt, trying to persuade him out from under the coffee table, he barked joyously, darting out to take refuge under a chair.

She followed him, shooting Aksel an apologetic glance. His broad grin didn't help. Clearly he found this funny.

'He thinks this is a game. You're just reinforcing that by joining in with him. Come and drink your coffee, he'll come to you soon enough.'

Right. The coffee. Flora had been putting off the moment when good manners dictated that she'd have to take her first sip. But what Aksel said made sense, and he obviously had some experience in the matter. Flora sat down, reaching for her mug.

'This is…nice.' It *was* nice. Slightly sweeter than she was used to and with clear tones of taste and scent. Not what she'd expected at all.

'It's a light roast. This is a traditional Norwegian method of making it.'

'The easiest way when you're travelling as well.' A good cup of coffee that could be made without the need for filters or machines. Flora took another mouthful, and found that it was even more flavoursome than the first.

'That too. Only I don't travel any more.' He seemed to want to make that point very clear, and Flora thought that she heard regret in his tone. She wanted to ask, but Dougal chose that moment to come trotting out from under the chair to nuzzle at Aksel's legs.

He leaned forward, picking the little dog up and talk-

ing quietly to him in Norwegian. Dougal seemed to understand the gist of it, although Flora had no idea what
the conversation was about, and Aksel had him out of
the dog coat with no fuss or resistance.

'That works.' She shot Aksel a smile and he nodded,
lifting Dougal down from his lap so that he could join
Kari by the fire.

'You're not from Scotland, are you?' He gave a half-
smile in response to Flora's querying look. 'Your accent
sounds more English.'

He had a good ear. Aksel's English was very good,
but not many people could distinguish between accents
in a second language.

'My father's a diplomat, and I went to an English
school in Italy. But both my parents are Scots, my dad
comes from one of the villages a few miles from here.
Cluchlochry feels like home.'

He nodded. 'Tell me about the clinic.'

'Surely Dr Sinclair's told you all you need to know...'

'Yes, he has.' Aksel shot her a thoughtful look, and
Flora nodded. Of course he wanted to talk about the
place that was going to be Mette's home for the next six
weeks. Aksel might be nice to look at—strike that, the
man was downright gorgeous—but in truth the clinic
was about all they had in common.

The first thing that Aksel had noticed about Flora
was her red coat, standing out in the feeble light of a
cold Saturday morning. The second, third and fourth
things had come in rapid and breathtaking succession.
Her fair hair, which curled around her face. The warmth

in her honey-brown eyes. Her smile. The feeling in the pit of his stomach told him that he liked her smile, very much.

It was more than enough to convince Aksel to keep his distance. He'd always thought that dating a woman should be considered a privilege, and it was one that he'd now lost. Lisle had made it very clear that he wasn't worthy of it, by not even telling him that they'd conceived a child together. And now that he *had* found out about his daughter, Mette was his one and only priority.

But when he'd realised that Flora worked at the clinic, keeping his distance took on a new perspective. He should forget about the insistent craving that her scent awakened, it was just an echo from a past he'd left behind. He'd made up his mind that being a part of the clinic's community was a way to help Mette. And his way into that community had just turned up on his doorstep in the unlikely form of an angel, struggling to control an unruly puppy.

He'd concentrated on making friends with Dougal first, as that was far less challenging than looking into Flora's eyes. And when she'd started to talk about the work of the children's unit of the clinic, he'd concentrated on how that would help his daughter. *His daughter.* Aksel still couldn't even think the words without having to remind himself that he really did have a daughter.

'I've arranged with Dr Sinclair that Mette will be staying at the clinic full time for the first week, to give her a chance to settle in. After that, she'll be spending time at the weekend and several nights a week here, with me.'

'Oh. I see.' Flora's eyebrows shot up in surprise.

Aksel knew that the arrangement was out of the ordinary. Dr Sinclair had explained to him that most residents benefited from the immersive experience that the clinic offered, but he'd listened carefully to Aksel's concerns about being separated from Mette. The sensitive way that the issue had been handled was one of the reasons that Aksel had chosen the Heatherglen Castle Clinic.

Flora was clearly wondering why Mette was being treated differently from other patients, but she didn't ask. Aksel added that to the ever-growing list of things he liked about her. She trusted the people she worked with, and was too professional to second-guess their decisions.

'Mette and I are still working on…things…' *He* was the one who needed to do the work. He was still practically a stranger to Mette, and he had to work to prove that she could trust him, and that he'd always be there for her.

'Well, I'm sure that whatever you and Dr Sinclair have agreed is best.' She drained her cup and set it down on the small table next to her chair. 'I'm going to the clinic to catch up on a few things this afternoon. Would you mind if I dropped in to see her, just to say hello and welcome her?'

'Thank you. That's very kind…' Sudden joy, at the thought of seeing Flora again turned his heartbeat into a reckless, crazy ricochet. 'I'll be going in to see her this afternoon as well.'

'Oh…' Flora shot him an awkward smile, as if she hadn't expected that eventuality. 'Would you like a lift?'

'Thanks, but Kari needs a walk.' Kari raised her head slightly, directing her melting brown gaze at Aksel. Flora appeared to be taking the excuse at face value, but there was no getting past Kari.

He'd explain. On the way to the clinic, he'd tell Kari about yet another dark place in his heart, the one which made it impossible for Aksel to get too close to Flora. He'd confide his regrets and Kari would listen, the way she always did, without comment.

Dougal had been persuaded to say goodbye to his newfound friends and had followed Flora through the gap in the hedge, back to her own front door. When they were inside, she let him off the lead and he made his usual dash into the kitchen and around the sitting room, just to check that nothing had changed while he'd been away.

She leaned back against the door, resisting the temptation to flip the night latch. Locking Aksel out was all she wanted to do at the moment, but it was too late. He was already giving her that strong, silent look of his. Already striding through her imagination as if he owned it. At the moment, he did.

But if Flora knew anything about relationships, she knew that losing the first battle meant nothing. Aksel might have taken her by surprise, and breached her defences, but she was ready for him now.

Not like Tom... Eighteen, and loving the new challenges of being away from home at university. Her first proper boyfriend. So many firsts...

And then, the final, devastating first time. Flora had gone with Tom to visit his family for a week, and found his parents welcoming and keen to know all about her and her family. But when she'd spoken of her beloved brother, they hadn't listened to anything she'd said about Alec's dry humour, his love of books or how proud Flora was of his tenacious determination to live his life to the full. The only two words they'd heard were 'cystic fibrosis'.

Tom's parents had convinced him that his relationship with Flora must end. She had desperately tried to explain. She might carry the defective gene that caused cystic fibrosis, but she might not and if her children developed the condition then it would be a result of her partner also carrying the gene. Tom had listened impassively.

Then Flora had realised. Tom had already understood that, and so had his parents. Pleading with him to change his mind and take her back would have been a betrayal, of both Alec and herself. She'd gone upstairs and packed her bags, leaving without another word.

'What do you think, Dougal?' The puppy had returned to her side, obviously puzzled that she was still here in the hallway, and probably wondering if she was *ever* going to find her way to the jar in the kitchen that held the dog treats.

No answer. Maybe Dougal had that one right. He'd been abandoned too, and he knew the value of a warm hearth and a little kindness. Flora had found a home here, and she needed nothing else but her work.

'We're going to find you a home too, Dougal. Somewhere really nice with people who love you.' Flora walked into the kitchen, opening the jar of dog treats and giving Dougal one, and then reaching for a bar of chocolate for herself.

Chocolate was a great deal more predictable in the gamut of feel-good experiences. Aksel might be blood-meltingly sexy, and far too beautiful for anyone's peace of mind, but the few fleeting affairs she'd had since the break-up with Tom had shown Flora that desire and mistrust were awkward bedfellows. It was as if a switch had been flipped, and her body had lost its ability to respond. Sex had left her unsatisfied, and she'd given up on it.

If you could trust someone enough...

It was far too big an *if.* She'd kept the reason for her break-up with Tom a secret, knowing that it would hurt Alec and her parents beyond belief. They didn't deserve that, and neither did she. It was better to accept that being alone wasn't so bad and to channel all her energies into her work and being a part of the community here in Cluchlochry.

The next time she saw Aksel, she'd be prepared, and think of him only as a new neighbour and the father of one of the clinic's patients. When it came to thoughtless pleasure, she had chocolate, which made Aksel Olson's smile officially redundant.

Chapter 2

Aksel had walked the two miles to the clinic, with Kari trotting placidly beside him. It had done nothing to clear his head. Flora's smile still seemed to follow him everywhere, like a fine mist of scent that had been mistakenly sprayed in his direction and clung to his clothes. He was unaware of it for minutes on end, and then suddenly it hit him again. Fleeting and ephemeral, and yet enough to make him catch his breath before the illusion was once again lost.

His feet scrunched on the curved gravel drive. Castle Heatherglen Clinic was a real castle, its weathered stone walls and slate roof blending almost organically with the backdrop of rolling countryside and snow-dappled mountains. The Laird, Charles Ross-Wylde had added a new chapter to its long history and transformed his home into a rehabilitation clinic that offered its patients the best medical care, and welcomed them with a warm heart.

The children's unit was a little less grand than the rest of the building, and the sumptuous accommodation and sweeping staircases had been replaced by bright, comfortable rooms arranged around a well-equipped play area. Aksel had come prepared with a list of things that Mette might like to do, and suitable topics of conversation that might please her. But she seemed restless and bored today, not wanting to sit and listen while he read from her storybooks, and laying aside the toys he presented to her. Aksel's heart ached for all that his daughter had been through.

The awkward silence was broken by a knock at the door. Mette ignored it, and Aksel called for whoever it was to come in. Maybe it was one of the play specialists, who were on duty every day, and who might help him amuse his daughter.

Mette looked up towards the door, an instinctive reaction, even though she couldn't see anything that wasn't within a few feet of her.

'Hi, Mette. My name's Flora. May I come and visit you for a little while?' Flora glanced at Aksel and he wondered whether his relief at seeing her had shown on his face.

'Flora's our neighbour in the village, Mette.' He volunteered the information in English, and Mette displayed no interest. Flora sat down on the floor next to them, close enough for Mette to be able to see her face.

'I work here, at the clinic. I'm a physiotherapist.' Mette's head tilted enquiringly towards Flora at the sound of a word she didn't know. 'That means that I help people who are hurt to feel well again.'

'Where do they hurt...?' Mette frowned.

'All sorts of places. Their arms might hurt, or their legs. Sometimes it's their backs or their hips.'

Mette nodded sagely. She'd grown used to being surrounded by doctors and various other medical specialists, and while Aksel valued their kindness, it wasn't what he wanted for his daughter.

'Have you come to make me better?'

The question almost tore his heart out. No one could make Mette better, and he wondered how Flora could answer a question that left him lost for words.

'No, sweetie. I'm sorry, but I can't make your eyes better.' Flora pulled a sad face, the look in her eyes seeming to match his own feelings exactly. 'You have a doctor of your own to look after you. Dr Sinclair is very important around here, and he only looks after *very* important people…'

Flora leaned forward, imparting the information almost in a whisper, as if it were some kind of secret. She was making it sound as if Mette was someone special, not just a patient or a child who couldn't be helped.

'*I've* come because I heard that you were here, all the way from Norway. I'd like to be friends with you, if that's all right?'

Maybe it was the smile that did it. Aksel wouldn't be all that surprised, he'd already fallen victim to Flora's smile. Mette moved a little closer to her, reaching out as if to feel the warmth of the sun.

'I have a little something that I thought you might like…' Flora produced a carrier bag from behind her back, giving a little shiver of excitement. Mette was hooked now, and she took the bag.

'What is it?' There was something inside, and Mette

pulled out a parcel, wrapped in shiny paper that caught the light.

'Open it up and see.'

Mette didn't want to tear the wrappings and Flora waited patiently, guiding her fingers towards the clear tape that held it down. It peeled off easily, and Mette got the paper off in one piece, laying it carefully to one side, and started to inspect her gift.

A rag doll, with a brightly coloured dress and a wide smile stitched onto her face. Mette smiled, clutching the doll tightly to her chest.

'Why don't you show her to your dad?'

'Papa, look.' Mette held out the doll, and Aksel's heart began to thump in his chest. It wasn't the gift that had made Mette smile, but the way it had been given. The way it was wrapped so carefully, and the warmth of Flora's manner.

'It's beautiful… Thank you, Flora.'

'*She's* beautiful, Papa,' Mette corrected him.

'Yes, of course. Sorry. What's her name?'

Mette thought for a moment. 'Annette.' His daughter pronounced the name with a Norwegian inflection and Aksel repeated the English version for Flora.

'That's a lovely name. It sounds even better the way you say it…' Flora waited, and Mette responded, saying the name again so that Flora could mimic her.

This was all so easy, suddenly. Mette laughed over the way that Flora struggled to get her tongue around the Norwegian pronunciation, and when Flora stretched out her arms Mette gave her a hug. So simple, so natural, without any of the thought that Aksel put into his hugs. None of the wondering whether he was going too fast, or too slowly.

But, then, Flora didn't have agonised hope to contend with. Or the feeling that he didn't deserve Mette's hugs. Aksel watched as Mette showed Flora her toys, noticing that Flora didn't help Mette as much as he did, and that his daughter responded to that by becoming more animated.

'What's that?' Flora pointed to a box of jumbo-sized dominoes and Mette opened it, tipping the contents onto the floor. 'Oh, dominoes! I *love* dominoes...'

'Would you like to play?' The words slipped out before Aksel could stop them. He wanted to watch her with Mette for just a little longer.

Flora treated the request as if it was an invitation to a tour of the seven wonders of the world. Mette couldn't resist her excited smile and gave an emphatic '*Yes*!'

'Shall we do that thing first...?' Mette took a few uncertain steps towards Flora, clearly wanting to know what *that thing* was. Aksel wanted to know too. 'Where you stand them all up in a row and then knock them down again?'

Flora started to gather the dominoes together, putting them in a pile on the floor. 'It's such fun. Your papa will show you, I can never get them to balance properly.'

That was a ruse to get him involved. But Flora could manipulate him as much as she liked if this was the result. Aksel sat down on the floor, and started to line the dominoes up in a spiral pattern, seeing his own hand shake with emotion as he did so. Flora and Mette were both watching him intently, Mette bending forward to see.

'Spirals, eh? Show-off...' Flora murmured the words and Aksel felt his shoulders relax suddenly. Maybe this wasn't so difficult after all.

When Flora walked out to her car, it was already getting dark. She'd stayed longer than she'd intended with Aksel and Mette, and the work that she'd expected to take an hour had taken two. That might be something to do with the daydreaming. Aksel's bulk and strength and the gentle vulnerability that little blonde-haired, blue-eyed Mette brought out in him were downright mouth-watering.

He was so anxious to please and yet so awkward with his daughter. Aksel watched over Mette's every move, ready to catch her if there was even the smallest likelihood that she might fall. He meant well, but he was smothering her.

Not your business, Flora. Dr Sinclair will deal with it.

Lyle Sinclair had a way of taking patients or their families aside and gently suggesting new ways of looking at things. And Lyle would have the advantage of not feeling quite so hot under the collar at the mere thought of a conversation with Aksel.

'Flora!'

Flora closed her eyes in resignation at the sound of his voice. However hard she tried to escape him... When she turned and saw him striding across the car park towards her, she didn't want to escape him at all.

'I wanted to thank you.'

He'd done that already. More than once, and in as many words as Aksel seemed capable of.

'It was my pleasure. I always bring a little gift for the children, to make them feel welcome.' She'd told him that already, too. They could go on for ever like this, repeating the same things over and over again.

'I...' He spread his hands in a gesture of helplessness. 'You have a way with children.'

He made it sound as if it was some kind of supernatural power. Flora frowned. 'Children are just...people. Only they're usually a bit more fun.'

'You have a way with *people,* then.'

It was a nice compliment, especially since it was accompanied by his smile. Something was bugging him, but she wasn't the right person to speak to about it. She had too much baggage...

Baggage or experience? Experience was something that she could use to help her get things right this time. She'd been an impressionable teenager when she'd loved Tom, but she knew better now. There was no cosmic rule that said she had to fall for Aksel, and she could handle the regrets over never being able to trust a man enough to build a relationship. If that meant that she'd never be able to sit on the floor and play dominoes with her own child, she could deal with that, too.

Flora turned, opening the rear door of her car and dumping her bags in the footwell. Then she faced him. If all he had to throw at her were longing and regret, she'd already made her peace with them, a long time ago.

'You've said "Thank you" already, there's no need

for us to stand in the cold here while you say it again. What's bugging you?'

That was obviously confronting. But the slight twitch at the corners of his mouth told Flora that challenge was one of the things that he thrived on.

He took a breath, as if preparing himself. 'My relationship with Mette's mother was over before Mette was born and we never lived together as a family.'

What was he trying to say? That he'd been an absent father who hardly knew his own child? His obvious commitment to his daughter made that difficult to believe.

'And now?'

'I can't bring her mother back, or her sight. But I'd give anything to make her happy and...' He shrugged. 'It's not working. When I saw you with her this afternoon, I saw how much it wasn't working.'

Flora thought quickly. Aksel needed the kind of professional help that didn't fall within her area of expertise.

'Maybe you should talk to Lyle Sinclair. The clinic has a family counsellor who deals with just these kinds of issues, and Lyle could organise a session for you both.'

He shook his head abruptly. 'Mette's just fine the way she is. I won't put her into counselling just because *I* need to change.'

'Maybe it's not about change, but just getting to know each other better. Kathy uses storytelling a lot in her sessions, to make things fun. I'm sure you have plenty of stories about the places you've been—'

'No.' That sounded like a hard limit. 'That part of my life is over. Mette needs to know that I'll be there for her, always. That I'm not about to leave, and go to places that she can't.'

His heart was in the right place, but his head was way off course, and lost without a map or compass. This was something she *could* help with; Flora had grown up with a brother who hadn't always been able to do the things that she had. When Alec had been ill, she'd learned how to go out into the world, and to bring something back to share with her brother when she got home.

'Who says that you can't go together?' Flora gave an imperious twitch of her finger, indicating that he should follow her, and started to walk.

Flora seemed impatient with him, as if he was stubbornly refusing to see a simple fact that was obvious to her. On one level, Aksel just wanted to see her smile again. But on another, much more urgent level, he reckoned that Flora could be just as annoyed as she liked, if only it meant that she'd tell him what he was doing wrong. The first lesson he needed to learn was how to follow, rather than lead, and he walked beside her silently.

They reached the gravel driveway outside the clinic, and Flora stopped. 'You think that Mette doesn't know what it's like to be an explorer?'

The warmth in her eyes had been replaced by fire. Aksel swallowed down the thought that he liked that fire, and concentrated on the point that Flora seemed about to make.

'You're going to tell me different, aren't you?'

'Just think about it. She can feel the gravel under her

feet, and she can hear it scrunch. If she bends down, she can probably see it. She can feel the snow…' Flora broke off, turning her face up towards the flakes that had started to drift down, and one landed on her cheek. Aksel resisted the temptation to brush it away with his finger, and it melted almost immediately.

'But she can't see any of this.' He turned towards the mountains in the distance. He'd give his own sight if Mette could just appreciate the beauty of the world around her.

'Exactly. That's where you come in. She needs someone to explore with her, and tell her about the things she can't see for herself.'

'And if it's upsetting for her?'

'Then you respond to what she's feeling and stop. Just as long as it's Mette who's upset by it, and not you.'

She had a point, and this was a challenge he couldn't resist. Aksel's head was beginning to buzz with ideas. 'Maybe I could take a photograph of them. She might be able to hold that up close and see it.'

'*Now* you're thinking… Speak to Lyle and find out whether he thinks that might work for Mette.' Flora seemed to know that she'd lit a fuse and she wasn't taking cover. She wanted more from him.

'Maybe she'd like to go this way.' He started to walk towards the small, sheltered garden at the side of the property and found that Flora was no longer with him. She was standing still, her hands in her pockets, and one eyebrow raised slightly.

If that was the way she wanted to play it. Aksel returned to her side, holding out his arm. 'I'm going to have to guide her there, of course.'

She nodded, slipping her hand into the crook of his elbow. A frisson of excitement accompanied the feel of her falling into step beside him, and Aksel turned his mind to describing the things around them. The darkening bulk of the stone built castle. The sky, still red from the setting sun, and the clouds off to the east, which promised more snow for tonight.

She slipped so easily into a child-like wonder at the things around her. Aksel was considering asking Flora if she might accompany him and Mette when they set out on their own voyage of exploration, but he guessed what her answer might be.

No. You have to do it yourself.

'Careful…!' He'd seen her reach for a rose bush to one side of the path, and Aksel automatically caught her hand, pulling it away. 'It has thorns.'

Something that had been simmering deep beneath the surface began to swell, almost engulfing him. The thought of rose petals, wet with summer rain and vainly attempting to rival the softness of Flora's cheeks, made him shiver.

'All roses do.' She turned her gaze onto him, and Aksel saw a sudden sadness, quickly hidden. 'Will you let Mette miss the rose because of its thorns?'

That was a hard thought to contemplate. Aksel guided her hand, so that her fingers could brush the leaves. 'You must be gentle. In the summer, the rose is the softest of blooms, but the thorns will still hurt you.'

He let her fingers explore the leaves and then the

stem, touching the thorns carefully. It seemed to him that the thorns of this world had done Flora some damage, but that she still chose to see roses. She had room in her heart for both Mette and for Dougal, and yet she lived alone. He wanted to ask why, but he didn't dare.

Flora looked up at him suddenly. 'What's next for us to explore, then?'

A whole spectrum of senses and experiences, none of which involved asking personal questions. Aksel took her to the trunk of an old tree, which twisted against the castle wall, and she followed the rough curves of its bark with her fingers. He explained the eerie wail of a fox, drifting towards them from somewhere beyond his own range of vision. The temptation to draw her closer, and let his body shelter her against the wind, hammered against him.

'I can hear water...' Flora seemed intent on playing this game out.

'Over here.' A small stream trickled past the flower beds, curving its way out into the surrounding countryside. Flora's excitement seemed real, and he wondered whether she was play-acting or not.

'I don't think I can get across...' Mette wouldn't be able to jump to the other side, so neither could Flora.

The temptation was just too great. He could justify it by saying that this was what he would have done with Mette, or he could just give in to it and enjoy. Right now, the urge to just enjoy was thundering in his veins.

'I could carry you.' He called her bluff, wondering who'd be the first to blink.

'You're sure you won't drop me?'

He was about to tell her that he'd carried heavier weights, over much more difficult terrain, and then he realised that Flora was looking him up and down. This was a challenge that he couldn't back off from.

'Let's find out.' He wound his arm around her back, waiting for her to respond, and Flora linked her hands behind his neck. Then he picked her up in his arms.

Stepping across the narrow stream was nothing. Having her close was everything, a dizzying, heady sensation that made Aksel forget about anything else. Her scent invaded his senses and all he wanted to do was hold Flora for as long as she'd allow it.

He wondered if she could feel the resonance of his heart pounding against his ribs. Feeling her arms tighten around him, he looked into her face and suddenly he was lost. Her gaze met his, seeming to understand everything, all of his hope and fears and his many, many uncertainties. He might be struggling to keep his head above water, but she was the rock that he clung to.

None of that mattered. Her eyes were dark in the twilight, her lips slightly parted. The only thing that Aksel could think about was how her kiss might taste.

He resisted. It seemed that Flora was too. This was all wrong, but he couldn't make a move to stop it.

'Are you going to put me down now?' She murmured the words, still holding him tight in the spell of her gaze. Aksel moved automatically, setting her back on her feet, and for a moment he saw disappointment in her eyes. Then she smiled.

'Where shall we go next?'

Their voyage of exploration wasn't over. And Aksel

had discovered one, basic truth. That he must navigate carefully between the dangerous waters of Flora's eyes, and the absolute need to do his best for Mette.

'Over there.' Light was pooling around a glazed door, which led back into the castle. He needed that light, in order to forget the way that shadows had caressed Flora's face, in a way that he never could.

Chapter 3

Flora opened her eyes. Sunday morning. A time to relax and think about nothing.

Nothing wasn't going to work. That was when Aksel invaded her thoughts. The night-time dreams of a perfect family, which were usually brushed off so easily when she woke, had been fleshed out with faces. Aksel had been there, and her children had their father's ice-blue eyes. The image had made her heart ache.

And she'd come so close yesterday. Almost done it...

Almost didn't matter. She hadn't kissed him and she wasn't going to. She'd flirted a bit—Flora could admit to that. They'd shared a moment, it was impossible to deny that either. But they'd drawn back from it, like grown-up, thinking people. It took trust to make a relationship, and that was the one thing that Flora couldn't feel any more.

She got out of bed, wrapping her warm dressing gown around her and opening the curtains. Not picturing Aksel at all. Actually, she didn't need to imagine he was there, because he was the first thing she saw when she looked out over the land that bordered the village.

Kari was racing to fetch a ball that he'd just flung into the air, and he turned, as if aware of her gaze on him. Seeing her at the window, he waved.

Great. Not only was he intruding into her dreams, he seemed to have taken over her waking moments now. Flora waved back, turning from the window.

Somehow, Aksel managed to follow her into the shower. Wet-haired, with rivulets of water trickling over his chest. Then downstairs, as butter melted on her toast, he was standing by the stove, making coffee in that little copper kettle of his.

'If he's going to stalk me, then perhaps he should do the washing-up...' Dougal was busy demolishing the contents of his bowl, and gave Flora's comment the disregard that it deserved. Aksel wasn't stalking her. She was doing this all by herself.

The doorbell rang and Dougal rushed out into the hallway, knocking over his water bowl in the process. He was pawing at the front door, barking excitedly, and Flora bent down to pick him up. Then she saw Aksel's dark shadow on the other side of the obscured glass. She jumped back, yelping in surprise, and the shadow suddenly seemed to back away too.

She opened the door, trying to compose herself. At least the real Aksel bothered to wait on the doorstep and didn't just waltz in as if he owned the place.

'Is this too early...?' Today he was clean-shaven, with just the top half of his hair caught back, leaving the rest to flow around his shoulders. How on earth did he get such gorgeous hair to look so masculine? Flora dismissed the question for later, and concentrated on the one he'd asked.

'No. Not at all.' A cold wind was whipping through into the house, and Flora stood back from the door. 'Come in.'

She led the way through to the kitchen, and both he and Kari stepped neatly around the puddle of spilt water from Dougal's bowl. He insisted that he didn't want coffee, and that she should sit down and have her breakfast while he cleared up the mess. Flora sat, taking a gulp from her mug while he fetched a cloth and wiped up the water, washing the bowl in the sink before refilling it for Dougal.

'I assume you didn't just pop in to wipe my kitchen floor for me?' Who knew that a man could look sexy doing housework? If she wasn't very careful, she would find herself fantasising about that, too.

'No. I came to ask you a favour.'

'Fire away.' Flora waved him to a seat, and picked up her toast.

'I did some reorganisation this morning, to prepare for when Mette comes back to the cottage to stay with me.' He frowned, clearly not very pleased with the results. 'I wondered if you might take a look, and tell me what you think? I won't keep you long.'

This was where the fantasy stopped. Mette was a patient at the clinic, and Aksel was a father in need of some help. It was safer, more comfortable ground, even if it was less thrilling. Flora got to her feet.

'Okay. Let's have a look.'

* * *

Aksel picked Dougal up in his arms, and all four of them squeezed through the hole in the hedge, Flora shivering as the wind tugged at her sweater. Dougal followed Kari into the sitting room, and He led the way up the stairs. Flora was surprised when he opened the door to the left because this cottage was the mirror image of hers, with the smaller bedroom and a bathroom to the right. She followed him inside.

Aksel had obviously made an effort. There was a toy box with a row of cuddly animals lined up on the top. A single bed stood at the other end of the room with the wardrobe and chest of drawers.

'This is nice. I can see you've covered all the health and safety aspects.' The room was immaculately tidy, which would help Mette find what she wanted. He'd obviously been thinking about trip hazards and sharp edges, and all of the wall sockets had protectors fitted.

'That's easy enough.' Aksel was looking around the room with a dissatisfied gaze. 'It's not very pretty, though, is it?'

It was a bit stark. But that could be fixed easily. 'Why did you choose this room for Mette?'

'It's the biggest.'

'Big isn't always best. In a very large room like this, Mette might find it difficult to orientate herself.'

Aksel thought for a moment, and then nodded, striding across the hallway and opening the door of the other bedroom. Inside, Flora could see a large double bed, which must have come from the main bedroom. This room too was scrupulously tidy, as if Aksel had decided to camp here for the night and would be moving on soon.

He looked around, assessing her suggestion. 'I think you're right. I'll move everything back the way it was.'

'Would you like a hand?' The heavy bedframe must have been a bit of a struggle.

'Thanks, but I'll manage. What else?'

'Well… I'm no expert…'

'Give me your next-door-neighbour opinion.' His smile sliced through all of Flora's resolutions not to interfere too much and she puffed out a breath, looking around.

'You're not here for long so you don't want to make any permanent changes. But it would be great to be able to change the tone and brightness of the light in here to suit her needs. Maybe get some lamps with programmable bulbs that you can take with you when you go?'

He nodded. 'That's a great idea. What else?'

'Taking her toy box downstairs and just having a few cuddly toys up here for bedtime might get her used to the idea that upstairs is for sleeping. If you use bright colours that she can see, it'll help guide her around the room. And what about some textures, a comforter or a bedspread…?'

He walked across to the nightstand next to his bed, picking up a notebook and flipping it open. 'Lights…' He scribbled a note. 'Colours… Textures… Bedspread.'

Flora nodded. 'If you got her a nice bedspread, then perhaps she could use it here and on her bed at the clinic. Then, if she wakes up in the night, she'll have something that feels familiar right there.'

Aksel nodded, scribbling another entry in the notebook. 'Good idea. Anything else?'

'What does Mette like?'

That seemed the hardest question of all to answer. 'Um… Sparkly things, mostly. And she likes it when I read to her. She always wants the same stories over and over again.'

'The ones her mother read to her?'

'Yes. I think they help her to feel more secure.'

'Then use them as a guide. Maybe choose some things that feature in her favourite stories.'

'That's a great idea, thank you.' He made another note in his notebook before putting it into the back pocket of his jeans and striding back to the main bedroom. 'I'll take the toy box downstairs now. If you could suggest a place for it…'

He was trying so hard. Maybe that was the problem, he wanted to make everything perfect for Mette and couldn't be satisfied with anything less. Flora watched as he cleared the cuddly animals from the top of the toy box, trying not to notice how small they looked in his large, gentle hands.

'Oh…wait, I'll give you a hand…' Aksel had lifted the large wooden box alone, hardly seeming to notice its weight.

'That's all right. If you'll just stand aside.'

She could do that. Flora jumped out of his way, noticing the flex of muscle beneath his shirt as he manoeuvred the box through the doorway. She followed him as he carried it downstairs, swallowing down the lump in her throat. Aksel's strong frame was impressive when he was at rest, but in action it was stunning.

'Over there, maybe…?' He was standing in the centre of the sitting room, looking around with a perplexed look on his face. Flora shifted one of the chairs that stood around the fireside, and he finally put the box down, one hand rubbing his shoulder as he straightened up.

'Is your shoulder all right?' He raised an eyebrow, and Flora felt herself redden. Okay, so she'd been looking at his shoulders. 'Professional interest. I'm a physiotherapist, remember?'

'It's fine. It was just a little stiff this morning.'

His tone told Flora to leave it, so she did. 'Maybe we could move one of the lights so that when Mette opens the box she can see inside better.'

Suddenly Aksel grinned. 'Kari…'

The dog raised her head, moving from relaxed fireside mode to work mode immediately. In response to a command in Norwegian, she trotted over to the box and inserted her paw into a semi-circular hole cut into the side, under the lid. Flora heard a click and the lid swung open smoothly, its motion clearly controlled by a counterbalance mechanism.

The ease of opening was just the beginning. As the box opened, light flooded the inside of the box, and Flora could see that there were small LEDs around the edge, shaded at the top so that they would shine downwards and not dazzle Mette. The contents were carefully arranged in plastic baskets, so that she would be able to find whatever she wanted.

'That's fantastic! Wherever did you get this?'

'I made it. There was nothing on the market that quite suited Mette's needs.' Aksel was clearly pleased with Flora's approval.

She knelt down beside the box, inspecting it carefully. The lid opened easily enough for a child…or a dog…to lift it and the counterbalance mechanism meant that once open there was no danger of it slamming shut on small fingers. The lights came on when the lid opened and flicked off again as it closed, and they illuminated the contents of the box in a soft, clear light.

And the box itself was a masterpiece, made of wooden panels that were smooth and warm to the touch. It was quite plain but that was part of its beauty. The timber had obviously been carefully chosen and its swirling grain made this piece one of a kind.

'Mette must love it.' It was a gift that only a loving and thoughtful father could have made. And someone who was a skilled craftsman as well.

He nodded, looking around the room restlessly as if searching for the next thing that needed to be done. Aksel's response to any problem was to act on it, and he was obviously struggling with the things he could do nothing about. No wonder he was carrying some tension in his shoulders.

'We could go and do some shopping, if you wanted. It won't take long to pick out a few things to brighten Mette's bedroom up.'

'Would you mind…?' He was halfway towards the door, obviously ready to turn thought into action as soon as possible, and then stopped himself. 'Perhaps another time. Whenever it's convenient for you.'

Flora allowed herself a smile. 'Now's fine. I'll go and get my coat.'

Aksel had been struggling to get the fantasy out of his head ever since he'd opened his eyes this morning. Rumpled sheets and Flora's cheeks, flushed with sleep.

Yesterday had shown him how easy it would be to slip into loving intimacy with Flora, but her reaction had told him that she didn't want that any more than he did. The word *impossible* usually made his blood fire in his veins at the thought of proving that nothing was impossible, and it had taken Flora's look of quiet certainty to convince him that there was something in this world that truly was impossible.

He could deal with that. If he just concentrated on having her as a friend, and forgot all about wanting her as a lover, then it would be easy. When she returned, wearing a dark green coat with a red scarf, and holding Dougal's dog coat and lead, he ignored the way that the cottage seemed suddenly full of light and warmth again.

'Why don't you leave him here? They'll be fine together.' The puppy was curled up in front of the fire with Kari, and didn't seem disposed to move.

'You think so?' Flora tickled Dougal's head and he squirmed sleepily, snuggling against Kari. 'Yes. I guess they will.'

She drove in much the same way as she held a conversation. Quick and decisive, her eyes fixed firmly on where she was going. Aksel guessed that Flora wasn't much used to watching the world go by, she wanted always to be moving, and he wondered whether she ever took some time out to just sit and feel the world turn beneath her. He guessed not.

For a woman that he'd just decided *not* to be too involved with, he was noticing a great deal about her. Flora wasn't content with the just-crawled-out-of-bed look for a Sunday morning. She'd brushed her hair until it shone and wore a little make-up. More probably than was apparent, it was skilfully applied to make the most of her natural beauty. She wore high-heeled boots with her skinny jeans, and when she moved Aksel caught the scent of something he couldn't place. Clean, with a hint of flowers and slightly musky, it curled around him, beckoning his body to respond.

'So… Mette's never lived with you before?' She asked the question when they'd got out of the winding country lanes and onto the main road.

'No.' Aksel couldn't think of anything to say to describe a situation that was complicated, to say the least.

'Sorry…' She flipped her gaze to him for a moment, and Aksel almost shivered in its warmth. 'I didn't mean to pry.'

'It's all right. It's no secret. Just a little difficult to explain.'

'Ah. I'll leave it there, then.'

Flora lapsed into silence. 'Difficult to explain' didn't appear to daunt her, she seemed the kind of person who could accept almost anything. He imagined that her patients must find it very easy to confide in her. All their hopes and their most secret despair. Suddenly, he wanted to talk.

'I didn't know that I had a daughter until after Mette's mother died.'

Nothing registered in Flora's face, but he saw her fingers grip the steering wheel a little tighter. Maybe she was wondering what kind of man hadn't known about his own daughter. He wouldn't blame her—he frequently tormented himself with that thought.

'That must be…challenging.'

Her answer was just the thing a medical professional would say. Non-judgemental, allowing for the possibility of pain and yet assuming nothing. Aksel wanted more than that, he wanted Flora to judge him. If she found him wanting then it would be nothing he hadn't already accused himself of. And if she found a way to declare him innocent it would mean a great deal to him.

'What do you think?' He asked the question as if it didn't mean much, but felt a quiver deep in the pit of his stomach.

No reaction. But as she changed gear, the car jolted a little, as if it was reflecting her mood.

'I'd find it very difficult.'

Aksel nodded. Clearly Flora wasn't going to be persuaded to give an opinion on the matter and maybe that was wise. Maybe he should let it drop.

'In…lots of ways.' She murmured the words, as if they might blow up in her face. Flora wanted to know more but she wasn't going to ask.

'Lisle and I split up before either of us knew she was pregnant. I was due to go away for a while, I was leading an expedition into the Andes.' Suddenly his courage failed him. 'It's a fascinating place...'

'I'm sure.' Her slight frown told Aksel that she wasn't really interested in one of the largest mountain ranges in the world, its volcanic peaks, the highest navigable lake on the planet or the incredible biodiversity. To her, the wonders of the world were nothing in comparison to the mysteries of the human heart, and she was the kind of woman who trod boldly in that unknown territory.

He took a breath, staring at the road ahead. 'When I got back, I heard that Lisle had gone to Oslo for a new job. I think that the job might have been an excuse...'

Flora gave a little nod. 'It does sound that way.'

There was compassion in her voice. Most people questioned why Lisle should have gone to such lengths to keep her pregnancy a secret from him, but Flora didn't seem disposed to make any judgements yet.

'I never saw her again. The first I knew of Mette's existence was when her parents called me, telling me about the accident.'

'That must have been a shock.'

It had changed his world. Tipped it upside down and focussed every last piece of his attention on the child he'd never known he had. '*Shock* is an understatement.'

She flipped a glance at him, then turned her gaze back onto the road ahead. But in that moment Aksel saw warmth in her eyes and it spurred him on, as if it was the glimmer of an evening campfire at the end of a long road.

'Olaf and Agnetha are good people. They never really agreed with Lisle's decision not to tell me about

Mette, although they respected it while she was alive. When she died, they decided that Mette needed to know more than just what Lisle had told her. That she had a father but that he was an adventurer, away exploring the world.'

Flora nodded, her lips forming into a tight line. 'And so you finally got to meet her.'

'Not straight away. Mette was in hospital for a while. She had no other serious injuries, she was still in her car seat when the rescue services arrived, but one of the front headrests had come loose and hit her in the face. The blow damaged her optic nerves...'

The memory of having to stand outside Mette's room, watching through the glass partition as Agnetha sat with her granddaughter, was still as sharp as a knife. He'd understood the importance of taking things slowly, but reaching out to touch the cool, hard surface of the glass that had separated them had been agony. Aksel gripped his hands together hard to stop them from shaking.

'Olaf and Agnetha were naturally anxious to take things at whatever pace was best for Mette and I was in complete agreement with that. I dropped everything and went to Oslo, but it was two weeks before they made the decision to introduce me to her. They were the longest two weeks of my life.'

'I imagine so. It must have been very hard for them, too.'

'Yes, it was. They knew me from when I'd been seeing Lisle, but they wanted to make sure that I wouldn't hurt Mette any more than she'd already been hurt. Letting me get to know her was a risk.'

'But they took it. Good for them.'

'Not until I'd convinced them that I wouldn't walk in, shower Mette with presents and then leave again. That was why Lisle didn't tell me about her pregnancy. Because I was always leaving...'

Aksel could hear the bitterness in his own voice. The helpless anger that Lisle hadn't known that a child would make all the difference to him. She'd only seen the man who'd wanted to go out and meet the world, and she'd done what she'd felt she had to do in response to that.

'She must have cared a lot about you.'

That was a new idea. Aksel had been more comfortable with the thought that the only emotion he'd engendered in Lisle's heart was dislike. 'What makes you say that?'

'If the thought of you leaving was such an issue to her, then it must have hurt.'

Guilt was never very far from the surface these days, but now it felt as if it was eating him up. 'I didn't think of it that way.'

'You're angry with her? For not telling you about Mette?'

Yes, he was angry. Rage had consumed him, but he'd hidden it for Olaf and Agnetha's sake. And now he hid it for Mette's sake.

'Mette loves her mother. I have to respect that.'

He was caught off balance suddenly as Flora swerved left into the service road that led to a large car park.

That was the story of his life at the moment, letting other people take the driving seat and finding himself struggling to cope with the twists and turns in the road. She caught sight of a parking spot, accelerating to get to it before anyone else did, and turned into it. Aksel waited for her to reverse and straighten up, and then realised that the car was already perfectly straight and within the white lines.

'I'd want to scream. I mean, I'd go out and find a place where no one could hear me, and *really* scream. Until I was hoarse.'

So she knew something of the healing nature of the wilderness. Aksel hadn't told anyone why he'd taken the train out of Oslo towards Bergen, or that he'd set out alone in the darkness to trek to the edge of one of the magnificent fjords, roaring his anger and pain out across the water.

'I didn't scream, I yelled. But apart from that, you have it right.'

She gave a soft chuckle, regarding him silently for a moment. 'And then you went back home and read all the manuals? Did your best to be a good father, without any of the training and experience that most men get along the way?'

That was exactly how Aksel felt at times. He'd loved Mette from the first moment he'd seen her. But sometimes he found it hard to communicate with her.

'I've made a career out of dealing with the unexpected.'

Flora smiled and the warmth in the car turned suddenly to sticky heat. If he didn't move now, he was going to fall prey to the insistent urge to reach forward and touch her. Aksel got out of the car, feeling the wind's sharp caress on his face.

Flora grabbed her handbag from the back seat, getting out of the driver's seat, and Aksel took his notebook from his pocket, skimming through the list he'd made. 'I should get some Christmas-tree decorations as well while we're here.'

She turned to him, a look of mock horror on her face. 'You don't have any?'

Aksel shrugged. 'I'm used to moving around a lot. Whenever I'm home for Christmas, I go to my sister's.'

'Perfect. I love buying tree decorations, and if I buy any more I won't be able to fit them on the tree.' She scanned the row of shops that skirted the car park, obviously keen to get on with the task in hand. 'It's a good thing we came today, all the best ones will be gone soon.'

Chapter 4

It was unlikely that *anything* would be gone from the shops for a while yet. The stores that lined the shopping precinct were full of merchandise for Christmas, and rapidly filling up with people. Flora ignored that self-evident fact. It was never too early for Christmas.

Unlikely as it might be, Aksel seemed slightly lost. As someone who could find his way to both the North and South poles, a few shops should be child's play. But he was looking around as if a deep crevasse had opened up between him and where he wanted to be and he wasn't sure how to navigate it. Flora made for the entrance to the nearest store.

'What sort of decorations did you have in mind?' The in-store Christmas shop shone with lights and glitter, and was already full of shoppers.

'Um… Can I leave myself in your hands?'

Nice thought. Flora would have to make sure it stayed just a thought. She smiled brightly at him and made for some glass baubles, finding herself pushed up against Aksel in the crush of people.

'These are nice…'

'We'll take them. What about these?' He picked up a packet of twisted glass icicles.

'They're lovely.' Flora dropped a packet for herself into the basket, despite having decided that she already had too many tree decorations.

As they left the shop, Aksel gazed longingly at the entrance to the DIY store, but Flora walked determinedly past it, and he fell into step beside her.

An hour later they'd filled the shopping bags that Flora had brought with her, and Aksel was laden down with them.

He peered over her shoulder as Flora consulted the list he'd torn from his notebook, ticking off what they already had and putting a star next to the more specialised home-support items that the clinic could supply him with. That left the bedspread.

'I saw a shop in the village that sells quilts. They looked nice.' He ventured a suggestion.

'Mary Monroe's quilts are gorgeous. But they're handmade so they're expensive. You can get a nice bedspread for much less at one of the big stores here...'

Aksel shook his head. 'I liked the look of the place in the village.'

'Right. We'll try that first, then.'

Aksel was shaping up to be the perfect shopping companion, patient and decisive. He didn't need to sit down for coffee every twenty minutes, and he was able to carry any number of bags. Maybe if she thought of him that way, the nagging thump of her heart would subside a little. It was a known fact that women had lovers and shopping companions, and that the two territories never overlapped.

It wasn't easy to hold the line, though. When he loaded the bags into the boot of the car, Flora couldn't help noticing those shoulders. Again. And the fifteen-minute drive back to the village gave her plenty of time to feel the scent of fresh air and pine cones do its work. By the time they drew up outside Village Quilts she felt almost dizzy with desire.

A little more shopping would sort that out. Shopping beat sex every time. And this was the kind of shop where you had to bring all your concentration to bear on the matter in hand. Mary Monroe prided herself on making sure that she was on first-name terms with all her customers, and if they could be persuaded to sit on one of the rickety chairs while she sorted through her entire stock to come up with the perfect quilt, then all the better.

But Aksel wasn't going to be confined to a chair. The introductions were made and he sat down but then sprang to his feet again. 'Let me help you with that, Mary.'

Mary was over a foot shorter than him, slight and grey-haired. But she was agile enough on the ladder that she needed to reach the top shelves, and never accepted help.

'Thank you.' Mary capitulated suddenly. Maybe she'd decided that sixty was a good age to slow down a bit, but she'd never shown any sign of doing so. And when Flora rose from her chair to assist, Mary gave her a stern glare that implied no further help was needed.

Aksel lifted the pile of heavy quilts down from the top shelf and Mary stood back. Maybe she was admiring his shoulders, too.

'Your little girl is partially blind...' Mary surveyed the pile thoughtfully.

'Yes. Something that's textured might be good for her.' Flora decided that this didn't really fall into the category of help, it was just volunteering some information.

'What about a raw-edged quilt?' Mary pulled a couple from the pile, unfolding them. 'You see the raw edges of each piece of fabric are left on the top, and form a pattern.'

The quilts were rich and thick, and each square was surrounded by frayed edges of fabric and padding. Aksel ran his fingers across the surface of one and smiled. 'This will do her very nicely. Do you have something a bit more colourful? Mette can see strong colours better.'

'That pile, up there.' Mary didn't even move, and Aksel lifted the quilts down from the shelf. Flora rose, unfolding some of the quilts.

'This one's beautiful, Mary!' The quilt had twelve square sections, each one appliquéd with flowers. Mary beamed.

'I made that one myself. It's a calendar quilt...'

Flora could see now that the flowers in each square corresponded to a month in the year. December was a group of Christmas trees on snowy white ground, the dark blue sky scattered with stars.

'Not really what you're looking for.' Mary tugged at

a raw-edged quilt that was made from fabrics in a variety of reds and greens. 'How about this one?'

Aksel nodded, turning to Flora. 'What do you think.'

'Do you like it?'

'Very much.' He ran his fingers over the quilt, smiling. 'I'll take this one.'

'I have more to show you.' Mary liked her customers to see her full stock before making any decisions, but Aksel's smile and the quick shake of his head convinced her that, in this instance, they didn't need to go through that process.

'I like this one, too.' He turned his attention back to the calendar quilt, examining the different squares. 'These are all Scottish plants and flowers?'

'Yes, that's right. I design my quilts to reflect what I see around me. But this one doesn't have the texture that your daughter might like.'

'It would be something to remind us of our trip to Scotland. Perhaps I could hang it on the wall in her room. May I take this one too?'

'No, you may not.' Mary put her hands on her hips. 'My quilts are made with love, and that's why they'll keep you warm. They are *not* supposed to be hung on the wall.'

'If I were to promise to keep it in my sitting room? Something to wrap Mette in on cold winter nights and remind us both of the warm welcome we've had here. The raw-edged one will stay on her bed.' Aksel gave Mary an imploring look and she capitulated suddenly.

'That would be quite fine. You're sure you want both?'

Aksel nodded. If Mary could be an unstoppable force

at times, she at least knew when she'd come into contact with an immovable object. Something had to give, and she did so cheerfully.

'You'll give this one to your daughter as a present?' She started to fold the raw-edged quilt.

'Yes.'

'I've got some pretty paper in the back that'll do very nicely. I'll just slip it into the bag and you can do the wrapping yourself.' Mary bustled through a door behind the counter, leaving them alone.

'You're sure?' Flora ran her hand over the quilts. They were both lovely, but this was a big expense, and she was feeling a little guilty for suggesting it.

'I'm sure. I'll have a whole house to furnish back in Norway, and these will help make it a home for Mette.'

'You don't have a place there already?'

'I've never been in one place long enough to consider buying a house. Mette and I have been staying with Olaf and Agnetha—their house is familiar to her and they have more than enough room. I've bought a house close by so that we can visit often.'

Flora wanted to hug him. He'd been through a lot, and he was trying so hard to make a success of the new role he'd taken on in life. She watched as Mary reappeared, bearing a large carrier bag for Aksel and taking the card that he produced from his wallet.

They stepped outside into the pale sunshine and started to walk back towards Flora's car.

'I'll give the quilt to Mette tomorrow when you're at the clinic. Will you come and help me?'

'No! It's *your* present. Aren't you going to see her

this afternoon?' Flora would have loved to see Mette's face when she opened the quilt, but this was Aksel's moment.

'Yes. I just thought…' He shrugged. 'Maybe it would be more special to her if you were there.'

'It's your present. And you're her father. She can show it to me when I come and visit.' Flora frowned. 'You really haven't had that much time alone with her, have you?'

Aksel cleared his throat awkwardly. 'Almost none. I relied a lot more heavily on Olaf and Agnetha to help me than I realised.'

'And how is Mette ever going to feel safe and secure with you if you can't even give her a present on your own? You've got to get over this feeling that you're not enough for her, Aksel.' Maybe that was a little too direct. But Aksel always seemed to appreciate her candour.

'Point taken. In that case, I don't suppose you have a roll of sticky tape you could lend me?'

'Yes, I have several. You can never have too much sticky tape this close to Christmas.'

He chuckled quietly. 'You'd be happy to celebrate Christmas once a month, wouldn't you?'

Flora thought for a moment. The idea was tempting. 'Christmas is special, and once a year is just fine. It gives me loads of time to look forward to it.'

'There's that. I'm looking forward to my first Christmas with Mette.'

'You're not panicking yet?'

'I'm panicking. I just disguise it well.'

Flora grinned up at him. 'It'll be fine. Better than fine, it'll be brilliant. Christmas at the castle is always lovely.'

'Just your kind of place, then.'

Yes, it was. Cluchlochry was home, and her work at the clinic was stimulating and rewarding. Flora had almost managed to convince herself that she had everything that she wanted. Until Aksel had come along...

She felt in her pocket for her car keys, watching as Aksel stowed the quilts in the back seat with the rest of their shopping. She'd found peace here. An out-of-the-way shelter from the harsh truths of life, where she could ignore the fact that she sometimes felt she was only half living. And Aksel was threatening to destroy that peace and plunge her into a maelstrom of what-ifs and maybes. She wouldn't let him.

Aksel had spent a restless night just a few metres away from her. Even the thick stone wall between Flora's bedroom and his couldn't dull the feeling that anytime now she might burst through, bringing light and laughter. He imagined her in red pyjamas with red lips. And, despite himself, he imagined her out of those red pyjamas as well.

He set out before dawn with Kari, walking to the canine therapy centre, which was situated in the grounds of the Heatherglen Castle Estate. As they trekked past the clinic, Aksel imagined Mette, stirring sleepily under her quilt. She'd loved it, flinging her arms around his neck and kissing him. Each kiss from his little girl was still special, and every time he thought about it, his fingers moved involuntarily to his cheek, feeling the tingle of pleasure.

Esme Ross-Wylde was already in her office, and took him to meet his new charges, dogs of all kinds that were being trained as PAT dogs. For the next few weeks Aksel would be helping Esme out with some of the veterinary duties, and he busied himself reading up on the notes for each dog.

A commotion of barking and voices just before nine o'clock heralded Flora's arrival with Dougal, and Aksel resisted the temptation to walk out of the surgery and say hello. There was a moment of relative peace and then Esme appeared, holding Dougal's lead tightly.

'Flora tells me that Kari's made friends with this wee whirlwind.' She nodded down at Dougal, raising her eyebrows when, on Aksel's command, Kari rose from her corner and trotted over to Dougal. The little dog calmed immediately.

'Yes. He just needs plenty of attention at the moment.'

'I don't suppose you could take him for a while, could you? Give everyone else a bit of peace? He's a great asset when it comes to teaching the dogs to ignore other dogs, but he's getting in the way a bit at the moment.'

Aksel nodded and Esme smiled. 'Thanks. You know that Flora works at the clinic...?' The question seemed to carry with it an ulterior motive.

'Yes, she came to introduce herself on Saturday, and she's been helping me settle in. We went shopping for Mette yesterday.'

Esme chuckled. 'Shopping's one of Flora's greatest talents. Along with physiotherapy, of course.'

'We found everything that we needed.' The idea that yesterday hadn't been particularly special or much out of the ordinary for Flora was suddenly disappointing. It had been special to him, and the look on Mette's face when he'd helped her unwrap her new quilt had been more precious than anything.

'I've no need to make any introductions, then. I've been talking to the manager of a sheltered housing complex near here—her name's Eileen Ross. We're looking at setting up a dog visiting scheme there and I thought that might be something I could hand over to you. Flora visits every week for a physiotherapy clinic, maybe you could go along with her tomorrow and see how the place operates.'

'I'd be very happy to take that on. I've seen a number of these schemes before, and I know that the elderly benefit a great deal from contact with animals.' The tingle of excitement that ran down his spine wasn't solely at the thought of the medical benefits of the visit.

'So I can put this on the ever-growing list of things that you'll take responsibility for while you're here?'

Aksel nodded. He wasn't aware of such a list and wondered whether it was all in Esme's head. She ran a tight ship here at the centre, and he'd already realised that she was committed to exploring new possibilities whenever she could.

'Leave it with me. I'll have a report for you next week.'

'Marvellous. I'll give Flora a call and let her know

that's what we're planning. Is an eight-thirty start all right for you?'

'That's fine. Is the sheltered housing complex within walking distance from Cluchlochry?'

Esme chuckled. 'It depends what you call walking distance. I doubt Flora would think so. You don't have a car?'

'No.'

'We have an old SUV that you can use while you're here. It's a bit bashed around and it needs a good clean, but it'll get you from A to B.'

'Thank you, that's very kind. I'll pick it up in the morning if that's okay.'

'Yes, that's fine. I'll leave the keys at Reception for you.'

Chapter 5

Flora had allowed herself to believe that going to
Mette's room at lunchtime, when she knew Aksel would
be there, was just a matter of confirming their visit to
the sheltered housing complex tomorrow morning. But
when she found him carefully threading Mette's fingers
into a pair of red and white woollen gloves, the matter slipped her mind. The two of them were obviously
planning on going somewhere as Mette was bundled
up in a red coat and a hat that matched her gloves, and
Aksel had on a weatherproof jacket.

'Hi, Mette.' Flora concentrated on the little girl, giving Aksel a brief smile, before she bent down towards
Mette, close enough that she could see her. 'You look
nice and warm. Are you going somewhere?'

Mette replied in Norwegian. Her English was good
enough to communicate with all the staff here, but
sometimes she forgot when she needed to use it.

'English, Mette.' Aksel gave his daughter a fond
smile. If there had ever been any doubt about his commitment to the little girl, it was all there in his eyes.
'We're going on an expedition.'

'Papa says there's a river, and we have to jump across it.' Mette volunteered the information, and Flora felt a tingle run down her spine at the thought of the trickle of water, and how she'd crossed it in Aksel's arms.

Aksel flashed her a grin. 'Dr Sinclair thought that your idea was a good one.'

Okay. Flora wondered whether Aksel had shared her other ideas, and hoped that Lyle wouldn't think she'd been interfering. She'd just been trying to help...

'Don't look so alarmed. I told him that I'd asked you for some ideas and that you'd been very kind.' He smiled.

Fair enough. It was disconcerting that he'd been able to gauge her thoughts so easily from her reaction, and she wished that he'd do as everyone else did, and wait for her to voice them. But Aksel was nothing if not honest, and it was probably beyond him not to say what was on his mind.

Before she could think of a suitable answer, Lyle Sinclair appeared in the doorway, holding a flask and a large box of sandwiches. The kitchen staff never missed an opportunity to feed anyone up, and it appeared that Aksel was already on their culinary radar.

'Hello, Mette. You're off to explore with your dad, are you?' He put the sandwiches down and bent towards the little girl, who looked up at him and nodded. Lyle looked around, as if wholly satisfied with the arrangement.

'Are you going too, Flora?'

'Um... No. Probably best to leave them to it.' This was something that Aksel and Mette needed to do alone.

And any reminder of the almost-kissing-him incident was to be avoided.

'Yes, of course.' Lyle beamed at her. His quiet, gentle manner was more ebullient than usual, and Flora suspected that had a great deal to do with Cass Bellow's return from the States.

'How is Cass? I haven't seen her yet.'

'She's fine.' Lyle seemed to light up at the mention of her name. 'A little achy still, she was hoping you might have some time to see her in the next couple of days.'

'How about tomorrow afternoon? Would you like me to give her a call?'

'No, that's fine, I'll let her know and get her to call you and arrange a time. In the meantime, I won't keep you. I'll see you later, Mette.' Lyle touched Mette's hand in farewell and swept back out of the room.

'What's going on there?' Aksel had been watching quietly.

'Just a little romance. Actually, quite a lot of it, from what I've heard.' Flora liked Cass a lot, and she was happy for Lyle.

'That's nice.' Aksel's face showed no emotion as he turned his attention back to Mette's gloves, picking up the one she'd discarded on the floor. Clearly he was about as impressed with the idea of romance as Flora was, and that made things a great deal easier between them.

'You're really not going to come with us?' He didn't look up, concentrating on winding Mette's scarf around her neck.

'I'll come and wave you off.' Flora grinned at Mette.

'You've got to have someone wave you goodbye if you're going on an expedition.'

Aksel put the sandwiches into a daypack and made a show of going through its contents with Mette, explaining that the most important part of any expedition was to make sure it was properly provisioned. This particular journey required three glitter pens, a packet of sweets and Mette's rag doll.

Downstairs, Mette solemnly let the receptionist know where they were going and when they'd be back, and that they'd be documenting their journey thoroughly with photographs. Flora accompanied them outside, wrapping her arms around herself against the cold.

'I want to ride, Papa.'

'All right.' Aksel bent down, lifting Mette up and settling her securely on his shoulders, and she squealed with glee. He said something in Norwegian, clearly instructing Mette to hold on tight, and she flung her arms around his head.

He was standing completely still, blinded suddenly. Flora laughed, moving quickly to remove Mette's arms from over his eyes. 'Not like that, sweetheart. Papa can't see.'

'Thanks.' Aksel shot her a slow smile, and it happened again. That gorgeous, slightly dizzy feeling, as if they were the only two people on the planet, and they understood each other completely.

Flora wrenched her gaze away from his, reaching up to pull Mette's hat down firmly over her ears. The little girl chuckled, tapping the top of her father's head in an obvious signal to start walking.

Flora waved them goodbye, calling after them, and Aksel turned so that Mette could wave one last time. She watched them until they disappeared around the corner of the building, two explorers off to test the limits of Mette's world. Maybe Aksel's too.

Aksel had wondered whether Flora might come to say goodnight to Mette when she finished work. His disappointment when she didn't wasn't altogether on behalf of his daughter, however much he tried to convince himself that it was.

They had a connection. It was one of those things that just happened, forged out of nothing between two people who hardly knew each other. He could do nothing about it, but that didn't mean he had to act on it either. The days when he'd had only himself to consider were gone.

The evening ritual of reading Mette a story and then carrying her over to her bed calmed him a little. As he settled her down, cosy and warm under the quilt, he heard a quiet tap on the door and it opened a fraction.

'What are you still doing here?' Flora's working day had finished hours ago, but he couldn't help the little quiver of joy that gripped his heart.

'I've been working late. I just wondered how your expedition went.'

'We went across a big river! And back again.' Mette was suddenly wide awake again. 'Will you come with us next time, Tante Flora?'

Flora blushed, telling Mette that she would. Aksel wondered whether it gave her as much pleasure to hear the little girl call her *Tante* as it did when she called him Papa. He'd decided with Olaf and Agnetha that they wouldn't push her, and that Mette should call him whatever she felt comfortable with, but the first time she'd used Papa, Aksel hadn't been able to hide his tears.

'It means aunt. Don't be embarrassed, she calls a lot of people *tante* or *onkel*.' Flora's reluctance to be seen to be too close to the little girl in front of Dr Sinclair had been obvious.

'And I was hoping it was just me...' Flora smiled as if it was a joke, but Aksel saw a flash of longing in her eyes, which was hidden as quickly as it had appeared.

'Not usually so quickly.' Aksel tried to take the thought back, turning to his daughter and arranging the bedcovers over her again. 'Are you ready to say goodnight, Mette?'

'I want Tante Flora to say it with me...' Mette reached for the cabinet by the side of her bed, carefully running her fingers across its edge. Aksel bit back the instinct to help her, waiting patiently for her to find what she wanted by touch. The clinic staff had told him that he should let her do as much as she could by herself, but each time he had to pause and watch her struggling to do something that came so naturally to other children, he felt consumed with the sadness of all that Mette had lost.

'It's okay...' Flora whispered the words. They were for him, not Mette, and when he looked at her, he saw understanding. She could see how much this hurt, and was enforcing the message that it was what he must do, to allow Mette to learn how to explore her world.

Not easy. He mouthed the words, and Flora nodded.

'I know. You're doing great.'

Mette had found what she wanted, and she clutched the small electric light in her hand as she snuggled back under the covers. When she tipped it to one side, light glimmered inside the glass, as if a candle had been lit.

She hadn't done that for a few days, and Aksel hadn't pushed the issue, leaving Mette to do as she wanted. Maybe it was Flora's presence, her warmth, that had made Mette think of her mother tonight.

'Say goodnight to Mama.' Mette directed the words at Flora and she glanced questioningly at Aksel.

'Her grandmother gave her this. Mette switches it on when she wants to talk to Lisle and then we pretend to blow out the candle.'

'That's a lovely thing to do.' Flora's smile showed that she understood that this was an honour that Mette usually didn't share with people outside the family.

They each said their goodnights, Mette including Tante Flora in hers. Flora leaned forward, kissing Mette, and then turned, leaving Aksel to kiss his daughter goodnight alone.

She was waiting outside the door, though. The connection, which grew stronger each time he saw her, had told Aksel that she'd be there and it hadn't let him down yet.

'Would you like a lift home?'

Aksel shook his head. 'No. Thanks, but I want to go and have a word with Dr Sinclair. He said he'd still be here.'

'I can wait.'

'I'd prefer to walk. It clears my head.' It also didn't carry with it the temptation to ask Flora into his cottage for a nightcap. By the time he got home, he would have persuaded himself that the light that burned in her porch in the evenings was something that he could resist.

'I think I prefer a head full of clutter to walking in the cold and dark.' She gave him a wry smile and started to walk slowly towards the main staircase.

There was no one around, and they were dawdling companionably along the corridor. He could ask her now...

A sixth sense warned Aksel that he couldn't. Someone like Flora must have men lining up to ask her out, but she obviously had no partner. No children either. He wanted to ask about the welcome gifts she gave to all the kids at the clinic, and the quickly veiled sadness he'd seen in her eyes. But he didn't have the words, and something told him that even if he did, Flora would shut his enquiries down.

A couple of nurses walked past them, and Flora acknowledged them with a smile. The moment was gone.

'So... You're still okay for eight thirty tomorrow? To visit the housing complex?'

Flora nodded. 'I'll be ready.'

'Esme's offered me the use of one of the therapy centre's vehicles, so I'll drop in there to get the keys first thing and then pick you up.'

'Oh, great. I'll see you then.' She gave him a little wave, making for the main staircase, and Aksel watched her go.

Flora was an enigma. Beautiful and clever, she

seemed to live inside a sparkling cocoon of warmth. When she was busy, which seemed to be most of the time, it was entirely believable to suppose that she had everything she wanted.

But he'd seen her with Mette, and he'd seen the mask slip. Beneath it all was loneliness, and a hint of sadness that he couldn't comprehend. Maybe he saw it because he too was searching for a way forward in life. Or perhaps the connection between them, which he'd given up trying to deny, allowed him to see her more clearly.

But this chance to work together would set his head straight. Aksel had made up his mind that it would banish the thought that Flora could be anything else to him, other than a friend and colleague. And when he made up his mind to do something, he usually succeeded.

Chapter 6

Flora saw the battered SUV draw up outside at ten to eight the following morning. Aksel was early, and she gulped down her coffee, hurrying into the hall to fetch Dougal's lead. But the expected knock on her door didn't come.

When she looked again, she saw Aksel had opened the bonnet of the SUV and was peering at the engine. He made a few adjustments and then started the engine again. It sounded a bit less throaty than it had before.

That was a relief. The therapy centre's SUV had done more miles than anyone cared to count, and although it was reliable it could probably do with a service. Aksel looked at the engine again, wiping something down with a rag from his back pocket and then seemed satisfied, closing the bonnet and switching off the engine. Then he walked up the front path of his cottage, disappearing inside.

Fair enough. He'd said half past eight, and that would give her time to make herself some toast. She put Dougal's lead back in the hall and he gave her a dejected look.

'We'll be going soon, Dougal.' The little dog tipped

his head up towards her at the mention of his name and Flora bent to stroke his head.

When she wandered back into the sitting room, still eating the last of her toast, she saw that Aksel was outside again, in the car and that it was rocking slightly as he moved around inside it. Flora put her coat on and Dougal once again sprang to the alert, realising that this time they really were going to go.

'What are you doing?' Flora rapped on the vehicle's window, and Aksel straightened up.

'Just…tidying up a bit. I didn't realise this car was such a mess when I offered you a lift.'

He tucked a cloth and a bottle of spray cleaner under the driver's seat and opened the car door. The scent of kitchen cleaner wafted out, and something about Aksel's manner suggested that he'd really rather not have been caught doing this.

'It sounds as if it's running a lot better.' Flora wondered if she should volunteer her car for the journey, but it seemed ungrateful after he'd spent time on the SUV.

'I made a few adjustments. The spark plugs really need to be replaced, I'll stop and get some if we pass somewhere that sells car parts. They'll be okay for the distance we have to do.'

'I'm sure they will. It's not exactly a trip into the wilderness. And if the SUV breaks down, we can always call the garage.'

He grinned suddenly, as if she'd understood exactly what he was thinking. 'Force of habit. When you're miles away from anywhere, you need a well-maintained vehicle. I'll just go and fetch Kari.'

The dogs were installed on the cushioned area behind the boot divider, amidst a clamour of excited barking from Dougal. Aksel stowed Flora's bag of medical supplies on the back seat, and then gave the passenger door a sharp tug to open it. Flora climbed in, noticing that both the seat and the mat in the footwell were spotlessly clean.

'You didn't need to do all this…'

'You don't want to get your coat dirty.' Aksel looked a little awkward at the suggestion he'd done anything. He closed the passenger door and rounded the front of the vehicle.

All the same, it would have been a nice gesture on anyone's part, and on Aksel's it was all the sweeter. He clearly hadn't given the same attention to his own seat, and Flora leaned over to brush some of the mud off it before he got in.

'Anything I should know about the sheltered housing?' He settled himself into the driver's seat, ignoring the remains of the mud, and twisted the ignition key. The engine started the first time.

'It's a group of thirty double and single units, designed to give elderly people as much independence as possible. Residents have their own front doors, and each unit has a bedroom, a sitting room and a kitchenette. There's a common lounge, and a dining room for those who don't want to cook, and care staff are on hand at all times to give help when needed.'

'And what's your part in all of this?'

'I'm the Tuesday exercise lady. Mondays is chiropody, Wednesdays hairdressing. The mobile library comes on a Thursday, and Friday is shopping list day.'

'And everyone gets a rest at the weekend?'

'Kind of. Saturday is film night, and that can get a bit rowdy.'

He chuckled. 'So you just hold an exercise class?'

'No, I hold one-to-one consultations as well. I have a lady with a frozen shoulder and one who's recovering from a fractured wrist at the moment. And I also hold sessions for family members during the evenings and at weekends to show them how to assist their elderly relatives and help keep them as active as possible. Just a little of the right exercise makes a huge difference.'

'It sounds like a good place.' He manoeuvred into the drive-through entrance of the canine therapy centre and retrieved Dougal's lead from the back seat. 'I'm almost tempted to book myself in for a couple of weeks.'

'You don't strike me as the kind of person who likes a quiet life.'

Aksel shot her a sideways glance, the corners of his mouth quirking down for a moment. 'I'm leaving what I used to be behind. Remember?'

He got out of the car, opening the tailgate and lifting Dougal out, leading him towards the glass sided entrance. Dougal bounded up to the young man at the reception desk, and Aksel gave him a smiling wave. Flora wondered exactly who he was trying to fool. Everything about Aksel suggested movement, the irresistible urge to go from A to B.

'So you're not convinced that Mette will benefit from sharing your experiences?' By the time he'd returned to the car, Flora had phrased the question in her head already so that it didn't sound too confronting.

He chuckled. 'Spare me the tact, Flora. Say what's on your mind.'

'All right. I think you're selling yourself short. And Mette.'

He started the car again. 'It's one thing to take her on pretend expeditions. But I have to change, I can't leave her behind and travel for months at a time.'

'No, of course you can't. But that doesn't mean that ~~you~~ have to give up who you are. You can be an explorer who stays home...'

'That's a lot harder than it sounds.'

She could hear the anger in his voice. The loss.

'Is losing yourself really going to help Mette?'

'I don't know. All I know is that who I used to be kept me apart from her for five years. I can't forgive myself for that, and I don't want to be that person any more.'

His lips were set in a hard line and his tone reeked of finality. There was no point in arguing, and maybe she shouldn't be getting so involved with his feelings. She sat back in her seat, watching the reflection of the castle disappear behind them in the rear-view mirror.

It wasn't fair, but Aksel couldn't help being angry. Flora had no right to constantly question his decisions, Mette wasn't her child. If she'd been faced with the same choice that he had, she'd understand.

But he couldn't hold onto his anger for very long, because he suspected that Flora *did* understand. She'd seen his guilt and feeling of inadequacy when faced with the task of bringing up a child. She saw that he loved Mette, too, and that he would do whatever it took to make her happy. And she saw that even though he was ashamed to admit it, he still sometimes regretted the loss of his old life.

In that old life, the one he'd firmly turned his back on, he would have loved the way that she understood him so well. He would have nurtured the connection, and if it led to something more he would have welcomed it. But now, even the thought of that made him feel as if he was betraying Mette. The anger that he directed at Flora should really be directed at himself.

By the time they drew up outside the modern two-storey building, nestling amongst landscaped gardens, he'd found the ability to smile again. It wasn't difficult when he looked at Flora. She got out of the car, shouldering her heavy bag before he had a chance to take it from her.

'The exercise does me good.' She grinned at him.

'All that weight on one shoulder?' He gave her a look of mock reproach. 'If I were a physiotherapist, I'm sure that I'd have something to say about that.'

She tossed her head. 'Just as well you're not, then. Leave the musculoskeletal issues to me, and I won't give Kari any commands.'

'She won't listen to you anyway, she understands Norwegian.'

'If you're going to be like that…' Flora wrinkled her nose in Aksel's direction, and then directed her attention to Kari. 'Kari, *gi labb.*'

Her pronunciation left a bit to be desired, but Kari

got the message. She held out her paw and Flora took it, grimacing a little at the weight of the bag as she bent over. As she patted Kari's head, Aksel caught the strap of the bag, taking it from her.

'If you're going to speak Norwegian to my dog, then all bets are off.' He slung the bag over his shoulder, feeling a stab of pain as he did so. He ignored it, hoping that Flora hadn't noticed.

Inside the building, a woman at a large reception desk greeted Flora, and they signed the visitors' book.

'Here's your list for today. Mr King says that he has a crawling pain in his leg.'

'Okay. I'll take a look at that, then.' Flora seemed undeterred by the description. 'I'll go and see Mrs Crawford first.'

'I think you'll find she's a great deal better. She said that she'd been able to raise her arm enough to brush her hair the other day.' The smiling receptionist was clearly one of those key people in any establishment who knew exactly what was going on with everyone.

'Great. Thanks. My colleague's here for a meeting with Eileen. Is she around?'

'Yes, she's in her office.' The receptionist stood, leaning over the desk. 'Is that your dog? She's gorgeous. May I stroke her?'

'Of course. Her name's Kari.'

'I'll leave you to it…' Flora shot him a smile, and grabbed the strap of her bag from his shoulder. Aksel watched as she walked away from him. Bad sign. If she turned back and he found himself smiling, that would be an even worse sign.

* * *

Flora had gone on her way, warmed by the smile that Aksel had given her, but stopped at the lift and looked back. It was impossible not to look back at him, he was so darned easy on the eye. And the way he seemed to be struggling with himself only made him even more intriguing.

Fortunately, Mrs Crawford was waiting to see her, and Flora could turn her thoughts to the improvement in her frozen shoulder. Aksel was still lurking in the part of her brain where he seemed to have taken up permanent residence, but he was quiet for the moment.

'Your shoulder seems much better, Helen, you have a lot more movement in it now. Are you still having to take painkillers to get to sleep?'

Helen leaned forward in her chair, giving her a confiding smile. 'Last night I didn't feel I needed them so I put them in the drawer beside my bed.'

'Right. You do know that you can just tell the carer you don't need them and she'll take them away again?' Flora made a mental note to retrieve the tablets before she left and have them disposed of.

'She'd come all the way up here. And I might need them at some other time. It's *my* medication, but they act as if it's all up to them whether I take it.'

Flora had heard the complaint before. Drugs were carefully overseen and dispensed when needed, and it was one of the things that Helen had been used to making her own decisions about.

'They have to do that, they'll get in all kinds of trouble if they don't store medicines safely and keep a record. Some people here forget whether or not they've taken their medication and take too much or too little.' *Some people* was vague enough to imply that Flora didn't include Helen in that.

'I suppose so. It's very annoying, though.'

'I know. Give the carers a break, they have to keep to the rules or they'll get into trouble.' Flora appealed to Helen's better nature.

Helen nodded. 'I wouldn't want them to get into trouble over me. They have enough to do and they're very kind.'

'Right, then. I'll write in your notes that the carer is to offer you the painkillers and ask whether you want them or not. Is that okay?' Flora moved round so that Helen could see over her shoulder. She liked to know what was being written about her.

'All right, dear.' Helen tapped the paper with one finger. 'Put that it's up to me whether I take them or not.'

Flora added the note, and Helen nodded in approval. She'd raised four children, and worked in the village pharmacy for thirty years to supplement the family income, and even though her three sons and daughter were determined that she should be well looked after now, she resisted any perceived loss of independence.

'Who's the young man you arrived with? He's very tall.' Helen's living-room window overlooked the drive, and she liked to keep an eye on arrivals and departures.

'That's Aksel Olsen. He's from the canine therapy centre at the castle. They're talking about setting up a dog visiting scheme.'

'To help train the dogs? I could help with that, but I'm not sure that many of the others could.'

'Well, those who can't help might benefit from having the companionship of an animal. Don't you think?'

Helen thought for a moment and nodded. 'Yes, I think they will. Where's he from? His name isn't Scottish.'

'He's Norwegian. The dog understands Norwegian, too. He's trained Kari as an assistance dog for his daughter.'

'He has a daughter? Then he has a wife, too?' Helen was clearly trying to make the question sound innocent.

'No. No wife.'

'Really?' Helen beamed. 'Well, he might be looking for one. And it's about time you found yourself someone nice and had some bairns of your own.'

'I'm happy as I am, Helen. I have everything I want.' The assertion sounded old and tired, as if she was trying to convince herself of something. Flora wondered how many times she'd have to tell herself that before she really believed that Aksel was no exception to the rule she lived by. That there was no exception to the rule. Fear of rejection made the practicalities of falling in love and having a family impossible.

Helen brushed her words aside. 'He's very good looking. And tall. And such a mane of hair, it makes him look rather dashing. I dare say that he'd be able to sweep *someone* off to lots of exciting places.'

'He's actually better looking close up. Blue eyes.' Flora gave in to the weight of the inevitable, and Helen clapped her hands together gleefully.

'I like blue eyes. Mountain blue or ocean blue?'

Flora considered the question. 'I'd say mountain blue. Like ice.'

'Oh, very nice. And is he kind?'

Flora had worked through her list of patients, and when she arrived back in the communal sitting room, she found that Helen had decided to take part in the exercise class today. It was a first, and Flora wondered whether it was an attempt to get a closer look at Aksel's blue eyes and broad shoulders, and make a better assessment of both his kindness and his capacity to sweep a girl off her feet.

'Right, ladies and gentlemen.' Everyone was here and seated in a semi-circle around her, ready for the gentle mobility exercises. 'I brought along a new CD, ballads from the sixties.'

A rumble of approval went round, and Flora slipped the CD into the player. Carefully chosen songs that reflected the right rhythm for the exercises.

'We'll start with our arms. Everyone, apart from Helen, raise your arms. Reach up as high as you can...' Flora demonstrated by raising her own arms in time to the music.

The response was polite rather than enthusiastic, but the music and a little encouragement would warm things up. 'That's lovely, Ella, try the other arm now. Helen, you're sitting this one out... Now gently lower your arms. And up again...'

This time there was a murmur of laughter and the response was a lot more energetic. '*Very* good. Once more.'

A sudden movement from Helen caught her eye, and

Flora turned, following the direction of her pointing finger. Everyone was laughing now.

Aksel was leaning in the wide doorway, smiling, looking far more delicious than he had any right to. And in front of him Kari had obligingly raised one paw, lowering it again and raising the other.

Flora put her hands on her hips and walked over to him. Behind her she could hear chatter over the strains of the music.

'You know what this means, don't you?'

Aksel shook his head, flashing her an innocent look.

'There's a spare chair right there, next to Helen.' She may as well give Helen the chance to look him over in greater detail. 'Go and sit in it.'

'Yes, ma'am.' His eyes flashed with the ice-blue warmth that she'd told Helen about, and Aksel went to sit down. Kari trotted to her side, obviously having decided that she was the star of the show.

'Right. Let's do one more arm raise.' Flora raised her arms again and Kari followed suit, raising one paw. There was more laughter, and everyone reached for the sky.

'Well done, everyone. Aksel, I think you can do a bit better than that next time...'

Flora always kept a careful eye on everyone during her exercise classes to gauge how well they were moving and that no one was overdoing things. And this time Aksel was included in that. His left arm was fully mobile but he wasn't extending his right arm fully upwards, and she guessed that it was still hurting him. His neck seemed a little stiff as well.

Kari was loving all the attention, and when the ex-

ercise session was finished she trotted forward, eager
to get to know everyone. Flora started to pack up her
things, leaving Aksel to lead Kari around the semi-circle and introduce her.

She'd expected that Eileen would be keeping her eye
on things, and saw her standing quietly at the doorway.

'What do you think?' Suddenly it mattered to her
that the dog visiting scheme was a success. That Aksel
should feel useful and accepted here, rather than dwelling on all the things that he felt he'd done wrong.

Eileen nodded. 'The written plan for the scheme was
very thorough and I liked the thought behind it. This
is the acid test.'

Flora looked around. Kari was in off-duty mode,
which meant that she was free to respond to someone
other than her handler. She was greeting everyone with an
outstretched paw, and receiving smiles and pats in return.

'It looks good to me. Kari certainly made everyone
a bit more enthusiastic about the exercises.' Aksel had
done his part in that, too. He'd joined in without a murmur, smiling and joking with everyone. His charm had
contributed almost as much as Kari's accomplishments.

'It looks *very* good.' Eileen seemed to have already
made her decision. 'It might be a while before he's allowed to leave.'

It was a while, and by the time Aksel had torn himself away, promising everyone that he'd return, Flora
was looking at her watch. She needed to be back at the
clinic for her afternoon sessions.

As soon as he was out of the sitting room, Aksel
called Kari to heel, picking up her bag and making pur-

posefully for the reception area. He signalled a hurried goodbye to the receptionist, telling Eileen that he'd be in touch, and managed to insinuate himself between Flora and the front door so that she had no choice but to allow him to open it for her.

'How was your morning?' He gave her a broad smile. 'Did you manage to get to the bottom of Mr King's crawling leg?'

'Uh? Oh…yes, the carers keep telling him that the elastic on his favourite socks is too tight, but he won't listen. I changed them and gave his leg a rub and that fixed the crawling. You seem to have enjoyed yourself.'

'Yes, I did.'

'I see that your shoulder's still bothering you.'

'It's fine. It doesn't hurt.'

Pull the other one. There was a clear imbalance between the way that he was using his right and left arms, and Aksel seemed determined to ignore it. Just as he was determined to ignore everything else he wanted or needed. But she shouldn't push it. The clinic was full of therapists and movement specialists, and if he wanted help he could easily ask for it.

'We'll get straight back…' He dumped her bag on the back seat and started the engine. 'I saw you looking at your watch.'

'Yes, I've got afternoon sessions that I need to get back for. And if we hurry we should be back in time for you to have lunch with Mette.'

He nodded, the sharp crunch of gravel coming from beneath the tyres of the SUV as he accelerated out of the driveway.

Chapter 7

Flora knew that Aksel was at the clinic that afternoon, but she didn't drop into Mette's room during her break. It was bad enough that her thoughts seemed to be stalking him, without her body following suit.

Cass had come for her physiotherapy session, glowing with a happiness that matched Lyle's exactly. She'd come to the clinic as a patient, after sustaining injuries to her arm and leg during a search-and-rescue assignment. Then she'd met Lyle Sinclair. Sparks had flown, and the two had fallen head over heels in love. Lyle had been inconsolable when Cass had returned home to America, but now she was back in Cluchlochry for good. She'd spent most of the forty-minute physiotherapy session telling Flora about their plans for the future.

'The movement in your leg is a great deal better. I'm really pleased with your improvement.'

Cass sat up, grinning. 'I hardly even think about it now, only when it begins to ache. Lyle says I should still be careful…'

'Well, you don't need me to tell you that he's right,

you should be taking care. But being happy helps you to heal, too.'

'Then I'll be better in no time.' Cass slid off the treatment couch, planting her feet on the floor. 'Especially as I have you to help me...'

It had been an easy session. Flora stood at the door to the treatment room, watching Cass's gait as she walked away, and Aksel intruded into her thoughts once again. Cass was so happy, and looking forward to the future, and it showed in the way she moved. Aksel was like a coiled spring, dreading the future. No wonder he had aches and pains. Tension was quite literally tearing him apart.

He might be able to ignore it, but Flora couldn't any more. His shoulder could probably be fixed quite easily at this stage, but if he did nothing it would only get more painful and more difficult to treat. This was what she did best, and if she really wanted to help him, it was the most obvious place to start.

Aksel drew up outside his cottage, trying not to notice that Flora's porch light was on. He'd decided that he wouldn't seek her out at the clinic this afternoon, and it felt almost saintly to deprive himself of that pleasure.

As he got out of the SUV, opening the tailgate to let Kari out, he saw her door open and Flora marched down the path towards him, her arms wrapped around her body in a futile attempt to shelter herself from the wind. She looked determined and utterly beautiful as she faced him, her cheeks beginning to redden from the cold and small flakes of snow sticking to her hair. Aksel decided that sainthood was overrated.

'The car sounds better than it did this morning.' That was clearly just an opening gambit, and not what she'd come outside to say.

'Yes, I changed the spark plugs.' The SUV's rusty growl had turned into a healthier-sounding purr now. Aksel closed the tailgate and reached into the passenger footwell for his shopping bags, trying not to wince as his shoulder pulled painfully.

'And have you done anything about your shoulder? I'm not taking any excuses this time.'

'In that case...no, I haven't.'

'Come inside.' She motioned towards her cottage with a no-nonsense gesture that no amount of arguing was going to overcome. He hesitated and she frowned.

'If you don't come inside now, I'm going to turn into an icicle. You don't want to have to chip me off the pavement and thaw me out, do you?'

It was obviously meant as a threat, but the idea had a certain appeal. Particularly the thawing-out part. Aksel dismissed the thought, nudging the car door shut, and Kari followed him to Flora's doorstep. When she opened the door, Dougal came hurtling out of the sitting room to greet them.

He watched as she stood in front of the hall mirror, brushing half-melted snowflakes from her shoulders and hair. 'I appreciate the concern, but there's really no need. These things tend to rectify themselves.'

She turned on him suddenly. 'What's the problem, Aksel? You have a stiff shoulder, and I'm a qualified physiotherapist. Or are you not allowed to have anything wrong with you?'

She was just a little bit too close to the truth and it stung. He wanted to be the one that Mette could rely on completely. Strong and unbreakable. But there was no point in denying any more that his shoulder felt neither of those things at the moment.

'Okay, I…appreciate the offer and… Actually, I would like you to take a look at it if you wouldn't mind. It has been a little painful over the last few days.' He put his shopping bags down, taking a bottle of wine from one. 'Don't suppose you'd like some of this first?'

She rolled her eyes. 'No, I don't suppose I would. I'm not in the habit of drinking while I'm working.'

That put him in his place. But when he walked into the sitting room, he saw that a backless chair was placed in front of the fire. She'd been concerned about him and waiting for him to come home. The thought hit him hard, spreading its warmth through his veins as he sat down.

Suddenly all he wanted was her touch.

'Take your sweater off and let me have a look.' Flora congratulated herself on how professional her tone sounded. It was exactly how this was going to be.

She stood behind him, gingerly laying her fingers on his shoulder. 'You're very tense…'

Flora was feeling a little tense herself suddenly. The lines of his shoulder felt as strong as they looked, and there was only the thin material of his T-shirt between her fingers and his skin.

'It's been a long day.'

'What happened?'

He turned suddenly and Flora snatched her fingers

away, stepping back involuntarily. She couldn't touch him when the smouldering blue ice of his gaze was on her.

'I didn't come here to tell you my troubles.'

'I know. Turn around and tell me anyway.'

He turned back and she continued her examination. There was a moment of silence and she concentrated on visualising the structure and musculature of his shoulder. Suddenly Aksel spoke.

'Dr Sinclair took me through the results of Mette's latest MRI scan today. It's clear now that there isn't going to be any more improvement in her sight.'

'There was hope that there might be?' Flora pulled the neck of his T-shirt to one side, reaching to run her fingers along his clavicle.

'No, not really. The doctors in Norway told me that her condition was stable now, and there was very little chance of any change. It was unreasonable of me to hold out any hope.'

'But you did anyway, because you're her dad.'

'Yes. I wasn't expecting to come here and cry on your shoulder about it, though.'

'You can't expect muscles to heal when you're this tense, Aksel.'

Flora felt him take a breath, and he seemed to relax a little. As she pressed her thumb on the back of his shoulder he winced. 'It's a little sore there.'

She imagined it was *very* sore. The shoulder must be a lot more painful than he was letting on. 'You have a few small lumps on your collarbone. That's usually a sign that it's been broken recently.'

'Nearly a year ago.'

'And what happened? Did you get some medical

treatment when you did it, or were you miles away from the nearest doctor?'

He chuckled. 'No. Actually, I'd gone skiing for the New Year. There was a doctor on hand and he treated it immediately.'

'Good. That seems to have healed well, but the muscles in your shoulders are very tight. I can give you some exercises that will help ease them out.'

'Thanks.' He reached for his sweater.

'I can work the muscles out a bit for you if you'd like. It'll reduce the discomfort.' It was also going to take every ounce of her resolve to stay professional, but she could do that.

'That would be great. Thank you.'

She was just debating whether it would be wise to ask him to remove his T-shirt so that she could see what she was doing a little better when he pulled it over his head. Flora watched spellbound as he took an elastic band from his pocket, twisting his hair up off his shoulders.

His skin was golden, a shade lighter than his hair. Slim hips and a broad, strong chest came as no surprise, but Aksel had to be seen to be believed. He was beautiful, and yet completely unselfconscious.

'Okay. Just relax…' The advice was for herself as well as Aksel. This was just a simple medical massage, which might make him feel a little sore in the morning but would promote healing. And she wanted very badly to heal him.

He could feel the warmth of the fire on his skin. Aksel closed his eyes, trying not to think about her touch. Warm, caressing and… He caught his breath as she concentrated her attention on the spot that hurt most.

'Sorry. I can feel how sore it must be there…'

'It's okay.' He didn't want her to stop. Flora seemed to know all of his sore points, the things that tore at his heart and battered his soul. He wondered whether all of her patients felt the connection that seemed to be flowing through her fingers and spreading out across his skin.

He felt almost as if he was floating. Disengaged from his body and the cares of the day. Just her touch, firm and assured.

'My brother has cystic fibrosis.' She'd been silent for a while, working out the muscles in his shoulder, and the observation came out of nowhere.

'That's why you became a physiotherapist?'

'It was what made me first think of the idea. Alec's physiotherapist taught him techniques to clear the mucus from his airways, and he benefited a great deal from it.'

'It's a difficult condition to live with, though.' Aksel sensed that Flora had something more to say.

He heard her take a breath. 'I know how badly you want to help Mette, and how helpless you feel. I've been through all that with Alec. You're tying yourself in knots and that shows, here in your shoulder.'

'It's… I can't change how I feel, Flora.'

'I know. I'm not asking you to. Mette's lost a great deal, more than any child should have to. All she has left is you, and you owe it to her to take care of yourself.'

Aksel thought for a moment, trying to get his head around the idea. 'It sounds…as if you have a point to make.'

He heard her laugh quietly, and a shiver ran down his spine. 'My point is that you feel so guilty that your lifestyle kept you from her all those years that you just want to throw it all away. I can understand that, I've felt guilty about going out and doing things when Alec was ill in bed. But my mum used to tell me that if I didn't go, then I couldn't come home again and tell Alec all about it. You can share the things you've done with Mette, too. Don't be afraid to give her the real you.'

'And that'll make my shoulder better?' Flora might just be right.

'Maybe. I think the massage and exercise might help as well.'

She gripped his arm, rotating it carefully, seeming satisfied with the result. Then she handed him his T-shirt and Aksel pulled it over his head. The movement felt easier than it had for days.

'That feels better, thank you. Can we have that glass of wine now?'

She hesitated. 'It's not something I'd usually advise after a physiotherapy session. Water's better in terms of reducing inflammation.'

'Noted. Since I'm going to ignore your advice and have a glass anyway, you can either send me back to my cottage to drink alone, or join me.'

'In that case, I'd say it's my duty to keep an eye on you. I might need to save you from yourself.'

Aksel chuckled, getting to his feet.

* * *

The Advent candle burned on the mantelpiece. Another nineteen days to go. Aksel was sitting next to her on the sofa, and although they'd left as much space between them as possible, it still felt as if they might touch. Christmas was coming, and at the moment all that called to mind was mistletoe.

'Tell me about your family.' He sipped his wine, his tone lazy and relaxed now. He'd obviously forgiven her for forcing him to face the facts that he'd been so assiduously ignoring.

'There isn't much to tell. There's the four of us, and we travelled so much when I was a kid that we didn't see much of the rest of the family. Just at holiday time.'

'Where are your parents now?'

'They're in Italy. Dad's going to be retiring in a couple of years, so I'm not sure what will happen then. He always said he wanted to come back to Scotland. But my brother's married and lives in England, and they're trying for a child. I can't see my mum wanting to be too far away from a new grandchild.'

'What does your brother do?'

'He's a university lecturer. He fell in love with English literature when he went to Durham University, and then fell in love with his wife. The cystic fibrosis has slowed him down at times, but it's never stopped him from doing what he wants to do.'

'That's a nice way of putting it. It's what I want for Mette.'

'She can do more than you think. One day maybe she'll be leading you off on a trip around the world.'

The yearning in his face made Flora want to reach out and touch him. 'I'd like that very much.'

'My brother's never compromised…' Flora shrugged. 'It's caused its share of heartache, but we've faced it as a family.'

He nodded. There was never a need to over-explain with Aksel. He understood her and she understood him. That didn't mean they necessarily had to like what the other was saying, but the connection between them meant that neither could disregard it.

'So… You already know what frightens me. What are you afraid of?'

It was such a natural question, but one that was hard to answer. 'I'm afraid that the in vitro fertilisation for my brother and his wife will fail. They can't get pregnant on their own because of the cystic fibrosis. They'll deal with it, if it happens…'

'So that's a fear that you can face.' He was dissatisfied with her reply. 'What about the ones you can't face?'

'I have everything I want.' That must sound as much like an excuse to Aksel as it did to her. She had everything that she dared reach out for, and that was going to have to be enough.

'Having everything you want sounds nice.'

'I have a fireside, and a glass of wine. It'll be Christmas soon…' And Aksel was here. But however much she wanted to add him to the list, she couldn't.

'And…?' He reached out, allowing the tips of his fingers to touch hers. Her gaze met his and in an exquisite moment of clarity she knew exactly what he was asking.

She wanted to but she couldn't. Flora couldn't bring herself to trust any man enough to give herself to him. And the froth and excitement of a no-strings affair… It seemed great from the outside. But inside, when all the longing turned into disappointment and frustration, it hurt so much more than if it had never happened.

She moved her hand away from his, and he nodded. 'I'm sorry. I forgot all about my patient ethics for a moment.'

Flora couldn't help smiling. 'I thought *I* was the one who was supposed to be professional.'

'Oh, and I can't have ethics? I'm sure there's something in the patients' handbook about respecting your medical professional and not making a pass at them.' He grinned, his eyes dancing with blue fire.

He acknowledged the things that she didn't dare to. And he made it sound as if it was okay to feel something, as long as they both understood that actions didn't automatically follow.

'Fair point. Would it compromise your patient ethics to top up my glass?'

He chuckled. 'I don't think so. I'll do it anyway.'

This was nice. Sitting in front of the fire, drinking wine. Able to voice their thoughts and allow them to slip away. It was the best kind of friendship, and one that she didn't want to lose. Taking things any further would only mess it up.

Chapter 8

Flora had understood his unspoken question, and Aksel had understood her answer. Maybe she'd also understood that in the electric warmth of her touch, he'd got a little carried away.

She wanted to stay friends. That was fine. It was probably the wisest course of action, and it was just as well that one of them had kept their head. Making love with her might well have turned into the kind of explosive need that had no part in his life since he'd found Mette.

Friends was good. It meant that he could seek her out at the clinic the next day and ask her about the trucks that had been arriving on the estate, wondering aloud if she was interested in accompanying him and Mette on another voyage of discovery.

'The Christmas carnival is a bit of a fixture here. They set it up every year. There's usually an ice skating rink.' They were walking across the grass, with Mette between them, each holding one of his daughter's hands so that she didn't fall on the uneven ground.

'I want to skate!' Mette piped up, and Aksel swallowed down the impulse to say no. The clinic was proving as much of a learning experience for him as it was for Mette, and he was beginning to understand that, *Yes, let's make that happen* was the default position.

'That sounds fun.' Flora's answer wasn't unexpected. 'Perhaps you can skate with your papa.'

Okay. He could handle that. Keeping a tight hold on his daughter and guiding her around the edge of the rink. He doubted whether Kari would be all that happy on the ice.

It wasn't hard to orientate themselves as the carnival site was a blaze of light and activity. Most of the attractions were set up, apart from a few finishing touches, and Aksel recognised a few of the clinic staff using their lunch hour to try out the skating rink. The booth for skate hire wasn't open yet, and Mette was mollified with a promise that he would take her skating as soon as it was.

'We could take a look at the maze.' Flora gestured towards a tall hedge, decked with fairy lights, which lay on one side of the carnival booths.

'There's a maze?'

'Yes, it was re-planted a few years ago, using the plans of the original one that stood in the grounds. They decided to put it here so it could be part of the Christmas carnival.'

It looked impressive. Aksel bent down, explaining in Norwegian what a maze was, and Mette started to jump up and down.

'I want to go. I want to go…'

'Let's ask, shall we?' Flora approached a man stand-

ing at the entrance, who Aksel recognised by sight as
having come from the village. He turned towards Aksel
and Mette, waving them towards the entrance.

It was entirely unsurprising that Aksel forged ahead
of them into the maze. The paths were slightly narrower
than last year, the hedges having grown since then, and
they were tall enough that even he couldn't see over the
top now. They were all walking blind.

'Where do we go, Papa?'

He stopped, looking around. There was a dead end in
front of them, and paths leading to the right and the left.

'I'm…not sure.'

'Why don't you lead the way, then, Mette? We have
to try and see if we can find our way to the centre.'

Aksel shot her a questioning look, and then understanding showed in his face. 'Yes, good idea. Why don't
you tell us which way to go?'

He stepped back behind Mette, who stretched out
her hand, finding the branches to one side of her. Kari
watched over her, walking by her side, as she carefully
walked ahead, following the line of the hedge right up
to the dead end, and then turning back and to her right.

'I think she's got the right idea.' Flora fell into step
beside Aksel, whispering the words to him.

'Will this work? Following the wall to your right…?'
he whispered back,

Flora shot him an outraged look. 'Of course it will.
We'll get there if we just stay with Mette.'

'Papa…?' Mette hesitated, suddenly unsure of herself.

'It's okay, Mette. Just keep going, we're right behind you.' He reached forward, touching his daughter's shoulder to let her know that he was there, and she nodded, confident again.

Mette led them unerringly to the centre of the maze, where a small six-sided structure built in stone was decked with fairy lights. Kari guided her towards it, and she walked around it until she found the arched doorway.

'We can go inside, Mette.' Aksel was right behind her, patiently waiting for Mette to find her own way, and he'd seen the notice pinned to one side of the arch. 'We can climb to the top of the tower if you want to.'

The tower at the centre of the maze had a curving stone staircase inside, and from the viewing platform at the top it was possible to see the whole maze, the walkways picked out by sparkling fairy lights. Mette might not be able to see them, but she could still climb, and still feel that she was the queen of this particular castle.

Aksel guided her ahead of him, ducking under the arch and letting Mette find the handrail and climb the steps. Flora followed, Kari loping up the steps at her side. The four of them could just squeeze onto the small viewing platform at the top, bounded by crenellated stonework.

'Papa! I found the way!' Mette squealed with excitement, and Aksel lifted her up in his arms.

'Ja elskling…' He was hugging the little girl tightly, and he seemed to have tears in his eyes. 'I'm so proud of you, Mette.'

'I'm an explorer too, Papa.'

Aksel seemed to be lost for words. Flora wanted so

badly to put her arms around them both, but this was their moment. Mette had used some of the techniques that the clinic was teaching her, and they'd worked for all of them in the maze. And Aksel had found that for all his height and strength, and even though he could see, he'd not known which way to go any more than Mette had.

Flora waited while they savoured their triumph. Then she reached out, touching Mette's hand to catch her attention.

'Are you going to lead us back out again now?'

'She'd better. I don't know the way.' Aksel's voice was thick with emotion still.

Mette regarded him solemnly. 'What if I get lost, Papa?'

'You won't.' He set Mette back down on her feet, turning to guide her carefully down the staircase.

By the time they'd navigated their way out of the maze, the stallholders had almost finished setting up for the opening later on that afternoon, and the proprietor of the village tea shop was pleased to sell them sausage rolls, warm from the small oven on his stall, and made with homemade beef sausagemeat.

They wandered between the lines of stalls, and when Mette had finished eating, Aksel lifted her up onto his shoulders. Then he caught sight of it, stopping suddenly and staring at the open-sided tent.

'What's that?' He couldn't take his eyes off the large blocks of ice under the awning.

'You want to go and have a look? I'll stay here with

Mette.' Flora had a feeling that this was something that Aksel would like to explore on his own.

'I...' He turned, but seemed unable to find enough momentum to walk away. Looking back, he nodded. 'Yes. If you don't mind.'

'Of course not. We can go and get some doughnuts to take back with us.'

'I'll be back in a minute.' He lifted Mette down from his shoulders and Flora took her hand, watching as Aksel strode across to the tent. She'd be very surprised if he was back in a minute.

They chose and purchased their doughnuts, and Flora looked back towards the tent to see Aksel deep in conversation with Ted Mackie, the estate manager. Ted was eyeing him up, clearly deciding whether it would be okay to let Aksel loose with a chainsaw. Flora resisted the temptation to run up to Ted, take him by the lapels of his coat, and tell him that if Aksel could be trusted to get to both Poles and back, he could be trusted with power tools. And that he really needed to do something like this.

'What's Papa doing?' Mette was unable to see her father.

'He's right over there, at one of the other stalls. Shall we go and see?' Aksel had taken the pair of work gloves that Ted had proffered, and was passing them from one hand to the other as he talked. He was tempted. Flora could see that he was *very* tempted.

She walked slowly over to the tent, wondering whether that would give Aksel time to give in to the temptation. She could see him checking out the chainsaw and running his hand over one of the large blocks of ice. Ted was nodding in agreement to something he'd said.

'Hi. We've got doughnuts.' Aksel jumped when Flora spoke, too immersed in his conversation to have noticed them approaching. Flora tried hard not to smirk.

'Oh… I suppose…' He handed the gloves back to Ted ruefully. 'I'd really like to give this a go but…'

Ted flashed Flora a glance. 'Shame. It would be good to have something to show people. It would give us a start.'

'I'd like to but…' Aksel turned, masking the regret in his face with a smile. 'We need to get you back to the clinic, Mette. You've got a play date this afternoon.'

One of the well-organised play sessions, which would help Mette to make the most of her limited sight. They were very well supervised, and Mette was already making friends at the clinic. Aksel really wasn't needed.

'If you'd like to stay here, I can take Mette back.'

'We bought you a doughnut, Papa. So you don't get hungry.'

'Thank you.' He grinned down at Mette, taking the paper bag that she was holding out towards him. 'I should come back with you, though.'

Ted had bent down to Mette and took her hand, leading her over to the blocks of ice so that she could run her hand over them to feel the icy coldness beneath her fingertips. Aksel looked about to follow, and Flora caught his sleeve.

'She can do that by herself, Aksel. Ted's looking after her.'

'I know, but…' His forehead creased into a frown. 'I'm crowding her, aren't I?'

'You're spending time with her, so that you can make a relationship. That's great.' Aksel shot her an unconvinced look. 'And, yes, you are crowding her a bit. She's learning how to explore her world.'

'And this is what the therapists at the clinic are teaching her.' He looked over at Mette thoughtfully.

'That's our job, all of us. We may have specific roles, but we all have the same aim.' Everyone who worked here on the estate was a part of that. Ted took the children on nature walks during the summer, and Mrs Renwick, the cook at the castle, held regular cookery classes for both adults and children.

'All the same, Mette's far more important than this…'

'Yes, she is. She's important to all of us, and she's just starting to feel at home at the clinic. She has a play date this afternoon, and she's going to have a great time. You can either interfere with that, or you can stay here and make her something nice.'

He narrowed his eyes. 'Are you just saying that because you know I want to stay?'

'I'm saying this because staying's okay. Mette has other things to do this afternoon.'

Aksel was frowning, now. 'I was rather hoping that she'd learn to need me.'

Flora puffed out an exasperated breath. 'She *does* need you, Aksel. She needs you to be her father, which means you're always there for her. It doesn't mean that you have to follow her around all the time. The whole point of her being here is to learn to be independent.'

Most people would have hummed and hawed about it a bit. But Aksel had the information he needed, and it was typical of him to make his decision and act on it.

'You're killing me. You know that.' He turned on his heel, walking over to Mette.

'Ted says that I can make an ice sculpture. Would you like me to make one for you this afternoon, while Tante Flora takes you back to the castle to play?'

'Yes, Papa!' Mette obviously thought that was a good idea, too.

'Okay. What would you like me to make, then?'

Flora winced. Maybe it would have been better to give Mette some suggestions, rather than allow a child's imagination to run rampant.

'A reindeer. Mama took me to see the reindeer.'

'A reindeer?' Ted chuckled, removing his flat cap to scratch his head. 'That'll be interesting. What do you think, Aksel?'

Aksel shrugged. 'If she wants a reindeer, then… I can do a reindeer.'

'Would you like me to bring Mette back here after I've finished work?' Flora reckoned that Aksel might need a bit of extra time to work out how to sculpt four legs and a pair of antlers.

'Um… Yes. That would be great, thank you.'

'Right.' Flora took Mette's hand. 'Shall we stay and watch Papa get started on your reindeer, Mette, and then we'll go back to the castle.'

Mette nodded, following Flora to a safe distance, while Ted gave Aksel the gloves and a pair of safety glasses. Running him through a few safety rules was probably unnecessary, but Ted was nothing if not thorough, and Aksel listened carefully. Then he turned towards the block of ice that Ted had indicated, standing back for a moment to contemplate his first move, before starting up the chainsaw.

Mette tugged her hat down over her ears in response to the noise. 'What's Papa doing?'

'He's cutting some ice off the top. To make the reindeer's back.'

Aksel had clearly decided to start with the easy part, and was making an incision on one side of the block of ice that ran half way along its length. Then he made a similar incision from the top, freeing a large piece of ice, which he lifted down onto the ground. He switched off the chainsaw, engaging the safety mechanism, and beckoned to Flora and Mette.

'See this big block he's sawn off. It's almost as big as you are.' She kept hold of Mette's hand, letting her feel the size of the block. 'I can't wait to see what it'll be like when we get back.'

'Neither can I,' Ted interjected. He was clearly wondering how Aksel was going to sculpt a pair of antlers too.

'You're *all* killing me…' Aksel muttered the words under his breath, but he was grinning broadly. He was clearly in his element.

He bent down, kissing Mette goodbye and telling her to enjoy her afternoon. Flora took her hand and walked away, knowing that Aksel was watching them go. It wasn't until she'd turned into one of the walkways between the stalls that she heard the chainsaw start up again.

* * *

Mette had told everyone about how her papa was using a chainsaw to make her a reindeer out of ice. When Flora arrived back at the children's unit to pick her up, the nursery nurses and some of the children already had their hats and coats on.

'Are we ready, then?' Lyle was wearing a thick windcheater and was clearly intending to join the party. Flora hoped that they wouldn't be disappointed.

'Should we phone Ted first? To see if it's finished?' And possibly to make sure that the reindeer hadn't collapsed and they'd be greeted by an amorphous pile of ice.

Lyle chuckled. 'Aksel called me earlier for some orthopaedic advice.'

'He's hurt himself?' Flora hoped that Aksel hadn't overdone things and damaged his shoulder.

'No, it was more a matter of how thick the reindeer's legs needed to be to support the weight of the body. Interesting equation. I called Ted just now, and he says that it's all going rather well.'

Lyle looked round as Cass entered the room, displaying the sixth sense of a lover who always knew when his partner was nearby.

'I can't wait to see it.' Cass's green eyes flashed with mischief. 'There's something very sexy about a man using power tools…'

Yes, there was. And there was something almost overwhelmingly sexy about Aksel using power tools. Combine that with large blocks of ice, and it was enough to melt the most frozen heart.

'You think so? I might have to have a go, then.' Lyle raised an eyebrow and Cass laughed.

They all trooped out of the main entrance to the clinic, Mette holding her hand. It was dark now and the lights of the carnival shone brightly ahead of them, people straggling along the path that led down from the castle.

The first evening of the carnival was, as always, well attended. Charles Ross-Wylde was there, fulfilling his duties as Laird and host by greeting everyone and then melting quietly away to leave them to their fun. His sister Esme had brought a couple of the dogs from the canine therapy centre, and was clearly taking the opportunity to make sure that they weren't distracted by the lights and sounds around them.

Mette tugged at Flora's hand, remembering which way they needed to walk to get to the ice sculpture. As they approached, Flora could see Ted adjusting the lights that were placed at the bottom of the sculpture to show it off to its best effect. And Aksel's tall, unmistakeable silhouette standing back a little.

He turned, seeming to sense that they were there, and walked towards them. Shooting Flora a smile, he addressed Mette.

'Would you like to come and see your reindeer?'

'Yes, Papa!'

Flora watched as he led his daughter over to the reindeer, letting her stand close so that she could see the lights reflected in the ice. It was beautiful, standing tall and proud, a full set of antlers on its head. The lights glistened through the ice, making it seem almost alive.

Over the noise of the carnival, Flora could hear Mette's excited chatter. Lyle came to inspect the reindeer and Mette took his hand, pulling him closer to take a look. Aksel stood back, leaving his daughter with Lyle and Cass, and walked over to Flora.

'That is downright amazing.' Flora grinned up at him.

'I had a bit of help. One of the antlers snapped off, and Ted and I had to re-attach it. And Dr Sinclair's anatomical knowledge was invaluable.'

'Yes, I heard about that. I'm a little more interested in *your* anatomy.' Flora frowned. She could have phrased that a little better. Somehow, a perfectly innocent enquiry about his shoulder seemed to have turned into a barely disguised chat-up line.

'My shoulder's fine. If that's what you mean.' The slight quirk of his lips showed that Aksel was quite prepared to call her bluff, and Flora decided to ignore the invitation.

'I'm glad you haven't undone the work I did on it.'

'It might be a bit stiff in the morning…'

Flora returned his smile. 'If it is, I'll be officially reporting you to Lyle for some more orthopaedic advice.' A repetition of last night was probably to be avoided.

'You make that sound like a threat.'

'Don't worry. It is.'

Chapter 9

Aksel woke up the following morning feeling more refreshed from sleep than he had in a long time. It was a bright, clear day, and although his shoulder was a little sore, it was nothing that a hot shower and some stretching exercises wouldn't banish. He was ready for the day, and the day seemed that much better for the possibility that it might bring another chance to see Flora.

He wasn't disappointed. When he arrived at the clinic, after a morning's work at the therapy centre, he found that Mette was absorbed in a learning game with one of the children's therapy assistants. He kissed his daughter and told her that he wouldn't interrupt, and then wandered aimlessly down to one of the patient sitting rooms.

He saw Flora sitting in one of the wing-backed chairs by the great fireplace, which had been made bright and welcoming with an arrangement of Christmas greenery. He recognised the sandy-haired man in the chair opposite. One of the children's play leaders had told him that this was Andy Wallace and that he didn't much like to be touched, in a broad hint that Aksel should steer Mette clear of him.

Flora was leaning towards Andy, and the two seemed to be deep in conversation. Aksel turned to walk away, but then Flora looked up and beckoned him over.

Andy didn't offer to shake hands when Flora introduced the two men but nodded quietly in Aksel's direction, clearly taking his time to sum him up.

'We're just having tea. Would you like to join us?' Flora smiled at him.

There was no *just* about it. Flora had been talking quietly to Andy, no doubt discussing the next step of what looked like a long road back to full health. Andy's leg was supported by a surgical brace and his eyes seemed haunted. But if Flora thought that it was okay for him to join them, then he trusted her.

'Thank you. Can I get you a refill?' He gestured to the two empty cups on the small table between them.

'Not for me, thanks. Andy?'

Andy proffered his cup, and Aksel carried it over to the side table where coffee and tea were laid out. He put a fresh herbal teabag into Andy's cup and reached for a coffee capsule for himself. Flora leaned forward, saying a few words to Andy, and he nodded. All the same, when Aksel operated the coffee machine, Andy jumped slightly at the noise.

'Where's Mette?' Flora turned to him as he sat down.

'She's…got something going with the play assistants. Apparently I'm surplus to requirements at the moment.' Aksel made a joke of it, but it stung more than he cared to admit.

Flora nodded, smiling at Andy. 'Aksel's not used to that.'

Andy let out a short, barked laugh. 'I can identify with *surplus to requirements*.' He nodded down at his leg, clearly frustrated by his own lack of mobility.

'It's nothing…' The comparison was embarrassing; Andy clearly had life-changing injuries.

'Don't let Flora hear you say that. She has a keen nose for *nothing*.' Andy gave a wry smile, and Flora grinned back at him.

'Nothing's a code word around here. Meaning something.' Flora's observation sounded like a quiet joke, and Aksel wondered if it was aimed at him or Andy. Probably both of them.

'In that case, it's something. And I'm handling it.' Aksel's smiling retort made both Andy and Flora laugh. He was beginning to like Andy, and Aksel pulled out his phone, flipping to the picture he'd taken yesterday and handing the phone to Andy.

'Oh, she's a bonny wee lass. What's that she's standing next to?'

Flora smiled. 'Ted Mackie has an ice-sculpting stall at the carnival. With chainsaws. Aksel made the mistake of telling Mette that he'd sculpt whatever she wanted for her, and he ended up having to do a reindeer.'

Andy chuckled. 'You made a decent job of it. Why is your daughter here?'

'She was in a car accident, and she's lost most of her sight. Anything that's more than a few feet away from her is just a blur.'

'You've done the best thing for her, bringing her to the

clinic. They'll help her make the most of what she has.' Andy's reaction was like a breath of fresh air. Someone who knew the nature of suffering but didn't dwell on it, and who preferred to look at what could be done for Mette, and not express horror at what couldn't be changed.

'Thanks. That's good to hear.'

Flora had leaned back in her chair, seemingly in no hurry to go anywhere. The talk drifted into quiet, getting-to-know-you mode. Andy had been in the army and had travelled a lot, and the two men swapped stories about places they'd both visited. Andy's story about patching up a broken-down SUV from the only materials to hand struck a chord with Aksel, and the two men laughed over it. And Aksel's story about the mystery of the missing coffee supplies made Andy chuckle.

Finally, Flora looked at her watch. 'I hate to break this up, but it's time for your physio now, Andy.' She was clearly pleased with the way things had gone. And Aksel had enjoyed their talk. Andy had a well-developed sense of humour, and he'd led an interesting life.

Andy rolled his eyes. 'Another chance for you to torment me?' He clearly thought a lot of Flora.

'Yes, that's right. I don't get paid if I can't find something to torment my patients with.' Flora gave Andy a bright smile, helping him to his feet and pulling in front of him the walking frame that stood by the side of his chair.

'I'd like to see the pictures of your expedition to the Andes.' Andy turned to Aksel.

'Sure. I'll bring them in tomorrow. Is it okay for me to bring Mette with me?' Aksel wondered if a child might be too much for Andy but he smiled.

Martin County Library:
Fairmont - Adult -

Title: Her Christmas gift / Annie Claydon &
                             Teri Wilson.

Barcode:
                             30613004061747

Date   Wed Jan 19 2022 05:56PM

From: 890

'I'd like that. As long as she doesn't find me boring.' Andy glanced down at his leg. Aksel shook his head, sure that if anyone could see past Andy's injuries then his daughter could.

Flora broke in briskly. 'If you send me the pictures, I can print them out for you. Perhaps Mette will be able to see them better that way?'

'Thanks. I think she will.'

The two men nodded goodbye, and Flora followed as Andy walked slowly towards the doorway. She turned, giving Aksel a grin.

'If you're at a loose end, you can always go and sculpt something else. I'm very partial to unicorns, and now you have this down to a fine art it should be child's play…'

'Don't listen to her, man.' Andy called out the words. 'She's far too bossy.'

Bossy and beautiful. Soft and sweet and yet surprisingly strong. Intelligent, warm… The list just went on. Aksel had given up trying to complete it, because there was always more to say about Flora.

He called out an acknowledgement to Andy, wondering if Flora had lip-read the words that had formed silently on his lips. Or maybe she'd tapped into the connection between them and she just knew, because she shot him a look of amused surprise.

You want a unicorn…? If that was what Flora wanted, then that's what she'd get.

The ice unicorn stood next to the reindeer, and Ted Mackie had told Aksel that it had attracted both attention and admiration. He hadn't told Flora about it, even though she was the one person that it was intended to please. She was sure enough to hear about it, and he hoped she'd know it was *her* unicorn.

He'd arranged a schedule with Lyle for when he should bring Mette home. Both of them agreed that Mette was settling in well, and Aksel was anxious that she wouldn't miss any of the activities that the clinic ran for its patients.

'Are you sure you're happy with this? It's a little less than we originally envisaged.' Lyle gave him a searching look, and Aksel realised that his own attitude had changed since they'd last spoken about this. The question was less of a tug of war and more a meeting of minds now.

'I'm very happy with it. My relationship with Mette has been much better since she's been here. I have you to thank for that. She's gained a lot of confidence.' Aksel had wondered if he should say that Flora had given *him* the confidence to see that.

Lyle had nodded, smiling. 'I'm glad you feel that way. I think that your daily visits are very important for Mette, she knows that you're always there for her.'

He'd gone to the children's unit to see Mette and she'd greeted him with a hug and a kiss. When he'd asked her if she'd like to spend the day with him tomorrow, she'd tugged at the play assistant's arm excitedly, telling her that she was going to explore a new place with her papa.

Then he'd texted Flora, asking her if she was free. There had been no mention of unicorns, which had been a little disappointing, but her 'Yes' had made up for that.

* * *

Aksel arrived at the clinic just as the children were finishing their breakfast. He packed some things into his day-pack, although in truth nothing was needed. But Mette liked the idea of packing for a journey.

His shoulder had improved a great deal. The massage had done wonders and he suspected that Flora's wake-up call had something to do with it as well. He lifted Mette up onto his shoulders, perched on top of his day-pack, and felt his stride lengthen as they started the two-mile walk home, the rhythm of his steps quieting his heart. Aksel began to tell Mette the story of his trip up to a remote village in the Andes.

'Were there crocodiles, Papa?'

Not that he'd noticed. But, then, Mette's idea of a crocodile was her smiling stuffed toy. 'Yes, there were crocodiles. We gave them some chocolate so they wouldn't eat us.'

'And penguins?'

'Yes. We had to go fishing and catch them some tea, so they'd tell us the right way to the village.' If he was going to enter into the realms of fantasy, then he may as well just go for it.

'Did your feet hurt?'

'A little bit. I had a big blister on my toe.' He'd made a rookie mistake on the way back down, allowing water to get inside one of his boots, and frostbite had taken hold.

'Did it get better, Papa?'

'Yes, it got better. And when we reached the village, at the top of the high snowy mountain, the people there welcomed us and gave us food and comfortable beds, with warm quilts like yours.'

Mette whooped with joy, and the achievement seemed greater than the walk up to the isolated village, in terrible weather conditions, had been.

They had warm drinks together when they arrived back at the cottage, and Mette insisted on keeping her hat on, since she too was an explorer. Then there was a knock at the door, and Flora burst into the cottage, bringing the same sunlight with her that she took everywhere.

'I like the new look.' She grinned up at him and Aksel's hand shot awkwardly to the small plait that ran from his right temple and was caught into the elastic band that held the rest of his hair back.

'Mette's rag doll has plaits…' He shrugged as if it was nothing. When Mette had demanded that she be allowed to plait his hair this morning, it had felt like another step towards intimacy with his daughter, and he hadn't had the heart to unravel the uneven braid.

'I'm glad you kept it. She has excellent taste.' Flora obviously approved wholeheartedly. 'I hear that Ted Mackie's acquired an ice unicorn…'

Aksel wondered if she really hadn't been to see it, or she was just teasing. 'Has he?' He decided to play things cool.

'It's beautiful. I have about a million pictures of it.' She stood on her toes, kissing his cheek so briefly that he only realised she'd done it after the fact. 'Thank you.'

His cheek tingled from the touch of her lips as he followed Flora into the sitting room, where Mette was playing with Kari. Aksel decided that the hours spent sculpting the unicorn had been well worth it, and that he'd be tempted to create a whole menagerie of fantastic creatures in exchange for one more fleeting kiss.

It was agreed that they would walk down to the marketplace to see the village Christmas tree and the Christmas market. Aksel called Kari, putting on the yellow vest that denoted that she was at work now.

'Mette's already using Kari as her assistance dog?'

'No, but Esme suggested that it might be a good idea to let her see her at work a bit, just to get her used to the idea. Where's Dougal?'

'I took him up to the therapy centre, they're minding him. I didn't want him to get under Mette's feet.' Flora took a green and red striped bobble hat from the pocket of her red coat, pulling it down over her ears, and Aksel chuckled. She looked delightful.

'What are you? One of Santa's elves?'

'Right in one.' She shot him an innocent look, tugging at the hat. 'What gave me away?'

Chapter 10

Cluchlochry's market square was paved with cobble-stones, and boasted an old market cross, worn and battered by many winters. The market was already in full swing, with fairy lights hung around the canvas-topped stalls, and the village Christmas tree standing proudly in one corner, smothered in lights. As this was a Saturday morning, carol singers and a band had turned out to give the market a festive air.

The band struck up a melody that Mette recognised, and she started to sing along in Norwegian. Aksel lifted her up out of the crush of people, and heard Flora singing too, in English. At the end of the carol she joined in with the round of applause for the band, and Mette flung her arms up, wriggling with delight.

'Shall we go over to the village hall first?' Flora indicated a stone building next to the church. 'There are lots of stalls in there as well.'

Aksel nodded his agreement, and Flora led the way, while he followed with Mette. Kari trotted by her side, and every now and then the little girl held out her hand, putting it on Kari's back. It was a start. Soon, hopefully, Mette would be learning to rely on Kari to guide her.

Inside, it looked as if there had been some kind of competition between the stallholders to see who could get the most Christmas decorations into their allotted space. Aksel saw a large reindeer twinkling above one of them, and decided not to point it out to Mette, in case she wanted to take it home with her.

'Oh, look.' Flora had caught sight of yet another stall that she wanted to visit. 'I heard that Aileen was here, we should go and see her knitwear. She might have something that Mette would like.'

Aksel nodded his agreement, and Flora led him over to the stall, introducing him to Aileen Sinclair, an older woman with greying hair, confiding the information that Aileen was Lyle's mother and that she did a *lot* of knitting. That was self-evident from the racks of hats and scarves, and the sweaters laid out on two tables. Aileen smiled at him, sizing him up with an experienced eye.

'I don't know whether I can find anything to fit you, hen.' Aileen seemed willing to try all the same, sorting through a small pile of chunky cableknit sweaters. 'No, there isn't much call for extra-large, and Mrs Bell bought the last one for her son. If there's something you like, we can always make it up for you.'

'Thank you.' Aksel began to dutifully look through the sweaters. 'Actually, we were looking for something for my daughter.'

Flora lifted Mette up so that she could run her hand across the fine, lace knitted children's jumpers. Aileen greeted Mette with another of her beaming smiles, producing a tape measure from her pocket, and began to measure Mette's arms.

'What colour do you like, Mette?' Flora always asked Mette what she liked rather than suggesting things to her.

'Red.' Mette had caught sight of Aileen's bright red sweater, under her coat.

'Very good choice. Maybe a lacy one?' Aileen glanced at Flora and she nodded.

Piles of sweaters were looked through, knocked over and then re-stacked, in what looked like a completely arbitrary search. Finally three pretty sweaters, which looked to be around Mette's size, were laid out on top of the others.

'What do you think, Aksel?' Flora turned to him questioningly.

'They're all very nice.' Aksel wasn't prepared to commit himself any further than that and Flora frowned at him.

'You're no help.'

'Everyone should stick to what they're good at.' And Flora was very good at shopping. She always seemed to pick out the nicest things, buying the best she could afford and yet not over-spending. That was why she always looked immaculate.

He watched as Flora encouraged Mette to run her hand across each of the sweaters to feel their softness and warmth. She picked one, and Flora unzipped her coat so that Aileen could hold it up against her and make sure it fitted properly. The general consensus of opinion seemed to be that this was the perfect sweater, and Aksel reached into his pocket for his wallet.

He was too slow. As Aileen wrapped the sweater carefully in pretty paper, sticky-taping the ends down, Flora had whipped a note from her purse and handed it over.

'Thank you. I'll get your change.' Aileen plumped the package into a paper carrier bag and gave it to Mette.

'Don't worry about the change, Aileen. You don't charge enough for these already, I still have the one I bought from you three years ago. You'd make a lot more money if you didn't make them to last.'

Aileen flushed with pleasure. The sweaters were clearly more a labour of love than a money-making exercise.

Mette whirled around, eager to show Aksel her carrier bag, and Flora caught her before she lost her balance. He examined the bag, declared it wonderful, and Aileen bade them a cheery goodbye.

Then it was on to the other stalls. Flora was endlessly patient, letting Mette sniff each one of the home-made soaps on offer and choose the one she liked the best. The avuncular man at the fudge stall offered them some samples to taste, and Aksel was allowed to make the choice of which to buy. The indoor market was a whirl of colours, tastes, textures and smells, and Aksel found himself enjoying it as much as Mette obviously was.

'Are you hungry yet?' Flora clearly was or she wouldn't have asked the question. 'There's a pub on the other side of the green that serves family lunches whenever the market's open.'

A family lunch. That sounded good, and not just because Aksel was hungry too. He could really get used to this feeling of belonging, with both Mette *and* Flora.

'Good idea. They won't mind us taking Kari in?' Despite her yellow service coat, Kari wasn't working as Mette's assistance dog just yet.

'No, of course not. They're used to people coming in with dogs from the canine therapy centre, and they welcome them.'

Flora managed to find a table close to one of the roaring fires, and while she stripped off Mette's coat, Aksel went to the bar, ordering thick vegetable soup with crusty bread, and two glasses of Christmas punch. When he returned with the tray, Mette and Flora were investigating their purchases together. This seemed to be an integral part of the shopping experience, and Mette was copying Flora, inserting her finger into the corner of each package so that they could catch a glimpse of what was inside.

'Why don't you open them?' Aksel began to clear a space on the table between them, and Flora shot him a horrified look.

'Hush! We can't open them until we get home.'

'Ah. All right.' Aksel found that the thought of Flora and Mette spreading out their purchases for a second and more thorough inspection was just as enticing as this was. This complex ritual was more than just going out and shopping for something that met your needs. It was about bonding and sharing, and the excitement of finding a sweater that was the right colour and design, and fitted perfectly.

He was learning that there were many things he *could* share with Mette, and wondered if this would ever be one of them. At the moment, it seemed an impossible set of rules and conventions, which were as complicated as any he'd seen on his travels. It occurred to him that Mette really needed a mother, and the thought wasn't as difficult to come to terms with as it had been. He could be a good father, without having to do everything himself.

Flora and Mette were whispering together, and he couldn't hear what they were saying over the swell of conversation around them. Then Flora turned to him, her eyes shining.

'We're giving you ten out of ten. Possibly ten and a half.'

That sounded great, but he wasn't sure what he'd done to deserve it. 'What for?'

'For being our ideal shopping companion.' Flora didn't seem disposed to break the score down, but Mette had no such reservations.

'Because you carry the bags, Papa. And you don't rush, and you buy soup. And fudge.'

Aksel hadn't realised that this could cause him so much pride. And pleasure. 'Thank you. I'm…honoured.'

Mette gave him a nod, which said that he was quite right to feel that way, having been given such an accolade. Flora smiled, and suddenly his whole world became warm and full of sparkle.

'The Christmas tableau will be open by the time we've finished. And then I'd like to pop over to Mary's stall if you don't mind. I heard she has some nice little things for Christmas gifts.'

'That sounds great. I'd like that.' He wasn't quite sure what a Christmas tableau was, but he'd go with the flow. Aksel leaned back in his seat, stretching his legs out towards the fire. Making sense of the proceedings didn't much matter, he'd been voted ten out of ten as a shopping companion, and that was a great deal more than good enough.

The Christmas tableau turned out to be housed in a three-sided wooden structure outside the church. Inside were Mary and Joseph, an assortment of shepherds and three kings, along with one of the dogs from the therapy centre. Aksel wasn't quite sure how it had ended up there, but he assumed its presence had something to do with Esme, and that she'd probably had a hand in choosing its festive, red and white dog coat.

'Mette!' As they opened the gate to the churchyard, the shortest and broadest of the three kings started to wave, handing a jewelled box to one of the other kings and ducking past the crowd that was forming around the tableau.

Mette turned her head, recognising the voice, and tugged at Aksel's hand. 'It's Carrie. Where is she?'

It was the first time that Aksel had heard Mette say anything like that. Usually she ignored the things she couldn't see, and she'd been known to throw a temper tantrum when she couldn't find something she wanted.

'She's coming over to you now, sweetheart.' Flora volunteered the information, and Mette nodded. Now that the king was a little closer, he realised it *was* Carrie, one of the children's nurses from the clinic, and almost unrecognisable under a false beard and a large jewelled hat. Her small frame was completely disguised by what looked like several layers of bulky clothes under her costume.

'Hi, Carrie. Keeping warm?' Flora grinned at her.

'I'm a bit hot, actually.' Carrie pushed her beard up, propping it incongruously on the rim of her hat, and bent down to greet Mette. 'The costume was a bit big so I've got two coats on underneath this. Along with a thick sweater *and* thermal underwear.'

'Sounds reasonable to me. You've got a couple of hours out here. The shepherds are already looking a bit chilly.'

'Don't worry about them. The vicar's brought a couple of Thermos flasks along, and we've got an outdoor heater behind the manger, that's why everyone's crowding around it. You'd be surprised how warm it gets after a while.' Carrie volunteered the information and Flora laughed.

'That's good to know. I'll make sure I'm standing next to the heater when it's my turn.'

It was impossible that Flora wouldn't take a turn, she was so much a part of the life of the village. Aksel wondered what she'd be dressing up as and decided to wait and see.

'Would you like to come and see the stable, Mette?' Carrie bent down towards her. 'We've got a rabbit...'

'Yes, please.' Mette took her hand, waving to Aksel as Carrie led her away.

'A rabbit?' Aksel murmured the words as he watched her go.

'The vicar's not afraid to improvise, and I don't think there were any sheep available.' Flora chuckled. 'And anyway, don't you think it's the best stable you've ever seen?'

It was. The costumes were great, and there was a sturdy manger and lots of straw. A couple of other children, besides Mette, had been led up to the tableau by their parents, and had been welcomed inside by the shepherds and kings. Carrie was carefully showing Mette around, talking to her and allowing her to touch everything. The place shone with sparkling lights to recreate stars, and the warmth and love of a small community.

'Yes. The very best.'

Chapter 11

Aksel was relaxed and smiling as they watched Mette explore the stable with Carrie. So different from the man Flora had first met. The clinic tended to do that to patients and their families. Flora had seen so many people arrive looking tense and afraid, and had watched the secure and welcoming environment soothe their fears and allow them to begin to move forward. It was always good to see, but she'd never been so happy about it as she was now.

It was hard not to wonder what things might have been like if she and Aksel had met before they'd both been changed by the world. Whether they might have been able to make a family for more than just the space of a day. But for all the hope that the clinic brought to people's hearts, there was also the understanding that some things couldn't be changed, and it was necessary to make the best of them. She should enjoy today for what it was, and let it go.

Carrie delivered Mette back to her father, and she chattered brightly about having seen the rabbit and stroked it, as they walked towards Mary's stall. It was a riot of colour. Along with a few small quilts, there were fabric bags, with appliquéd flowers, patchwork lavender bags tied with ribbon, and quilted hats with earflaps. Mary was, unusually, not in the thick of things but sitting on a rickety stool and leaving her husband and Jackie, the young mum who helped out in the shop on Saturdays, to deal with the customers.

Flora greeted her with a smile. 'Hello, Mary. It's cold enough out here…'

Mary was sitting with her hands in her pockets, and her woollen hat pulled down over her ears and brow. Most of the stallholders prided themselves on being out in all weather, however cold, but maybe Mary should consider going into the pub for a while to get warm.

Mary nodded, her expression one of deep thought.

'These look wonderful.' Flora indicated the lavender bags and Aksel hoisted Mette up so she could smell them. 'How much are they?'

Mary smiled suddenly. 'Thruppence.'

Okay…. Flora had never heard of thruppenny lavender bags being a thing, but there were three in each bundle. They'd be tagged with a price anyway. Mary went back to staring in her husband's direction and Flora wondered if maybe they'd had an argument about something.

Hats were tried on, lavender sniffed, and the fabric bags admired. They found a hat for Mette, its bright reds and greens matching her coat, and Aksel encouraged Flora to treat herself to one of the fabric bags. It would be perfect for carrying some of the smaller items that she used most regularly in the course of her job,

and it would be nice to visit the residents at the sheltered living complex carrying a bag that didn't scream
that it was *medical*.

Mary smiled at her, and Flora put the bag and the
hat down in front of her. 'I'd like to take these, Mary.'

'Ah, yes.' Mary sprang to her feet. 'The hat's for…
the little girl.'

It was unlike Mary to forget a name. 'Yes, it's for
Mette.'

'Of course. Red.' Mary stared at the hat and then
seemed to come to her senses. 'That's two pounds for
the hat, plus three and fourpence for the bag. Fourteen
and six altogether, dear.'

Mary held out her hand to receive the money. Something was very wrong. Flora leaned across, studying
her face in the reflection of the fairy lights above their
heads.

'Are you all right, Mary?'

'I just have a bit of a headache, dear. How much did
I say it was?'

Mary *wasn't* all right. Flora glanced at Aksel and
saw concern on his face too. Even if he didn't follow
the vagaries of pounds, shillings and pence, it was obvious that Mary was confused and calculating the bill
in coins that had been obsolete for almost fifty years.

Flora squeezed around the edge of the stall, taking
Mary's hand. It felt ice-cold in hers. 'Mary, can you sit
down for me, please?'

'No, dear.'

'What's the matter?' Mary's husband, John, had left

the customer he was serving and come over to see what was happening.

'I don't know. Mary doesn't seem well, has she hit her head or anything recently?'

John Monroe had been a county court judge before he'd retired, and his avuncular manner covered an ability to sum up a situation quickly and take action.

'Sit down, hen.' He guided Mary to the stool, keeping his arm around her when she sank down onto it, and turning to Flora. 'She bumped her head when we were setting up the stall. She said it was nothing, and she seemed fine…'

'Okay, where?' Flora gently peeled off Mary's hat and realised she hadn't needed to ask. A large bump was forming on the side of her head.

'We need to get her into the warm, John.' Flora looked around at the crowded market. 'Go and fetch the vicar. I think that the church is the best place.'

John hesitated, not wanting to leave Mary, and Flora caught his arm. 'Go now, please.'

Aksel had dropped their shopping bags and Jackie stowed them away under the stall. Mette seemed to understand that something was wrong, and she stood quietly, her arms around Kari's neck. Jackie took her hand and Aksel bent down next to Mary, supporting her on the stool. Flora pulled out her phone.

'I'm going to call Charles.' She hoped that she wasn't overreacting but in her heart she knew that she wasn't. And she knew that Charles Ross-Wylde would rather she called, if she thought someone needed his help.

Charles answered on the second ring, and Flora

quickly told him what had happened, answering his questions and breathing a sigh of relief when he told her he'd be there as soon as he could. She ended the call, and Aksel glanced up at her.

'Charles is on his way, and he's going to call an ambulance.' Flora murmured the words quietly, so that Mary didn't hear. 'This may be a bad concussion or a brain bleed, so we must be very careful with her and take her somewhere warm and quiet.'

'Fourteen and six... Fourteen...and...seven...' Mary seemed to be in a world of her own, and Aksel nodded, concern flashing in his eyes.

The vicar arrived, along with Carrie, who was redfaced and breathless from running, her beard hanging from one ear. She took Mette's hand and Aksel turned to her.

'Will you take her, please, Carrie?'

'Of course. You see to Mary, and I'll look after Mette and Kari.'

'I'll go and open up the church lounge.' The vicar was fumbling under his shepherd's costume for his keys. 'It's nice and warm in there.'

Now all they had to do was to persuade Mary to go with them. Flora knelt down beside her. 'Mary, we're going to the church.'

'Are we?' Mary gazed dreamily around her, as if she wasn't quite sure what direction that was. 'All right.'

Mary went to stand up, swaying suddenly as she lost her balance. Aksel caught her, lifting her up, and she lay still and compliant in his arms.

People were gathering around the stall, some offering help. The only help they could give was to stand back, and Flora cleared a path for Aksel. As everyone began to realise what was happening, the crowd melted away in front of them, leaving them a clear route to the church.

They walked around the side of the ancient building to a more modern annexe. The vicar was waiting for them, holding the swing doors open, and he ushered Aksel through to the quiet, comfortable lounge. There was a long, upholstered bench seat at one side of the room, and Aksel carefully laid Mary down, while Flora fetched a cushion for her head.

'Mary, love….' John knelt down beside her and took her hand, but Mary snatched it away. Aksel laid his hand on John's shoulder.

'She's confused, John. We just need to keep her calm at the moment.'

'Is there any tea?' Mary tried to sit up, and Aksel gently guided her back down again.

'The vicar's just making some. He'll be along in a minute.' His answer seemed to satisfy Mary, and she lay back. Aksel kept talking to her, reassuring her and keeping her quiet.

Flora's phone rang and she pulled it from her pocket. Charles sounded as if he was in the car, and she quickly told him where to find them.

'That's great. I'll be there soon, and an ambulance is on its way too…' The call fizzled and cut out, and Flora put her phone back into her pocket. Maybe Charles had just driven into a black spot, or maybe he'd said all he wanted to say.

'What's the matter with her, Flora?' John was standing beside her, waiting for her to end the call.

'I'm not sure, but it seems to be a result of the bump on her head.' Flora didn't want to distress John even further by listing the things it could be. 'We need to keep her quiet. Charles is on his way and the ambulance will be here soon.'

'What have I done…?' Tears misted John's eyes. 'She said it was nothing. She seemed a bit subdued, but I thought she was just cold. I was going to take her to the pub for lunch as soon as I'd finished with the customer I was serving.'

'It's okay. In these situations people often try to deny there's anything wrong with them and they'll hide their symptoms. And they'll push away the people they love most. We'll get her to the hospital and they'll help her.' There was nothing more that Flora could say. If this was what she thought it was, then Mary was gravely ill.

John nodded. 'Is there *anything* I can do?'

'Has Mary taken any medication? Did she take something for the headache?'

'She didn't say she had one. And, no, she tries to avoid taking painkillers if she can.'

That could be a blessing in this particular situation. 'No aspirin, or anything like that? Please try to be sure.'

'No. Nothing. I've been with her all day, she hasn't taken anything.' John shook his head.

'Okay, that's good.' Flora smiled encouragingly at him. 'Now, I want you to sit down and write down exactly when Mary bumped her head, and how she's seemed since. Please include everything, whether you think it's important or not.'

'Right you are.'

Maybe John knew that Flora was giving him something to do but he tore a blank sheet from one of the stack of parish magazines that lay on top of the piano and hurried over to a chair, taking a pen from his jacket pocket. Maybe the details would come in useful…

Flora knelt down beside Aksel. 'You should go and get Mette now. I can manage.'

Flora didn't want him to leave. Her own medical knowledge was enough to care for Mary until Charles arrived, but he was so calm. So reassuringly capable. But however much Mary might need him, however much Flora *did* need him, she knew that he couldn't leave Mette.

'One minute…' He got to his feet, striding towards the door. A brief, quiet conversation with someone outside, and he returned.

'You're sure you want to stay?' Aksel had obviously made a decision and from the look on his face it troubled him a little. But he'd come back.

'Carrie's going to take Mette and Kari back to the clinic and I'll meet her there later. She's in very good hands.'

'Yes, she is. Thank you.'

He gave a little nod, and knelt back down beside Mary, taking her hand. Flora had to think now. She had to remember all the advanced first-aid courses she'd been on, and the physiology and pathology elements of her degree course. She took a deep breath.

Leaning forward, she looked for any blood or fluid discharge from Mary's ears and nose. Checked that she was conscious and alert, and noticed that her pupils were of an unequal size and that a bruise was forming behind her ear. Then she picked up Mary's hand.

'Can you squeeze my hand, Mary?'

The pressure from Mary's fingers was barely noticeable.

'As tight as you can.'

'I think I must have hurt it.' Mary looked up at her, unthinking, blank trust written on her face. It tore at Flora's heart, and she knew that she must do everything she could to help Mary.

'Let me massage it for you.' It wouldn't do her head injury any good, but it would keep Mary calm, and that was important.

'Thank you. I feel a bit sick.'

Aksel carefully moved Mary, sitting her up, and Flora grabbed the rubbish bin, emptying it out on the floor. Mary retched weakly, and then relaxed.

'That's better. I'm sorry…'

'It's okay. You're okay now.' Flora made sure that Mary's mouth was clear, and Aksel gently laid her down in the recovery position. Flora was aware that John was watching them, and couldn't imagine his agony, but she had to concentrate on Mary.

She talked to Mary, soothing her, watching her every reaction. It seemed a very long time before the door opened and the vicar ushered Charles into the room.

John shot to his feet, watching and listening. Flora carefully relayed all the information she had to Charles, and he nodded, bending down towards Mary to examine her. Mary began to fret again, and by the time he'd finished she was trying to push him away. Charles beckoned to Flora.

'Can you keep her quiet?'

'Yes.' Flora knelt down, taking Mary's hand, and she seemed to settle. She heard Charles talking softly to John behind her, and then the arrival of the ambulance crew. Then she had to move back as the paramedics lifted Mary carefully onto a stretcher.

'I couldn't have done better myself, Flora. Well done.' Charles didn't wait for her answer, turning to usher John out of the room.

The lights from the ambulance outshone the fairy lights on the stalls in the marketplace. The noise and bustle seemed to have quietened down, and many of the stallholders watched as Mary was lifted into the ambulance and Charles and John followed.

Suddenly she felt Aksel's arm around her shoulders. As the ambulance negotiated the narrow street around the perimeter of the market square, people began to crowd around her, wanting to know what had happened to Mary.

'I'm sorry, we can't say exactly what's happened, that's for the doctors at the hospital to decide. Mary's in good hands.' Aksel gave the answer that Flora was shaking too much to give. Then he hurried her over to Mary's stall.

'Jackie, will you be okay to pack up the stall?'

Jackie nodded. 'Yes, I've called my husband and he's on his way down with his mates. They'll be here in a minute. How's Mary?'

'I'm afraid we don't know, but Charles Ross-Wylde is with her and she's in very good hands.' Aksel repeated the very limited reassurance that he'd given to everyone else.

'Okay. I'll wait for news. Carrie came and took your shopping bags, she's taken them back to the clinic with Mette.'

'Thanks, Jackie. Are you sure you'll be all right on your own?'

'Yes, of course. Look, there's my husband now.'

Jackie waved, and Aksel nodded. He turned away, his arm tightly around Flora.

'Do you want to go the long way home? Or take the more direct route?'

'What's the long way? Via Istanbul?'

Aksel chuckled. 'No, via the clinic. I'm going to go home and pick up the SUV, then go to see Mette. I'll either walk you home or you can come with me.'

'I'll come with you.' Being at home alone didn't much appeal at the moment. 'Thanks for staying with me, Aksel. I know you didn't want to leave Mette.'

'No, I didn't. But Mette was all right and I reckoned I might be needed here.'

'Yes, you were.' Flora was going through all of the things she'd done in her head, trying to think of something that she'd missed. Something she might have done better.

'Mary's going to be all right. Largely because of you...'

'You're just saying that. I'm not a doctor.'

'No, but you used your medical knowledge to do as

much as any doctor on the scene could have. You kept her quiet, you made sure she didn't choke. You acted professionally and decisively.'

'But if something happens to her...' Flora didn't want to think about it. If there was something that she'd missed, and Mary didn't survive this... She couldn't bear to think about it.

He stopped walking, turning to face her. His eyes seemed dark, and his shadow all-encompassing.

'Listen. Mary was surrounded by people, and no one realised there was something wrong. If you hadn't noticed and done something about it, this wouldn't have ended as well as it has. You were the one who gave her a chance, Flora.'

His trust in her reached the dark corners of her heart. 'You were pretty cool-headed yourself.'

'Well, I've been in a few situations before.'

Flora would bet he had. 'I don't know what I would have done without you.'

He chuckled. 'I do. You would have done exactly the same—taken care of Mary, checked all her symptoms, and acted quickly. I might not cross the line from animal medicine into human medicine, but those things are essential in any kind of emergency.'

'You make me feel so much better.' He'd lifted a heavy weight from her shoulders. Whatever happened now, she'd know that she'd done all she could.

'Mary was lucky that you were there, Flora. Never think otherwise.'

They'd reached the SUV, parked outside his cottage, and Aksel felt in his pocket for the keys and opened the door for Flora. He was clearly keen to see Mette. *She* wanted to see Mette. Both of them had found a place in her heart, and now she didn't want to let them go.

The process of winding down had taken a while, but helping Mette to unpack the bags that lay in the corner of the room had helped. Aksel had been persuaded to tell a story about his travels, and she found herself joining in with Mette's excitement at the twists and turns of his narrative.

As they were leaving her phone rang. She pulled it out of her pocket, seeing Charles's number on the display, and when she answered, she heard John's voice on the line.

She listened carefully to what he had to say, feeling the tension ebb out of her. 'That's really good news, John...'

'Words can't express my gratitude, for what you did this afternoon Flora...' John's voice was breaking with emotion.

'I'm glad I could help. Make sure you get some rest tonight, you'll be able to see her in the morning. I'll come as soon as she's allowed visitors.' Flora ended the call, aware suddenly that Aksel was staring at her, waiting to hear John's news.

'This isn't bad news, is it?'

Flora shook her head. 'No, it's very good news. We were right about it being a brain haemorrhage and Mary was taken into surgery straight away. The operation was a success, and they're hopeful that, in time, Mary will make a full recovery.'

'That's wonderful. How's John, does he need a lift from the hospital? I can go there now and take him home.'

'No, he's okay. Charles is still there and he got someone from the estate to fetch his car from the village and bring it to the hospital. Benefits of being the Laird.' A great weight seemed to have been lifted from Flora's chest, and she felt that she could really breathe again. 'John said…he was glad that I'd been there.'

'Yes. I was glad you were there, too. Let's go home, shall we?'

It seemed so natural to just nod and take his arm. As if the home that they were going to was *their* home and not two separate cottages. As they walked out of the clinic together, towards the battered SUV, it didn't seem to matter that she was leaning on his arm. Just for tonight, until she reached her own front door, she could rely on Aksel's strength and support.

Chapter 12

Flora had been wondering whether to ask Aksel over for Sunday lunch, but she'd seen him set out towards the clinic with Kari by his side at eleven o'clock. She opened the refrigerator, staring at its contents. Suddenly she didn't feel like going to the trouble of cooking.

She made herself a sandwich, rounding it off with apple pie and ice cream as she watched a film on TV. Then she picked up a book, curling up on the sofa with Dougal and working her way through a couple of chapters.

The doorbell rang, and she opened her front door to find Aksel standing in the front porch. 'Shouldn't you be at the clinic?' The question slipped out before she'd had time to think.

'I went in a little early today and had lunch with Mette. I left her making paper angels with the other children.'

There was always something going on at the clinic, and Mette had obviously been drawn into the Sunday afternoon activities. 'That's good. The world always needs more paper angels.'

He nodded. 'Would you like to come for a walk?'

'A walk? I was planning to sit by the fire and make a few welcome gifts for the kids.'

'Sounds nice. A lot less chilly.' Something in his eyes beckoned her.

'The forecast's for snow later on this evening.'

He nodded, looking up at the sky. 'That looks about right. Are you coming?'

It was a challenge. Aksel was asking her to trust him, and in Flora's experience trusting a man didn't usually end well.

But Aksel was different. And what could happen on a windy, snowy hillside? Certainly nothing that involved exposing even a square inch of flesh.

'Why not? Come in, I'll get my coat.'

'You'll need a pair of sturdy shoes.' He glanced at the shoe rack in the hall.

'Even *I* wouldn't tackle the countryside in high heels. I have walking boots.' They were right at the back of the wardrobe, and Flora made for the stairs.

When she came back downstairs, his gaze flipped from her boots to the thick waterproof coat she wore and he gave a little nod of approval. As he strode across the road and towards the woods ahead of them, Flora struggled to keep up and he slowed a little.

'Where are we going?'

'I thought up to the old keep.' He pointed to the hill-top that overlooked the village, where piles of stones and a few remnants of wall were all that was left of the original castle seat of the Ross-Wylde family. 'Is that too far?'

It looked a long way. The most direct route from the

village was up a steep incline, and Aksel was clearly heading for the gentler slope at the other side, which meant they had to go through the woods first.

'I can make it.' She wasn't going to admit to any doubts. 'Looks like a nice route for a Sunday afternoon.'

He kept his face impressively straight. If Aksel had any doubts about her stamina, he'd obviously decided to set them aside in response to her bravado. Perhaps he reckoned that he could always carry her for part of the way.

'I think so.' His stride lengthened again, as if he'd calculated the exact speed they'd need to go to get back by teatime. Flora fell into step with him, finding that the faster pace wasn't as punishing as it seemed, and they walked together along the path that led into the trees.

The light slowly began to fail. Flora hoped they'd be home soon, although Aksel didn't seem averse to stumbling around in the countryside after dark. She felt her heel begin to rub inside her boot and wondered if she hadn't bitten off more than she could chew.

Only their footsteps sounded in the path through the trees. It was oddly calming to walk beside him in silence, both travelling in the same direction without any need for words. Their heads both turned together as the screaming bark of a fox came from off to their left, and in the gathering gloom beneath the trees Flora began to hear the rustle of small creatures, which she generally didn't stop to notice.

He stopped at the far end of the wood, and Flora was grateful for the chance to catch her breath. Aksel was staring ahead of him at a red-gold sunset flaming across the horizon. It was nothing new, she'd seen sunsets before. But stumbling upon this one seemed different.

'You're limping. Sit down.' He indicated a tree trunk.

Flora had thought she was making a pretty good job of *not* limping. 'I'm okay.'

'First rule of walking. Look after your feet. Sit.' He was brooking no argument and Flora plumped herself down on the makeshift seat. Aksel knelt in front of her, picking up her foot, and testing the boot to see if it would shift.

'Ow! Of course it's going to hurt if you do that...' she protested, and he ignored her, unlacing the boot. He stripped off her thin sock, the cold air making her toes curl.

'You're getting a blister.' He balanced her foot on his knee, reaching into his pocket and pulling out a blister plaster. It occurred to Flora that maybe he'd come prepared for her as she couldn't imagine that he ever suffered from blisters.

All the same, it was welcome. He stuck the plaster around her heel, and then pulled a pair of thick walking socks from his pocket.

'Your feet are moving around in your boots. These should help.'

'I thought walking boots were meant to be roomy.' She stared at the socks. They had *definitely* been brought along for her benefit.

'They're meant to fit. When your foot slips around in them, that's going to cause blisters.' He slid her boot back on and relaced it. 'How does that feel?'

She had to admit it. 'Better. Thanks.'

He nodded, unlacing her other boot. Running his fingers around her heel to satisfy himself that there were no blisters, he held the other sock out and she slid her foot into it. She reached for her boot, and he gave her a sudden smile.

'Let me do it. You need to lace them a bit tighter.'

Flora gave in to the inevitable. 'Rookie mistake?'

'Yes.' His habitual honesty wasn't making her feel any better.

'You might mention that it can happen to anyone. With new boots.' The boots weren't exactly new, but they hadn't been used much.

'It *can* happen to anyone. I let water get into one of my boots once, and lost the tips of two toes to frostbite.'

'Hmm. Careless.'

He looked up at her, smiling suddenly. 'Yes, it was. Looking at the way your teammates are walking comes as second nature because your feet are the only things you have to carry you home.'

They weren't exactly in the middle of nowhere. One of the roads through the estate was over to their right, and Flora had her phone in her pocket, so she could always call a taxi. But as Aksel got to his feet, holding out his hand to help her up, that seemed about as impossible as if they'd been at the South Pole.

She took a couple of steps. 'That's much more comfortable.'

'Good. Let me know if they start to hurt again, I have more plasters.'

Of course he did. If there was a next time, she'd make him hand over the plasters and lace her boots herself. She'd show him that she could walk just as far as he could. Or at least to the top of the hill and back down again.

As the ground began to rise, Flora's determination was tested again. She put her head down, concentrating on just taking one step after another. The incline on the far side of the hill hadn't looked that punishing, but it was a different matter when you were walking up it.

Aksel stopped a few times, holding out his hand towards her, and she ignored him. She could do this herself. It was beginning to get really dark now, and snow started to sting her face. This was *not* a pleasant Sunday afternoon stroll.

Finally they made it to the top and Aksel stopped, looking around at the looming shapes of the stones. Flora would have let out a cheer if she'd had the breath to do it.

'Perhaps we should take a rest now. Before we go back down.'

Yes! It was cold up here, but there must be some place where the stones would shelter them. Flora's legs were shaking and she suddenly felt that she couldn't take another step. She followed him over to where a tree had grown up amongst the stones, its trunk almost a part of them, and sat down on a rock, worn smooth and flat from its exposed location. Heaven. Only heaven wasn't quite so cold.

'I won't be a minute. Stay there.'

She nodded. Wild horses couldn't get her to move now. Aksel strode away, the beam of his torch moving to and fro among the stones. He seemed to be looking for something. Flora bent over, putting her hands up to her ears to warm them.

When he returned he was carrying an armful of dry sticks and moss. Putting them down in front of her, he started to arrange them carefully in two piles.

'What are you going to do now? Rub two sticks together to make a fire?' Actually, a fire seemed like a very good idea. It was sheltered enough here from the snow, which was blowing almost horizontally now.

'I could do, if you want. But this is easier.' He produced a battered tin from his pocket, opening it and taking out a flint and steel. Expertly striking the flint along the length of the steel, a spark flashed, lighting the pile of tinder that he'd made. He carefully transferred the embers to the nest of branches, and flames sprang up.

This was *definitely* a good idea. Flora held her hands out towards the fire, feeling it begin to warm her face as Aksel fuelled it with some of the branches he'd set to one side. She felt herself beginning to smile, despite all he'd put her through.

'This is nice.' When he sat down next to her she gave him a smile.

'Better than your fire at home?' His tone suggested that he thought she'd probably say no.

'Yes. In a strange kind of way.' Flora was beginning to see how this appealed to Aksel. They'd only travelled a short way, but even though she could still see the lights of the village below her, she felt as if she was looking down from an entirely different planet. The effort of getting here had stripped everything away, and she felt unencumbered. Free, even.

Chapter 13

Aksel had pushed her hard, setting a pace that would stretch even an experienced walker. He'd wanted her exhausted, unable to sustain the smiles and the kindnesses that she hid behind and defended herself with. But Flora was a lot tougher than he'd calculated. She'd brushed away all his attempts to help her, and kept going until they'd got to the top of the hill.

But her smile *was* different now. As she warmed herself in front of the fire, Aksel could see her fatigue, and the quiet triumph in meeting the challenge and getting here. He'd found the real Flora, and he wasn't going to let her go if he could help it.

The blaze seemed to chase away the darkness that stood beyond it, illuminating the faces of the rocks piled around them as if this small shelter was the only place in the world. Right now, he wished it could be, because Flora was there with him.

'Now that we're here…' she flashed him a knowing smile '…what is it you want me to say?'

She knew exactly what he'd done. And it seemed that she didn't see the need for tact any more.

'Say whatever you want to say. What's said around a camp fire generally stays there.'

She thought for a moment. 'All right, then, since you probably have a lot more experience of camp-fire truth or dare games, you can start. What's the thing you most want?'

Tricky question. Aksel wanted a lot of things, but he concentrated on the one that he could wish for with a good conscience.

'Keeping Mette from harm.'

'That's a good one. You'll be needing to get some practice in before she hits her teens.'

'What's that supposed to mean?' Aksel explored the idea for a moment and then held up his hand to silence Flora. 'On second thoughts, I don't think I want to know.'

'That's just as well, really. Nothing prepares any of us for our teens.'

She was smiling, but there was quiet sadness in her tone. Aksel decided that if he didn't call her bluff now, he was never going to. This wasn't about Mette any more, it was all about Flora.

'All right. I'm going to turn the question on its head. What would you avoid if you could go back in time?'

'How long have you got?'

'There's plenty of fuel for the fire here. I'll listen for as long as I can convince you to stay.'

She stared into the fire, giving a little sigh. 'Okay. Number one is don't fret over spots. Number two is don't fall in love.'

'The spots I can do something about. I'm not sure

that I'm the one to advise anyone about how not to fall in love.' Aksel was rapidly losing control of his own feelings for Flora.

'All you can do is be there for her when she finds herself with a broken heart.'

The thought was terrifying. But he wouldn't have to contend with Mette's teenage years just yet, and the question of Flora's heart was a more pressing one at the moment. He would never forgive himself if he lost this chance to ask.

'Who broke yours?'

'Mine?' Her voice broke a little over the word.

'Yes. What was his name?'

'Thomas Grant. I was nineteen. What was the name of the first girl who dumped you?'

Aksel thought hard. 'I don't remember. I went away on a summer camping trip with my friends, and by the time I got back she was with someone else. I don't think I broke her heart, and she didn't break mine.'

'If you can't remember her name, she probably didn't.' Flora was trying to keep this light, but these memories were obviously sad ones.'

'So… Thomas Grant. What did he do?'

'He…' Flora shrugged, as if it didn't matter. Aksel could tell that it did. He waited, hoping against agonised hope that if she looked into her own heart, and maybe his, she'd find some reason to go on.

'I went to university in Edinburgh to study physiotherapy. He was in the year above me, studying history…' She let out a sigh. 'I fell in love with him. I didn't tell my parents for a while, they were in Italy and I thought I'd introduce him to them first. I think my mum probably worked it out, though, and so Dad would have known as well.'

'An open secret, then.' It didn't sound so bad, but this had clearly hurt Flora. Aksel supposed that most really bad love affairs started well. The only real way to avoid hurt, was never to fall in love.

'Yes. We decided to tell our parents over the summer. We'd been talking about living together during our second year and…he seemed very serious. He even spoke about getting engaged. So I asked him to come to Italy with me for a fortnight. Mum and Dad really liked him and we had a great holiday. Alec wasn't too well that summer…'

Something prickled at the back of Aksel's neck. He knew that the end of this story wasn't a good one, and wondered what it could have to do with Flora's brother. His hand shook as he picked up a stick, poking the fire.

'You know, don't you, that cystic fibrosis is an inherited condition?' She turned to look at him suddenly.

'Yes.' Aksel searched his brain, locating the correct answer. 'It's a recessive gene, which means that both parents have to carry the gene before there's any possibility of a child developing cystic fibrosis.'

'Yes, that's right. Tom knew that my brother had cystic fibrosis, I never made any secret of it and I'd explained that since both my parents have the gene there was a good chance that I'd inherited it from one of them. Not from both, as my brother did, because I don't have the condition.'

'There's also a chance you haven't.'

She nodded. 'There's a twenty five percent chance of inheriting the gene from both parents. Fifty percent of inheriting it from one parent, and a twenty five percent chance of inheriting it from neither parent. The odds are against me.'

She didn't know. The realisation thundered through his head, like stampeding horses. Aksel hadn't really thought about it, but taking the test to find out whether she'd inherited the faulty gene seemed the logical thing to do, and he wondered why Flora hadn't. He opened his mouth and then closed it again, not sure how to phrase the question.

'When we came home to Scotland, we went to stay with his parents for a week. I told them about myself, and talked about my family. Tom told me later that I shouldn't have said anything. His parents didn't want their grandchildren to run the risk of inheriting my genes.'

'But that's not something you have to keep a secret...' Aksel had tried to just let her tell the story, without intervening, but this was too much. Anger and outrage pulsed in his veins.

'No. I don't think so either.'

'But... Forgive me if this is the wrong thing to say, I'm sure your whole family would rather that your brother didn't have cystic fibrosis. That doesn't mean it would be better if your parents had never married, or your brother hadn't been born.'

Tears suddenly began to roll down her cheeks. Maybe he *had* said the wrong thing. 'Thank you. That's exactly how I feel.'

'So they were wrong.' Surely *someone* must have told her that. 'What did your parents say?'

'Nothing. I didn't tell them, or Alec. It would have really hurt them, and I couldn't tell my own brother that someone thought he wasn't good enough. He's a fine man, and he's found someone who loves him and wants to raise a family with him.'

The defiance in her voice almost tore his heart out. Flora had stayed silent in order to keep her brother from hurt. She'd borne it all by herself, and her tears told him that with no way to talk about it and work it through, the wound she'd been dealt had festered.

'Did he listen? To his parents?'

'Yes, he listened. It probably had a lot to do with the fact that they were funding his grant, and they threatened to withdraw their support if he didn't give me up.'

'Don't make excuses for him, Flora. Don't tell me that it's okay to even contemplate the thought that my daughter, or your brother, are worth less than anyone else.'

She laid her hand on his arm, and Aksel realised that he was shaking with rage. Maybe that was what she needed to see. Maybe this had hurt her for so long because she'd never talked about it, and never had the comfort of anyone else's reaction.

'No one's ever going to tell Mette that she's anything other than perfect. I'm not going to tell Alec that either.'

She'd missed herself out. Flora was perfect too, whether or not she carried the gene. But, still, she hadn't found out…

'You don't know whether you carry the gene or not, do you?'

She shook her head miserably.

'Flora, it's no betrayal of your brother to want to know.'

'I know that. In my head.' She placed her hand over her heart. 'Not here…'

Suddenly it was all very clear to him. 'You just want someone to trust you, don't you?'

Surprise showed in her face. 'I never thought of it that way. But, yes, if I take the test I want someone who'll stick by me whatever the result. If it turns out that I don't carry the gene, then I'll never know what would have happened if I did, will I? I suppose that's just foolishness on my part.'

It was the foolishness of a woman who'd been badly hurt. One that Aksel could respect, and in that moment he found he could love it too, because it was Flora's.

'Anyone who really knew you would trust you, Flora. *I* trust you.'

She gave a little laugh. 'Are you making me an offer?'

Yes. He'd offer himself to her in a split second, no thought needed. But he couldn't gauge her mood, and the possibility that she might not be entirely serious made him cautious.

'I just meant that you can't allow this to stop you from taking what you want from life. You deserve a lot more than this.'

The sudden anger wasn't something that Flora usually felt. There was dull regret and the occasional throb of pain, but this was bright and alive. And it hurt, cutting into her like a newly sharpened blade.

'And that's why you brought me up here, is it? To take me apart, piece by piece?' On this hilltop, with the village laid out below them like a child's toy, it felt as if she could sense the world spinning. And it was spinning a great deal faster at the thought that Aksel wanted to know what made her tick.

'I brought you here because…it's possible to walk away from the everyday. To see things more clearly than you might otherwise. And because I wanted to know why someone as beautiful and accomplished as you are seems so sad.'

No. She couldn't hear this. Aksel needed to take the rose-coloured spectacles off and understand who she really was.

'I'm *not* sad. I just see things the way they are.'

'That no one's ever going to accept you for who you are? That's just not true, Flora.'

'Well that's not my experience. And for your information, I didn't give up on men completely, I just…approach with caution.'

He shook his head, giving a sudden snort of laughter. 'I've never thought that sex was much like stopping at a busy road junction.'

Trust Aksel. But his bluntness was always refreshing. She'd been skirting around the word and now that he'd said it… They were talking about sex. And unless Flora was very much mistaken, this wasn't a conversation about sex generally, it was about the two of them having sex. Despite all the reasons why it shouldn't, the thought warmed her.

'I'm not going to have sex with you, Aksel. I can't...' Flora didn't have the words to tell him why and she buried her face in her hands in frustration.'

'You don't have to give me any reasons. *No* is enough.'

Not many men took rejection the way that Aksel did. He'd pushed her on so many other things but this was where he drew the line. His smile let slip a trace of regret, but he accepted what she said as her final answer.

It wasn't final, though. Everything they were to each other, all the things they'd shared came crashing in on Flora. She couldn't let him believe that she didn't want him. The problem was hers, and she had to own it.

'It's not you. It's me.'

'It's a good decision, Flora. We've both been hurt. I'm leaving in five weeks, and you'll be staying here.'

And despite all that she wanted him. Maybe *because* of it. A relationship that had to end in five weeks didn't seem quite so challenging as something that might end because her genetic make-up, something she couldn't change, wasn't deemed good enough.

'But I *want* to explain...'

His face softened suddenly. 'There's no better place to do that than at a camp fire.'

'After Tom left me I had a few no-strings affairs, with men I knew. I thought it would help me get over him, but...they just didn't turn out right.' Flora couldn't bring herself to be more specific than that. She was broken, and even Aksel couldn't mend her.

'They ended badly?' Aksel came to the wrong conclusion, which was hardly surprising. She was going to have to explain.

'No, they ended well, it was all very civilised. But things didn't work physically. For me, I mean…'

He was looking at her steadily. She could almost see his brain working, trying to fit each piece of the puzzle together, and when he did, she saw that too.

'I think that when two people have sex, an orgasm is something that you create together.'

Sex and *orgasm*. All in the same sentence and without a trace of embarrassment or hesitation. That made life a lot easier.

'I don't want to fake it with you, Aksel. And that's all I know how to do now.'

Tears began to roll down her cheeks. She wanted to be with him, and all that she'd lost hurt, in a way it never had before. Flora heard the scrape of Aksel's all-weather jacket as he reached for her, and she shied away.

'The way I see it is that we have a connection. I don't know why or how, but I do know that I want to be close to you, in whatever way seems right. Do you feel that?' The tenderness in his face made her want to cry even more.

'I feel it. But it's too late…' Flora made one last attempt to fight the growing warmth that wanted so much more than she was able to give.

'Maybe I just ask you to my place for a glass of wine. We put our feet up in front of the fire…'

Frustration made her open her mouth before she'd put her brain in gear. 'You don't get it, Aksel. I want wild and wonderful sex with you, and frankly a glass of wine doesn't even come close...' Flora clapped her hand over her mouth before she blurted anything else out.

The trace of a smile hovered around his lips. 'You're killing me, Flora. You know that, don't you?'

'I know. I'm sorry.'

'That's okay. You're worth every moment of it.' Aksel leaned forward, murmuring in her ear, 'Close your eyes. I won't touch you, just imagine...'

Here, alone with him on a windy hilltop, warmed by the crackling flames of a fire, Flora could do that. She could leave her anger behind, along with everything that stood between them, and visualise his kiss and the feel of his fingers tracing her skin. She shivered with pleasure, opening her eyes again.

'You're smiling.' He was smiling too. The knowledge that he'd been watching her face, knowing that she was thinking of him, sent tingles of sensuality down her spine.

'That was a great kiss. One of the best.'

He raised his eyebrows. 'So we kissed? I'm glad you liked it. Any chance I might get to participate in the next one?'

He was closer now, and Flora closed her eyes again. This time she didn't have to imagine the feel of his lips on hers. They were tender at first, like the brush of a feather, and when she responded to him the kiss deepened. She grabbed the front of his jacket, pulling him close, and felt his arms wrap around her.

Arousal hit her hard. The kind of physical yearning

that she'd searched for so many times and which had eluded her. It was impossible to be cold with Aksel.

'That was much better. There are some things I can't imagine all on my own.'

He grinned suddenly. 'I liked it much better, too.'

'Would you like…to continue this? Somewhere more comfortable?'

'Will you promise me one thing?' He hesitated.

'What's that?'

'Don't fake it with me, Flora. However this turns out is okay, but I need you to be honest with me.'

She stretched up, kissing his cheek. 'No secrets, no lies. It's what I want, too.'

The thought that Flora had trusted him enough to feel that this time might be different was both a pleasure and a challenge. Aksel kicked earth onto the smouldering remains of the fire and shouldered his backpack, holding her hand to guide her down the steepest part of the hill, which led most directly to her cottage.

Flora unlocked her front door, stepping inside and turning to meet his gaze when he didn't follow her.

'Have you changed your mind?'

'No. But it's okay for you to change yours. At any time.'

She replied by pulling him inside and kicking the door shut behind them, then stretching up to kiss him. It was impossible that she didn't feel the electricity that buzzed between them and when she gave a little gasp of pleasure, unzipping his jacket so that they could nuzzle closer, it felt dizzyingly arousing. He wanted her so badly, and she seemed to want him. The thought that he might not be able to please her as he wanted to clawed suddenly at his heart.

Maybe he shouldn't take that too personally. Flora had been quick enough to tell him that he wasn't in charge of everything that happened around him. He would be a kind and considerate lover, and if things didn't work out the way they wanted, he'd try not to be paralysed by guilt.

'I'll love you the best that I can…' The urgent promise tore from his lips.

'I know you will. That's all I want.' She took his hand and led him up the stairs.

Chapter 14

He was letting her dictate the pace. Caught between urgent passion and nagging fear, Flora had no idea what she wanted that pace to be. Aksel pulled back the patchwork quilt that covered her bed and sat down, waiting for her to come to him.

She opened the wooden box that stood on top of the chest of drawers, rummaging amongst the collection of single earrings and pieces of paper that she shouldn't lose. Right at the bottom, she found the packet of condoms.

'I have these. I hope they're not out of date…' Her laugh sounded shrill and nervous.

'Let's see.' He held out his hand, and she dropped the packet into it. Aksel examined it carefully and then shot her a grin. 'They're okay for another six months.'

'Good. Maybe we'll save one for later.' The joke didn't sound as funny as she'd hoped. In fact, it sounded stupid and needy, but his slow smile never wavered.

Aksel caught her hand, pressing it to his lips. She sank down onto his knee and he embraced her, kissing her again, and suddenly there was only him. Undressing her slowly. Allowing him to patiently explore all the things that pleased her was going to be a long journey, full of many delights.

'Stop…' She'd let out a sigh of approval when he got to the fourth button of her shirt, and he paused, laying his finger across her lips. 'Be still. Be quiet, for as long as you can.'

'How will you know the difference?' In Flora's rather limited experience, most men wanted as much affirmation as they could get.

He gave a small shrug. 'If I don't know the difference when I hear it, then I really shouldn't be here.'

Flora put her arms possessively around his neck. This guy was *not* going anywhere. And if he wanted her to fight the rising passion until there was no choice but to give in to it, then that was what she would do.

She kept silent, even though her limbs were shaking as he undressed her. The touch of his skin against hers almost made her cry out, but she swallowed the sound. Flora had never had a man attend to her pleasure so assiduously before, and while the physical effect of that was evident in the growing hunger she felt, the emotional effect was far more potent.

He moved back onto the bed, sitting up against the pillows, and lifting her astride him. Face to face, both able to see and touch wherever they pleased. She reached round to the nape of his neck, undoing the band that was tied around his hair, and letting it fall forward.

'Is that what you want?' He smiled suddenly.

'Yes.' She kissed him again. 'I want that too.'

Aksel laughed softly. 'What else?'

It was an impossible question. 'It's too long a list. I don't think I know where to start…'

'How about here, then?'

She felt his arm coil around her back, pulling her against his chest. His other hand covered her breast, and she felt the brush of his hair against her shoulder as he kissed her neck. Flora closed her eyes, trying to contain her excitement.

She couldn't help it. Her own ragged cry took her by surprise. Wordless, unmodulated, it was as if Mother Nature had climbed in through a window and stripped away everything but instinct and pleasure. She felt Aksel harden, as if this was what he'd been waiting for. If she'd known that it would feel so good, she'd have been waiting for it too.

'I want you so much, Flora…'

But he was going to wait until she was ready. Flora reached for the condoms, her hands shaking. When she touched him, to roll one on, she saw his eyes darken suddenly, an involuntary reaction that told her that he too was fighting to keep the last vestiges of control.

When she lifted her body up and took him inside, Aksel groaned, his head snapping back. And his large gentle hands spread across her back.

This time things were going to be different. No faking it, and… No thought either. She was thinking too much. Flora felt herself tremble in his arms, returning his kisses as the tension built. A soft, rolling tide that must surely grow.

He sensed it too. The fragile, tingling feeling rose and then dissipated, leaving her shaken but still unsatisfied. All the same, it was something. More than she'd experienced for a long time.

Aksel didn't question her, but as he held her against his chest she could hear his heartbeat. He wanted to know.

'It was nice… Something.'

'Not everything, though?' His chest heaved, with the same disappointment that Flora felt. Nagging frustration turned once more to hunger.

'Can we try again?' He was still inside her. Flora knew that he must feel that hunger too.

'Maybe we should stop. I don't want to hurt you.'

'You won't. I want to try again, and this time I… don't want you to be so gentle.'

He hesitated. Flora knew that she was asking a lot of him. *Just take me. Make me come.* Maybe that was too much weight of expectation to put on any man.

But she knew that he wanted to. She wriggled out of his arms, moving away from him. Bound now only by gaze.

'Don't you want me?'

'Are you crazy, Flora? You're everything any man could want, and far more than I have a right to take…'

'But I'm asking you to do it anyway.'

For one moment, she thought he'd turn away from her. And then he moved, so quickly that he'd caught her up and pinned her down on the bed before she knew quite what was happening. His eyes were dark, tender and fierce all at the same time.

'Take my hand.' His elbows were planted on either side of her, and she reached up, feeling his fingers curl around hers in what seemed a lot like a promise. What-ever happened next, he'd be right there with her.

They'd faced passion together, and then faced disap-pointment. The kind of disappointment that a man—Aksel, anyway—found difficult to forget. If Flora hadn't already given him a good talking to about the nature of guilt, he'd be feeling far too responsible, and much too guilty to do this.

But when he'd tipped her onto her back, she'd gasped with delight, smiling up at him and putting her hand in his when he asked her. Trapped in her gaze, entering her for the second time was even better than the first. Better than anything he'd ever done, and it felt liable to overshadow anything he ever *would* do again.

She wrapped her legs around his back, and he felt her skin against his, warm and welcoming. He began to move, and her eyes darkened as her pupils dilated. Her body responded to his, a thin sheen of perspiration forming on her brow.

Aksel watched her carefully, revelling in all the little signs of her arousal. Suddenly she gasped, her whole body quivering for a moment in anticipation and her hand gripping his tightly. And then that sweet, sweet feeling as Flora clung to him, choking out his name.

It broke him. His own orgasm tore through him, leav-ing him breathless, his heart hammering in his chest. When he was able to focus his eyes again, the one thing he'd most wanted was right in front of him.

'You're smiling.'

Flora reached up, her fingertips caressing the side of his face. 'So are you.'

'Yes.' Aksel had the feeling that it was one of those big, stupid after-sex smiles. One that nothing in this world could wipe from his face. 'I'm not even going to ask. I know you weren't faking that.'

The thought seemed to please her. As if she'd wanted him to feel the force of her orgasm, without having to be told.

'I loved it. Every moment.'

'I loved it too.'

Her hand was still in his, and he raised it to his lips, kissing her fingers. Easing away from her for a moment, he arranged the pillows and she snuggled against him, laying her head on his chest, so soft and warm in his arms. Aksel let out a sigh of absolute contentment.

Flora had slept soundly, and she woke before dawn. The clock on the bedside table glowed the numbers six and twelve in the darkness. Twelve minutes past six was more Aksel's wake-up call than it was hers.

But he was still asleep. And she felt wide awake and more ready to meet the day than she usually did at this time in the morning.

She moved, stretching her limbs, and his eyelids fluttered open. Those blue eyes, the ones that had taken her to a place she'd been afraid to go last night.

Afraid... The clarity of early morning thoughts wondered whether it might just be the case that she'd been afraid all these years. Afraid to give herself to a man who didn't trust her enough for her to trust him back.

But she'd given herself to Aksel. In one overwhelming burst of passion that really should have been accompanied by booming cannons, waving flags, and perhaps a small earthquake. And she couldn't help smiling every time she thought about it.

He stretched, and she felt the smooth ripple of muscle. Then he reached for her hand, the way he had last night. He was still here, with her. Still protecting her from the doubts and fears.

'God morgen.' He leaned over, kissing her brow.

He'd lapsed into Norwegian a few times last night as they'd lain curled together in the darkness. It was as if his thoughts didn't wait to be translated before they reached his tongue, and although Flora didn't know what he'd said, the way he'd said it had left her in no doubt. They had been words of love, whispered in the quiet warmth of an embrace, and meant to be felt rather than heard.

'Are you…?' Did he feel as good as she did? Did he want this moment to last before the day began to edge it out? Flora couldn't think of a way of saying that in any language.

He chuckled, flexing his limbs again. 'I am. Are you?'

'Yes. I am too.'

All she needed was to lie here with him, holding his hand. But the sound of paws scrabbling at the kitchen door broke the silence.

'That's Dougal. He won't stop until I let him out…' Flora reluctantly tried to disentangle herself from Aksel's embrace, but he held on to her.

'I'll go. If you'd like to stay here, then I'll make you some breakfast.'

That would be nice, but even the time it took to make a couple of pieces of toast would be too long an absence. Flora let go of his hand and sat up. Even that was too much distance and she bent to kiss him again.

'I'll go. Are you hungry?'

He shook his head. 'Coffee or juice would be nice.'

She could let Dougal out, give him some food and water, and make coffee in two minutes flat if she hurried. 'Will you still be naked when I get back?'

Aksel grinned. 'You can count on it.'

She took the road into the estate as fast as the freezing morning would allow, and dropped Aksel off at the therapy centre at ten to nine, leaving him to take Dougal inside. If anyone noticed, then giving a next-door neighbour a lift into work couldn't excite any comment. She made it up to her office at one minute to nine, tearing off her coat and sitting down at her desk. Her first session of the morning wasn't until half past nine, and she could at least look as if she was at work, even though her mind was elsewhere.

Her whole body felt different, as if it was still bathed in Aksel's smile. Science told her that it was probably the effect of feel-good neuro-transmitters and hormones, but rational thought had its limitations. Aksel seemed to have no limitations at all.

When she closed her eyes, she could still feel him. He'd brushed off her suggestion that surely there wasn't anything more he might explore, and had taken her on a sensory journey that had proved her wrong. Aksel made foreplay into an exquisite art, and he obviously enjoyed it just as much as she did.

'Flora, we've a new patient….' Her eyes snapped open again to see Charles Ross-Wylde staring at her from the doorway. 'Are you all right?'

'Oh. Yes, I'm fine. Just concentrating.' Flora wondered if it looked as if she'd just spent two hours having stupendous sex. In the three years she'd been here, she'd never seen Charles show any interest in anything other than work, and he might not understand.

'Yes. Of course. As long as you're not feeling unwell.'

'No!' She could have sounded a little less emphatic about that as Charles was beginning to look puzzled. Best get down to business. 'You've a new patient for me to see…?'

The day wasn't without its victories. Andy Wallace had mentioned that Aksel had popped in, bringing Mette with him, and that they'd talked about ice carving and the long road that led across the Andes. The friendship seemed to have given Andy the final push to take his first step unaided.

Flora had tried to conceal her blushes when Andy had talked about Aksel, but he was in the habit of watching everyone closely. When they'd finished their session together, Andy had asked her to give Aksel his best when she saw him, smiling quietly when Flora had said she would.

Dougal seemed a little calmer when she picked him

up from the centre, and didn't make his usual frenetic dash around the cottage. He lay down in front of the fire, growling quietly.

'What's the matter, Dougal?' Flora bent down to stroke him, and he gave her his usual response, his tail thumping against the hearth. She walked into the kitchen, wondering if he'd follow, and he bounded past her, pawing at the cupboard where she kept his food. Whatever it was, it didn't seem to have affected his appetite.

She knew that Aksel would come. He'd be late, staying at the clinic until Mette was ready to go to bed, but he'd come. She heard the sound of the battered SUV outside, and smiled. He usually walked back from the castle, but tonight he was in a hurry.

The doorbell rang and she opened the door. Aksel was leaning against the opening of the porch, grinning.

'Are you coming in?'

'Are you going to ask me in?' There didn't seem to be any doubt in his mind that she would.

'Since you're holding a bottle of wine, then yes.'

He stepped inside, and Flora took the bottle from his hand, putting it down on the hall table. Without giving him the chance to take off his coat, she kissed him.

'I thought you wanted the wine,' he teased her, kissing her again hungrily.

'Isn't that just an excuse? To call round?'

'Yes, it's an excuse. Although if you'd prefer to just sit around the fire and drink it…' Aksel seemed determined to give her the choice, even though their kisses had already shown that neither of them wanted to spend the rest of evening anywhere else than in bed.

'No. I want you stone-cold sober. Upstairs.'

Aksel chuckled. 'I'll have you stone-cold sober, too. And calling out my name, the way you did last night.'

The thought was almost too much, but there was still something she had to do. Dougal was lying in front of the fire, still making those odd growling sounds.

'Will you take a look at Dougal first?'

'Of course. What's the matter with him?' Aksel walked into the sitting room, bending down to greet Dougal.

'I'm not sure. He's eating fine, and he doesn't seem to be in any pain. But he's making these odd noises.'

Aksel nodded, trying to stop Dougal from licking him as he examined him. Then he nodded in satisfaction. 'There's absolutely nothing wrong with him. He's trying to purr.'

'What?' That didn't sound like much of a diagnosis. 'Like a cat?'

'Yes.' Aksel tickled Dougal behind his ears and he rolled on his back, squirming in delight and growling. 'When I arrived at work this morning, I went to the office to finish up my report for Esme on the dog visiting scheme. I took Dougal with me to keep him out of the way as everyone was busy.'

'And you have a cat in the office at the canine therapy centre? Isn't that a bit of an explosive mix?'

Aksel shrugged, getting to his feet. 'Cats and dogs aren't necessarily natural enemies. A dog's instinct is to chase smaller animals, and a cat's instinct is to sense that as an attack, and flee. It's all a big misunderstanding, really.'

'Okay, so there was a cat at the centre...'

'Yes, someone brought it in, thinking that they might take it. Esme wasn't about to turn it away because... Esme doesn't know *how* to turn an animal in need away. And Dougal's natural instinct seems to be to make friends with everything that moves, and so by the end of the morning the two of them were curled up together. The cat was purring away and Dougal... I guess he was just trying to make friends.'

'So now we've got a dog that thinks he's a cat on our hands.' Flora looked down at Dougal, and he trotted up to her, rubbing his head against her leg.

'Maybe he'll grow out of it.'

Maybe. It made the little dog even more loveable, if that was at all possible. And talking of loveable...

'So... Mette and Kari are at the castle, and they're both fast asleep by now. Dougal's okay, apart from a few minor identity issues.' She approached Aksel, reaching up to wrap her arms around his neck. 'That just leaves you and me.'

'And more than twelve hours before it's time to go back to work.' Aksel grinned, and picked her up in his arms.

Chapter 15

They lay on the bed together, naked. Aksel had made love to her, and each time he did, it was more mind-blowing than the last. Things were going to have to plateau at some point, or Flora's nerve endings were going to fry.

'You know, don't you? When someone you're with has an orgasm.' Flora wondered whether the other guys she'd been with had known too. Maybe they had, and just hadn't cared.

'I do with you.' He grinned lazily. 'I suppose you want to know how.'

Yes, she did. Very much, because it seemed to please him so much. 'Tell me.'

'Your pupils dilate. You start to burn up, and you cry out for me. Then your muscles start to contract...'

'You like that?' Flora traced her fingertips across the ripple of muscles in his chest.

'You know I do. And you can't fake any of that.'

'Strictly speaking... I think you could try.'

'No, you wouldn't fool me.' Aksel curled his arm

around her, pulling her a little closer. 'What we have is honesty, and I'd know if that ever changed.'

It was a good answer. They *were* honest with each other. It had been something that had just happened from day one. Perhaps it was that which had guided them past all the traps and obstacles, and led them here.

'Well, honestly...' Flora propped herself up on one arm so that she could look into his eyes '...you are the most perfect, beautiful man I've ever seen.'

He didn't believe that. Aksel thought that his body was a workhorse that got him from one place to another, along with anything he carried with him. Vanity didn't occur to him.

'I'd urge you to make an appointment with your optician if you think I'm perfect.'

'You have a great body. *Very* nice arms.'

'Uneven toes...' He wiggled the toes on his left foot, two of which had been amputated above the distal phalangeal joint.

'Not very uneven. You only lost the tips of your toes, and they tell a story.'

'One that I won't forget in a hurry. Frostbite's painful.'

'And the mark on your arm?'

'That's where I was bitten by a snake. In South America.'

'And this one?' Flora ran her finger across a scar on his side.

'I was in a truck that tipped over while fording a river. The current turned out to be a bit stronger than we anticipated.'

'And you have a couple of small lumps along your clavicle where you broke it. The muscles in your shoulders are a little tight because you worry. A little tension in your back because Mette loves it when you carry her on your shoulders. Most people's bodies reflect who they are, and how they've lived, and yours is perfect.'

'And you… You really *are* perfect, Flora. You're made of warmth and love, and that makes you flawlessly beautiful.' He chuckled. 'Apart from that little scar on your knee.'

'It's not as good a story as yours are. I fell off my bike when I was a kid.'

Aksel reached up, pulling her down for a kiss. 'It's a great story. The scar's charming, along with the rest of you.'

Flora ran her fingers through his hair. Thick and blond, most women would kill for hair like that.

'Okay…so what's with the hair, then?' He knew that she liked it spread over his shoulders, instead of tied back, especially when they made love.

'It makes you look free, like a wild creature. Is that why you grew it so long?'

He shrugged. 'I don't know. Maybe I just never got around to cutting it. I like the sound of that, though.'

She kissed him again. 'Don't get around to cutting it, Aksel. That's perfect too.'

Aksel was happy. He felt free when he made love to Flora. And even when they weren't making love, the contentment that he felt whenever he was in her company was making him feel that maybe there was a little life left in his battered, careworn heart.

Tonight he'd be sleeping apart from Flora, though. He'd arranged to bring Mette home for the afternoon, and she'd stay the night with him at the cottage, before returning to the clinic the next morning. It had gone without saying that this was something that he needed to do alone.

He'd decided on some games, and had bought all of Mette's favourite foods. When he arrived home with her, he spread the colourful quilt on her bed, walking her around the cottage to remind her of the layout.

Everything just clicked into place, as if he'd been there all of Mette's life. She enjoyed her afternoon, and dozed in his arms as he told her the story about how crocodiles and penguins had helped him to reach the top of a high mountain in safety.

'I want to say goodnight to Mama.'

Aksel realised suddenly that in his determination to get everything right, he'd forgotten all about Mette's electric candle and had left it by her bed at the clinic. But it was important that his daughter felt she could speak to her mother whenever she wanted to. He reached for one of the Christmas candles that Flora had arranged on his mantelpiece, putting it into the grate.

'We'll use Tante Flora's candle, shall we? Just for tonight.'

Mette nodded, and Aksel fetched matches from the kitchen and lit the candle. They sat together on the hearthrug, saying their goodnights, and Mette leaned forward and blew out the candle. Aksel carried her up-stairs, settled her into her bed and kissed her goodnight.

At a loose end now, and not wanting to go down-stairs just yet in case Mette stirred, he went to his own bedroom and lay down on the bed, staring at the ceil-ing. This was the first night that he'd been completely alone with her, and it was a responsibility that brought both happiness and a measure of terror.

Aksel woke up to the feeling of something tugging at his arm. Opening his eyes, he realised that Kari had hold of his sweater in her jaws and was pulling as hard as she could to make him wake up and get off the bed. A moment later the smoke alarm started to screech a warning that made his blood run cold.

'Mette…' He catapulted himself off the bed and into her room. The bedclothes were drawn to one side and Mette was nowhere to be seen. Remembering that chil-dren had a habit of hiding when they sensed danger, he wrenched open the wardrobe doors, but she wasn't there either.

As he ran downstairs, he could smell smoke, but he couldn't see where it was coming from. Mette was curled up at the bottom of the stairs, crying, and he picked her up, quickly wrapped her in his coat, then opened the front door and ran with her to the end of the path.

'Papa. Kari made me go away from the fire.'

Cold remorse froze his heart suddenly. He could see a flicker of flame through the sitting-room window. Kari must have herded Mette out of danger, shutting the door behind them as she'd been taught. He held his daughter close, feeling tears run down his face.

'It's all right, Mette. Everything's all right. You're safe...'

The sound of an alarm beeping somewhere woke Flora up. It wasn't coming from inside the cottage, and she rolled drowsily out of bed, sliding her feet into her slippers and peering out of the window. She saw Aksel outside with Mette in his arms, Kari sitting obediently at his feet.

Running downstairs, she grabbed her coat, not stopping to put it on. As soon as she was outside, the faint smell of smoke hit her and she hurried over to Aksel.

'Are you both all right?'

He raised his face towards her, and Flora saw tears. Mette realised that she was there, although she must be practically blind in the darkness, and reached out from the warm cradle of his arms.

'Papa says we're safe.' Aksel seemed too overwhelmed to speak, and Mette volunteered the information.

'That's right. You're safe now.'

She looked up at Aksel questioningly, and he brushed his hand across his face. 'There's a fire, I think it's pretty much contained to the sitting room. Will you take Mette while I go and have a look.'

'No, Aksel. Wait for the fire brigade. Have you called them?'

'My phone's inside. Please, take her.'

It seemed that Aksel was more comfortable with

dealing with the situation than he was with taking care of his daughter right now. Flora wondered how the fire had started. She took Mette, holding the little girl tight in her arms.

'Papa's just looking to see how big the fire is.' As Aksel walked back up the path, peering through the front windows, Mette craned round to keep him in view.

'It's all right, he's quite safe. He isn't getting too close, so the fire won't burn him.'

Mette seemed more confident of that than Flora felt. 'My papa fights crocodiles.'

'There you are, then. If he can fight crocodiles then a little fire will be easy…'

She watched, holding her breath as Aksel walked back towards them, his face set in a look of grim determination.

'It's just the hearth rug at the moment. Will you look after Mette while I go and put it out?'

'You should leave it, until the fire brigade gets here. We'll go inside and call them now…'

'I can put it out, there's a fire extinguisher in the kitchen. And if we leave it, then it may spread to the chimney. I don't know how long it's been since it's been swept, and I want to avoid that.'

A chimney fire could easily spread to her cottage. Flora dismissed the thought. What mattered was that they were all safe. 'No, Aksel…'

He was going anyway. She may as well accept it, and work with what was inevitable. Flora transferred Mette into his arms for a moment while she wriggled out of her own coat, wrapping it around the little girl so that his was no longer needed.

'If you must go, put your coat on, it'll protect your arms. And put a pair of boots on as well.'

He looked down at his feet, seeming to realise for the first time that he was only wearing a pair of socks. 'Okay. You're right. You'll take Mette inside?'

She was shivering, her pyjamas giving no protection against the wind. But she wasn't moving until she saw that Aksel was safe. 'If you must go, go now. Before the fire gets any worse. And no heroics, Aksel. Back off if it looks to be getting worse.'

He nodded. Giving Kari a curt command, he strode back up the path, opening the door to his cottage.

Kari was on the alert now, sniffing the air and looking around. Aksel had clearly ordered the dog to protect them, and she was taking her task seriously. Flora hugged Mette close, pulling her coat down around the child's feet.

'Papa's just going to put out the fire. He won't be a minute.' She said the words as if it was nothing. Maybe it *was* nothing to Aksel, but right now it seemed a great deal to her.

She watched as Aksel's dark figure approached the fire. A plume of shadows emitted from the fire extinguisher and the flames died almost immediately. He disappeared for a moment and then reappeared with a bucket, tipping its contents over the ashes to make sure that the fire was well and truly out.

Okay. Everything was okay, and now all she wanted

to do was to get warm. By the time Aksel reappeared her teeth were chattering.

'Everything all right?'

'No.' He took his coat off and wrapped it around her. 'You're freezing.'

'The fire's out, though…' He was hurrying her towards her own front door, his arm around her shoulders.

'Yes. I made sure of it.' Aksel pushed the door open and glorious warmth surrounded her suddenly. 'Come and sit down.'

He was gentle and attentive, but his eyes were dead. Whatever he felt was locked behind an impervious barrier.

'Stay with Mette and I'll make a hot drink.' Flora was trying to stop shivering.

'No, I'll do that. You sit and get warm.' He picked up the woollen blanket that was folded across the back of the sofa and waited until Flora had sat down, then tucked it around her and Mette. Then he disappeared into the kitchen.

He came back with two cups of tea, and Flora drank hers while he went upstairs to the bathroom to wash his hands and face. When he came back and sat down, Mette crawled across the sofa, snuggling against him and yawning. Flora waited for the little girl to fall asleep before she asked the inevitable question.

'What happened?'

'I was asleep upstairs. Kari and Mette were downstairs, and Kari herded Mette out into the hallway and shut the door. Then she came to wake me up.' He held out his hand, and Kari ambled over to him. He fondled the dog's ears and she laid her head in his lap.

'You taught her to do that?'

He nodded. 'I didn't even know that Mette was out of bed.'

'What was she doing downstairs?'

'From the looks of it, she'd gone downstairs and lit a candle in the grate. It must have fallen over onto the hearth rug...' His voice cracked and broke with emotion.

'Where did she get the matches from?' Aksel had clearly already tried and convicted himself, without even listening to the case for the defence.

'They were in one of the high cupboards in the kitchen. I didn't think she could get to them, but when I went back inside I saw that she'd dragged a chair across the room. She must have climbed up on it, then got up onto the counter top and into the cupboard.'

It was quite an achievement for a six-year-old with poor sight. 'What made her so determined to light a candle in the middle of the night?' Flora's hand flew to her mouth. She knew the answer.

'When I packed her things, I forgot her electric candle. So I lit a real one for her. It's all my...' He fell silent as Flora flapped her hand urgently at him.

'Don't. You're not to say it. It's *not* your fault.'

'That's not borne out by the facts.' His face was blank, as if he'd accepted his guilt without any question.

Flora took a breath. Whatever she said now had to be convincing. 'Look, Aksel, I talk to a lot of parents in the course of my work. The one thing that everyone agrees on is that you can't watch your children twenty-four hours a day. It isn't possible. But you've come up with a good second-best, and you trained Kari to watch over her.'

He narrowed his eyes. 'You're just making excuses for me.'

'No, I'm not. You let her say goodnight to her mother, Aksel, she needs to do that. And you put the matches away, somewhere that should have been out of her reach.'

'She *did* reach them, though.'

'Well, you might be able to take part of the blame for that one. She takes after her father in being resourceful. I imagine she has all kinds of challenges up her sleeve…'

'All right. You're making me panic now.'

If he didn't like that, then he *really* wasn't going to like the next part. 'You need to let her know, Aksel, that she mustn't play with matches.'

He sighed. 'Yes. I know. Her grandmother always told her off when she was naughty…'

'Yeah, right. You can't rely on her to be the bad guy now.'

Right on cue, Mette shifted fitfully in his arms, opening her eyes. 'Papa, the fire's out?'

'Yes.'

'Did you save all the crocodiles, and the penguins?' Mette was awake again now, and probably ready to play. Aksel's face took on an agonised look, knowing that the time had come for him to be the bad guy.

'Yes, the crocodiles and penguins are all fine. Mette, there's something I have to say to you.'

Mette's gaze slid guiltily towards Flora and she struggled not to react. Aksel had to do this by himself.

'I love you very much, Mette, and you know that you can talk to Mama any time you want.' He started with the positive. 'But you mustn't touch matches or light candles when I'm not there. And you mustn't climb up onto cupboards either. You could hurt yourself very badly.'

A large tear rolled down Mette's cheek. Flora could almost see Aksel's heart breaking.

'Is the fire my fault, Papa?'

'No. It's my fault. I didn't tell you not to do those things, and I should have. But I want you to promise not to do them again.' He waited a moment for Mette to respond. 'You have to say it, please, Mette. "I promise…"'

Mette turned the corners of her mouth down in a look of abject dismay. Even Flora wanted to forgive her immediately, and she wondered whether getting to the North Pole had presented quite as much of a challenge to Aksel as this.

'I promise, Papa.' Another tear rolled down her cheek and Aksel nodded.

'Thank you.' Finally he broke, cuddling Mette to his chest. 'I love you very much.'

'I love you too, Papa.'

'What was it you wanted to say to Mama?' He kissed the top of his daughter's head.

'I forgot to tell her all about our house. And that I like my room…'

'All right. We'll go back to the clinic and find your candle. And you can tell Mama all about it.'

'When?'

'Right now, Mette.'

Mette nodded, satisfied with his answer, and curled up in his arms, her eyelids drooping again drowsily. Flora handed him the woollen blanket and he wrapped his daughter in it, leaving her to sleep. Finally his gaze found Flora's.

'Forget wrestling crocodiles. That was the most difficult thing…'

'*Have* you wrestled a crocodile?'

'Actually, no. Mette thinks I have, but that's not as dangerous as it sounds because she thinks that her cuddly crocodile is a true-to-life representation. I tell her a story about crocodiles and penguins that I met when I was in the Andes.'

'Right. Even I could wrestle a cuddly toy. I didn't know there were crocodiles in the Andes.'

'There aren't. She added a few things in as we went along. The penguins act as tour guides and show you the right way to go.'

'Penguins are always the good guys.'

He nodded, finally allowing himself a smile. 'I'm going to take her back to the clinic, now.'

'What? It's three in the morning, Aksel. Why don't you just stay here?'

'I said that we'd go now so that she can talk to Lisle. And I want her to wake up somewhere that's familiar to her.'

'But…' Flora saw the logic of it but this felt wrong.

'She's asleep. It seems a shame to take her out into the cold now when you can let her sleep and take her back first thing in the morning.'

'You heard me promise her, Flora. I'll stay the night so that I'll be there whenever she wakes up. You can't help me with this.'

There was more to this than just practicality. More than a promise. She could feel Aksel slipping away from her, torn by his guilt and the feeling that he'd let his daughter down.

Flora had to let him go. He'd feel differently about this in the morning and realise that he could be a father to Mette and a lover to her as well.

'Okay. You'll be back in the morning?'

'Yes.' He reached for her, and Flora slid towards him on the sofa. His kiss was tender, but it held none of the fire of their nights together.

'You're tired. You'll sleep in?'

If she could sleep at all. Dread began to pulse through her. What if he decided that this was where their relationship had to end? She pushed the thought away. She *had* to trust Aksel. There was no other choice.

'I'll phone in and take a couple of hours off work, I don't have any patients to see in the morning. I'll be here when you get back.'

He nodded. 'I'll come as soon as I can.'

Chapter 16

Flora was up early and let herself into Aksel's cottage with the spare key that he'd left with her. The place stank of smoke, and there were deposits of soot all around the sitting room, but apart from that the damage was relatively minor. She tidied the kitchen, putting away the evidence of Mette having climbed up to reach the matches, and tipped the remains of the hearth rug into a rubbish bag. Then she brewed a cup of strong coffee to jolt her tired and aching limbs into action and started to clean.

Ten minutes after she'd returned to her own cottage for more coffee and some breakfast, Flora heard the throaty roar of the SUV outside in the lane. Running out to embrace him seemed as if it would only make the awful what-ifs of last night a reality again, and she forced herself to sit down at the kitchen table and wait for him to come to her.

When he did, he looked as tired as she felt. But the first thing he did, when she let him into the cottage, was hug her. His body seemed stiff and unresponsive, but it was still a hug. Things were going to be all right.

'I appreciate the clean-up, but I was hoping to find

you'd slept in this morning.' He sat down at the kitchen table while she made him coffee.

'Your early mornings are starting to rub off on me.' It wouldn't do to tell him she'd been awake most of the night, worrying. Normal was good at the moment, even if she was going to have to fake it.

She put his coffee down in front of him and sat down. 'So how's Mette?'

'Fine. She told me that a fire's a very second-league adventure. Fighting crocodiles is much more exciting.' He smiled suddenly, and Flora laughed.

'Shame. If we could have tempted a few out of the loch then you could have done that too.'

He laughed, but there was no humour in his eyes. They were going through the motions of believing in life again, without any of the certainty.

'Aksel, I… What happened last night was a terrible accident. Mette's all right and so are you.'

'Yes. I know.' He might know it, but he didn't seem to believe it.

'You're a good father. You can keep her safe. We'll do it together, we'll go through the whole cottage and check everything… We can learn from this and make sure that it doesn't happen again.'

He looked at her blankly. 'We?'

'Yes, *we*. You're not alone with this, we'll do it together.'

'*I* need to do it, Flora. When I go back to Oslo…' They both knew what happened then. When he went back to Oslo, she would stay here in Cluchlochry, and it would be an end to their relationship. Aksel couldn't bring himself to rely on her.

She'd thought about this. It was far too early to say anything, but maybe it needed to be said now. Maybe they both needed to know that their relationship didn't have to be set in stone, and that it did have a future.

'When you go back to Oslo, there's nothing to stop me from visiting, is there?' Flora decided to start slowly with this.

He looked up at her. The look in his eyes told Flora that maybe she hadn't started slowly enough.

'I just… It seems so very arbitrary, to put an end date on this. What we have.'

'We'll always have it, Flora. There's no end date on that.'

It was a nice thought. A romantic thought, which didn't bear examination. Over time, the things they'd shared would be tarnished and forgotten.

'That's not what I meant. I was thinking in a more… literal sense.' Flora's heart began to beat fast. This wasn't going quite the way she'd hoped, and she was beginning to dread what Aksel might say.

'You're thinking of coming to Norway?'

'Well… I'm a free agent. I can come and see you, can't I?'

This wasn't about Mette any more. It was about Aksel's determination to do things on his own. About hers to find someone who trusted her. It was a bright winter morning, warm and cosy inside with snow falling outside the window, but Flora could feel the chill now, instead of the heat.

He was still and silent for a moment. When he looked at her, Flora could only see the mountain man, doggedly trudging forward, whatever the cost. Whatever he left behind.

'Do you seriously think that if you came to Norway, I'd ever let you go?'

Flora swallowed hard. That sounded like a *no*.

'Okay.' She shrugged, as if it didn't matter to her. 'That's okay, I won't come, then.'

'Flora…' He reached across the table, laying his hand on her arm. The sudden warmth in his eyes only made her angry and she pulled away from him.

'I heard what you said, Aksel.' He didn't want her. Actually, not wanting her would have been relatively okay. Flora knew that he wanted her but that he was fighting it.

'I didn't mean…' He let out a breath, frustration showing in his face. Clearly he didn't know quite what he meant. Or maybe he did, and he wasn't going to say it. In a moment of horrible clarity Flora knew exactly what he meant.

Aksel wouldn't take the risk of things becoming permanent between them. She'd trusted him, and he was pushing her away now. They'd tried to be happy—and surely they both deserved it. But Aksel was going to turn his back on that and let her down.

'Don't worry about it. I know what you're saying to me. That you're in control of this, and it comes to an end when you go. Well, I'm taking control of it and it ends now. I'm going to work.'

'Flora…' he called after her, but Flora had already walked out of the kitchen. Pulling on her coat, she picked up Dougal's lead, which was all she needed to do to prompt him to scrabble at the front door.

He'd made her feel him. He'd been inside her, in more ways than just physically, and she'd dared to enjoy it. Dared to want more. When he caught her up in the hallway, and she turned to look at him, she still loved him. It would always be this way with Aksel, and she had to make the break now, for her own sanity's sake.

'Can't we talk about this?'

'I think we've said all we need to say, haven't we? If you see me again, just look the other way, Aksel. I don't want to speak to you, ever again.'

She pulled open the front door, slamming it in his face. Aksel would be gone by the time she got home from work this evening, and hopefully he'd take what she'd said seriously. If they saw each other in the village, or at the clinic, she'd be looking the other way, and so should he.

He'd messed up. Big time. Aksel had been in some very tight spots, but he couldn't remember one as terrifying and hopeless as this.

He'd spent most of the night sitting in the chair next to Mette's bed, staring into the darkness and wondering how he could make things right. How he could be a father to Mette, and love Flora as well. He'd come to no conclusion.

Last night's fire wasn't the issue. But it had shaken him and dredged up feelings that he'd struggled to bury. Lisle's lies. His guilt over not having been there for Mette. And when Flora had spoken of coming to Norway to visit…

He knew what she'd been doing. She'd been trying to patch things up and convince them both that nothing was the matter. Flora always tried to mend what was broken, and he loved her for it. But she deserved someone better than him. Now that he was responsible for Mette, could he ever be the man that Flora could trust?

The question hammered at him, almost driving him to his knees. He'd travelled a long way, and it had seemed that he'd finally found the thing that he hadn't even known he'd been looking for. Did he really have to turn his back on Flora? Aksel couldn't bear it, but if it had to be done, then it was better for it to be done now.

He took a gulp of his coffee, tipping the rest into the sink and clearing up the kitchen. Then he signalled to Kari to follow him out into the cold, crisp morning air. As Aksel shut Flora's front door behind him, he knew only two things for sure. That this hurt far more than anything he'd experienced before. And that now he had to go on the most important journey of his life. One that he'd told himself he'd never make, and which might just change everything.

Anger had propelled Flora through the morning. But anger was hard to sustain, particularly where Aksel was concerned. When she couldn't help thinking about his touch, the honesty in his clear blue eyes, and the way he gave himself to her…

But now he'd taken it all away. As the day wore on, each minute heavy on her hands, the sharp cutting edge of her fury gave way to a dull ache of pain. She hurried

home after work, trying not to notice that his cottage
was quiet and dark, no lights showing from the windows.

Flora spent a sleepless night, thinking what might
have been, and wondering if a miracle might happen
to somehow bring it all back again. The feeble light of
morning brought her answer. It had been good between
them, and Aksel was the man she'd always wanted. But
he couldn't handle the guilt of feeling himself torn in
two directions, and Flora couldn't handle trusting him
and then having him push her away.

She'd decided that she must go and see Mette, because it wouldn't be fair to just desert the little girl.
Making sure that Aksel wasn't at the clinic that morning, she spent an hour with Mette, putting on a happy
face even though she was dying inside, and then went
back to her treatment room, locking the door so that
she could cry bitter tears.

It seemed that Aksel had got the message. He knew
that she didn't want to see him, and he was avoiding
her too. He was perceptive enough to know that things
weren't going to work out between them, and it was
better to break things off now. He might even be happy
about that. Flora was a claim on his time and attention
that he didn't need right now.

The second time she passed his cottage, on the way
to her own front door, was no easier than the first. It
looked as empty as it had last night, and Flora wondered
whether he'd found somewhere else to stay.

But then she'd gone to the window to close the curtains and seen the light flickering at the top of the hill,
partly obscured by the ruins of the old keep. Flora knew

exactly where Aksel was now. This was his signal fire, and it was meant for her.

He might have just phoned... If Aksel had called her then she could have dismissed the call, and that would have been an end to it. But the fire at the top of the hill burned on, seeming to imprint itself on her retinas even when she wasn't staring out of the window at it.

She needed something to take her mind off it. Her Christmas card list was always a good bet, and she fetched it, along with the boxes of cards that she'd bought, sitting down purposefully in front of the fire with a pen and a cup of tea. But her hand shook as she wrote. Wishing friends and family a happy Christmas always made her smile but, knowing that this year she'd be spending hers without Aksel, the Christmas greetings only emphasised her own hollow loneliness.

She gathered the cards up, deciding to leave them for another day. Drawing the curtains apart, she saw the light of the fire still twinkling out in the gloom...

Aksel had built the fire knowing that Flora would see it. And knowing that he'd stay here all night if he had to, and then the following night, and each night until she came. However long it took, he'd be here when Flora finally decided to climb the hill.

Maybe it wouldn't be tonight. It was getting late, and the lights of her cottage had been flicking on and off, tracing what seemed to be an irregular and undecided progress from room to room. Soon the on and off of the lights upstairs would signal that Flora had gone to bed, which left little chance that she'd come to him tonight.

All the same, he'd be here. Wrapped in his sleeping bag, until the first rays of dawn told him that he had to move now, work the cold stiffness from his limbs, and get on with another day.

His fire was burning low, and he went to fetch more fuel from the pile of branches that he'd stacked up nearby. The blaze began to climb through the dry twigs, brightening as it went, and he missed the one thing he had been waiting and watching for. When he looked down toward the village again, Flora's porch light was on.

He cursed his own inattentiveness, reaching for his backpack. His trembling fingers fumbled with the small binoculars, and he almost dropped them on the ground. Focussing them down towards Flora's cottage, he saw her standing in her porch, wearing her walking boots and thick, waterproof jacket, and looking up in his direction. Aksel almost recoiled, even though he knew that she couldn't see him. And then she went back inside the cottage again.

He bit back his disappointment. It had been too much to expect from this first night. But then she reappeared, pulling a hat onto her head, and as she started to walk away from the cottage a small thread of light issued from her hand. He smiled, glad that she'd remembered to bring a torch with her.

Aksel tried to calm himself by wondering which route she'd take. The most direct was the steepest, and it would be an easier walk to circle around the bottom of the hill before climbing it. She crossed the bridge that led from the village to the estate and disappeared for a moment behind a clump of bushes. And then he saw her again, climbing the steep, stony ground and making straight for him.

He waited, his eyes fixed on the small form labouring up the hill. When she fell, and the torch rolled skittishly back a few feet down the slope, he sprang to his feet, cursing himself for bringing her out here in the dark. But before he could run towards her, she was on her feet again, retrieving the torch.

Aksel forced himself to sit back down on the stony bench he'd made beside the fire. He *had* to wait, even though it was agony to watch Flora struggle like this. He had to trust that she'd come to him, and she had to know that she would too, however hard the journey.

His heart beat like a battering ram, and he suddenly found it difficult to breathe. The fire crackled and spat, flames flaring up into the night. The moment he'd longed for so desperately would be here soon, and despite working through every possible thing she might say to him, and what he might say in reply, he was completely unprepared.

When she finally made it to the top of the hill, she seemed rather too out of breath to say anything. Flora switched off her torch, putting her hands on her hips in a stance that indicated she wasn't going to take any nonsense from him.

'It's warmer by the fire...' He ventured the words and she frowned.

'This had better be good, Aksel. If you think I came up here in the middle of the night to hear something you might have said anywhere...'

'When might I have said it? You told me you never wanted to speak to me again.'

The logic had seemed perfect to him, but it only seemed to make her more angry. 'You could have slipped a note under my front door. It's not so far for either of us to walk.'

'I trusted you to come to me.'

She stared at him. 'I really wish you hadn't said that.'

Because it was the one thing he could have said to stop her from walking away from him? A sharp barb of hope bit into his heart.

'Sit down. Please.'

Flora pressed her lips together, hesitating for agonising moments. Then she marched over to the stone slab that he was sitting on, plumping herself down on the far end so that their shoulders didn't touch.

She was angry still, but at least she was sitting down. Aksel wasn't sure where to start, but before he could organise his thoughts, Flora did it for him.

'Where have you been, Aksel? You haven't been at the cottage and Mette told me that you weren't coming in to see her today.'

'You went to see Mette?' Of course she had. Flora wouldn't let a little thing like a broken heart get in the way of making sure that a child wasn't hurt by her absence. And from the way that she seemed to hate him so much, Aksel was in no doubt that her heart was just as wounded as his.

'Yes. I made sure that you weren't there already.'

Good. Hate was a lot more akin to love than indifference was. 'I was in Oslo.'

'Oslo? For two days?'

'Just a day. I went to see Mette yesterday afternoon

and left straight from there. I got back a couple of hours ago. The flight only takes an hour from Glasgow.'

She turned the edges of her mouth down. 'And it was such a long way when I was thinking of making the trip.'

He deserved that. 'I meant it when I said that I wouldn't be able to let you go, and that this is your home. I went to Oslo to talk with Olaf and Agnetha. About making this *my* home and Mette's.'

'You need their permission?' He could hear the fight beginning to go out of Flora's tone. She was starting to crumble, and if she wasn't in his arms yet, then maybe she would be if he gave it time.

'No, I don't. I'm Mette's father, and I make decisions about what's best for her, you taught me that. I wanted their blessing, and to reassure them that moving here didn't mean that they wouldn't get to see her.'

Flora stared at him. 'And…?'

'They told me that they expected me to get a house with a nice guest room, because they'll be visiting.'

A tear ran down her cheek. 'Aksel, please. What exactly are you saying?'

Now was the time. He had to be bold, because Flora couldn't be. He had to trust her, and show her that she could trust him. Aksel hung onto her hand for dear life.

'There's so much I want to say to you. But it all boils down to one thing.'

Flora had stumbled up a hill in the pitch darkness, and probably skinned her knees. If, in the process, she'd come to realise that nothing could keep her away from

Aksel, she wanted to hear what he had to say for himself first.

The flickering flames bathed his face in warmth, throwing the lines of worry across his forehead into sharp relief. The taut lines of his body showed that he was just as agitated as she was.

'What's the one thing?'

'I love you.'

That was good. It was very good because, despite herself, she loved him.

'Seriously?' Maybe he could be persuaded to say it again…

'Yes, seriously. I love you, Flora.' He was smiling at her in the firelight.

'I…love you too.'

He didn't argue. Putting his arms around her, he enveloped her in a hug.

'I was so horrible to you. I'm sorry, Aksel.' The things she'd said made Flora shiver now.

'You were afraid. I was afraid too, and our fear was all that we could see. But I'd be the bravest guy in the world if you'd just forgive me.'

'You mean I'm more scary than wrestling crocodiles?'

'Much more. But the thing that scares me most is losing you.'

Flora kissed him. So much nicer than words. But even the wild pleasure of feeling him close, embraced in his fire on a cold, dark night, couldn't entirely wipe away the feeling that there were some things they really did need to talk about.

'Aksel… What if…?'

'What-ifs don't matter.' He kissed her again, and Flora broke away from him with an effort.

'They *do* matter, Aksel. I need to know. I want you to say it, because I can't keep wondering what might happen if we make a go of this, and decide to have children some day.'

'I'd like children very much. A boy, maybe. Or a girl. One or more of each would be more than acceptable...' He was grinning broadly now.

'Stop it! Don't even say that if you can't also say that there's a risk that one or more of our children might have cystic fibrosis.'

He took her hands between his. 'I know that there *may* be a risk, but only if I carry the gene as well. I love you and I trust you. It's not that I don't care about these possibilities, I just have no doubts that we can face it and do the right thing. And there are other things we need to do first.'

He trusted her. He'd take her as she was, with all the doubts that raised, and he'd make them into certainties. 'What other things do we need to do first?'

'First, I need to tell you that I intend to marry you. I'll work very hard towards making you so happy that you won't be able to resist asking...'

'What? I have to ask you?'

Aksel nodded. 'You have to ask me, because you already know what my answer will be. I'll wait.'

'You're very sure of yourself.'

'I'm very sure of *you*. And I'll be doing my best to wear you down...' He took her into his arms and kissed her. He'd answered none of her questions, but they were all irrelevant now. The only thing that mattered was that they loved each other.

'And how are you going to do that?'

He gave her a gorgeous grin. 'Close your eyes and imagine…'

Aksel wasn't sure whether he had a right to be this happy. But he'd take it. He'd stamped the fire out hastily, lucky not to singe his boots in the process, and he and Flora had hurried back down the hill. The only question that was left to ask was whether they'd spend the night in his bed or hers.

He reckoned that last night had to count towards the *wearing down* process. And then this morning, when they'd made love again, before rushing to work.

If Lyle noticed the coincidence of Aksel wanting to take Mette out after lunch and Flora asking for the afternoon off, he'd said nothing. The old SUV was now running smoothly and even though the outside left a little to be desired, it was now thoroughly clean inside and had a child seat in the back.

'Where are we going?' Flora felt as excited as Mette was.

'Wait and see.' Aksel took the road leading to the other side of the estate, through snow-covered grasslands, and then they bumped a little way across country to the half-acre plantation of Christmas trees. The larger ones, for the castle and the village marketplace had already been felled, but there were plenty of smaller ones that would fit nicely in Flora's cottage. He left Flora to help Mette out of the car seat, and opened the boot to retrieve the chainsaw he'd borrowed from Ted Mackie.

'No!' Flora clapped her hand over her mouth in horror when she saw him eyeing the plantation. 'We can't do that…isn't tree rustling some kind of crime?'

'I got permission from Charles. He says I can take whichever tree I want. Anyway, trees can't run away, so I'm sure it wouldn't technically be rustling.'

'Is it Christmas Eve tomorrow?' Mette started to jiggle up and down in excitement.

'In Scotland we can put up our tree as soon as we like, we don't have to wait until the day before Christmas Eve.'

Mette's eyes grew rounder. 'I *like* Scotland, Papa. Do we have *two* Christmases?'

'No, but there's Hogmanay.' Aksel grinned as Mette looked perplexed. 'You'll have to wait and see what that is.'

Mette nodded, and Aksel leaned towards Flora, her soft scent curling around him. 'I like Scotland, too.'

They took their time choosing, wandering through the plantation hand in hand, while Mette relied on Kari to guide her through the snow. Mette declared that she wanted a tree tall enough for her to climb up to the sky, and Aksel explained that they couldn't get one like that into the cottage. In the end, Flora settled the argument by choosing one they all liked.

'Stand back…' He started up the chainsaw, grinning at Flora, and then cut a 'V' shape in the trunk. Flora hung tightly onto Mette's hand as she screamed excitedly. The tree fell exactly where Aksel had indicated it would.

He'd brought some netting, and Aksel wrapped the tree up in it, bending the larger branches upwards. Then he lifted the tree onto one shoulder to take it to the car. The raw power in his body never failed to thrill Flora. But there was more now. They were becoming a family.

'How long do I have to hold out for? Before I ask you to marry me?' Mette was busy scooping snow up to make a snowman, and Flora watched as Aksel loaded the tree into the car.

'Be strong.' He grinned at her. 'I'm finding that persuading you is much nicer than I'd thought. I have a few more things in mind.'

'What are they?'

'Breakfast in bed on Christmas morning. A Hogmanay kiss. Taking you back to Norway to meet my family after the New Year.'

Flora had always thought that the most romantic proposal must be a surprise. But planning it like this was even better than she'd dreamed. 'That sounds wonderful. Don't think that I won't be thinking of some things to persuade you.'

'So how long before we give in?' He leaned forward, growling the words into her ear as if they were a challenge.

'I think that decorating the tree's going to be the first big test of our resolve. Christmas Eve might prove very tempting…'

'Yes. That'll be difficult.' He took her hand, pulling off her glove and pressing her fingers to his lips.

'You'll be ready with your answer?' Flora smiled up at him.

'Oh, yes.' He wrapped his arms around her, kissing her. 'I'll be ready.'

Epilogue

Oslo, one year later

It was the night before Christmas Eve, and the family had gathered for Christmas. The big tree at Olaf and Agnetha's house was the centrepiece of the celebrations, and both Aksel's and Flora's parents were spending Christmas here this year. Everyone had admired the appliquéd Christmas stockings, a present from Mary Monroe, who had made a complete recovery and was back working at her beloved quilt shop three days a week.

Mette had fallen asleep as soon as her head had touched the pillow, and Aksel and Flora had tiptoed next door to their own room.

'Mum was telling me how welcome your parents have made her and Dad. They've been showing them around Oslo.' Flora slid onto the bed, propping herself up on the pillows next to Aksel, and he put his arm around her.

'I'm glad they get on so well. And with Olaf and Agnetha too.'

Flora nodded. 'I'm really going to miss this year. We did so much.'

They'd arranged a wedding and bought a house, one of the large stone-built properties just outside the village. Mette understood that her new family would always be there for her, and was gaining in confidence and exploring her world a little more each day. Aksel had been working at the canine therapy centre, after the previous vet had decided not to return from her maternity leave, and helping Ted Mackie organise adventure trips on the estate for the clinic's residents.

'I've got something to get us started on next year. I had an email from Charles this morning. He's signed the papers for the land, and it's now officially ours. We can start to build in the New Year.'

This had been Aksel's dream project, and Flora had fallen in love with it too. The small parcel of barren land, right on the edge of the estate, was no good for anything other than being ideally situated to build. Charles had sold it for a nominal amount, after Aksel had approached him with his plans for an adventure centre for people with disabilities.

'So it's a reality. That's fantastic!' Flora hugged him tight.

'Charles is as excited about it as I am. He offered to make a contribution towards the building costs, but I told him that if he wanted to do something, he could turn up and help dig out the foundations. He liked that idea much better.'

'I'm glad you decided that you weren't going to entirely give up on exploring. Even if these trips will be a little different.'

'They'll be even more challenging.' Aksel took her hand, pressing her fingers to his lips. 'And I'll never be away from my family for too long.'

'Well, maybe your family will just pack their bags every once in a while and come with you.'

He grinned. 'You know I'd love that.'

'I have something for you as well.' Flora reached under the pillow, giving him the small, carefully wrapped package.

'Am I supposed to open this now?' He grinned at her.

'Yes.' She watched as he tore the paper, then turned the little fabric crocodile with sharp embroidered teeth over in his hands.

'All right. You've given me a crocodile to wrestle…?' He'd got the message and he was smiling at the thought of whatever challenge she was going to present him with now. 'Whatever it is you have in mind, the answer's yes.'

Flora nudged him in the ribs. 'You don't know what the question is yet.'

'It'll be Christmas Eve soon. And I trust you…'

It was his trust that had brought Flora to this point. They'd talked about this, and he'd told her that she'd know when the time was right. And she *did* know.

'You said that when we decided to start a family, we'd both take the test for the cystic fibrosis gene. Together…'

A broad grin spread across his face. He knew now exactly what she wanted.

'Yes. I did.'

'Are you ready, Aksel?'

He nodded. 'I've been ready for a long time. You?'

'I'm ready. If it turns out that we both carry the gene we have lots of options. Would it be irresponsible of me to say that we don't need to decide anything now? We'll know what to do if and when we find ourselves in that situation?'

'Nope. Life's one big exploration. You can't know what's ahead of you, but if you're travelling with someone you trust, you can be sure that you'll face it together.'

This felt like the first step in a journey that Flora couldn't wait to make. She kissed him, nestling into the warmth of his arms.

'So I'm going to be a dad again.' Aksel hugged her tight. 'I'm not going to miss a moment of it this time. I'll find someone else to lead the trips...'

'Whatever happens, it won't be for a little while. And when it does, you can have both, Aksel, you don't have to choose.' Sometimes she still had to remind him of that.

'How do you do it, Flora? Every time I think that I'm about as happy as it's possible to be, you manage to make me happier.'

'Trust me Aksel. There's a lot more to come, for both of us.'

He laughed, pure joy spilling out of him. 'Oh, I trust you. Always.'

* * * * *

Teri Wilson is a *Publishers Weekly* bestselling author of romance and romantic comedy. Several of Teri's books have been adapted into Hallmark Channel Original Movies, most notably *Unleashing Mr. Darcy*. She is also a recipient of the prestigious RITA® Award for excellence in romantic fiction for her novel *The Bachelor's Baby Surprise*. Teri has a major weakness for cute animals and pretty dresses, and she loves following the British royal family. Visit Teri at teriwilson.net.

Visit the Author Profile page at Harlequin.com for more titles.

A DADDY BY CHRISTMAS

Teri Wilson

In loving memory of my dad, Bob Wilson.

Chapter 1

The puppy was the last straw.

Chloe Wilde's bad luck streak kicked off a little over a week ago while performing with the Rockettes during the annual Thanksgiving Day parade. She'd taken a tumble and accidentally ruined the dance troupe's legendary toy soldier routine on live television. Things had progressed from bad to worse ever since, and now, just twenty-four days before Christmas, she'd reached rock bottom.

"I don't understand." One of the sequined antlers on Chloe's glittering derby hat drooped into her line of vision and she pushed it away, aiming her fiercest glower at the woman who'd just given her the bad news. Not that glowering while dressed as a high-kicking reindeer was an easy task. It wasn't, but after everything Chloe had been through lately, she excelled at it. "I've been visiting this puppy every day for twelve days. I filled out an adoption application a week ago, and you yourself called me last night and told me I'd been approved."

That phone call had been the first good thing that had happened to her in *days*. Weeks, if she was really being honest with herself. But that was okay, because starting today, she wouldn't have to face the worst Christmas of her adult life by herself. She'd have a snuggly, adorable puppy by her side.

Or so she thought.

The man standing beside Chloe cleared his throat. "She called me yesterday afternoon and told me the same thing."

"Just because she called you first doesn't mean the puppy is yours." Chloe took a time-out from her refusal to acknowledge the man's presence to glare at him.

She wished he weren't so handsome. Those piercing blue eyes were a little difficult to ignore, as was his perfect square jaw. His clothes were impeccable—very tailored, very Wall Street. And the dusting of snow on the shoulders of his dark wool coat made him seem ultramanly for some reason. Under normal circumstances, she'd have thought he looked like the kind of man who would turn up wielding a little blue box in a Tiffany's Christmas advertisement.

But these weren't normal circumstances, and he wasn't holding a little blue box. He was holding a puppy. *Her* puppy.

"Actually, that's exactly what it means. She called me first, and a verbal agreement was made wherein I would take possession of the puppy." He arched a brow. "Therefore the puppy is mine."

Who talked like that?

Chloe turned her back to him and refocused her attention on the animal shelter's adoption counselor, who thus far hadn't been much help. But Chloe wasn't going down without a fight.

"Are you really going to let him take my puppy? Listen to him. He says he wants to adopt a pet, but he sounds like he's talking about a business merger."

The adoption counselor's gaze swiveled back and forth between the two of them as if she were watching a snowball fight.

"She's not your dog. I'm adopting her. I've got the papers right here." Using his free hand, the man pulled an envelope from the inside pocket of his suit jacket and placed it on the counter.

Chloe didn't bother opening it. Instead, she pulled an identical packet of papers from her dance bag and slammed it on the counter next to his envelope.

"I've got papers, too." She crossed her arms, causing the jingle bell cuffs on the long brown velvet sleeves of her costume to clang, echoing loudly in the tiled shelter lobby.

The man's mouth twitched into a half grin, which, to Chloe's dismay, made him even more attractive. "Nice outfit, by the way."

She jammed her hands on her velvet-clad hips, ignoring the jingly commotion she made every time she moved. "I'll have you know that this is an official Rockettes reindeer costume, steeped in Christmas tradition dating back to the 1930s. I'm basically a New York treasure. So laugh it up, puppy thief."

He cut his gaze toward her, and his smile faded. "Once again, I'm not a puppy thief."

"Says the man who refuses to let go of my puppy."

Chloe cast a longing glance at the tiny Yorkie mix. "You know who you are? You're Cruella De Vil in pinstripes."

"Pinstripes haven't been in style in years," he muttered.

"Note taken, Cruella."

"You know what?" The adoption counselor finally chimed in. "I think I should probably go get the manager so she can help us figure out how to proceed."

"Excellent. Thank you so much." Chloe nodded. Out of the corner of her eye, she could see the twinkle lights on her antlers blinking.

Oops. She could have sworn she'd switched those off.

Her nemesis turned toward her. Chloe still didn't quite trust herself to look at him without swooning, but she couldn't keep pretending he was invisible when they were the only two people in the room.

His gaze flitted to her antlers. "Are you really a Rockette?"

"Yes." She nodded. *Jingle, jingle, jingle.*

"That's quite impressive."

"Thank you." She cleared her throat.

It wasn't a lie. Not technically.

On paper, she was still a Rockette. She just wasn't allowed to perform anymore. Much to her humiliation, she now had the lovely task of standing in Times Square in her reindeer costume two hours a day to hand out flyers to tourists to encourage them to go to the annual Rockettes Christmas show at Radio City Music Hall.

Oh, how the mighty had fallen.

For the past four years, she'd been living her dream. She'd high-kicked her way through the last four Christmases—three shows a day for five weeks straight. Twice, she'd even traveled overseas with the Rockettes to perform in their USO tour. And now she'd been relegated to Times Square. She might as well put on an Elmo costume and a Santa hat and call it a day.

The worst part about being demoted wasn't the humiliation, nor was it the drastically reduced paycheck. Although she was going to have to do something about the latter really soon.

More troubling than either her dwindling bank account or her shame at the 50,000-plus YouTube views of her Thanksgiving Day toy soldier mishap was the prospect of telling her family she was no longer dancing. The Wildes weren't a scary bunch. Quite the opposite, actually. They were loving and supportive, especially Chloe's mother, Emily, who'd started the Wilde School of Dance over forty years ago and still taught nearly every day.

As much as Chloe hated to admit it, she'd taken advantage of all that family devotion. She'd used her busy rehearsal schedule as an excuse to miss nearly all the weekly dinners at the Wilde brownstone for the past few years. Every Thanksgiving and every Christmas, she'd been too busy performing at the parade or at Radio City to be a part of the family holiday celebrations. She couldn't even remember the last time she'd set foot in the dance school.

Her brother and sister liked to joke about it, calling her the ghost of Christmas past, but her mom never complained. No one had, even though Chloe knew she could have made more of an effort. What had she been thinking? Hadn't her dad's sudden death from a heart attack taught her not to take family for granted?

She was a horrible person. She couldn't even bring herself to tell the Wildes the truth. No wonder fate had thrown a puppy thief into her path. She deserved this, didn't she?

Her gaze slid toward the dog's scruffy little face and her tiny button nose. So adorable. Somehow her cuteness seemed magnified in the arms of Chloe's strapping rival.

She felt her chin start to wobble.

Stay strong.

The only thing that would make this episode more upsetting would be if she broke down and cried.

"Were you telling the truth just now? Have you actually visited this dog every day for the past twelve days?"

She peered up at the man and squared her shoulders. "Yes. Did you think I was lying?"

Chloe would never lie to the adoption counselor's face like that. Lies of omission were apparently her thing, specifically lying by omission to her own flesh and blood.

He sighed and said nothing in response.

Chloe's heart gave a little zing. Was he beginning to crack?

"I already bought her a dog bed," Chloe said. "It's red-and-white-striped, like a candy cane."

"I wouldn't expect anything else from a woman dressed as Rudolph." His frown stayed firmly in place, but Chloe thought she spotted a twinkle in his eyes that hadn't been there before.

He was either about to give in and let her have the puppy, or he was flirting with her in order to get her to throw in the towel. For a second, Chloe wasn't sure which scenario she preferred.

She blinked.

Had she lost her mind? She wasn't going to let a few kind words and an eye twinkle crack her composure. Even if the eye twinkle was just shy of a full-on smolder.

That puppy was hers.

"Nice try," she said tartly. "But I'm not here to play games."

"No reindeer games." He gave her a solemn nod. "Got it."

The man was hardly playing fair, damn him.

"Good," she said.

Then she looked away, lest he see the smile on her face.

An awkward silence fell between them, punctuated every so often by the bells on Chloe's costume. She tried her best to keep her gaze focused on the countertop and the adoption papers she'd filled out in careful handwriting the night before. But the puppy started making cute little whimpering noises, and she couldn't help it. She had to look.

The tiny dog was gnawing on the handsome man's thumb, which would have been completely adorable if he'd been paying any attention whatsoever to the animal. He wasn't, though. His brow was furrowed, and he was staring into space, distracted.

Chloe rolled her eyes. He was probably thinking

about the stock market or suing someone or the recent demise of pinstripes. "Why do you want this dog, anyway? You don't really seem like the Yorkie type."

He glanced at the dog and then at her. "What type do I seem like?"

A golden retriever, maybe. Or an Irish setter. A classic sort of dog that would look good curled in front of a fireplace or with its head sticking out of a town car.

"I haven't given it any thought," she lied.

He peered at her for a long, loaded moment, as if he could see inside her head. Finally, he said, "The puppy is an early Christmas gift."

"A *Christmas gift*?" Chloe blinked in indignation. "Do the people here at the shelter know that? Pets are living creatures. You can't just give them away as presents. That's the height of irresponsibility."

He shifted the puppy to his other arm, farther away from her. "Rest assured, the shelter staff knows. I'm taking full responsibility for the dog."

"So…what, then? She's a gift for your wife?" Chloe's gaze flitted to his left hand.

No ring.

"No wife," he said. Then he frowned, as if his bachelorhood was a surprise. Or a problem that needed to be fixed.

Chloe's face went hot for reasons she didn't care to contemplate.

She took a deep breath. Action was required. If she didn't stop thinking about this mysterious man's relationship status and *do* something, she'd be going home to an empty apartment, complete with an empty candy cane–striped dog bed.

Her own bed would be empty, too, but that was fine. Preferable, actually. Although why she was suddenly thinking about the unoccupied half of her antique sleigh bed was a mystery.

Sure it is.

She took another glance at the puppy thief holding her Yorkie mix and melted a little bit. The two of them looked like they belonged on that Instagram account her dancer friends were always going on about—Hot Men and Mutts.

She swallowed. "Look, is there any way we could work this out ourselves before the shelter manager gets involved? The puppy is a gift. Couldn't you just pick out another one? I love that dog. What can I do to change your mind? Anything?"

Surely there was something he wanted, although Chloe couldn't imagine what it might be.

She lifted her chin and looked him directly in his eyes, so he'd know she meant business. No reindeer games.

Then she tilted her head, prompting him to say something. Anything.

Make me an offer.

His gaze narrowed and sharpened. For a second or two, he focused on her with such intensity that she forgot how to breathe.

So there is *something he wants, after all.*

When at last he gave her the answer she'd been waiting for, he didn't crack a smile.

"Marry me."

* * *

Anders Kent wanted to take the words back the minute they'd left his mouth.

Marry me.

What had he been thinking? He'd just proposed to a complete and total stranger in a sterile room that smelled like soap and puppy chow. A stranger who was *dressed as a reindeer.* And now she was looking at him as if he was the crazy one.

Oh, the irony.

He wasn't crazy. Nor was he impulsive, all evidence to the contrary. He was simply desperate. Which was also ironic, considering Anders's name popped up in the tabloids from time to time as one of New York's most sought-after bachelors. Anders Kent had an office with a corner window in Wall Street's premier investment banking firm and a penthouse overlooking Central Park West. If he wanted something, he generally found a way to get it. Romantic entanglements included.

But his current predicament didn't have anything to do with romance. Far from it. There wasn't anything remotely romantic about sitting across a desk from your attorney and being told you had thirty days to find a wife.

Anders had been given just such an ultimatum at nine o'clock this morning, and his head had been spinning ever since.

Marriage?

No.

Hell no.

Anders didn't want to get married—to *anyone*, least

of all the hostile woman beside him who looked as if she was on the verge of prying Lolly's puppy right out of his arms.

"What did you just say?" She swallowed, and the jingle bells at her throat did a little dance.

"Nothing." Anders shook his head. He sure as hell wasn't going to repeat himself. He shouldn't have opened his mouth to begin with.

You don't even know this woman's name.

His gut churned. In the brief span of time since he'd left his lawyer's office, something strange had happened to Anders. He'd begun to weigh every woman he came across as a potential wife…as if he truly had any intention to go through with the insane requirement.

He wouldn't. Couldn't. He'd fight it. He'd throw every dollar he had at fighting it until he won.

But legal battles took time. More often than not, they took years. And Anders didn't have years. He had a month.

"It didn't sound like nothing. It definitely sounded like a big fat *something*." The woman's eyes grew wide, panicked.

She'd gotten his message, loud and clear.

He should have phrased it differently, though. He was proposing a business arrangement, not an actual marriage.

Yes, he needed a wife. But not a real one, just a stand-in. A temporary wife. After Lolly's guardianship was properly settled, everything could go back to normal.

His chest tightened. *Normal* was a pipe dream. It didn't exist anymore. His life wouldn't be normal ever again.

He took a tense inhalation and looked away from the dancing reindeer. "Never mind."

"Never mind?" She threw her arms in the air. *Jingle, jingle, jingle.* "You can't just ask someone to marry you and then take it back. This isn't the season finale of *The Bachelor.*"

"I've never seen that show," he said woodenly.

He couldn't marry this woman. She watched garbage television. She was bubbly, brash and far too emotional. She was a bleeding heart who spent her free time visiting shelter dogs. Plus, she obviously despised him.

It would never work.

Unless…

He frowned.

Unless the fact that they were so clearly ill-suited for one another would be an advantage. He couldn't marry anyone he actually found attractive. That would be a recipe for disaster. And he definitely wasn't attracted to the reindeer.

He *shouldn't* be attracted to her, anyway.

A surge of something that felt far too much like desire flowed through his veins. What the hell was wrong with him?

"I'm not going to marry you for a puppy," she said hotly. She looked him up and down. "No matter how… nice…the two of you look together."

She swallowed and averted her gaze, giving Anders an unobstructed view of the graceful curve of her neck.

Definitely a dancer, he thought. Her posture, coupled with the way she moved, was undeniably balletic. Beautiful, even in that silly costume.

"I thought you said I didn't look like the Yorkie type," he said.

Her cheeks went pink, but before she could respond the door swung open and a no-nonsense-looking woman wearing a T-shirt with Adopt, Don't Shop printed across the front of it extended her hand.

"Hello, Miss Wilde. Mr. Kent. I'm the shelter manager." She looked back and forth between them. "I understand there's been a mistake."

Anders nodded and glanced at Rudolph—whose actual name was Miss Wilde, apparently—and braced himself for the tirade that was sure to come. She hadn't let the adoption counselor get a word in edgewise. Why would she hold her tongue now?

But she didn't say a thing. Instead, she crossed her arms and stared daggers at him while the shelter manager reviewed their respective paperwork.

He'd dodged a bullet. There were countless single women in New York. He didn't know what had possessed him to propose to this one.

Still, there was a sadness in her eyes that made him feel like his heart was being squeezed in a vise. Anders had seen enough sadness in recent days that it made him want to do something to take away that melancholy look in her eyes—something that was sure to make her smile.

"Here," he said, holding the little dog toward her.

He had more than enough to worry about without adding alleged puppy thievery to the list. He'd simply have to find another dog for Lolly. It was sure to be easier than finding a wife.

"She's yours."

Chapter 2

The tiny dog squirmed in Chloe's arms as she watched the brooding man—her erstwhile fiancé—cross the length of the lobby and walk out the door in just three bold strides.

What just happened?

Wordlessly, she stared after him until the shelter manager cleared her throat.

"Well," she said. "I guess that settles that. The dog is yours if you still want her."

Chloe snapped back to the matter at hand. "I do. Definitely."

Of course she still wanted the puppy. She was just having a hard time switching gears from being proposed to by a total stranger to once again thinking about the logistics of puppy ownership.

"That was weird, though, wasn't it?" Chloe held the dog closer to her chest. The tiny animal smelled like shampoo and puppy breath, which was a comforting and welcome switch from the gritty aroma of Times Square. "Don't you think so?"

"Um." The shelter manager's smile faded. "I really couldn't say."

"That's right. You missed the crazy part." The puppy started gnawing on Chloe's thumb. Somewhere in her purse, she had a chew toy she'd purchased for a moment like this one, but she was too rattled to look for it. "He asked me to *marry* him."

The shelter manager gave a little start. "Oh, I didn't realize you and Mr. Kent knew each other."

Kent.

So that was his name. It swirled through her thoughts like a snowflake until she found herself combining it with hers.

Chloe Kent.

Mrs. Chloe Kent.

Her face went hot. "We don't. I've never seen him before in my life."

"Oh."

Chloe sneaked a glance at his paperwork, still sitting on the counter where he'd left it. "Anders Kent" was printed neatly in the name box.

"He just upped and asked me to marry him, and then he took it back." Chloe huffed out a sigh.

Of course this would happen to her. The hits just kept on coming. Instead of getting a normal proposal from a normal man—her ex, Steven, for instance—she got one from a total crackpot who promptly changed his mind.

Except he hadn't seemed like a crackpot. He actually seemed sort of charming, especially when he was holding the puppy. But come on, what handsome man didn't seem charming with a cute dog in his arms?

"Not that I considered it for even a second. It seems exceedingly rude to withdraw a proposal, though. I'm just saying." The puppy started to whine in her arms, so she bounced up and down a bit. *Jingle, jingle, jingle.* "Surely you agree."

The shelter manager sighed. "Honestly, as long as the puppy goes to a good home, I don't really care."

"Right. Of course." Why was she telling this woman about her almost-engagement to a perfect stranger?

More specifically, why couldn't she let the stunning incident go? She shouldn't be dwelling on it. It was a *non*-incident, as evidenced by the mysterious Anders Kent's speedy retraction, followed by his hasty exit.

"Do you want the dog or not?" The exasperated woman slid a paper across the counter toward Chloe.

"Absolutely." She scrawled her name on the designated line.

After all, she was here to adopt a puppy, not to get engaged.

Not now.

Not ever.

"Mr. Kent." Edith Summers, Anders's personal assistant, stood as he strode into the paneled entryway to his office. "We weren't expecting you to come in today."

Anders paused and nodded graciously at the older woman. He wasn't typically one for small talk in the workplace, but he hadn't seen Mrs. Summers since the funeral and her presence at that ghastly affair had been more comforting than he'd expected. Burying his brother and sister-in-law was by no means easy, but seeing his assistant sitting in the second pew, wearing her customary pearls and stoic, maternal expression, had made him feel a little less alone. A little less untethered.

"I changed my mind." Anders smiled stiffly.

He should say something. He should thank her, or at the very minimum, acknowledge her presence on that darkest of days. But just over Mrs. Summers's shoulder, Anders spotted his brother's name on the smooth oak door to the office next to his own, and the words died on his tongue.

Mrs. Summers followed his gaze, then squared her shoulders and cleared her throat. She'd been Anders's assistant long enough to know that what he needed now was normalcy. And normalcy meant work. It meant numbers and spreadsheets and meetings with investors. It meant being at his desk from sunup to sundown...

But that would have to change now, wouldn't it?

"Very well. I'll get you a cup of coffee and then we can go over your schedule," Mrs. Summers said.

"Thank you." He held her gaze long enough to impart all the things he couldn't say—thank you for being there, thank you for not trying to make him talk about his feelings or force him to go home. The list was long.

"Of course." Her eyes flashed with sympathy, and Anders's chest wound itself into a hard, suffocating tangle as she bustled past him toward the executive break room.

How long would it be this way?

How long would it be before he could stand in this place where he once felt so capable, so impenetrable, and not feel like his heart had just been put through a paper shredder?

Months. Years, maybe.

Lolly's sweet, innocent face rose to the forefront of his consciousness, and he knew with excruciating clarity that no amount of time would be sufficient. He'd feel this way for a lifetime. He'd carry the loss to his grave.

But he couldn't think about that now. Lolly was depending on him. His niece was only five years old, too young to grasp the permanence of what had just happened to her...what had happened to them both. Anders, on the other hand, was all too aware.

He was even more aware of feeling that he wasn't quite up to the task of raising a child. Anders didn't know the first thing about being a father. Not that he would ever come close to replacing Grant and Olivia in Lolly's life. But having lost his own parents at an early age, he knew that children as young as his niece didn't understand words like *guardian* and *custody*. Even if Lolly continued calling him Uncle Anders, he'd become so much more than that. He'd be the one to teach her how to ride a bicycle and help her with her homework. He'd be the one cheering at her high school graduation and pulling his hair out when she learned how to drive. He'd be the one to walk her down the aisle at her wedding.

For all practical purposes, he'd be her father. He'd spend the rest of his life walking in his younger brother's shoes.

If he was lucky.

"Shall I set up a meeting between you and the estate

lawyer?" Mrs. Summers placed a double cappuccino with perfect foam on the desk in front of Anders and took a seat in one of the leather wingback guest chairs facing him. As usual, she held the tablet she used to keep track of his calendar in one hand and a pair of reading glasses in the other.

"Already done. I saw him this morning." Anders stared into his coffee. It was going to take a lot more than caffeine to get him through the next few weeks.

"Oh." His secretary blinked. "Everything all right, then?"

Anders took a deep breath and considered how much, exactly, he should share with his secretary. On one hand, she was his employee. On the other, she might be the closest thing he had to a friend now that his brother—who also happened to be his business partner—was gone. Such was the life of a workaholic.

"Not really," he said quietly.

The phone on Mrs. Summers's desk began to ring, but when she popped out of her chair to go answer it, Anders motioned for her to stay put.

"Leave it. Just let it roll to voice mail." He took a sip of his cappuccino. She'd gone easy on the foam this time, and it slid down his throat, hot and bitter. Just like his mood.

Mrs. Summers frowned. "You're beginning to worry me, Mr. Kent. Is something wrong?"

Nothing that a wife wouldn't fix.

He closed his eyes and saw the puzzled face of the woman from the animal shelter—her wide brown eyes and lush pink lips, arranged in a perfect O of surprise.

Marry me.

God, he'd actually said that, hadn't he? The past week had been rough, no doubt about it. It was astounding how much a single phone call could change things, could eviscerate your life so cleanly as if it were a blade of some sort. A knife to the gut.

But until this morning, Anders had been hanging on. He'd had to, for Lolly's sake and for the sake of the business. Grief was a luxury he couldn't afford. Not now, not yet. Besides, if he let himself bend beneath the crushing weight of loss, he wouldn't be able to get back up—not after the things he'd said to Grant the night before the accident.

Anders and his brother rarely argued, and when they did, it was typically about the business. As two of the name partners in one of the most influential investment banking firms on Wall Street, they always had one another's back, but that didn't mean blind support. They challenged each other. They made each other better.

Their last argument had been different, though. Anders had gone too far—he'd made it personal. There'd been raised voices and slammed doors, and then nothing but an uncomfortable silence after Grant stormed out of the building. It had been their most heated exchange to date, but that was okay. They were brothers, for crying out loud. Grant would get over it.

But he couldn't get over it, because now he was gone. And Anders couldn't even bring himself to set foot in his dead brother's empty office.

It was easier to stay on this side of that closed door. Safer.

Anders had managed to push their final confrontation into the darkest corner of his consciousness that he could find, and at first, it had been remarkably easy. He'd had a funeral to plan and Grant's in-laws to deal with and a new, tiny person sleeping in his penthouse.

He was beginning to crack now. That much was obvious. Tiny fissures were forming in the carefully constructed wall he'd managed to build around the memory of his last conversation with Grant. Any minute now, it would all come flooding back. The effort to keep it at bay was crippling, as evidenced by his spontaneous marriage proposal to a woman dressed in a reindeer costume.

"There are some issues with Lolly's guardianship." Anders swallowed. The knot that had formed in his throat during the funeral service was still sitting like a stone.

Mrs. Summers shook her head. "I don't understand. You're her godfather."

"Yes, I am." He'd dutifully attended the church service at St. Patrick's Cathedral and poured water over Lolly's fragile newborn head. It had been a done deal.

Or so he'd thought.

He took another scalding gulp of his cappuccino. Then he set the china cup back down on the desk with enough force that liquid sloshed over the rim. "As it turns out, the legalities of the matter are a bit more complicated."

"How so?"

"When Grant and Olivia drafted their wills, they

made my guardianship of Lolly conditional. The only way I can be awarded full custody is if I'm married."

The tablet slid out of Mrs. Summers's hand and fell to the floor with a clunk. She didn't bother picking it up. "Married?"

"Married." He nodded. Maybe if they both kept repeating the word, the reality of his situation would sink in.

"But…" The older woman's voice drifted off, which was probably for the best. Anders could only imagine the trajectory of her thoughts.

But you haven't been on more than three dates with the same woman in years.

But you're a workaholic.

And to quote his brother…

But you're dead inside.

"Exactly," Anders said, because it didn't really matter which objection caused her hesitation. They all fit.

"So that's it, then? What happens to Lolly?"

"Lolly's staying put." They'd take her away over his dead body. He'd made a promise to his brother that rainy day in St. Patrick's Cathedral, and he intended to keep it. He owed Grant that much. It was the least he could do. "I just have to find a wife."

The shocked expression on Mrs. Summers's face gave way to one of perplexed amusement. "Find a wife? It's as simple as that, is it?"

"Yes." He gave her a curt nod.

Simple was a necessity.

Frankly, the more Anders thought about it, the more he liked the idea of an arranged marriage. A temporary wife was exactly what he needed. He'd handle it like a basic merger. After all, those were his specialty. No messy emotions, no expectations—just a simple business transaction between two consenting adults.

Two consenting adults who wouldn't sleep together or have any other sort of romantic entanglement.

Maybe I really am dead inside.

Fine. So be it.

Maybe Grant had hit the nail on the head when he'd made that astute accusation right before he turned on his heel and stormed out of the office five days ago. Anders hoped he had. He'd love nothing more than to remain in his current state of numbness for the rest of his godforsaken life.

"My husband and I only knew each other for six months before we got married, and he was the love of my life." Mrs. Summers gave Anders a watery smile. "You're absolutely right. It doesn't have to be complicated."

Anders swallowed around the rock in his throat. "I don't have six months. I have until Christmas."

She gaped at him, and he took advantage of her silence to abruptly fill her in on the rest of it. Having this conversation was more humbling than he'd anticipated. "If I'm not married by the end of the calendar year, Lolly goes to the alternate guardians—Olivia's sister and her husband. Lolly can't go to them. They live in Kansas, and her entire life would be upended. Plus, they've already got five kids of their own, and while I'm sure they're competent parents, they weren't my brother's first choice."

Nor was Anders, technically. Grant and Olivia wanted Lolly raised by Anders *plus one*, as if the matter of guardianship could be worded like a wedding invitation.

Was it even legal? Possibly, according to his lawyer. But they didn't have time to battle it out in court.

Even if they had, Anders would have had to speculate in front of a judge and jury why his own brother would place such a condition on his role in Lolly's life in the event she became orphaned. He would be forced to admit that the provision in the will had taken him by surprise, but he knew precisely why it was there.

If Grant and Olivia couldn't be there for Lolly, they wanted her to grow up in a nuclear family—a home with a mom and dad. But that wasn't the only reason. They knew that Anders loved their daughter, but they also knew he couldn't be trusted to get up and walk away from Wall Street at a reasonable hour every day. Work was his first love, his only love. And that wasn't good enough for Lolly.

Hell, even Anders knew it wasn't.

He would change. Had they really thought he wouldn't? He'd turn his life inside out and upside down for that little girl.

Yet here you sit.

The paneled walls of his office felt as if they were closing in around him. Anders fixated on the smooth surface of his desk and breathing in and out until the feeling passed.

When at last he looked up, the tablet was back in

Mrs. Summers's hands again and her glasses were perched on the end of her nose.

"Tell me how I can help," she said.

A fleeting sense of relief passed through him. Help was precisely what he needed, and Mrs. Summers was efficient beyond measure. He could do this. He had to. "Get me the names and contact information for every woman I've dated in the past twelve months."

"Yes, sir." She jotted something down with her stylus.

"Better make that the past eighteen months, just to be safe." He took a deep inhalation. It felt good to have a plan, even if said plan was a long shot. Reaching out to old girlfriends made more sense than proposing to strangers.

"If I might make a suggestion, sir. Perhaps you should consider..." Mrs. Summers tipped her head in the direction of the office across the hall from Anders's, which belonged to another partner in the firm—Penelope Reed.

Anders grew still. He hadn't realized anyone in the office knew about the arrangement he had with Penelope. So much for subtlety.

"No." He shook his head.

It wasn't completely out of the question, but Penelope was his last resort. True, they occasionally shared a bed. And true, their relationship was strings-free, as businesslike as a coupling could possibly be.

But marrying someone within the firm was a terrible idea. They could hide the occasional one-night stand, but a marriage was another matter entirely.

"Very well." Mrs. Summers nodded. "It was just an idea."

"I'll keep it in mind." He shifted uncomfortably in his chair and wondered what it meant that he'd felt more comfortable proposing to a stranger than to a woman he bedded from time to time. Nothing good, that was for sure. "In the meantime, I also need to find another puppy."

Mrs. Summers peered at him over the top of her glasses. "Did you miss your appointment at the animal shelter this afternoon? I thought I'd programmed it into your BlackBerry."

"No, I was there. But the shelter made some kind of mistake. They promised the dog to someone else." For a brief, blissful moment, Anders's attention strayed from his messy life, and he thought about the graceful woman in the reindeer costume—her soulful eyes, holly berry lips and perfect, impertinent mouth. Somewhere in the back of his head, he could have sworn he heard jingle bells.

"What a shame. Lolly would have loved that little dog." His assistant pressed a hand to her heart.

Anders had screwed up a lot of things lately. His list of mistakes was longer than the line to take pictures with Santa at Macy's, but he had a feeling he'd done the right thing when he'd walked away from the animal shelter empty-handed. Maybe he wasn't as big of a Scrooge as everyone thought he was.

Dead inside.

A headache bloomed at the back of Anders's skull.

"There are other puppies. I suspect it worked out for the best."

Mrs. Summers narrowed her gaze, studied him for a beat and then nodded. "Things usually do."

Did they?

God, he hoped so.

"I think I'm going to take the rest of the afternoon off, after all." He stood, buttoned his suit jacket and shifted his weight from one foot to the other.

This office was his sanctuary. He'd always felt more at home at his desk, glued to the market's highs and lows, than he did at his luxury penthouse with its sweeping views of Central Park and the Natural History Museum. But today it felt different, strange… He wondered if it would ever feel like home again, and if it didn't, where he was supposed to find peace.

"Call the nanny and tell her I'm on the way to fetch Lolly." Maybe he'd take her to see the tree at Rockefeller Center or for a carriage ride through the park. Something Christmassy.

Like the Rockettes show at Radio City Music Hall?

His jaw clenched tight.

"Yes, Mr. Kent. And I'll look into the puppy situation and send you a list of available dogs that might be a good fit." Mrs. Summers looked up from her tablet. "Would you like me to try and find another Yorkie mix?"

He heard the woman's voice again—so confident, so cynical in her assessment of his character.

You really don't seem like the Yorkie type.

What did that even mean?

Did she picture him with something less fluffy and adorable, like a bulldog? Or a snake? More to the point, why had that assumption stuck with him and rubbed him so entirely the wrong way?

"Anything. I'm open to suggestions," he muttered. Then on second thought, he said, "Scratch that. I want a lapdog—something cute and affectionate, on the smaller side. A real cupcake of a dog."

Mrs. Summers stifled a smile. "Of course, sir."

"The sweeter, the better."

Chapter 3

The afternoon following Chloe's odd encounter at the animal shelter, she tucked her new puppy into a play-pen containing the candy cane–striped dog bed and a dozen or so new toys and then trudged her way through the snow-covered West Village to the Wilde School of Dance.

It was time to face the music.

She couldn't keep lying to her family about her job. Just this morning, she'd thought she spotted her cousin Ryan walking through Times Square while she'd been on flyer duty. She'd ducked behind one of the area's ubiquitous costumed characters—a minion in a Santa hat—but there was no hiding her blinking antlers.

Luckily, the man in the slim tailored suit hadn't been her cousin. Nor had it been her brother, Zander. To her immense relief, she also ruled out the possibility that he was the man who'd proposed to her yesterday—Anders Kent. This guy's shoulders weren't quite as broad, and the cut of his jaw was all wrong. His posture was far too laid-back and casual. He seemed like a regular person out for a stroll on his lunch break, whereas Anders had been brimming with intensity, much like the city itself—gritty and glamorous. So beautifully electric.

Not that she'd been thinking about him for the duration of her two-hour shift. She quite purposefully *hadn't*. But being on flyer duty was such a mindless job, and while she flashed her Rockette smile for the tourists and ground her teeth against the wind as it swept between the skyscrapers, he kept sneaking back into her consciousness. The harder she tried not to think about him, the clearer the memory of their interaction became, until it spun through her mind on constant repeat, like a favorite holiday movie. *Love Actually* or *It's a Wonderful Life.*

Chloe huffed out a sigh. If life was even remotely wonderful, she wouldn't be so hung up on a meaningless encounter with a stranger. Which was precisely why she had to stop pretending everything was fine and come to terms with reality. She was no longer a professional dancer. She might never perform that loathsome toy soldier routine again, and if she didn't humble herself and come clean with the rest of the Wildes, they were sure to find out some other way and her embarrassment would be multiplied tenfold. Emily Wilde was practically omniscient. It was a miracle Chloe's mother hadn't busted her already.

Sure enough, the minute Chloe pushed through the door of the Wilde School of Dance, she could feel Emily's eyes on her from clear across the room. Her mother was deep in conversation with a slim girl in a black leotard—one of her ballet students, no doubt—but her penetrating gaze was trained on Chloe.

Here we go.

Chloe smiled and attempted a flippy little wave, as if this was any ordinary day and she stopped by the studio all the time. She didn't, of course, making this whole situation more awkward and humbling than she could bear.

When was the last time she'd set foot inside this place? A while—even longer than she'd realized. She didn't recognize half the faces in the recital photographs hanging on the lobby walls, and the smooth maple floors had taken quite a beating since she'd twirled across them in pointe shoes as a teenager. The sofa in the parents' waiting area had a definite sag in its center that hadn't been there when Chloe spent hours sprawled across it doing her homework after school.

Was her mother still using the same blue record player and worn practice albums instead of a digital sound system? Yes, apparently. The turntable sat perched on a shelf in the corner of the main classroom, right where it had been since before Chloe was born.

At least Emily was no longer teaching back-to-back classes all day, every day. Chloe's sister-in-law, Allegra, had taken over the majority of the curriculum. From the looks of things, Allegra's intermediate ballet class had just ended. She waved at Chloe from behind the classroom's big picture window as happy ten-and eleven-year-olds in pink tights and soft ballet slippers spilled out of the studio, weaving around Chloe with girlish, balletic grace.

Her throat grew tight as a wave of nostalgia washed

over her. Everything was all so different, and yet still exactly the same as she remembered.

She'd grown up here. In total, she'd probably spent more time between these faded blue walls than she had in the grand family brownstone on Riverside Drive. If family lore was to be believed, she'd taken her first steps in her mother's office between boxes of tap shoes and recital costumes. Just months afterward, she'd learned to plié at the barre in the classroom with the old blue record player.

Chloe's first kiss had happened here, too—with a boy from the School of American Ballet Theatre during rehearsals for *Romeo and Juliet*. It had been a stage kiss, but her heart beat as wildly as hummingbird wings, and when the boy's lips first touched hers, she'd forgotten about pointed toes and the blister on her heel from her new pointe shoes.

The kiss might have been fake, but the warmth of his lips was real, as was the feeling that this school, this place that she knew so well, was etched permanently on her soul. She'd always come back here. It was her home.

I should have come back sooner.

She'd meant to. But somehow days turned into weeks and weeks turned into months, and then her father died. Walking in her childhood footsteps after his heart attack was just too painful, so she'd taken the easy way out and stayed away. She'd thrown herself fully into the Rockettes and, like everything in her life, the family dance school took a back seat to her career.

And now here she was—jobless, with no close friends, superficial relationships with her family members and no love life whatsoever now that Steven had so unceremoniously dumped her after the Thanksgiving parade mishap.

Perfect. She'd somehow become the horrible character in a Christmas movie who required divine intervention to become a decent person again. Except there wasn't an angel in sight, was there?

Again, Anders Kent's chiseled features flashed in her mind. She blinked. Hard.

"Chloe!" Allegra clicked the classroom door shut behind her and pulled Chloe into a hug. "What a wonderful surprise. What are you doing here? Isn't this your busy season? Aren't you performing ten times a day or something crazy like that?"

Before she could form a response, the teen ballerina bade Emily goodbye. Chloe stepped out of the hug and held her breath as her mother approached.

"Hello, dear. Isn't this a lovely surprise." Emily kissed her cheek, but the warm greeting didn't alleviate her sense of shame.

If anything, it made her feel worse.

"Hi, Mom. Allegra. It's great to see you both." Chloe could feel her smile start to tremble.

Don't cry. The only thing that could make her confession more painful was if she fell apart before she could get the words out.

"Are you okay, dear?" Emily glanced at the dainty antique watch strapped around her wrist. She'd been wearing it as long as Chloe could remember. "It's the middle of the day. Shouldn't you be performing in the matinee?"

This was it. This was the moment to spill the beans and admit she was the Rockette who'd become You-Tube famous for ruining the Thanksgiving Day parade.

She took a deep breath. "No, I'm actually not performing anymore. For now, anyway."

"What do you mean, you're not performing?" Emily's face fell.

The disappointment in her eyes was a knife to Chloe's heart. For all Chloe's mistakes, Emily had always been her biggest supporter. Chloe had missed months' worth of family dinners and get-togethers, but when it came to performing, she'd never failed to make her dancer mother proud. Until now.

"I'm on hiatus for a while." She swallowed and shifted her gaze over Emily's shoulder so she wouldn't have to see her mother's crushed expression, but then she found herself staring at a slick, glossy poster from one of her own Christmas shows.

The poster hung in a frame surrounded by photographs of herself in various Rockette costumes. The arrangement was practically a shrine.

"Oh dear, you're not injured, are you?" Emily's hand fluttered to her heart.

"Please don't worry, Mom. I'm fine." *I'm just a world-class coward.* She couldn't do it. She couldn't confess to being fired, not while she was standing there, facing the Chloe wall of fame.

Besides, her mom had just given her an excellent idea. An injury, even a small one, would buy her some time to make things right. She could start helping out at the school. She'd answer the phones, manage the dance moms—anything—and once she'd proved her devotion to her family again, she'd finally tell them everything.

Because she was definitely telling the truth, 100 percent. She was just delaying it a tiny bit longer.

Seriously? Just fess up already.

"It's only a sprain," she heard herself say, and immediately wished the floor would open up and swallow her whole.

Allegra gasped. "Oh, no. Please say it's not your ankle."

Chloe looked down at her feet. She'd worn Uggs, because it was freezing out, but if she'd had an injured ankle, it would be wrapped. She might even be on crutches. "Um, no. It's my calf."

"Your calf?" Emily lifted a brow.

"Yes. There's a terrible knot in it." Could she have come up with a more ridiculous lie? There was no way her mother was buying this.

"I see," Emily said quietly…so quietly that Chloe had the distinct impression that her mother really did understand what was happening, but was so unable to face the truth of the situation that she couldn't even say it out loud.

But if Emily sensed Chloe was being less than truthful, she didn't admit it.

"That's a shame, sweetheart. But whatever circumstances brought you back, I'm glad you're here." She smiled. "Really glad."

Chloe took a deep breath. "Me, too. I was actually hoping you could put me to work."

"Here at the studio?" Allegra said.

"Yes. I'd love to help run things around here with the two of you. I'll do whatever you need."

"But your calf…" Allegra's gaze drifted downward.

"She's right," Emily chimed in. "Your calf could get in the way of doing any teaching. Plus, I'm afraid we can't really afford it."

The school was having money troubles? No wonder things looked a little worse for wear. "I didn't realize…"

Of course she didn't. Maybe if she'd bothered to show up every now and then, she'd know what was going on.

"I think I might have an idea, but it would only be part-time," Emily said.

"That's okay." She needed a few hours a week off for flyer duty, anyway. "I'll do anything."

"We're doing *Baby Nutcracker* this year, and you'd be a perfect director."

"Baby Nutcracker?" Chloe had no idea what that meant, but she didn't ask. Whatever it was must have been added to the school's annual repertoire, and she didn't want to draw yet more attention to her prolonged absence. "That sounds like fun. I'd love to."

Emily and Allegra exchanged a glance.

"Are you sure? It might be part-time, but it's not an easy job," Allegra said.

"And you'd need to be around until Christmas Eve." Emily raised her brows, waiting for an answer.

Perfect. "I'm sure."

"Great. You can start right now." Emily brushed past her and held the door open for the crowd of parents with small children who'd appeared out of nowhere and were lined up on the sidewalk outside.

Wait. *What?*

"Now?" Chloe gulped.

"Now." Emily nodded.

Allegra leaned closer. "I'll help. You have no idea what you've gotten yourself into, do you?"

Thank God for sisters-in-law. "I'm clueless."

"*Baby Nutcracker* is a Christmas recital for the pre-ballet students, aged three to five." She pushed open the door to the main classroom and waved Chloe inside. "It's an abbreviated version of the traditional *Nutcracker* ballet—same music, same characters, just a bit shorter."

Preschoolers dressed as mice, nutcrackers and a sugarplum fairy? Yes, please. Who would turn down this job? "That sounds adorable."

Allegra crossed her arms. She seemed to be biting back a smirk. "When was the last time you taught pre-ballet?"

Was this a trick question? "Never. I might have helped out back when I was a teenager, but that's the extent of my teaching experience."

Chloe slipped out of her coat. Luckily, she'd worn a black wraparound sweater and yoga pants—clothes she could move in.

"You can borrow these." Allegra tossed her a pair of ballet shoes. "If you think your calf will be okay."

"Thanks." She swallowed and slipped the shoes on. "I'm excited. This should be fun."

"The little ones are precious, and the production is

definitely adorable. But they're a handful." She glanced over Chloe's shoulder. "And they're here."

Right. She could do this. She was usually onstage for a minimum of three shows a day for the entire month of December. Putting together a half-hour ballet recital for a few preschoolers would probably be easy by comparison.

You wanted to be involved, and now you are.

She took a deep breath and turned, following Allegra's gaze toward the picture window that overlooked the lobby. The space was suddenly packed with strollers and tiny bodies dressed in candy-colored ballet clothes. It looked like every mom in the Village had turned up with a toddler in tow.

How could they possibly have money problems? Enrollment seemed to be booming. "Allegra, how bad is the school struggling?"

"Pretty bad." Allegra sighed. "We had the big dance-athon fund-raiser a while back, so the business is out of the red. But we're still barely getting by. We've got just enough to pay the bills every month. I keep thinking that if we could give the studio a major face-lift, we could attract serious dance students. Maybe we could even hold a summer intensive for one of the dance companies."

"That's a great idea." But it would never happen in the school's current condition.

Chloe looked around again, and her gaze snagged on all the little things that needed to be fixed—the cracked walls, the scuffed floors, the faded furniture. Even the window overlooking the lobby had a tiny spiderweb of cracks in the corner. She frowned at it, until something beyond the glass caught her attention.

Correction: not something. Some*one*.

His head towered above the crowd, and his expression was as grim and intense as ever. Chloe had never seen anyone look so woefully out of place at a ballet studio before. It would have been comical if the sight of him hadn't been such a shock.

"Brace yourself. I'm going to open the door and let the kids inside." Allegra paused midway across the room. "Are you okay? You look like you've seen a ghost."

Not a ghost. A thief.

A *puppy* thief.

The man on the other side of the window finally glanced her way. He did a double take, and then his gaze collided with hers.

She forgot how to breathe for a second. All day long she'd kept imagining that she'd seen him, and now here he was in the flesh, as if she'd somehow conjured him.

Anders Kent.

Her would-be fiancé.

Chapter 4

Anders went still as their gazes locked through the picture window. Around him, chaos reigned as a dozen mothers wrestled their children out of snow boots and into pale pink ballet shoes and tutus. The floor was littered with coats, stray mittens and far more strollers than could safely fit into the small space. But he forgot all of it the moment he spotted the dancer on the other side of the glass.

Her.

She was dressed normally this time—no reindeer suit in sight—but he recognized her instantly. She had that same unforgettable graceful neck, same supple spine, same holly berry lips. Tiny earrings shaped liked candy canes dangled from her ears, brushing lightly against her skin in a way that made Anders forget he was standing in the middle of mommy-and-me chaos. He could only stand and stare, with all his attention focused on that swan-like curve, wondering what her body would feel like in his hands. Soft…warm.

His fingers balled into fists at his sides, and then she

waved, snapping him out of his trance. He lifted an eyebrow in acknowledgment.

Definitely the same woman, in all her Christmas-loving glory.

"Can we go in now?" Lolly tugged at his pant leg.

He looked down at her tiny feet, trying to figure out if he'd gotten her ballet shoes on the correct ones. He still wasn't certain. She seemed somewhat happy, though, and that was all that mattered. "Sure, pumpkin."

Most of the other kids charged into the classroom on their own, but Lolly wanted an escort. The morning after the accident, when Anders told her that her mommy and daddy were in heaven now and wouldn't be coming home, she'd clung to him and soaked his shirt with tears.

She'd been more like her usual chatty self in the past few days, but still had moments when she wanted to hold his hand, or be carried so that she could wrap her tiny arms around his neck. Anders had a feeling she just needed to know he wasn't going to disappear.

He wouldn't.

Not if he could help it.

Lolly led him into the classroom, but the minute they crossed the threshold, she dropped his hand to join her friends, sitting cross-legged in a cluster of frothy pink tulle in front of the large mirrored wall.

He lingered for a moment, hesitant to leave her there. And maybe a part of him—some shadow of his former self that remembered what it was like to wish for something, to want—didn't want to walk away from Miss Wilde again.

What are you doing? He had a mountain of tasks to accomplish today, starting with finding a way to convince Penelope Reed to marry him. He'd thought about the matter long and hard, and realistically, she was his only option.

He turned to go, but before he could take a step, the whimsical Miss Wilde tapped him on the shoulder.

"Going somewhere?" she said.

A smile tugged at his lips as he spun to face her. He barely recognized the sensation. It felt like years since he'd smiled. "Yes. Back to the office."

"I'm Chloe, by the way. We didn't get as far as names yesterday. Parents are welcome to stay and watch." Her soft brown eyes seemed almost hopeful.

He shook his head. "I can't. I…" *I've got to go get engaged.*

"Hello, Mr. Kent." Allegra, the dance teacher he'd met at Lolly's last recital, paused to stand beside Chloe. She glanced back and forth between them. "You two know each other?"

"No," said Anders, at the exact moment Chloe Wilde contradicted him by nodding and saying yes.

Then she frowned and glared at him in much the same way she had the day before when she'd accused him of being a puppy thief. "Seriously? You asked me to marry you yesterday and now you're pretending we don't know each other?"

Allegra coughed—loudly—but Anders's gaze remained glued to Chloe. "You're not going to let that go, are you?"

She smiled at him, and the curve of her red lips was

far too sweet. Visions of sugarplums danced in his head. "Nope."

"Wait—I'm confused." Allegra frowned. "What happened to Steven?"

"Who's Steven?" he asked, before he could stop himself.

Chloe's cheeks flared a lovely shade of pink. "He's no one."

Anders glanced at Allegra for confirmation, although why he cared about a person he'd never heard of before was a mystery.

Sure it is. You know *why.*

Allegra bit her lip and then caved under his gaze. "He's not exactly no one. Chloe, didn't you and Steven date for nearly three years?"

Something hardened in Anders's gut, and if he didn't know better, he would have recognized the feeling as jealousy.

Impossible. He didn't even know this woman. He'd laid eyes on her exactly twice, and both times he'd found her borderline annoying. Attractive, sure—he wasn't blind, after all. But he didn't typically go for the adorably quirky type, and if Chloe was anything, she was that. Compared to most women he dated, she was sort of a mess.

Then again, it wasn't as if those women were lining up to marry him. He'd spent the previous evening getting back in touch with his dates from the past few months, and at first, most of them had been happy to hear from him. But as soon as he'd brought up the whole marriage-of-convenience idea, their enthusiasm waned. He'd been hung up on more times than he could count.

Chloe squared her slender shoulders and gave her chin a defiant lift. "Steven and I broke up. It wasn't working out and we agreed to go our separate ways. No big deal."

Wrong. The flash of pain in Chloe's soft doe eyes told him it was a very big deal, but he didn't press for an explanation. He wasn't altogether sure why he was even still standing there.

"Wow, I had no idea. I'm so sorry. I don't really know what to say." Allegra's gaze flicked toward him again.

He held up his hands. "I had nothing to do with it."

How was this his life? He should be facilitating an acquisition right now, or better yet, proposing to Penelope Reed, instead of standing in a ballet school wondering why the enigmatic Chloe Wilde was suddenly single.

"I should go," he blurted.

Penelope was the logical choice, in spite of their working relationship. She was reliable and discreet. He knew precisely what he'd be getting into if she agreed to a business marriage with him. It would be clean, simple and orderly, which was precisely the sort of relationship he needed right now, even if it was temporary.

As if on cue, Lolly appeared. She'd broken away from the group of little girls sitting cross-legged in front of the mirror and was now standing at his feet with her arms wrapped around his shins.

Too soon.

He shouldn't have brought her here. She'd been

doing so well, and she'd been asking about going back to dance class, so he'd consulted his late brother's calendar and figured out Lolly's schedule. For a five-year-old, she was fiercely independent, brimming with confidence. Anders chalked it up to her Manhattan upbringing, but she was still just a child—a child who'd lost her mom and dad.

He should have waited another week or two. Better yet, he should have thrown that crazy schedule out the window and never come here.

But when Anders crouched down and peeled her slender arms from his legs, intent on scooping her up and walking out the door, she turned her back on him and gazed up at Chloe.

"Are you my teacher? I've never seen you here before," she said.

Chloe bent down so she was at eye level with Lolly. "I'm new." She pulled a face. "Sort of."

"Is that you on the picture outside?" Lolly pointed toward the lobby.

Of course Anders had noticed the framed poster of Chloe in her flirty Santa costume and silver tap shoes, along with the multitude of surrounding photographs from her performances with the Rockettes. It would have been impossible not to. Even if he'd somehow missed it, Lolly's reaction would have clued him in.

She'd looked at the poster with stars in her eyes as they'd walked past, and she'd apparently just realized the beautiful dancer from the picture was here in the flesh, standing in the same room.

"That's me," Chloe said brightly.

"You look like a Christmas princess." Lolly tilted her head and looked Chloe up and down. "*Are* you a Christmas princess?"

And just like that, Anders was in over his head. He hadn't even formulated a Santa Claus plan yet, much less given any thought to princesses and fairy tales and storybook endings. How on earth was he going to raise a little girl?

Hell, maybe his brother had been right when he'd added the marriage clause to the guardianship paragraph in his will. Anders didn't know the first thing about being a dad.

"Not exactly," Chloe said. And before Lolly's face could fall, she added, "Christmas is a magical time, though. Just like a real-life fairy tale. And you know what? The ballet we're putting together for Christmas Eve has all sorts of wonderful parts—fairies, dancing snowflakes and even a few snow queens."

Lolly's eyes went as wide as saucers, and when her tiny mouth curved into a smile that lit up her whole face, some of the tightness in Anders's chest unraveled. After days of struggling to take a full inhalation, he could almost breathe again.

"Can I be a queen?" Lolly's quiet voice was as reverent as if she were speaking to Cinderella herself.

"We'll see. But no matter what, you'll get to dress up in a pretty costume and dance and twirl in front of an audience." Chloe glanced at Anders and gave him a quick wink. So quick he almost thought he'd imagined it. "Your daddy here might even bring you flowers."

And with those words, everything within him

hardened again. They were a death blow. He couldn't breathe, couldn't speak, couldn't think. All he could do was stand there with his hands on Lolly's petite shoulders, choking on the truth while his ears roared.

Your daddy here...

Damn it.

Of course she'd assume he was Lolly's father. He should have seen it coming. Maybe he would have if he hadn't been so distracted by Chloe the Christmas Princess. And her perfectly bow-shaped, perfectly impertinent mouth.

He was mucking everything up.

Already.

"He's not my daddy," Lolly said, as casually as if she'd just announced the sky was blue.

"Oh." Chloe rested a hand on her chest, and for reasons he didn't want to contemplate, Anders's gaze darted to her unadorned ring finger. "I'm sorry. I thought..."

"He's my uncle." Lolly shrugged.

Anders gave her shoulders a gentle squeeze. "Why don't you go sit down, pumpkin? I think class is about to start."

"Okay." She threw her arms around him for a good-bye hug.

Anders bent low to hold her tight until she skipped back into place with the other children. When he straightened, he could see questions shining in Chloe's eyes—eyes that were the color of hot cocoa on frosty winter nights and seemed as if they could wrap around him like a blanket, enveloping him in warmth, making him feel at home.

Her lips parted, and he knew if he stayed, she'd ask about Lolly's mom and dad and he'd be forced to tell her everything, which was something he desperately didn't want to do. She'd been the first person in days who'd looked at him without a hint of pity in her gaze. He hadn't realized how much he'd needed a woman to look at him like that, but he had.

It made him feel human again. Like a man.

And it also made him wonder if he hadn't needed just any woman to see him as a man, but specifically *this* woman. If he'd been the type of person who believed in fairy tales, he might think that perhaps he'd been waiting for Chloe to prance into his life all along, reindeer suit and all.

But he wasn't.

Storybook endings were a fallacy. Anders had learned that lesson a hell of a long time ago, and now Lolly was learning it, too, in the most painful way possible. So once again, Anders turned his back on Chloe Wilde and left without so much as saying goodbye.

Chloe could barely concentrate as she ran the young children in her class through a simple round of pliés and tendus at the barre, followed by a giggly, boisterous round of chassés across the studio. For one thing, she couldn't believe the pitiful state of the wood floor beneath their tiny feet. A worn path extended from one corner of the room to the other, faded by decades of balletic turns and leaps.

Most dance schools didn't even have wood floors anymore. For years now, the trend had been performance floors—sheet vinyl laid over a sprung surface. Unlike wood, performance floors were slip resistant, resulting in fewer injuries and easier training for younger students. The elasticity absorbed shock and allowed dancers to leap higher. Emily should have replaced the floors years ago. No wonder enrollment was down.

But new floors cost thousands of dollars, and apparently money was more scarce around here than Chloe had realized. She wished she could do more to help.

She also wished she could stop thinking about Lolly Kent's handsome uncle. He'd been undeniably swoony at the animal shelter, holding the tiny puppy in his large, masculine hands. But seeing him with that precious little girl in his arms was almost more than Chloe could handle. It should be illegal for hot bachelors to walk around holding adorable children or tiny animals. Honestly.

His niece was a good dancer, too. She had great turnout for her age, but more important, she had charisma. Unlike technique, stage presence was something that couldn't be taught, and Lolly had it in spades. Chloe couldn't take her eyes off her, and it had nothing to do with Anders.

Not much, anyway.

It was only natural to be curious, though, wasn't it? And that was all she was experiencing—simple curiosity. Because it certainly wasn't attraction. She had far more important things to worry about at the moment than her nonexistent love life. Things like keeping track of all the lies she'd been telling lately. It was getting out of hand. If she didn't start telling the truth, she was going to need a spreadsheet to keep track of what came out of her mouth.

She had enough on her plate right now simply dealing with reviving her career, while at the same time doing something to alleviate all the guilt she felt about being the prodigal daughter. Also, as much as she hated to admit it, the breakup with Steven had gotten to her.

How could it not? Now that she was no longer performing, he thought she wasn't good enough. Deep down, she was starting to believe it, too. She'd devoted her whole life to dance. Without it, she wasn't sure who she was anymore.

Which was precisely why she had no interest in dating—or marrying—Anders Kent. Not that he'd asked… again.

Still, when a nanny showed up to collect Lolly after class, Chloe's heart practically sank to her ballet slippers. The undeniable stab of disappointment she felt at the prospect of not seeing him again was confirmation enough to stay away from the man. Steven had been safe. They'd been good together, but not *too* good. She'd enjoyed spending time with him, but there'd been no goose bumps when he kissed her good-night. No butterflies swarming in her belly when she saw him across a crowded room. If her father's sudden heart attack had taught her anything, it was that life had a way of yanking the rug out from under you when you least expected it. She didn't want to fall madly in love with anyone. Falling in like was just fine. Safe. Which meant her relationship with Steven had been perfect, except now it was over. And now she also got the definite impression that Anders Kent was anything but safe.

There was something quite dangerous about his cool blue eyes and his perfect bone structure. His odd habit of doing or saying something nice when she least expected it was definitely alarming. When he'd handed her the puppy at the animal shelter and then walked out the door empty-handed, there'd been butterflies aplenty fluttering around her insides.

So really, it was best if she never set eyes on him again. And she probably wouldn't. Uncles didn't typically tote their nieces to and from ballet class.

Maybe she should ask, though, just to be sure. If he was going to be coming to the studio on a regular basis, she needed to be prepared.

Purely so she could avoid him.

Obviously.

"Class went well, don't you think?" Chloe aimed a Windex bottle at the walled mirror, where sticky little handprints decorated the glass from barre-level down.

Allegra handed her a roll of paper towels. "It did. I knew you'd be great, but it never hurts to have reinforcements when so many small children are involved."

Chloe laughed. "You can say that again. At one point, I saw a little boy hanging upside down from the barre like a monkey."

"He sounds like a great candidate for the part of the mouse king. You can throw in some cute tumbling choreography. The parents will eat it up on performance night."

"So it's mostly family that comes to the performance?

Moms and dads, sisters and brothers…" She scrubbed hard at an invisible spot on the mirror. "Uncles."

Allegra met her gaze in the reflection and lifted a brow. "Any particular uncle you have in mind?"

Was she that obvious?

Yes, apparently she was. "No."

Allegra snorted.

"Fine. Maybe." Chloe wadded up her paper towel and lobbed it at Allegra's head.

She caught it midair. "That's what I thought. Tell me the truth—did Anders Kent really ask you to marry him?"

Why, oh why, had she felt the need to share that awkward moment? "It was just a joke."

Wasn't it?

Allegra frowned. "He's awfully intense. I don't get the impression he jokes around much, but I don't know him very well. Before the accident, we only saw him at recitals."

Before the accident?

Chloe swallowed. She wanted to press for more information, but at the same time, she was afraid to know more.

"It's so sad what happened, isn't it?" Allegra's voice went quiet, and the fear in the pit of Chloe's stomach crystallized into an overwhelming sense of dread. "To think that just a week ago, Lolly's mom was dropping her off at class. And now that sweet little girl is an orphan."

The Windex bottle nearly slipped through Chloe's fingers. "An orphan," she repeated woodenly.

"All because of a car accident. It's *tragic*. I suppose Anders will be appointed as her guardian since Grant was his brother, but you probably know all about that since the two of you are clearly acquainted." Allegra took the bottle of cleaner from Chloe's hands and put it back in the tiny storage cabinet in the corner of the classroom, oblivious to the fact that she'd suddenly become paralyzed.

A car accident.

It explained so much. It might even explain the out-of-the-blue proposal, although there had to be more to the story there. It *certainly* explained why Anders had been at the animal shelter to adopt a fluffy little puppy.

He'd been trying to comfort his niece. The dog had probably been Lolly's Christmas gift. He'd said so himself, hadn't he? And Chloe had been so wrapped up in her own problems that she'd chastised him for giving a puppy away as a present. She'd actually lectured him about responsible pet ownership, and he hadn't said a word. He'd just handed over the little dog and walked away.

"Anders is raising Lolly now, isn't he?" Allegra asked.

"Yes," Chloe said, as if she had intimate knowledge of the situation.

She didn't need anyone to tell her the truth. Deep down, she knew. Anders had lost his brother, and now he was suddenly a single dad to a grieving five-year-old little girl—a little girl who might have gotten a tiny Yorkie puppy for Christmas, if not for Chloe.

Who's the puppy thief now?

Chapter 5

"You wanted to see me?"

Anders closed his laptop and aimed his full attention at Penelope Reed hovering in the doorway of his office the following morning. "Yes. Please come in. Have a seat."

A fly on the wall would never suspect the two of them had ever shared a bed, but that was by design. Anders and Penelope weren't a couple, just two people who'd come to an understanding that suited them both. Which made him all the more convinced he was making the right choice.

Penelope would be the perfect wife, and the more he thought about it, the more convinced he'd become that no one at the office would even have to know. They could keep things private, and the marriage could simply be an extension of the unspoken agreement they already had. An addendum with mutually agreed upon terms and, most important, an expiration date.

She took a seat in one of the wingback chairs facing his desk, just as she'd done a thousand times before to discuss a stock offering or a merger.

"You look well, Anders. I'm happy you're back in the office." She shifted her gaze to her hands, folded neatly in her lap. "Apologies for not making it to the funeral. We had the Remington IPO, and I couldn't get away."

"I understand." Anders nodded.

In all honesty, her absence hadn't registered. He'd barely been aware of his surroundings on the day he'd buried Grant and Olivia. But it was fine. Penelope had never been the touchy-feely type, and there was no reason for that to change now.

But as he pulled open the top drawer of his desk, he heard the singsong lilt in Chloe Wilde's voice as she'd spoken to Lolly at the dance school the day before. He remembered the way Lolly had gazed up at her, eyes shining bright.

Are you a Christmas princess?

Penelope cleared her throat. "So what can I do for you?"

Anders's jaw tensed, and he pushed the sentimental memory away. *Focus.*

He needed someone reliable on his side. Someone he trusted. And that someone was most definitely *not* his niece's effusive dance teacher.

Besides, she'd already turned him down. And he was perfectly *fine* with her refusal. Relieved, actually.

"I have a proposal I wanted to discuss with you." Best to get right down to it. He'd wasted enough time in the past few days. "A business proposal...of sorts."

"I'm all ears." Penelope tilted her head.

She was a beautiful woman. No doubt about it. If Anders remembered correctly, she'd been a model for a few years before she'd gone to business school—in Paris, maybe. Or Tokyo. He wasn't quite sure.

But it was a flawless, cool kind of beauty, like one of Alfred Hitchcock's iconic blondes. Strange how he'd never noticed that before.

"I've prepared a contract for your review." He reached for the voluminous document that had been sitting in his drawer all morning like a bomb waiting to detonate, and his gaze snagged on the bold lettering printed across the margin of the top page.

Premarital Agreement.

His mouth went dry.

Why was this so difficult? He'd known Penelope for years. He'd proposed to Chloe within minutes of setting eyes on her, so asking Penelope to marry him should have been no trouble at all.

But he'd been shell-shocked from the meeting with the estate attorney when he'd hastily asked Chloe to be his wife. And it hadn't been a *genuine* proposal. He'd given more thought to what he'd had for lunch that day.

"So…" Penelope shifted in her chair and glanced at the vintage Tiffany desk clock on his credenza.

Anders smoothed down his tie and slid the contract toward her across the glossy surface of his desk. "It's all spelled out right here. The terms are negotiable, of course, other than the provisions spelled out in Section One."

She reached for the contract, but her hand froze mid-air as her gaze moved over the top of the page.

Clearly, he should have done a better job of preparing her for what was coming, but he was tired of putting it off, tired of sleepless nights, tired of wondering if he'd run out of time and Lolly would be taken away before the Christmas windows on Fifth Avenue came down.

So very, very tired.

"Anders, I don't understand." Penelope shook her head. "What is this? You want to marry me?"

No, actually. I don't.

He took a deep breath. "I need to get married. For Lolly."

"Oh." She gave him a thin-lipped smile. "So you're looking for a mommy figure for your orphaned niece."

"No. That's not it at all." He struggled to keep his tone even and businesslike.

He didn't care for her callous description of Lolly, but technically, it was true. And he'd botched enough marriage proposals in the past forty-eight hours to realize this one was off to a bad start. He needed a *yes*, whether he wanted one or not.

"In order to secure Lolly's guardianship, I have to be married by the end of the year," he said.

"The end of *this* year?" Penelope's brows crept up higher on her forehead.

"Yes." He nodded and took her stunned silence as the opportunity he needed to explain things. He laid out every detail of his proposed arrangement, from duration to compensation.

"Look," he concluded. "I know it's a lot to ask, but I don't have much time and I trust you, Penelope. We've successfully navigated a personal relationship for a while now, and I think we could make this transition rather seamlessly, in a way that could be beneficial to us both."

He leaned back in his chair and tried not to think

about what Grant would have had to say about such a proposal. A lot, probably. But he was doing what needed to be done, the only way he knew how. And to his great relief, Penelope nodded instead of renegotiating the terms. Now all they had to do was sign the paperwork and make an appointment at city hall.

But when he offered her the Mont Blanc pen from his suit pocket, she refused to take it.

"No," she said quietly and pushed the contract away before removing her fingertips from the edge of the crisp white pages, as if they'd burned her skin.

Anders frowned. "What do you mean, *no*?"

"I mean *no*." She stood. "I'm sorry, Anders. But I just can't do it."

"May I ask why not?" he asked calmly.

Too calmly.

He should be panicked right now. Christmas was in three short weeks, and he wasn't any closer to being married than he was two days ago.

But inexplicably, the knot of emotion in his chest felt more like relief than alarm.

It shouldn't be like this.

Even Anders knew this wasn't the way to choose a bride. Marriage was supposed to be a sacred vow, a lifetime commitment.

"I'm not cut out to be anyone's mommy, not even temporarily." Penelope shrugged. "And call me crazy, but if and when I get married someday, I want it to be for love."

Anders nodded. Maybe Penelope was more of a romantic than he'd realized.

Maybe you are, too.

He rubbed his eyes. Stress and exhaustion were messing with his head, not to mention the grief he was still doing his best to ignore. He'd grieve properly later, though. Once Lolly's guardianship was secure, he could grieve all he wanted.

Doesn't that sound like a joyous Christmas?

Christmas was the absolute last thing he had time for. If it were possible, Anders would snap his fingers and skip the rest of December altogether. No twinkling lights. No presents. No Christmas, period.

He sighed, opened his eyes and immediately wondered if the universe was playing some kind of joke on him. Or maybe he'd lost what little was left of his sanity, because he was suddenly seeing things.

Specifically, Chloe Wilde.

Standing in his office.

Dressed in her reindeer costume.

"Knock, knock," Chloe said, deflating a little beneath the weight of Anders's stare. "I hope I'm not interrupting anything."

She was *definitely* interrupting something. She had no idea what, but if the tense knot in Anders's jaw was any indication, it was big.

"You know what—never mind." She held Prancer's dog carrier more tightly against her chest. A barrier. "I'll come back later."

Or never.

This had been a monumentally bad idea. She should have just gone straight to Times Square for her afternoon flyer shift and forgotten about Anders Kent and his sad story altogether. Clearly, he didn't want her help.

"Wait." The woman standing beside Anders's desk held up an elegant hand. "Don't go. Mr. Kent and I are finished."

Chloe had no idea who the woman was, but she was gorgeous. Poised and classic, like a woman in a perfume commercial. Her polished chignon and sleek pencil skirt made Chloe even more aware that she was clad in brown faux Rudolph fur, if such a thing was even possible.

Plus, when the woman cast a final glance at Anders on the way out of his office, there was a quiet intimacy in her gaze that made Chloe's stomach churn.

She wasn't jealous. She couldn't be.

This impromptu visit had nothing to do with attraction. She was finished with dating after the Steven fiasco, and Anders Kent wasn't even her type. He was arrogant. He was also too cranky, too rich and far too handsome.

Although he had every right to be cranky, she thought with a pang.

Anyway, she was here for one reason and one reason only—to make things right.

"Miss Wilde," he said, once they were alone, and there was a weariness in his tone that made her heart ache.

She wished she could turn back the clock and go back to the afternoon at the animal shelter two days ago. If she'd known then what she knew now, she would have let him take the puppy. Only a monster would snatch a dog away from a child who'd just lost her parents.

Who's the puppy thief now?

But that was impossible, obviously. She wasn't George Bailey. She couldn't go back in time and do things differently. All she could do was let Lolly have Prancer.

"Here." She moved closer to Anders and set the pet carrier on his desk.

He looked at Prancer, and Chloe could hear the tiny dog's tail beating happily against the inside of the bag. "Perhaps you're mistaken, Miss Wilde. This is an investment banking firm, not a doggy day care."

Honestly, did he have to make this so difficult?

"Very funny. Look, I'm sorry to barge in here like this, but I was afraid if I didn't do it now, I'd chicken out and change my mind."

He studied her, and her cheeks burned with heat. She started sweating beneath the fur of her reindeer costume.

"Change your mind about what, exactly?" he said.

He truly didn't get it, did he?

"Prancer." She waved a hand at the dog, now attempting to break free from the pet carrier and crawl toward Anders across the paper-strewn desk. "The puppy. I want Lolly to have her."

His gaze softened, and for a brief, silvery moment, she caught a glimpse of sadness in the cool blue depths of his eyes, an emotion so profound, so hopeless, that her breath caught in her throat.

Then, as quickly as it had appeared, that heartbreaking flash of vulnerability was gone, and his chiseled face was once again a perfect, impenetrable mask.

"You named the puppy Prancer," he said flatly. "Why does that not surprise me a bit?"

She sat down in one of the stuffy chairs opposite

him. Not that he'd offered. "I did, but Lolly can rename her if she likes."

Her throat grew thick, and she pasted on a smile. Giving up the puppy wasn't going to be easy. She'd grown attached to the little ball of fur, especially since she'd helped bottle-feed Prancer when she was still at the shelter, too young to be adopted out.

But she'd be damned if Anders Kent would know how much she'd miss the precious little dog.

He shook his head, and his voice dropped an octave until it was low and deep enough to scrape her insides. "That won't be necessary."

"If she wants to keep the name, that's fine, too…"

"No." He shook his head again, and shockingly, his mouth curved into a smile. It was a Christmas miracle! "I mean I want you to keep the dog. I've found another puppy for Lolly. In fact, I'm stopping by the shelter this evening to pick her up."

"Oh, I see. Well, that's…" She swallowed. "…wonderful."

It *was* wonderful. It was the best possible news, given the circumstances. But for some strange reason, it struck Chloe as bittersweet.

"I appreciate the offer, though," Anders said. And then he looked at her again—*really* looked—until she forgot all about her silly reindeer costume and her derby hat with its velvet antlers and felt as if she was bared before him. An unwrapped gift.

She took a shaky inhalation and dropped her gaze.

That was when she saw it.

Premarital Agreement.

She stared at the words on the document sitting on Anders's desk until they swam together, forming a dark, inky pool. "What's this?"

None of your business, that's what.

Anders cleared his throat. "It's nothing."

Chloe stared at him until he looked away, and then she thought about the lovely woman who'd been standing beside his desk when she'd arrived. She thought about how natural the two of them had looked together, how perfectly matched they'd seemed. Like two blue-blooded peas in a pod.

"You're getting married?" she sputtered. The words were out of her mouth before she could stop them, and to her horror, they were laced with hurt.

She had no right to be upset. Still, what did the man do? Propose to every woman he met?

"No." Anders shook his head, then grimaced. "I mean, yes."

After a pause, he added, "I think."

Chloe lifted a brow. "How can you not know?"

"It's complicated." He reached for the sheaf of papers on the desk in front of her, but not before Chloe saw the names printed in the first paragraph.

This agreement is made by and between Anders Kent and Penelope Reed...

Below that, she saw a substantial dollar amount, which didn't quite make sense. He wanted to *pay* someone to marry him?

Chloe knew better than to ask any more questions. None of this was her business. But she couldn't seem to stop herself.

"Penelope Reed." She turned the name over in her mind. It sounded very sophisticated, very posh—the perfect sort of name for a bride someone like Anders would choose, as opposed to a person he'd only temporarily propose to. "Let me guess—that's the woman who was just in here, wasn't it."

He shoved the contract in one of the desk drawers and slammed it closed. "I'm not marrying Penelope Reed."

"But it was her, wasn't it?" Why did she care? More important, why was she still sitting here? She had less than an hour to get to Times Square, and the subway would be packed this time of day.

Anders sighed. "Yes, it was."

"And she turned you down?"

He glared at her.

"I'll take that as a yes."

"Look, Miss Wilde. I appreciate your offer regarding the dog. It was very thoughtful, but I have a lot on my plate right now…"

"Like finding a wife?" She couldn't resist. Something strange was going on, and she had to know what it was. And when she really thought about it, it sort of *was* her business, since for a split second, she'd been on his list of potential brides. "Why do you want to get married so badly, anyway? And why on earth would you offer someone money to be your wife?"

He narrowed his gaze at her. "Do you always ask so many questions?"

"Do you always propose to every woman who crosses your path?" she countered.

He crossed his arms, and she caught a glimpse of the

crisp French cuffs of his shirt, his understated platinum cuff links and just a sliver of his manly wrists. Her heart beat hard, and she looked away.

Who in their right mind got swoony over a man's wrist?

"If I tell you, will you and Prancer dash on out of here so I can get some work done?" He shot an amused glance at her antlers.

She shrugged one shoulder. "Maybe."

Definitely. If she didn't leave in exactly ten minutes, she'd be late for work.

Again, what was she still doing, sitting there in his office?

"I can't be appointed as Lolly's permanent guardian unless I'm married. I've got until Christmas to find a wife." He lifted a brow. "Happy now? Any more questions?"

So this was about Lolly.

Chloe's indignation melted away, replaced by a feeling much more complex, much more bittersweet. She couldn't quite put her finger on what it was, but it made her heart beat hard in her chest. And it made her think that maybe, just maybe, she could help Anders and his sweet little niece.

Plus, that dollar amount on the contract would go a long way toward improving the dance school.

"Just one." *This is crazy.* She swallowed. *Don't do it. Just get up and leave. Walk away while you still can.* But she knew she wouldn't—couldn't if she'd tried. "Why not me?"

Chapter 6

He didn't have a choice.

At least that was what Anders told himself when he agreed to marry Chloe Wilde. It was also what he told himself when she'd left Prancer in his care so she could go to work in her reindeer costume, which made for an interesting afternoon at the office. The havoc wrought by the Yorkie as Anders made conference calls and met with clients was astounding, especially given the dog's tiny size.

He'd had to call the animal shelter and cancel yet another pending puppy adoption, which meant he'd probably be blackballed from getting another pet for the rest of his life. But adding a wife and a dog to his household right after it had doubled in size seemed like more than enough to deal with at the moment.

On some level, he was aware that he could have said no. No to babysitting Chloe's dog. No to at least some of the chaos, but for reasons he didn't care to examine too closely, he hadn't. It was easier to keep believing that all the recent upheaval in his life was out of his control. Lolly needed him, therefore he needed Chloe. Again, he didn't have a choice.

But applying for a marriage license the following morning *felt* like one, especially when Chloe turned up to meet him on the front steps of the city clerk's office on Worth Street wearing a winter-white swing coat over a pretty pleated dress, and a flower tucked into her upswept hair. It occurred to him as he climbed the building's sweeping marble steps and made his way toward her that he'd never seen her in anything but her reindeer costume or dance clothes. And now here she was, looking as lovely as ever.

Like a bride.

His bride.

"Hi." She gave him an uncharacteristically bashful smile, and he was suddenly acutely aware of the sound of his own heartbeat, pounding relentlessly in his ears.

"Hi. You look…" He paused when he realized his hands were shaking, and tucked them into the pockets of his overcoat. "…beautiful."

"Thank you." Her cheeks flared pink. "I know we're not actually getting married today, only getting the license, but I figured I should probably look the part. Just a little, so it seems real. You know?"

Mission accomplished. Once they had the license and waited the mandatory twenty-four hours, they'd be husband and wife. It didn't get much more real than that.

"Look, I know we didn't discuss this, but I think it would be best if we kept things between us strictly platonic from here on out," she said, without meeting his gaze. "Don't you agree?"

"Absolutely." Inside his coat pockets, his hands balled into fists.

"So, no sex." At last she looked him in the eyes.

He held her gaze until the flush in her cheeks turned berry red. "I know what *platonic* means."

"Right." She swallowed, and he traced the movement up and down the slender column of her throat. "Just so we're clear."

"Crystal." It was a perfectly reasonable request, and if she hadn't brought it up, he definitely would have. The surest way to screw everything up would be to sleep together. But having it spelled out for him so succinctly was more unpleasant than he wanted to admit.

"I mean, not that we would have. You probably don't even want to."

"I don't," he lied.

"Perfect." She nodded. Snow flurries had begun to gather in her hair, and paired with the white blooms in her loosely gathered ballerina bun, it made her look like something out of a fairy tale. A Snow Queen. "Neither do I."

He wondered if she was lying, too, but then reminded himself it didn't matter because they wouldn't be going there under any circumstances. "It's settled, then. No sex."

"Good." Her gaze dropped to his mouth.

Yep, she's lying, too. He couldn't help but smile, despite the absurdity of the situation. "Good."

He nodded toward the building's revolving gilt door, where a bride and groom spun their way outside and stopped for a passionate kiss in the gently falling snow. "Shall we go in?"

Her gaze snagged on the couple. Then her lush lips parted, ever so softly. And damned if Anders didn't go hard.

What was happening?

She was gorgeous, but he'd known that all along. He'd been attracted to her since that first day at the animal shelter. If his life hadn't been such a spectacular mess at the moment, he would have no doubt acted on it by now.

But his life *was* a mess, and Chloe was the only person willing to help him straighten it out. Now wasn't the time for his libido to make an appearance after days of moving through life in a state of constant numbness.

"Yes, let's go." She brushed past him, and he inhaled a lungful of cold, cleansing air.

She'd mentioned sex, so now he was thinking about it. Plain and simple. His visceral reaction to her meant nothing whatsoever.

Sure it doesn't.

"Anders? Are you coming?" She glanced over her shoulder, and her pleated skirt swirled around her willowy legs.

His arousal showed zero signs of ebbing. If anything, he grew harder. But he managed to put one foot in front of the other and follow her inside.

The foyer split into two different directions—weddings to the left, licenses to the right. Anders placed his hand on the small of Chloe's back and guided her to the proper line.

It was an innocent gesture, just the barest of touches, but it filled him with inexplicable heat. Every nerve ending in his body seemed to gather at the small point of contact between the tips of his fingers and the delicate arch of her spine.

He snatched his hand away and buried it back in his coat pocket as they took their place behind dozens of happily engaged couples.

This is a terrible idea. The worst.

He should have stuck with his original plan and found someone to marry who was safe. Someone who he wasn't attracted to in the slightest, and more important, someone who wasn't already part of Lolly's life. How would it be possible for them to make a clean break when all this was over?

One thing at a time, he reminded himself. All the logistics were spelled out in the premarital agreement. The contract was absolutely crucial. It would protect them both...if only he'd remembered it.

He closed his eyes and sighed. How could he have forgotten something so important? "Damn it."

"Anders." Chloe's hand landed lightly on his forearm. "Everything okay?"

No. Everything was *not* okay. They were standing in line for a marriage license, and he didn't even know her middle name. "I forgot the contract."

She blinked. "What contract?"

"The premarital agreement," he muttered under his breath. How many other couples in this queue were having a similar discussion? Zero, probably.

"Oh, I thought that was just something between you and..." Her voice drifted off.

"Penelope," he said.

"Right." Chloe stiffened. "Her."

He lifted a brow. Was she *jealous*? Surely not.

"What?" She lifted her chin, eyes glittering.

"Nothing. You just seem…" He bit back a smile. Anders knew a jealous woman when he saw one, but he didn't want to embarrass her. Nor did he want to get into another discussion even remotely related to sexual attraction. "Never mind."

Her gaze narrowed. "Okay, but what were you saying? About the agreement?"

The contract. He'd forgotten about it *again*. "I meant to redraft it and bring it along today so we could sign it. I thought it would be best to have a notary here at the city clerk's office serve as our witness instead of one from my office."

"Because you don't want anyone from your office to know we're getting married?"

"I don't see why it's necessary. Isn't the plan to get married on paper with as little disturbance to our daily lives as possible?" Why did saying this out loud make him feel like the world's biggest cad? "I think that's what's best for Lolly."

"You're probably right." Chloe nodded.

Their gazes met and held, until he finally took a deep breath and looked away. "All of this is spelled out in the contract."

"You mean the one you forgot to write?" she said wryly.

"Yes."

The line moved forward again, until only one couple stood between them and the little slip of paper that would give them legal permission to marry.

Chloe turned to face him, and for a split second, he wondered what waiting in this queue would have felt like if they'd been a real couple. Would they have held hands during the long wait? Would they have whispered promises to one another and made plans for their future? Would he have cupped her face and kissed her when they finally reached the point where they stood now, on the brink of swearing in front of a government official that they'd chosen one another, that they would soon exchange vows?

He would. He could imagine it, clear as day in his mind's eye—her heart-shaped face, tipped upward toward his, the softening in her gaze as he lowered his mouth to hers, her slight intake of breath before their lips met. He could picture it so vividly that it almost seemed like a memory instead of some alternate version of reality. A fantasy that would never come true.

"It's fine. Don't worry about the agreement. I'm doing you a favor, and in return, you'll do one for me. The dance school can use that money." She smiled. "I trust you."

He gazed down at her and wondered if she had any inkling what those words meant to him. His own brother hadn't trusted him enough to grant him unconditional guardianship over Lolly, but Chloe was willing to walk down the aisle toward him without any sort of paperwork to protect her.

Anders was a stranger, and she was prepared to marry him. She could call it a favor if she liked, but they both knew it was more than that. So much more.

I trust you.

He reached for her hand and wove his fingers through hers. Somewhere deep inside him a dam was breaking, and he couldn't tell whether it was a good thing or a bad one, but didn't want to face it alone.

"Anders Astor Kent and Chloe Grace Wilde?" The clerk behind the counter looked up.

Chloe squeezed his hand as they stepped forward, and Anders realized he'd just learned something new, something serendipitous.

Grace.

His bride's middle name was Grace.

"How do you feel about Lolly Kent for the part of Clara?" Chloe slid the Tchaikovsky album back into its sleeve after *Baby Nutcracker* rehearsal the next day and did her best to sound nonchalant.

All the time she'd spent onstage must have made an actress out of her, because Allegra seemed oblivious.

"Sure." Allegra peeled her ballet shoes off and slid her feet into a pair of Uggs. "You're the director, remember. Emily put you in charge, and I'm just helping out. The casting is up to you."

Clara was the lead role, and while she wasn't technically a princess, whoever danced the part would be the star of the show. She'd also get to wear a tiara for most of the recital, which should satisfy Lolly's princess obsession.

"She's one of the oldest girls in the group, so I'm sure she could handle the simple choreography," Chloe said.

Allegra's gaze narrowed, ever so slightly.

"Plus, I just feel so bad for her, you know. She's only a little girl, and she's been through so much." Not to mention the fact that if she and Anders went through with the wedding, Lolly would sort of be her stepdaughter.

Her stomach did a little flip. *When* they went through with it, not *if.* They had the marriage license. Now it was simply a matter of waiting the mandatory twenty-four hours before they could go back to city hall and exchange vows.

It's really happening.

No one would know, obviously. She and Anders had agreed on that, for Lolly's sake. They'd decided not to tell anyone, except Anders's lawyer. It would be a marriage on paper only—a business transaction—for the sole purpose of satisfying the legal requirements for Lolly's guardianship. They weren't even going to share an apartment.

Which meant her awkward announcement that they wouldn't be sleeping together hadn't been necessary. Great. Now Anders probably thought she *wanted* to sleep with him. And she most definitely did *not*.

At least that was what she kept telling herself.

"Why are you still trying to convince me?" Allegra leaned her back against the ballet barre and crossed her arms. "I already told you it was fine."

"No reason." Chloe swallowed. Maybe she wasn't as talented acting-wise as she'd imagined.

"Are you sure? You're acting a little strange. Also, when Lolly's uncle came to pick her up just now, you two wouldn't even look at each other."

What were they supposed to do? Walk around in matching Bride and Groom T-shirts, joined at the hip? "There are a dozen kids in the *Baby Nutcracker* class. I'm sure I failed to make eye contact with a lot of the parents."

Allegra smirked. "Nope, just Anders Kent. It was almost like you were both going out of your way to avoid each other."

Probably because they were. Chloe was definitely

doing her best to avoid Anders. She wasn't sure she was physically capable of standing an arm's length away from him in the dance studio, meeting his gaze and pretending he was only a casual acquaintance when he was about to be her husband.

Your fake *husband.*

Why did she keep having to remind herself that this crazy engagement wasn't even a tiny bit real?

"Stop looking at me like that." She scowled at Allegra. "I barely know Anders Kent."

"He was the lone man in a sea of frazzled moms just now. A distractingly hot man, at that. I find it hard to believe you didn't notice."

"Well, I didn't." Chloe looked up from her clipboard and flashed Allegra a knowing grin. "But I'll be sure to tell my brother you think Anders is hot."

As if Zander would care. He'd worshipped the ground Allegra walked on since they were kids. Now that they were married, he was even more besotted.

Allegra laughed. "I'm married to your brother, but I'm not blind. I'm head over heels for Zander. You know that."

Chloe rolled her eyes. "Yes, I do. It's actually a little nauseating how happy you two are. Thanks for the reminder."

"Which is why I think the gorgeous Mr. Kent might be perfect for *you*." Allegra's tone softened. "Unless you're not ready to date because you're upset about Steven. What happened between you, anyway?"

Chloe flinched, and her grip tightened on the clipboard. She hadn't thought about Steven in a while. Days, maybe. Agreeing to marry a stranger was a surprisingly effective strategy for navigating a breakup. But the shock of hearing her ex's name out of the blue was like pressing a tender bruise.

She swallowed. "It just wasn't going anywhere."

But they had *been* going somewhere. Chloe had even thought Steven might propose over the holidays. He'd dropped a few hints about a surprise during her upcoming Christmas Eve performance at Radio City. Like a lovesick fool, she'd imagined him down on bended knee in the darkened theater, slipping a ring onto her finger during the curtain call.

She'd been wrong, of course. So. Very. Wrong. He'd never planned on proposing. He'd simply wanted to bring some important business associates to the show. He'd wanted to use her to dazzle his clients, not marry her. Once she'd been dropped from the performance roster, he'd clued her in to the "surprise."

And then he'd dumped her like she was a kid on Santa's naughty list.

"I'm here if you ever need to talk." Allegra wrapped a slender arm around Chloe's shoulders. "You know that, right?"

A lump lodged in Chloe's throat. Steven was right. She definitely belonged on the naughty list. She still hadn't fessed up to her family, and now she was piling lies on top of lies by keeping them in the dark about her unconventional wedding.

But that was okay, right? Because soon she'd be able to fix the floors and paint the walls and finish what Allegra had started with the dance marathon, and really turn things around at the Wilde School of Dance.

Then it would no longer matter that she'd been MIA for the better part of four years and made a mess of her career on live television. She could make up for all her mistakes. All the little white lies.

She just had to hold on until Lolly's custody hearing.

"Thank you. I love knowing I can talk to you. I really do, just like I'm grateful to Mom for the chance to help out around here."

"We're lucky to have you. You're a superstar!" Allegra nodded toward the lobby, where Chloe's smiling face beamed from the huge Rockettes poster. "Obviously, I hope your calf heals soon, but until it does, I love having you here. Plus, it gives Emily a little break."

Chloe couldn't bring herself to look at the poster anymore. She kept her gaze glued to her clipboard so she wouldn't be forced to face the constant reminder of how far her star had fallen. "Where is Mom, anyway?"

"She's supposed to be taking the day off, but if the vibrating phone in my pocket is any indication, she can't stand being away." Allegra reached into the pocket of her swishy ballet skirt and pulled out her cell phone. "Oh my God, she called four times during the past hour, even though she knew we had class."

"That's weird. I hope nothing's wrong." Dread snaked its way up Chloe's spine. She reached for her iPhone, where she'd placed it beside the record player.

The screen lit up with notifications. Six missed calls and three texts, all from her mother. "She's been trying to reach me, too."

Something definitely wasn't right.

"I've got a voice mail." Allegra pressed her phone to her ear, and after a second or two, her eyes widened and focused intently on Chloe.

She wasn't sure what the look meant, and she was genuinely afraid to ask. Instead, she scrolled through Emily's text messages. But instead of clearing things up, they left her more confused than ever.

Have you seen the paper today?

The paper?

The *New York Times*...they've made some kind of mistake.

Chloe was vaguely aware of Allegra saying something beside her, but she couldn't focus on the exact words. Her mother was obviously freaking out about something she'd seen in the *Times*, which could mean only one thing—they'd identified her as the dancer who'd ruined the Rockettes' most famous number during the Macy's parade.

Why now, though? Thanksgiving had been over a week ago.

She took a deep breath. Whatever article had gotten Emily all stirred up must be about something else. But what could be so urgent that she'd made multiple calls to both her and Allegra while she knew they were teaching the *Baby Nutcracker* class?

Chloe flipped to the next text message, hoping for clarity. But when she saw the shouty caps filling her screen, she froze and remembered the old adage—be careful what you wish for.

I KNOW YOU WOULDN'T BE PLANNING ON GET-TING MARRIED WITHOUT TELLING YOUR FAMILY.

She glanced up, heart pounding so hard and fast she almost couldn't breathe.

"I knew there was something going on between you and Anders Kent," Allegra said. And then she laughed. She actually *laughed*, as if Chloe wasn't about to drop dead from panic right in front of her. "But *engaged*? Already? The other day, when you said he'd proposed, I thought you were joking. Emily is about to come un-glued. I could barely understand her voice mail mes-sage, but I managed to catch the fact that you're getting married. You've got some explaining to do."

Oh God.

"I…" Her mouth opened and then closed. What could she possibly say?

He's paying me to marry him.

Technically, that was the truth. But wow, put so bluntly, it sounded terrible. Really, really terrible.

"You what?" Allegra lifted a brow.

Before Chloe could form a response, her phone pinged with another incoming text.

From Emily…again.

I'm on my way. I'll be there in five minutes or less.

Chapter 7

Emily must have been moving at the speed of light because she burst through the door of the dance school less than sixty seconds after Chloe received her text message.

Granted, it had been a long sixty seconds—the longest, most excruciating minute of her life as Allegra stared her down, waiting to hear all about how Chloe had managed to become engaged to a man she hadn't so much as spoken to when he'd come to pick up his daughter just moments ago. A man who she claimed was a total stranger.

"It's sort of a crazy story," Chloe said, pressing the heel of her hand against her breastbone.

Her heart was beating so hard she thought she might be having a coronary. She almost wished she were. At least if her heart stopped beating, Emily would forget about whatever she'd read in the paper that led her to believe Chloe and Anders were getting married.

Probably.

Or probably not.

Emily pushed through the door, clutching a copy of

the *New York Times* to her chest and out of breath. Her coat wasn't even buttoned. By all appearances, she'd either speed-walked or run all the way to the school from the brownstone.

"Oh boy," Allegra muttered under her breath.

Yeah. Chloe pressed harder on her breastbone, lest her heart beat right out of her chest. *Oh boy.*

"Chloe, what's going on? This columnist, Celestia Lane, made some sort of mistake, right? Or was it intentional erroneous reporting? Isn't she the reporter who made life so miserable for Zander last year?" Emily tossed the paper onto the reception desk and there, in black and white across the top of the popular *Vows* column, was the headline Manhattan Billionaire Anders Kent Granted Marriage License.

Manhattan billionaire?

Chloe didn't know billionaires were an actual thing. She thought they existed only in *Batman* movies and romance novels. No wonder he seemed so hung up on the premarital agreement. He probably thought she was trying to con him or something when she'd told him not to worry about it.

As if that was her most pressing worry at the moment. Chloe's name was in the very first sentence of the article, for the entire world to see. People all over the world read the *Vows* column, not just New York. It was famous for its Sunday coverage of all the society weddings and celebrity engagements. Sometimes during the week it contained juicy matrimonial gossip.

Like now.

"That's definitely the same reporter." Allegra rolled

her eyes. "She ran that whole series of columns about the Bennington and tried to make everyone believe it was cursed. This is obviously fake news. Why didn't you just say so, Chloe?"

She paused for a beat and then added, "It's kind of weird that the reporter used your name, though, out of all the women in New York."

Chloe took a deep breath. "It's not fake news. Not this time."

Celestia Lane definitely had a penchant for exaggerating. Zander's hotel had nearly gone bankrupt, all because she'd penned a series of articles about the Bennington's unusually high number of runaway brides. Allegra herself had been one of the brides who'd famously bolted from the hotel ballroom in a puffy white gown.

But that was a long time ago. The columnist may have manufactured the runaway bride curse, but this time her information was spot-on.

"So you're really marrying Anders Kent?" Allegra's jaw dropped.

Emily didn't say a word, and somehow her rigid posture and sudden silence was worse than if she'd yelled or screamed. But Chloe's mom had never been that kind of parent. It took a lot to make her upset, and when she finally reached her breaking point, she was much more likely to issue a calm, low reprimand than to raise her voice.

The fact that she couldn't seem to form words at all was definitely a bad sign. The worst.

"Mom, I can explain…" Could she, though? Could she really?

The phone in Chloe's hand pinged with a text, and she nearly dropped it. She'd forgotten she was even holding her cell until her cheery "Jingle Bells" text tone pierced the tense silence.

At last, Emily found her voice. "Who is it? Your secret fiancé?"

Chloe glanced down.

We need to talk. Meet me at Soho House at earliest possible opportunity? I'll send a driver to collect you.

Anders, indeed.

But he wasn't such a secret anymore.

So much for keeping things simple.

The news piece in the *Times* changed everything. As Anders's attorney so bluntly put it, everything about his relationship with Chloe needed to look real. Not just the wedding, but the marriage.

Everything.

Assuming, of course, that Chloe would still go through with their arrangement. Anders had a feeling she wouldn't, especially when she showed up at the Soho House looking every bit as shell-shocked as he felt.

Meeting her here suddenly seemed like a bad idea. If this was the end of their brief fake relationship, he'd much rather have ended things privately at his office instead of a trendy eatery. Soho House was a members-only establishment, but it was still filled with prying eyes. Three people had congratulated Anders on his engagement since he'd arrived ten minutes before.

"Hello." He rose from the table as she approached.

"Hi." She came around to his side of the table and wrapped her arms around him, enveloping him in a scent reminiscent of warm vanilla with just a touch of evergreen. Christmas on a snowy morning.

He had a sudden flash of memories from his childhood—the kind of Christmas mornings he hadn't experienced in years, with fresh baked cookies, a fire in the hearth and frost on the windows. They were the sort of memories he should be making for Lolly, especially now. What if he never had the chance again? What if this was the last Christmas she'd ever spend in New York?

Don't go there.

Chloe pressed her lips, impossibly soft, against his cheek, and as ludicrous as it seemed, that simple, innocent brush of her skin against his almost made him feel like everything might be okay. Like he could somehow keep Lolly's world—and his—from falling apart.

She pulled back and looked at him with wide, nervous eyes. Her voice dropped to a low murmur. "I hope that was okay. I just feel like since we're out in public and now everyone knows…"

Her cheeks blazed pink, and for the first time since he'd set eyes on the *Vows* column, the dull ache in his temples eased. The knot in his chest loosened, and he could breathe again. He wasn't sure why. According to his lawyer, Lolly's custody case had just gotten infinitely more complicated. Even if Chloe was still willing to walk down the aisle, they would have to pass for a believable couple until nearly the end of the month.

Until Christmas.

"It's fine." He slipped her hand in his, gave it a squeeze and then pulled back her chair. "Please, have a seat. Relax."

Relax…easier said than done. Although when he took his place beside her, Anders could imagine how nice it might be to spend time with her under normal circumstances. They'd been together only a handful of times, but he was already becoming accustomed to the way she moved—with a willowy grace that made even the simplest gestures more lovely. It soothed him somehow.

He took a deep inhalation and met her gaze with his. "I'm sorry."

A little furrow formed between her brows. "You're apologizing?"

Apparently, he was. He hadn't planned on it, but suddenly it seemed like a good idea. Necessary, even. "Yes, for the article. I had no idea it was going to happen, but on some level, I feel like I should have seen it coming."

Her gaze shifted to the menu sitting untouched on the table in front of her. "It's not your fault."

"The tabloids have taken an interest in my personal life in the past." He shook his head. "Still, I never expected this. The *Times*, for crying out loud. *Vows*."

"Seriously, don't blame yourself. It's as much my fault as it is yours." Her eyes met his again and held.

He hadn't a clue what she was talking about, but he was struck once again by the sadness in her eyes, just as he'd been at the animal shelter. But he realized now it was more than melancholy. Secrets swirled in the depths of her soft brown irises, and he reminded himself that, loveliness aside, he knew nothing about this woman.

Other than she's your only hope.

"Why would it be your fault?" Had she gone to the press?

Surely not. He felt guilty even suspecting her of doing such a thing.

"The reporter who wrote the piece did a series of articles about my brother's hotel a year ago. He's the CEO of the Bennington."

"The runaway bride curse?" He nodded. "She mentioned it in the article."

"Right. That's why I think it's my fault. I just can't figure out how she knew we were engaged."

Anders sighed. "As my attorney was quick to point out this morning, marriage licenses are public record. Anyone can look them up at the city clerk's office."

"Oh." Chloe's bottom lip slid between her teeth and despite everything—despite the fact that he still expected her to bow out of their agreement as soon as she'd heard the lawyer's assessment of their situation, despite the fact that Anders's well-ordered life was slipping slowly into an abyss and despite the fact that he'd sworn to himself not to touch her—he went still. Spellbound. And as much as he knew he shouldn't be aroused at a time like this, it was so damn nice just to *feel* again.

He'd been growing accustomed to the numbness associated with grief. He'd welcomed it. So long as he had work to do and problems to sort out—so long as he remained distracted and blissfully detached from his loss—he was fine. He could hold it together, and he could push away the memories of the things he'd said to his brother and the way Grant had looked at him before he'd stalked out of the office one final time.

There was a price to pay for that kind of numbness, though. Other things got lost in the hazy, unfeeling blur of his new existence. Things like joy. Laughter.

Lust.

He shouldn't want Chloe Wilde. He couldn't—not if he had a chance in hell of keeping his tiny, two-person family intact. But every so often, she had a way of making him feel alive again. And when it happened, it was like breaking through the surface of a deep, dark pool and taking the first gasping breath of air. It burned, but at the same time, it kept him going…gave him hope.

"So what happens, exactly?" she asked, and he forced his attention away from her mouth and back to her soulful eyes. "Do reporters sift through the marriage license records every day, trying to find newsworthy engagements?"

He gave her a grim smile. "That's exactly what they do, but don't blame yourself. I have a feeling Celestia Lane is far more interested in my recent family drama than your connection to the Bennington. From the looks of the article, she wants to paint me as some kind of romantic figure—a groom in mourning, saved by love."

The server approached their table, and Anders was grateful for the interruption. He hadn't brought Chloe here for a heart-to-heart. But as soon as he'd chosen a wine and they'd placed their orders, the waiter slipped away and they were alone again, with his words hanging between them.

A groom in mourning...

"Do you want to talk about it?" Chloe leaned closer, and the earnestness in her gaze made it impossible for him to cut her off.

The other women in his life knew better than to look at him like that—he wasn't an open book. Never had been, never would be. Which was precisely why his businesslike arrangement with Penelope worked out so nicely. Or it *had*, anyway.

"No, I don't want to talk about it. I—" His voice broke, and damn it if something inside him didn't break along with it.

He reached for his freshly poured wine and took a long swallow. When he placed his glass back down on the table, Chloe was still watching him with those tender eyes of hers, waiting for him to finish.

"Grant and I had an argument," he heard himself say. He couldn't stop himself; the truth just came spilling out. "The night of the car crash, before he left the office, we exchanged words. It got ugly."

"Anders, your relationship with your brother is made up of a lifetime of moments, not just his last day. Whatever happened, it's okay." She reached across the table and rested her hand on his. He held on tight to her fingertips, reluctant to release them, so he wouldn't have to sit there so excruciatingly alone after his confession.

Of all people, why her? He could have bared his soul to anyone, but instead he'd just told his darkest secret to his stranger fiancé. He wanted to believe it was so that she'd sympathize with him so much that she wouldn't walk away, that she'd stick by him and marry him even though the stakes had just risen dramatically.

But deep down he knew better. She was going to be his wife. For better or worse, she needed to know what she was getting into, even temporarily.

"I told him he was too focused on his family and he needed to spend more of his energy on work. Specifically, I said, 'You've got all the time in the world. Family can wait.'" Anders slid his hand away from hers and gripped the stem of his wineglass. The dark liquid sloshed perilously close to the rim in his trembling grasp. "Right before he walked out, he called me a monster."

He had to give Chloe credit; she didn't even flinch. Her expression remained as calm and pure as ever. Like a Christmas angel. Then she took a deep breath and said, "I got fired on Thanksgiving Day, and I've been lying to my family ever since."

Anders nearly choked on his Bordeaux. "What?"

"I messed up the legendary toy soldier routine." Her face went as red as a poinsettia. "You might have seen the video. It sort of went viral."

He nodded. "I think I did."

He knew what she was doing. She was trying to assuage his guilt by confessing to her own deep, dark secret. And her transgression was mild compared to his, so it shouldn't have worked. Somehow, it still did. Just a little bit.

"So yeah, I'm not actually a Rockette anymore. My mom and Allegra think I'm working at the studio now because I have a calf injury. I lied to both of their faces.

You're the only one who knows the truth." She stared into her wineglass. "Except for Steven, but he doesn't matter anymore."

There was that name again. Steven. The ex.

Anders couldn't help but wonder if the mysterious Steven truly no longer mattered. He hoped not. Purely for the sake of their arrangement, of course.

Liar. That's not the only reason.

"Can I ask you a question?" he said.

"Sure."

"What about the reindeer costume? Is that part of a cover-up, or do you simply enjoy wearing it?"

There was a beat of silence. Then the sound of her bell-like laughter broke through the somber mood that had settled over the table.

"The truth is more pathetic than you can imagine. I hand out flyers in Times Square for the Rockettes Christmas show." She smiled at him over her wineglass.

He winced. "Ouch."

"Trust me, it's as bad as you think it is. But it's a paycheck, and I keep thinking maybe I'll get back on the performance roster if they see how devoted I am."

The waiter returned with their food, and while he set their plates on the table, Anders tried to imagine standing in Times Square in costume for an afternoon. He wouldn't last a minute.

"So you'd go back to performing if you had the chance?" he asked, once they were alone again.

"Of course I would. Why wouldn't I?"

"I don't know." He shrugged. "You seem great with the kids at the dance studio. Lolly adores you."

Chloe grew quiet again, and the lightness of the moment faded away. The mention of Lolly had dragged them back to reality. For a moment it had felt like they were a regular couple out on a date, but they weren't.

"She adores you, too. You *do* know that, don't you?" Chloe's eyes shone bright in the warm glow of the restaurant. Behind her, snow beat against the window, and the sidewalk outside bustled with people carrying red and gold shopping bags. "Families are complicated. I never met your brother, but I know he loved you. If he didn't, he never would have left Lolly in your care. Not even conditionally."

But the condition was big, and it was time to tell her just how much of a commitment their fake marriage was going to entail.

He took a deep breath and then spelled it all out. "The article in the paper changes things. I met with my lawyer this morning and he said the press coverage of our engagement could look like a warning sign to the judge in the custody case. If we do this, it needs to look real. We'd have to have an actual wedding ceremony instead of getting married at city hall. And we'd have to do it immediately. Tomorrow, if possible. Afterward, you'd need to move into my apartment. From the outside, we'd have to look like newlyweds. At least until the custody hearing."

She had only one question. "Would I be able to tell my family the truth?"

Anders shook his head. "No, absolutely not. If the guardianship hearing doesn't go well, they might eventually be asked to testify in court."

"Okay." She nodded.

"Okay to the part about your family or okay to all of it?"

She took a deep breath. "All of it."

He angled his head. "You're absolutely sure?"

She nodded again. This was officially the easiest negotiation Anders had ever been a part of.

"Why are you doing this? You don't even know me." His gaze narrowed.

"Honestly, I could use the money. I'm unemployed at the moment, remember?" Her gaze shifted to her lap. "Besides, you seem like a decent person, and Lolly is precious. I know what it's like to lose a father. I wasn't as young as Lolly is now, but I want to help her. I want to help you both."

"Thank you," he said, and it felt wholly inadequate, but it was all he had to offer her.

Except that wasn't quite true. There was one other thing...

He reached into the inside pocket of his suit jacket, pulled out a little blue box tied with a white satin ribbon and slid it toward her across the table.

She stared at it and smiled, but didn't make a move to touch it.

Anders had never seen a woman afraid of a box from Tiffany's before. "Open it. It's yours."

She picked it up. Hesitated. "Can I ask you something first?"

And here it was—the moment when she changed her mind. Anders couldn't blame her. If he'd been in her position, he would have walked away before the appetizers arrived.

At least he thought he would. He wasn't quite sure of anything where Chloe was concerned.

"Ask away," he said.

She looked at the ring box and then back up at him. "Is this part of the contract?"

It wasn't, and suddenly that fact seemed significant.

He lifted a brow. "You mean the contract that still doesn't exist?"

She nodded. "Yep, that's one."

"Of course," he lied. "Just part of the package."

Because how could he tell her the truth? How could he admit that he'd bought her an engagement ring just because he'd wanted to? He'd managed to convince himself that it was no big deal. She was going to be his wife, after all. But the fact that he was trying to pass it off as part of a clause in a contract made him wonder if it was a far bigger deal than he wanted to believe.

"Right. That's what I thought." Her lips curved into a smile again, but it didn't quite reach her eyes.

And as she reached for the little blue box and untied its white satin bow with trembling fingers, Anders almost believed he spied a hint of disappointment in her gaze.

Chapter 8

"I need a favor." Chloe stood in the grand, glittering lobby of her brother's hotel and cut right to the chase.

Zander was a busy man, and she'd dropped by the Bennington without an appointment. Mercifully, he'd been free to see her.

He stood beneath the massive gold clock hanging from the ceiling, looking at her with unabashed amusement flickering in his gaze. "Does this have anything to do with your sudden, high-profile engagement?"

Of course he knew about Anders. The entire city did. "It does, actually."

"So it's true?" His eyebrows crept closer to his hairline. "Since Celestia Lane broke the story, I took it with a grain of salt. You're really getting married."

Zander glanced at her hand, where the Tiffany diamond on her ring finger sparkled as brightly as the Christmas tree at Rockefeller Center.

She'd come straight to the Bennington from Soho House, which meant she'd been wearing it for less than an hour. During the short ride from the restaurant, she kept stealing glances at it. Her engagement might have been fake, but the ring was the most beautiful piece of jewelry she'd ever seen. She realized she was absently caressing the band with the pad of her thumb, just as a real bride-to-be might do.

It needs to look real.

Mission accomplished. But should it *feel* as real as it did?

"Yes, I am." She cleared her throat. "I mean *we*. We're getting married—Anders and me."

So much for being believable.

"I see." His gaze narrowed. "Should I go into big-brother mode and ask if this is what you really want, or would you rather I keep my mouth shut and be supportive?"

She shot him a hopeful smile. "The latter, please."

He nodded. "Okay…"

"And if you could put in a good word with Mom, I'd really appreciate it." She couldn't face Emily. Chloe knew her mother, and the best way to handle her when she was upset was to give her some time and space.

Zander sighed. "How about a drink while we discuss these multiple favors I'm doing for you?"

Chloe never drank in the middle of the day, and she'd just had a glass of wine with Anders. On any given afternoon in December, Chloe was usually wearing tap shoes and running on nothing but protein bars and adrenaline. But the sommelier at the Bennington was their cousin-in-law Evangeline Wilde and her taste in wine was legendary.

"Sounds good," Chloe said.

Thirty minutes and an incredible glass of vintage

Chambertin Grand Cru later, she nodded as Zander
went over the list they'd made on a Bennington note-
pad while sitting at the bar.

"You want a cake, a dozen or so bottles of Dom Peri-
gnon, music, an officiant..." He jotted something down.
"What else am I missing?"

"Oh, flowers! Lolly will make an adorable flower girl."

"Flowers. Got it." He made another notation on the pad.

Couples got married at the Bennington all the time.
As soon as Anders had mentioned having a real wedding ceremony, she'd hoped Zander could throw something together. And now he'd promised he would—no
questions asked. If there was such thing as a brother-
of-the-year award, he'd have a lock on it.

"I'll make sure we've got a basket of petals for her to
toss, plus a bridal bouquet. Both ballrooms are already
decked out in Christmas decorations, so we probably
don't need anything else, flower-wise. We haven't even
talked about when this is happening, although something tells me it's soon." He glanced up, and Chloe
smiled back at him.

"*Really* soon. The sooner the better, actually," she
said. "How about tomorrow?"

"Tomorrow." He blinked. "We might need to open
another bottle of wine."

They did, and as she sipped, Zander assured her he
could put something festive and intimate together. He'd
even send out email invitations with the Bennington
crest to Anders's business associates.

"A Christmas wedding it is, then," he said.

Chloe gave him a quiet smile.

A holiday wedding sounded dreamy. Christmas had always been her favorite time of year, and she couldn't imagine anything as beautiful and moving as exchanging vows beneath a bough of evergreen and twinkle lights on a snowy December evening. She'd wear a sprig of mistletoe tucked into her upswept hair, and a string quartet would play a winsome Christmas song as she walked down the aisle toward her handsome groom.

Except Anders wasn't really her groom. It would all be pretend—just another holiday performance.

A lump formed in her throat for some silly reason. She dug her fingernails into her palm.

Get it together. You chose this.

Yes, she had. And she had no regrets. She was doing the right thing—a *good* thing. The dazzling engagement ring on her hand was messing with her head. That was all.

"A Christmas wedding sounds perfect." Her lips trembled, as if the smile might wobble off her face. "It's every girl's dream come true."

"Then I think we should toast on it." Zander's face split into a wide grin and he held up his glass. "Cheers to the happy couple."

"Cheers." And as Chloe clinked her wineglass against his, toasting to Anders and the fulfillment of her girlish hopes and dreams, she could hear a little voice in the back of her head. Whispering, warning…

Be careful what you wish for.

"You really didn't have to reserve a room for me." Chloe clutched her garment bag to her chest as Zander led her into the Bennington's lavish bridal suite the following afternoon. "I just needed someplace to get dressed. I never expected…" Her throat clogged as she took in the four-poster bed, the glittering crystal chandelier and the robin's egg spun-silk walls—something blue. "…this."

She felt like she was standing in Marie Antoinette's bedroom. There was even a plate of pastel-colored macarons on the dressing table, and beside it, a silver ice bucket engraved with the Bennington's logo cradled a bottle of champagne.

Somehow she doubted the room was dog-friendly, even though Prancer's head poked out of the bag slung over her shoulder. But she needed the puppy here with her for moral support. Other than Anders, the little Yorkie was the only living soul who knew the truth about what she was about to do.

"I know I didn't have to, but I wanted to." Zander wrapped an arm around her shoulders and gave her a squeeze. "You're my baby sister, and today is your wedding day. It's special."

Not quite as special as you think it is. "Thank you, but I'm not exactly a baby anymore."

"You'll always be my baby sister, though." He winked. "I hope your groom realizes that."

Chloe swallowed. Her brother would pummel Anders if he knew the truth. And then he'd probably lock her in this exquisite room and throw away the key so she wouldn't be able to go through with the wedding.

"He's a good man, Zander." Finally, she'd managed to say something truthful.

"I believe you. He must be, if you chose him." Zander pushed back the cuff of his dress shirt and checked his watch. "And he should be waiting downstairs right about now."

She tossed her garment bag and pet carrier onto the bed. Prancer wiggled out of it and pawed at the silk duvet cover.

Zander didn't bat an eye. His imaginary brother-of-the-year trophy was getting bigger by the minute.

"Great. I'll go down and introduce you," she said.

"Not so fast." He wagged a finger at her. "I've got a room reserved for him, too. We're doing this right. The groom can't see the bride before the wedding."

She jammed her hands on her hips. "Are you kidding me? That's a silly superstition. You of all people shouldn't believe in stuff like that."

Had the rumor about the Bennington's runaway bride curse taught him nothing?

Zander shrugged. "Like I said, you're my baby sister. It's tradition, and I don't want to risk any bad luck. You and Anders want to have a long and happy marriage, don't you?"

His right eyebrow shot up.

How about until just after Christmas? Would that be considered long?

Chloe forced a smile. "Of course we do."

"Then you're staying put. I'll deal with Anders. I haven't even met him yet. This will be good. It will give me a chance to get to know the man who's managed to sweep you off of your feet." He grinned, and something about the way he looked at her made the breath clog in her throat.

This was so much harder than she thought it would be—not the getting married part, but all the lies. She would have thought she'd be an expert at it by now, but lying to her family was beginning to get to her. They thought this was real. They thought she'd spend the rest of her life with Anders. They thought he'd be by her side on Christmas morning at the Wilde family brownstone, unwrapping gifts and sipping hot chocolate for years and years to come.

She took a deep breath and tried her best not to imagine what such a Christmas would be like, but images spun through her consciousness like snowflakes—Lolly setting out cookies for Santa Claus, Prancer tangled in the garland from the Christmas tree, Anders kissing her beneath the mistletoe.

God, what was wrong with her?

None of that would ever happen. They were pretending. It was just that the lie was so much more tempting to believe when her family was acting like she was living out some beautiful holiday love story.

She swallowed, with great difficulty. The only thing worse than lying to her own flesh and blood would be having to beg them to lie on her behalf. She couldn't ask them to perjure themselves at Lolly's guardianship hearing. She wouldn't.

"Okay, I'm on my way down. I'll see you in an hour or so, when you're ready to walk down the aisle." Zander paused with his hand on the doorknob. "Give me a call if you need anything, but don't worry. Mom's on her way, and she's got a surprise for you."

Chloe's stomach tumbled. She still hadn't seen her mother face-to-face since Emily had flown into the dance school in a panic over the *Vows* column, and frankly, she was a little terrified of having to explain her sudden nuptials. Zander had assured her he'd calmed Emily down, but still. The last thing Chloe needed was a surprise. "Wait—what are you talking about?"

But her brother didn't respond. His grin widened and he closed the door behind him, leaving her alone.

"Well, then." Chloe sighed and glanced at Prancer. The little dog was rolling around on the large bed, rubbing her little face on all the pillows, oblivious to Chloe's existential crisis.

"You're no help," she muttered and reached for the ice-cold bottle of champagne.

She popped the cork and poured a glass. Liquid courage. It couldn't hurt, could it?

A knock sounded on the door. "Chloe, it's me."

Her mother.

Chloe set down her champagne flute. Maybe a clear head was a better idea. "Coming."

She took a deep breath and opened the door, not altogether sure what to expect. Emily with her arms crossed and a look of profound disappointment on her face? Maybe even tears? *Please, no. Anything but that.*

Blessedly, she was greeted by neither of those nightmare scenarios. Emily stood smiling at the threshold, dressed to the nines in a floaty, mother-of-the-bride type dress and her hair in a fancy twist like she'd always worn back when she competed in ballroom dance competitions. She held a garment bag over her arm—a much longer one than the garment bag currently flung across the bed.

"Mom, you look gorgeous." Chloe didn't want to look at the garment bag, but she couldn't take her eyes off it. She was equal parts curious and terrified of whatever was inside. It was awfully big, and Emily was already dressed for the wedding, which meant it could contain only one thing.

She held the door open wide. "Come in."

Emily walked past her, while Prancer yipped and spun in excited circles on the bed.

"You brought the puppy?" Her mother laughed.

"Yes, I thought it might be fun for Lolly if Prancer was in the wedding."

"That's adorable." Emily inhaled a deep breath. "Look at you, already thinking about her like she's your daughter."

Chloe felt oddly like she might fall apart, so she wrapped her arms around her middle to keep herself together. Were she and Anders doing the right thing? Lolly was the sole reason for the marriage, and now they were being forced to drag her into it. Were they doing more harm than good? "She's a precious little girl. Anders loves her very much."

"I know he does. They've both been through a lot." Emily held up her hand. "Don't worry. I'm not going to try and talk you out of this or even ask if you're sure. If marrying Anders is really and truly what you want,

I'm here for you. We all are. This is your wedding day, a day for joy and love and happiness."

Relief coursed through Chloe, but it was short-lived, because then Emily held up the garment bag, the aforementioned surprise, just as Chloe feared.

"I brought you something." Tears shimmered in Emily's eyes.

"Is that a wedding gown?" Chloe's voice shook, and she gestured to the bed. "Because you really shouldn't have bought me anything. Maybe we can return it. This is supposed to be a simple ceremony, and I already had a white dress hanging in my closet. It will work."

She'd planned on wearing the same pleated chiffon number she'd worn to city hall when she and Anders had gotten the marriage license. It was perfectly fine, especially for a wedding that wasn't technically a wedding. Plus, she'd rather liked the way Anders had looked at her when she'd worn it, although that shouldn't have mattered a bit.

"Calm down." Her mother rolled her eyes. "I didn't spend any money."

She unzipped the garment bag, and a puff of white tulle spilled out. The gown was beautiful. It was also very familiar. Chloe had seen pictures of it in family albums and on the wall of the brownstone all her life. When she was a little girl, she'd dreamed of wearing it on her wedding day. Her mother had even let her try it on once when she was ten years old. It had nearly swallowed her whole, but being wrapped up in all that vintage tulle and lace had made her feel like a princess.

She squeezed her eyes shut tight as Lolly's words came rushing back to her.

Are you a Christmas princess?

She wasn't a princess. She wasn't even a Christmas bride. Not really.

She forced her eyes open and gave her mother a wobbly smile. "You want me to wear your wedding gown?"

"Of course I do, darling. You've always loved this dress." She took a step closer and cupped Chloe's cheek with her free hand. "If marrying Anders is what you want, then it's what I want, too. You'll wear it, won't you?"

She couldn't say no. If she did, it would be a huge red flag.

And her mother was right. Chloe had always pictured herself walking down the aisle in this very dress, only now that she thought about it, she'd never once imagined the man waiting for her at the end of the aisle would be Steven. But if he'd wanted to marry her, she would have said yes. Wouldn't she?

She twisted the ring on her finger—the one Anders had given her.

"I'd love to wear it." If Anders had taken a liking to her little white dress, his eyes would probably fall out of his head when she walked into the ballroom in this one.

Not that it mattered, except it would be nice if he looked at her with that glowy expression of adoration that grooms always had when they first saw their wives-to-be all decked out in bridal white. For her family's sake, obviously.

Liar.

Tears pricked her eyes. She'd been painfully aware of all the lies she'd been telling her family, but when had she started lying to herself?

"Do you think it will fit?" she said.

Maybe it wouldn't. Maybe it was like Cinderella's glass slipper and would fit only if fate willed it so.

Emily removed the dress fully from the bag. Age had changed its color from frosty white to a lovely, pale shade of blush, like a Valentine from days gone by or a timeless promise. Hundreds of tiny rhinestones scattered over the gown's full tulle skirt glittered in the soft light of the chandelier.

"Don't you worry, love." Emily pressed a hand to her heart. "Something tells me it will."

Chapter 9

The kindness of the Wildes was beginning to make Anders wonder if he was about to make a mistake. The biggest one of his life, perhaps.

Her brother had greeted him in the lobby with a wide grin, clapped him on the back and said, "I'm Zander. Welcome to the family."

Anders had felt like the biggest, worst impostor in the world. But no, he'd soon realized things were just getting started. He could sink to new, much lower depths as the day progressed. Like when Allegra arrived on the scene with a special flower girl dress for Lolly, and Emily Wilde grew misty-eyed as she pinned a flower to the lapel of his tuxedo.

Grant had been right. He was a monster. He'd given little to no actual thought to what this charade would do to Chloe's family. They expected her to be married to him for the rest of her life. They thought he was going to be a permanent part of their family.

They thought he loved her.

And he didn't, obviously. The overwhelming tightness that he felt in his chest when he thought about her and the way he almost felt like everything was going to be okay when she was around couldn't be love. People didn't fall in love in a matter of days. It just wasn't possible.

What he felt for Chloe was gratitude. Without her, he wouldn't have a chance of securing Lolly's custody. She was saving his family. She was saving *him*.

And how was he returning the favor? By hurting the people who cared about her.

He looked around the Bennington ballroom, where rows of white chairs connected by swags of evergreen and frosted holly berries held his friends and colleagues. Chloe's sister, Tessa, her cousin Ryan and his wife, Evangeline, along with their newborn baby and Allegra, were all lined up in the front row. Emily Wilde was at the back of the room, helping Lolly with Prancer's leash and the basket of white rose petals she would scatter down the aisle. Someone had even fashioned a tiny ring pillow for the dog to wear on its back.

It was all so heartfelt, like a scene out of a Hallmark movie.

Come January, these people will despise me.

As well they should. He was already beginning to despise himself.

He needed to see Chloe or at least talk to her. He needed her to remind him that she was fine with all this, that they were doing the right thing. He reached into the pocket of his tux for his cell phone, and as he dialed her number, he couldn't help but wonder when he'd started to rely on her so much. Because he had. He *needed* her, and not just for Lolly's sake.

Anders wasn't accustomed to needing someone. *Any-*

one. He'd been on his own since he was seventeen years old, with no one but Grant to rely on. And now Grant was gone, too. Sometimes he wondered what he'd done to deserve such a lonely life. What had prompted fate to be so cruel as to take their parents away when they were practically still kids, and then take Grant and Olivia in the same sudden manner a decade and a half later?

Then Anders would remember there was no such thing as fate. Nor was his life lonely. He'd been doing just fine, until lately. But soon he'd be fine again, as would Lolly. He just needed to get through today, and he definitely needed to stop thinking about things like fate and destiny. They were nothing but myths, just like love at first sight.

A vision of Chloe dressed in her silly reindeer costume and glaring at him as she accused him of being a puppy thief on the day they'd first met flashed in his mind.

His grip on his cell phone tightened. The call rolled to voice mail and Chloe's honeyed voice came through on the recording, and he sighed.

"It's time, man." A hand landed on his shoulder.

Anders looked up. Zander. "Now?"

"Now." Zander grinned and nodded toward the tower of white poinsettias, covered in twinkle lights and shaped like a massive Christmas tree, where a clergyman stood, waiting to make Anders a married man. "Are you ready to become my brother-in-law?"

Are you ready to make Chloe your wife?

Anders nodded. "I am."

The next few moments passed in a blur as he took his place beside the minister, the last of the guests filled the seats and music filled the air. A white grand piano had been brought in, where Julian Shine, Chloe's brother-in-law, played a gentle Christmas carol with just a touch of jazzy flair. Anders's chest had that terrible, tightly wound feeling again as Lolly came toward him up the aisle, dropping rose petals as she went. The silly dog tugged at the end of her leash, causing the ring pillow to slide around to her belly, and all the guests laughed.

Somehow it made him feel like more of a monster than ever.

This is wrong.

Then Chloe appeared, walking toward him on the arm of her brother, looking like something out of a dream. Only not the sort of dreams that he'd been having lately—nightmares that caused him to wake in a cold sweat, panicked at the thought of losing Lolly, of disappointing Grant again. Permanently.

This was a different kind of dream. The kind where a woman with laughter as sparkling as the summer sun high in the sky over Central Park wanted to promise to love, honor and cherish him for the rest of his life. The kind of dream where he'd gotten into an argument with a beautiful woman over a silly little dog, and now that woman wore his ring.

"Hi," she said, snapping him out of his trance when she came to a stop alongside him.

Zander gave him a look that somehow felt like both a warning and a blessing at the same time, before taking his seat. Chloe passed a bouquet of blue spruce and mistletoe to Lolly, who cradled it in her arms like a priceless treasure and sat down beside Emily Wilde.

Then it was just the two of them, hand in hand, as the minister talked about love and commitment and the meaning of forever. And by God, if this wasn't what a real wedding felt like, Anders didn't know what did.

The minister turned toward Chloe. "Do you, Chloe Wilde, take Anders Kent, to have and to hold, from this day forward, for better, for worse, for richer, for poorer, in sickness and in health, until death do you part?"

She looked up at Anders, and her eyes went misty. *Don't cry. Please don't.* He didn't know what those unshed tears meant—he only knew that he wouldn't be able to go through with it if she had even a trace of doubt about what they were doing.

"Are you sure about this?" he whispered. "It's okay if you're not. I'll find another way. I promise."

He didn't care if the minister heard him. He didn't care that the promise he'd just made was probably an empty one. He was running out of time.

Chloe smiled through her tears and she gripped his hand as if it were a lifeline. As if she wasn't just saving him, but they were somehow saving each other.

Then she turned to the minister and said, "I do."

It was over so quickly.

One moment, Chloe was walking down the aisle toward Anders with her heart beating wildly in her chest as he looked at her like she was a real bride and he was a real groom and this was a real wedding—the wedding of their dreams.

And then in a flash, there was a shiny new wedding band on her finger, right beside the diamond Anders had given her the day before, and the minister was smiling at them and saying, "Anders and Chloe have vowed, in our presence, to be loyal and loving toward each other. They have formalized the existence of the bond between them with words spoken and with the giving and receiving of rings."

Bond…they were bonded together. She and Anders Kent, who she'd met less than a week ago.

The clergyman's smile grew wider. "Therefore, it is my pleasure to now pronounce them husband and wife."

A forbidden thrill coursed through Chloe. Or was it just nerves? Right, that was what it was—nerves. She was going to have to kiss Anders now, right there in front of all her friends and family. *For the very first time.*

How on earth had she forgotten about the kiss? They should have practiced first, at least one time. First kisses were almost always awkward. She never knew which way to tilt her head, and they usually went on far too long, as if neither party wanted to be the first to pull away, even after they'd both begun to suffocate from lack of oxygen.

The odds of pulling this off and making it look natural were slim to none, but they didn't exactly have a choice. Regular newlyweds wouldn't exactly take a pass on their first kiss as a married couple.

She held her breath and waited for the minister to say it.

"Anders, you may now kiss your bride."

His bride.

His bride.

His.

Chloe's knees went a little weak as she lifted her gaze to Anders, peeking up at him through the thick fringe of her lashes. Right before she'd said her vows, he'd given her an out. He'd stopped looking at her as if she were a bride, and for a tentative sliver of a moment, he'd regarded her as something else—not quite a stranger, but not as a loved one, either. Not even a pretend loved one. But instead, more like someone he was destined to disappoint.

The moment had passed after she said "I do," and now he was watching her in a way that no one ever had before. Not Steven. Not the boy whose lips first touched hers all those years ago at the ballet school while they danced *Romeo and Juliet*. No man who'd kissed her had ever gazed at her with such hunger in his eyes. Such need, such blatant desire, like he wasn't about to kiss her, but to devour her whole.

It was almost frightening. Or rather, it should have been, considering it was a fake kiss to seal a fake marriage to her fake husband.

But as she draped her arms around his neck and lifted her mouth toward his—straining, seeking—she realized the fire skittering along her skin wasn't a sign of apprehension. It was pure anticipation. Pure longing. The exact sort of longing she saw looking back at her in Anders's moody blue eyes.

I am in so much trouble.

It was her final thought as her eyes fluttered closed in the excruciating moment before his mouth came down on hers—a moment that seemed to shimmer with promise, despite the ridiculousness of their situation. She

wondered if he felt it, too, or if she was alone in the re-
alization that this was a dangerous game they were playing, that it seemed impossible one of them wouldn't walk
away from their union in the days following Christmas
and face the New Year with a heart in tatters.

She wasn't alone. She could tell by the naked vulnerability in the tender way he touched her, so uncharacter-
istic for a man like Anders. A strong man. A careful one.
The kind of man who put his faith in words on a page
instead of in people. But there was no trace of that brand
of detachment in the first brush of his lips. It was as forgotten as the contract he couldn't seem to remember to
have her sign. Instead, there was want and heat and a
feeling so flush with desperation that her eyes filled with
tears again. This time, they were too numerous to blink
away. They flowed down her cheeks as she opened for
him, letting him consume her...taking him in.

Bonded together.

The words echoed in her consciousness, her heart
pounding in time with the sentiment.

That was what this was. More than a kiss, more than
her mouth seeking his. This was a bond. A promise. A
vow. *I do.* The words still lingered on his tongue as it
slid against hers, so decadently sweet. And beyond the
something borrowed and something blue, the kiss was
another thing, too. It was an invitation engraved upon
her heart. A question.

Do you want me?

Her fingertips tightened around the smooth collar of
his tuxedo jacket as his hands slid up the back of her

dress, burning her skin through the delicate lace covering her shoulder blades.

I do, I do, I do.

Somewhere in the periphery, a throat cleared. Chloe wasn't sure who it belonged to. She wasn't even sure how she'd managed to stay upright for the duration of that kiss, which somehow seemed to have lasted both a split second and an eternity.

Anders pulled back and rested his forehead against hers, his eyes twinkling with sapphire light.

"What was that?" she choked.

He brushed the pad of his thumb against her lower lip, where all the nerve endings in her body had gathered into one delicious place. And then he smiled. "That, my darling bride, was a kiss."

It was done.

The overwhelming sense of relief Anders expected to feel once the vows had been exchanged and the minister handed over the certificate of marriage never came. Instead, his heart brimmed with an emotion that felt suspiciously like joy as the short and simple ceremony gave way to a wedding reception. A party.

And why shouldn't he feel happy at a party? Wasn't that what parties were for?

Yet, as he shook hands with the partners from his office and accepted their congratulations, he couldn't seem to let go of Chloe's fingertips. Again, he told himself that was normal. Just part of the act. But he kept finding himself toying with the diamond on her finger, checking to make sure it was still there, that this day had actually been real.

And through it all—through the first dance and the cutting of the cake and the toast from Chloe's brother that made an unprecedented lump lodge in his throat—he couldn't shake the memory of the kiss.

It had rocked him to the core, that kiss.

If they hadn't been standing inches away from a clergyman, in full view of all of Chloe's nearest and dearest, he never would have ended it. If he hadn't made a solemn promise to himself, and to Chloe, not to touch her, he'd be upstairs right now in one of the Bennington's sumptuous king-size beds, tasting her again. Touching her…

Every tempting inch of her balletic body.

That couldn't happen, obviously. But Anders was suddenly excruciatingly aware of the fact that they'd be sharing a bedroom for the next few weeks. By Manhattan standards, his apartment was massive. It had a panoramic view of Central Park, lush with cherry blossoms in the springtime and frosted with whirling snowflakes and Christmas spirit during the winter. But the vast majority of its square footage was taken up by the expansive living room and its floor-to-ceiling windows. He had a grand total of two bedrooms, which had always been double the amount he actually needed.

Until he'd become a family man overnight.

Mrs. Summers had helped him transform the spare bedroom into a room for Lolly. It was more of an oasis than a bedroom, like a little girl's sparkly, pink fantasy-come-true, with a canopy bed and glow-in-the-dark stars on the ceiling. Which left the master bedroom to Anders, just like always.

Except now, Chloe would be coming home with him, and he couldn't very well ask her to sleep on the sofa. He would have gladly made himself at home on the living room couch, but he wondered what kind of example that set for Lolly. At the very least, it would prompt questions. Grant and Olivia had always been affectionate with one another. He couldn't see Grant spending many nights sleeping on the sofa.

But as it turned out, they wouldn't have to deal with the awkward matter of sleeping arrangements at his apartment. Not quite yet, because when the wedding reception wound down to a close and the purple New York twilight deepened to a velvety, inky blue, the Christmas shoppers lining the bustling sidewalks of Park Avenue found their way home and Zander Wilde tucked a card key into the inside pocket of Anders's tuxedo jacket.

"The honeymoon suite," he said, handing Anders yet another glass of sparkling champagne. "It's yours for the night. My treat."

"I can't accept," Anders protested, as visions of a heart-shaped bed and a bathtub built for two danced in his head.

Not likely, considering the Bennington was a five-star hotel. Still, even without the stereotypical romantic trappings, he wouldn't last five minutes in a honeymoon suite with Chloe. Not after that kiss.

"Don't be ridiculous. Of course you can. I own this hotel, remember? And you're family now." Zander's gaze narrowed. "Just promise me one thing."

Anders's jaw clenched. "What's that?"

"Keep making my sister happy. I've never seen Chloe glowing like she is today." Zander gave his chest a pat, right where the key to the honeymoon suite rested against his heart. "Don't worry about a thing. Julian and Tessa are taking Lolly and Prancer until tomorrow morning. Wild horses couldn't keep your niece away. Tessa is a principal dancer at the Manhattan Ballet, and she's promised Lolly a serious dress-up session in some of her old costumes. Let's all meet on the top floor for brunch tomorrow at Bennington 8."

Then he was gone, and Anders could only stand there with the key to the honeymoon suite in his pocket like a lead weight as he watched Chloe hugging her family members goodbye just feet away.

He wanted her. No question. He wanted her so badly that he couldn't stop thinking about all the things he longed to do to her in that lavish hotel suite. Most of all, he wanted to kiss her again. He needed it, just to see if the first time had been a fluke. Surely it was just the product of their unique circumstances. The past few days had been a wild ride, and he was running on some crazy mixture of loss and adrenaline. His mind and body were playing tricks on him, making him believe ever so slightly in the fairy tale they'd concocted.

Deep down, he knew he was fooling himself. It didn't matter why he wanted to kiss Chloe again or why he wanted to unfasten that delicate confection of a dress she was wearing and watch it fall into a pile of fluff at her feet. He just did. He wanted it with every broken part of his soul.

But Zander's words echoed in his head.

Keep making my sister happy.

They reminded him all too much of who he was, what he was—a monster, according to his own flesh and blood.

No sex. He'd made her a promise, and he intended to keep it.

Chapter 10

"Wow, can you believe this room?" Chloe spun in a slow circle, taking in the pale gold paneled walls, the creamy white crown molding—as abundant and extravagant as icing on a wedding cake—and what had to be the most massive bed she'd ever set eyes on. The honeymoon suite. *Oh God.* "I mean, have you ever seen anything like this?"

She attempted a light and carefree laugh, but it came out strained. Forced. "What am I saying? Of course you have."

Stop. Talking. What was wrong with her? She'd been babbling nonstop since they'd crossed the threshold. There was no telling what kind of nonsense would come out of her mouth next.

Anders folded his arms across his chest and gazed impassively at her. "Why would you think I'd spent any time whatsoever in a honeymoon suite before?"

"I don't." She shook her head. "I just meant you're probably used to nice surroundings. Sorry, I'm not sure what I'm even saying. I'm just…"

"Nervous?" He arched a brow in amusement.

"Yes, actually." She released a breath she hadn't realized she'd been holding. "I am."

"Don't be. You can relax." He unbuttoned his tuxedo jacket, slipped out of it and tossed it onto the opulent silk sofa in the suite's luxe sitting area. Then he walked toward her and gave her a little tap on the nose. "There's nothing to be nervous about, love. I made you a promise, remember?"

She swallowed. "Of course I remember."

No sex.

Whose terrible idea had that been? Oh yeah, hers.

He gave her a tight smile, raked his hand in his hair and meandered back to the sofa as if he didn't have a care in the world.

Seriously?

Chloe was suddenly livid—livid at Anders for kissing her like he had and livid at herself for liking it so much. She'd thought it had meant something. She wasn't sure what, exactly, but she knew it didn't involve Anders sleeping on the couch.

She stared daggers at him as he kicked off his shoes. His eyes narrowed, and then the corner of his mouth lifted into a half grin. Moving as slowly as possible, with the languid grace of some kind of predatory animal, he reached for one of the French cuffs of his shirt and unfastened the cuff link. Without tearing his gaze from hers, he dropped it into a little tray on the table beside the couch. It pierced the strained silence with a tiny clang. Platinum on china.

Chloe's face burned, but she didn't dare fan herself. If he could be happy sleeping on the sofa, she could be just as unaffected by his billionaire bachelor striptease. Except he wasn't a bachelor anymore, was he?

He was hers.

Sort of.

"You might want to turn around." He unfastened his other cuff link, slid his bow tie off and undid the top button of his immaculate white shirt. His fingertips paused at the next button down. Then his half grin morphed into a wide smile, with a touch of smolder for good measure. To her complete and utter mortification, he made a little spinning motion with one of his pointer fingers.

Two could play at that game.

Obediently, she turned around to face the wall. Then she ran her fingers through her hair and twirled it into a high bun, so her new husband-who-wasn't-really-her-husband could have a clear, unobstructed view of her back. A lifetime of being a dancer meant she could secure a ballerina bun with nothing but a twist of her wrist. She spent more time than necessary tucking the loose waves into place and then slid the tips of her fingers lazily down the side of her neck.

She knew he was watching her, even before she heard his sharp intake of breath. She could feel the heat of his gaze, as warm and sultry as a hot summer day. It felt like tiny little fires breaking out all over her skin, and it made her want him even more, if such a thing was possible. What was it about him that made her feel this way? So adored…so *seen*, when he'd never so much as touched her. He'd kissed her once, only because he had to, and she was a goner. It defied logic.

Deep down, though, she knew why. She wasn't a prop to Anders. She was a person. He knew all about her toy soldier fiasco, and he didn't care. He saw her and he *wanted* her, purely for who she was.

A tiny voice sounded in the back of her head, so tiny she almost didn't recognize it as her own. *Isn't this all supposed to be pretend?*

She pushed it away. There was nothing make-believe about the pounding of her pulse, nor was it an illusion when she reached behind her neck and unclasped the fastening of her dress. Only one thought spun through her mind as she paused and let the gown fall away, pooling at her feet in a whisper of dreams and lace. *This.... this...is real.*

"Are you sure about this?" Anders's breath was hot on the back of her neck. She wasn't sure how long he'd been standing there, or when he'd gotten up from the couch. All that mattered was that he had.

She peered at him over her bare shoulder. "That's the second time you've asked me that question today, Mr. Kent."

"And?" His eyes were unfathomably dark—darker than she'd ever seen them. Glittering pools of indigo blue. "What's your answer, Mrs. Kent?"

Dressed now in nothing but her lacy panties and her wedding rings, she turned to face the gloriously handsome man who was now her husband.

"The same as before." The same as it had been since that very first day at the animal shelter, whether or not she wanted to admit it. "Yes, please."

He kissed her, and it was a different kind of kiss

than the wild, untamed one that had sealed their vows. This kiss was slow and reverent—tender in a way that made her insides flutter, even as her body went molten.

Her hands slid over his crisp white tuxedo shirt, and she became excruciatingly aware of the fact that he was still dressed while she was almost entirely naked. If she'd been with someone else, she might have been embarrassed. But with Anders, she didn't feel an ounce of shame, nor a bit of the awkwardness that she'd always experienced with a new lover. She hoped it wasn't because Anders was her husband, since that would mean the lovely wedding and the romantic vows had gone straight to her head, when she knew better than to let that happen.

This man whose hands were now cupping her breasts, and whose mouth was making a decadent trail of kisses along the curve of her neck, wasn't her soul mate. He wasn't the love of her life, no matter how good it felt when he touched her or how quickened her breath became when his lips dipped lower and his tongue brushed softly against her nipple.

But the words they'd said to one another in front of their families and friends were heavy with meaning. They were the most intimate words of all, and whether she and Anders had meant them or not, it was as if their bodies had heard those words.

His hands slid to her waist, fingertips brushing lightly, gingerly, against her skin.

To have and to hold.

He dropped to his knees, his mouth moving lower, and lower still, until her panties were on the floor and he parted her thighs ever so gently, pressing a hot, open-mouthed kiss between her legs.

To love and to cherish.

Her head fell backward, and in the moment before she shattered, a sound came out of her mouth that she'd never heard herself make before. It was as if she'd become another person entirely—Chloe Wilde had ceased to exist and Chloe Kent, wild and romantic, had taken her place.

Till death do us part.

Anders carried Chloe to the bed and she mewed like a kitten into the crook of his neck. The cat who'd gotten the cream.

"Easy, love. We're just getting started," he murmured into her hair.

They had all night—a night to explore one another, to learn all the little ways to give each other pleasure. He wanted to know all of them. He wanted to memorize every inch of her balletic body and kiss every tantalizing curve. He needed to know her, *really* know her…this ethereal beauty of a woman who now shared his name.

He placed her gently on the smooth silk sheets and started to undress, but then paused, unable to move a muscle as he looked down at his wife, bare and beautiful. He couldn't take his eyes off her, and he wondered if it would always be like this…if looking at her would forever make him ache with need, if touching her porcelain skin would fill him with an emotion he couldn't name, one that almost made him forget that they weren't really man and wife. They were still just pretending.

He slid out of his clothes, and as she reached for him, the diamond on her finger shimmered in the darkness. He watched, mesmerized, as her elegant hand closed around his erection, making him moan.

With this ring, I thee wed.

His breath came hard and quick, and he tried to slow it down, to make himself last. As good as she made him feel, he didn't want to finish like this. He needed her legs wrapped around his waist. He needed to cover her willowy body with his.

He needed to be inside her.

For as long as we both shall live.

"I want you, Chloe," he growled, winding a lock of her hair around his finger, pushing it back from her face so he could look her in the eyes.

They'd gone liquid with desire, dark and heavy-lidded. Bedroom eyes. But he and Chloe had an agreement, and they were about to cross every last line they'd previously drawn in the sand. He wanted her to be sure, because if she wasn't, they'd stop right now. It wouldn't be easy, but he'd manage.

"Tell me you want me, love." He kissed her, and her lips tasted sugary sweet, like wedding cake and fizzy champagne. "I need to hear you say it."

"I want you, Anders." She nipped gently at his bottom lip, and he nearly came. It was a miracle that he hadn't already. "Desperately so."

No woman had ever made him feel this way before— half out of his mind with need. Something strange was happening, something that felt far more meaningful than it should have, but he didn't want to stop and analyze it. He'd been doing just that his entire life, and where had it gotten him?

Dumb luck had led him to Chloe Wilde. He didn't deserve her, and he'd never been quite so keenly aware of that fact as he was now, poised above her, ready to slide into her warm, perfect body.

Chloe reached for him again, guiding him to her entrance. He took a deep breath and pushed inside, pausing to give her a chance to adjust. Then, as he kissed her, she opened for him and he thrust his way home.

And two shall become one.

Chapter 11

What had they done?

Chloe had insisted on only one rule: keeping things platonic. Everyone knew what platonic meant. It was no big mystery. Platonic meant no kissing, no cuddling and absolutely no sex. Yet here she was, less than twelve hours after marrying Anders Kent, waking up naked in bed beside him.

Or more accurately, on top of him.

Oh God.

She slid off him and wrapped the sheet around herself, moving as gingerly as possible. She was afraid to slide out of the bed in case the movement woke him. The minute he was conscious, they needed to talk about the enormous mistake they'd just made. They needed to set new boundaries, reinstate the strict no-sex policy.

Chloe wasn't quite ready to have that conversation. Not while she was feeling so pleasantly warm and sated, wearing nothing but a Tiffany diamond.

Which your new husband had been contractually obligated to give you.

How could she have been so stupid? She'd somehow

managed to convince herself that the kiss at the wedding had meant something when it so obviously did not. Otherwise, she wouldn't have had to tempt him into sleeping with her. He would have been an active and willing participant from the second they'd walked into the honeymoon suite.

She glanced down at him, sleeping so soundly beside her. Funny, she could have sworn he'd once told her he never slept past five in the morning. Yet it had to be at least eight o'clock. The bedsheets were bathed in a pink glow from the morning sun's rays glinting off the surrounding skyscrapers. They'd never managed to close the velvet drapes before they'd fallen into bed. From the moment he'd put his hands on her, everything had become a blur of shimmering heat. Of sensation. Her mother's wedding gown was still in a pile on the floor, as if she'd stepped out of it only moments ago. The various parts of Anders's tuxedo littered the sitting area, from one end of the room to the other.

She bit back a smile. *This is what a real honeymoon suite looks like the morning after a wedding.*

Then she blinked. What was wrong with her? This was exactly what she'd been afraid of in that pivotal moment before Anders kissed her for the first time. She'd known she was in trouble. She'd sensed it as surely as she'd sensed the epic domino effect she'd set into motion when she'd stumbled during the toy soldier number in the Thanksgiving parade. Only then, the destruction had played out in slow motion. She'd watched, consciously aware of each wrong move, every tiny misstep, as one dancer after another fell to the ground.

Not this time. This time, she'd plunged headfirst into disaster. *Intentionally.* She'd known exactly what she was doing, from the minute he'd taken her hand and led her away from the ballroom. He hadn't seduced her as she'd expected him to, but no problem. She'd taken matters into her own hands.

This was how she'd end up with a broken heart. She wasn't the type of person who could indulge in meaningless sex. She wished she could. Oh, how she wished it, but she just wasn't wired that way. The whole fake marriage idea might have worked if she'd stuck to the rules, but now she wasn't so sure.

Could she really walk away from Anders and Lolly in less than a month?

You don't have a choice. You have to.

She glanced down at her temporary husband. His chest rose and fell with the languid grace of a dreamer, and the sternness in his features seemed softer somehow. More relaxed.

He looks happy. She swallowed hard around the knot in her throat. He looked happier than she'd ever seen him.

But what did she know? She was Anders's wife, but she'd known him for less than a week.

His eyes drifted open, first one and then the other, and then his mouth curved into a tender smile as he realized she'd been watching him sleep. Her heart clenched. *It's too late*, she thought. She was already in too deep. The thought of losing this, of losing *him*, already left her with a cavernous, hollow feeling in her heart.

This is why people shouldn't sleep with their pretend husbands.

She bit her bottom lip to keep it from quivering.

"Hey." Anders's brow furrowed and he slipped his hand beneath the sheet to cup her breast and run his thumb gently over her nipple. "Why do I get the feeling you're about to climb out of bed?"

Because I am. His touch drew a sigh out of her. Just one tender brush of his fingertips—that was all it took for her body to crave him again. She could feel it building inside. The want. The need.

"We have brunch, remember?" She forced herself to crawl away from him while she still could, and nearly tumbled to the floor in a tangle of sheets and desperation.

Over twenty years of dance classes and she couldn't even manage to get out of bed gracefully. Perfect.

She righted herself and pulled the sheet tighter around her bare body, consciously aware of the deepening frown on Anders's perfectly chiseled face. When at last she'd become steady on her feet, she flashed him a smile. A fake one, obviously, since pretending was all she knew how to do now.

He didn't move a muscle. He just stared at her as she silently willed her heart to close itself up like a book that could be read only one time and then tucked away and forgotten.

His gaze slid to the clock on the nightstand and then back to her. Was it her imagination or did her heart actually hurt when he looked at her now? *You have no one to blame but yourself.*

He'd asked her. More than once.

Are you sure?

Tell me you want me... I need to hear you say it.

She'd been sure. She'd never been so sure about anything in her life, never wanted anything as badly as she wanted him inside her. And that was precisely the problem.

"Brunch isn't for almost three hours." His voice was raw and delicious. It sounded like pure sex.

A rebellious shiver coursed through Chloe. This conversation would have been so much easier if he weren't naked.

Anders stood and closed the distance between them, and she couldn't force herself to look away from his long, lean body and its sculpted planes as he moved toward her.

She'd kissed those muscles. She'd dug her fingernails into that glorious flesh as he'd pushed his way inside her. In the mirror behind him, she could see little half-moon marks on his back—evidence of her longing, her passion. Passion that no man had ever brought out of her before. Only him. Only Anders.

What did it mean? What did *any of this* mean?

"Talk to me, love." He reached for her hand, then gingerly lifted it to his mouth and kissed the place where her wedding ring wrapped around her finger. "Tell me what's going on."

There was no way she could do this for two more weeks, not if he expected her to pack up her things and leave on Christmas Eve.

"Nothing." She pulled her hand away, pretending not

to notice the angry knot in his jaw as she did so. "It's just that the wedding is over now."

"And?" His gaze narrowed, and he peered at her as if daring her to continue.

She didn't have to. It wasn't too late to throw herself into his arms and kiss him, to start the morning over again. But if she did, what would happen the next morning? And the one after that?

What would happen when she woke up the day after Lolly's custody hearing and remembered everything had been for show?

"And last night was wonderful, but it should probably be a onetime thing." She stopped talking before she choked on a sob.

Out of the many, many lies she'd told in the past few weeks, this one was the biggest. It was the most devastating whopper of them all. She didn't want it to be a onetime thing. She wanted it to be more than that. She might even want it to be forever.

For as long as we both shall live.

What was she thinking? She still didn't know her husband. Not really. He'd just sexed the sense right out of her, which was yet another reason they shouldn't sleep together again. Ever.

Anders didn't say anything. He just stood there, studying her, as if he was trying to see inside her head.

Thank goodness he couldn't. They'd been married all of five minutes and she'd gone and reversed the script. But he didn't need to know that, did he? "I mean, that's what we agree on. Right?"

Say something.

If only he'd give her some indication that he felt the same way. One word…that was all it would take. But she couldn't just put herself out there if he didn't feel the same way. They'd agreed on a fake marriage. He'd even wanted her to sign a contract.

She peered up at him, breathless, willing him to argue with her. For a bittersweet second, she thought he might. In the morning light, his eyes were bluer than ever, as clear as the sparkling sea. And an invisible force seemed to pull her toward him, inviting her to dive right in.

But then he blinked, and it was gone. Whatever magical connection or genuine bond that had formed between them when they'd said *I do* fell away, and his expression hardened into stone.

Right before her eyes, he seemed to change from the man she'd spent the night with back into the brooding stranger she'd met at the animal shelter.

Anders was in no mood for brunch.

He wasn't sure how he could sip mimosas with the Wildes over French toast and gourmet waffles when he was still trying to unravel whatever had gone wrong the night before. Because something had *definitely* happened. He just wasn't sure what it was.

But he showed up and did his damnedest to smile and make small talk with Chloe and her family, because that was what husbands did, right? And Anders was Chloe's husband now. She was his *wife*.

In name only. He took a bitter gulp of black coffee. Why did the businesslike nature of their union grate so much? He'd known what he was getting into. They both had. There'd been no ambiguity about the rules—a platonic relationship, no sex. They'd never sworn not to have feelings for one another, but that had been a given. And now here he was, sitting beside Chloe the morning after their wedding, wanting nothing more than to reach for her hand under the table or brush the hair from her face and kiss her full on the lips for all the world to see.

Lolly wiggled her way between them, gripping Tessa's cell phone and chattering about her sleepover at Tessa and Julian's apartment. "And after we watched a dance movie, Tessa let me try on some of her costumes. We took pictures. Look!"

Chloe helped her scroll through images on the iPhone, and as adorable as they were, the nagging sense of regret in Anders's gut grew worse as he looked at them.

"I'm glad you had fun, sweetheart." He kissed the top of Lolly's head, careful to avoid the perfect ballerina bun Tessa had created for her.

"She's welcome anytime," Julian said, signing the words at the same time, since Tessa was deaf.

The whole family seemed to know American Sign Language, something he hadn't realized the day before during the busy buildup to the wedding. Lolly had apparently picked up a few basics during her sleepover, because when Anders reminded her to thank Tessa and Julian, she'd pressed her fingertips to her chin and brought them forward, almost like blowing a kiss—ASL for "thank you."

"Please come back soon, Lolly." Tessa mouthed the

words along with her hand gestures. "We loved having you."

Beside him, Lolly bounced up and down. "And will you come to my dance recital on Christmas Eve? Please? I'm going to be Clara from *The Nutcracker*."

Julian grinned at her. "Of course we will."

"We'll all be there, Lolly. I promise." Emily patted the chair beside her. "Why don't you come sit beside me until it's time to go home?"

Emily shot Anders a wink as Lolly scooted away and settled beside her. She was clearly trying to give him as much alone time as possible with Chloe until they took Lolly home, and the message wasn't lost on his wife. She glanced at him with wide eyes, no doubt wanting him to play along and act as if they were real newlyweds who couldn't keep their hands off each other.

He moved to slide an arm around her and her earlier words rang in his head.

Last night was wonderful, but it should probably be a onetime thing.

Anders didn't want it to be a onetime thing. From the moment he'd opened his eyes, all he could think about was reaching for her beside him, burying his hands in her softly tangled hair and making love to her again. He still couldn't quite wrap his mind around the fact that he'd misread the situation so profoundly.

Or had he?

The second his hand brushed against her back, a shiver coursed through her, sending a jolt of pure electric arousal straight to his groin. Her gaze shot to his, and in that brief, unguarded moment, he could see all the things she refused to say. Last night had meant something. She still wanted him—she might even want him as badly as he wanted her. She just didn't want to admit it.

He kept his arm draped around her shoulders and casually toyed with a lock of her hair, biting back a smile as her cheeks grew pink and she reached for her mimosa and took a healthy gulp.

"Have you two thought about a honeymoon?" Emily asked.

Anders arched a brow at Chloe. *Oh, I've thought about it. I'm thinking about it right now, and so are you, my darling bride.*

"Um…" Chloe's flush turned as red as Santa's plush suit.

"Give them time, Mom. Christmas is in less than two weeks. I'm sure they want to get through the holidays first." Allegra pointed her fork at Chloe. "Besides, you're in charge of *Baby Nutcracker*, remember? You can't go anywhere until after Christmas Eve."

"I'm not." Chloe's gaze darted toward Anders. Then she blinked and looked away.

Neither of them was going anywhere until after Christmas Eve, because that was the end date of their agreement. Lolly's guardianship hearing was first thing in the morning. Afterward, all bets were off.

The date rested so heavily on Anders's shoulders that he hadn't thought beyond it in weeks. It was as if the entire calendar ended right then and there.

Except now, he could almost see past it. Not entirely. He still had no idea what the days beyond Christmas

Eve would look like. He desperately hoped they included Lolly. She was the reason he'd ended up in this absurd situation to begin with, after all. Now that he was married, he could finally breathe again. He could allow himself to believe that it would all work out and Lolly could stay.

But he wasn't altogether sure why he was suddenly so acutely aware of the days, weeks and months to come. He only knew, sitting beside his complicated, beautiful wife at that joyous table in Bennington 8, surrounded by people who'd been lied to—kind people, good people—that the day before Christmas wasn't an end date.

It was a beginning.

Of what, he had no idea. He'd taken Chloe to bed, but their marriage was still a sham. Nothing had changed, and yet somehow everything had. Because despite the mess they'd made, and despite the fact that when Chloe let him take her hand and wind his fingers through hers, he knew it was just for show, the glittering diamond on her finger sparked something deep inside him. Something he hadn't felt in a very long time.

Hope. It was the hope of a fool—a man who'd abandoned his controlled, exacting existence and had been grasping at straws, making things up as he went along, making a mess of disastrous proportions.

But it was all he had, at least until Christmas.

"Your apartment is lovely." Chloe crossed her arms as she looked out over the snowy landscape of Central Park.

She could see ice-skaters spinning circles on the

pond below and horse-drawn carriages making a wide loop around the green-and-white-striped tents of the Christmas market in Columbus Circle. She'd never been in a penthouse like this before—or anywhere else, for that matter—with such a spectacular view of the city. It was breathtaking, like standing in the center of a snow globe.

It was also ridiculous, considering she'd married a man and was now seeing his home for the very first time.

Their home. For the time being, anyway.

How on earth had she gotten herself into this predicament?

"Thank you." Anders followed her gaze to the scene below, then turned his back on the window and raked a hand through his hair. He glanced around the massive master bedroom, looking at anything and everything, but not at her. "You can have the bed. I'll take the sofa."

"Oh." She swallowed. It was silly, wasn't it? They'd just made love the night before and now they weren't even going to sleep in the same bed. Surely that wasn't necessary. The bed was huge, a California king, big enough to spend an entire night side by side without ever touching one another.

Probably.

"You don't need to sleep on the couch." She shook her head, but it was too late.

Anders had already pulled a pillow and blankets from a sleek armoire and was busy arranging his makeshift bed.

Fine. If that was the way he wanted things, so be

it. At least having him a chaste ten feet away from the bed would make sticking to the no-sex rule a realistic possibility.

And she was determined not to break that rule again. As wonderful as last night had been, it had also been thoroughly confusing. For a minute, she'd actually begun to believe that they were really and truly married. She'd liked that feeling far more than she should have. And the pang in her heart at the sight of Anders's pillow on the sofa told her she'd done the right thing.

They were playing house. That was all this was, and she couldn't keep forgetting how it would end. She needed to protect her heart at all costs.

As if to prove her point, Anders shook his head and said, "It's for less than two weeks. I'll be fine."

"Right." She nodded, and smiled so hard that her cheeks started to hurt.

Anders didn't smile back. If anything, the furrow in his brow deepened as he strode into the expansive, spa-like bathroom and closed the door.

Chloe shimmied out of her dress and into her pair of black and carnation-pink polka-dot pajamas before he could emerge, and then pulled the covers up to her chin. The sheets were cold to the touch, and being in the enormous bed all by herself made her feel very suddenly, very acutely alone. She wished Prancer could curl up beside her. She'd broken every pet parenting rule known to man and let the puppy sleep with her after she'd brought her home, but now the little dog had taken up residence in Lolly's frilly canopy bed.

Lolly had begged, and Chloe immediately caved.

She didn't want to think about what that might mean when it was time to pack up her things and take Prancer back home with her, so she didn't. Instead, she aimed all her frustration at Anders as he exited the bathroom.

"Really?" She glared at his bare chest and the tight-fitting boxer briefs, slung so decadently low across his hips. "That's all you're wearing to bed?"

Her mouth dropped open, agog, before she could stop it, and for the first time since they'd left the Bennington and arrived at Anders's penthouse, his lips curved into a grin. Not just a cocky half smirk, but a full-on knowing smile. It was beyond annoying and just mortifying enough for Chloe to snap back to her senses and force her mouth closed.

"Yes, really." He planted his hands on his hips, drawing her attention even more directly to his chiseled abs—if such a thing was possible—and then lower, to the V-shaped muscle that disappeared below the waistband of his boxers. "Would you prefer I wear something else?"

Yes. Specifically, something *more*.

"Um, no. It's none of my business." Damn it, did her voice have to come out so breathy? She cleared her throat and continued. "It's freezing outside, though."

"Ah, so you're worried I might catch a cold." His smiled widened, as if he knew good and well that she was suddenly quite warm.

Damn him.

"Exactly." She'd rather play along and pretend she was worried about his health than admit the simple truth that having him nearly naked in the same room was, ahem, *distracting*.

She understood why they needed to share a bedroom. The judge at the guardianship hearing might question Lolly, and how would it look if she said Chloe and Anders didn't sleep together? Besides, the master suite was certainly big enough for the two of them. Although it seemed to be shrinking by the second the longer Anders stood there wearing next to nothing.

"Maybe you're right. I should probably put on something warmer. Flannel, maybe?"

She nodded. Flannel was exactly what this situation called for.

"Too bad I don't have any." He narrowed his gaze at her. "In case you haven't noticed, I'm not exactly the flannel-pajama type of husband."

Chloe's cheeks blazed with heat. He was baiting her, and she probably deserved it after the abrupt way she'd handled things earlier this morning at the Bennington. She doubted he'd touch her again, even if she asked him to. And she definitely wouldn't. But as she let herself remember what it had felt like to touch all that warm, male skin that was on such flagrant display in front of her, she couldn't help the way her gaze lowered from his eyes to his mouth.

She licked her lips. "What type are you?"

Their eyes locked, and for a long, loaded moment, neither of them said a word. Neither of them had to. She knew precisely what sort of memories were running through his head, because the same ones were running through hers. She'd been doing her best to push them away all day, but it was impossible. She couldn't look at him anymore without wanting him. Sleeping with him had been the worst possible mistake she could make. Why hadn't she realized that before she'd practically begged him to make love to her?

Actually, she'd been aware of the danger all along. She'd known giving herself to him would lead to trouble, but she'd done it anyway. Because she just couldn't help it. The more time she spent with Anders, the more attractive he became. He wasn't the cold, distant puppy thief she'd originally thought he was. She wished he were. It would make not sleeping with him so much easier.

"I'm the pretend type," he said. The rawness in his voice almost killed her. "Right?"

She didn't trust herself to speak, so she nodded instead.

"Right," he said quietly, turning toward the sofa.

She wasn't sure what time she finally fell asleep. For hours she lay awake in that cold, lonely bed, listening to the rhythmic sound of Anders's breathing and wishing things could be different. Wishing that, for once, she'd really be chosen by someone…by Anders.

This was going to be the longest two weeks of her life.

Chapter 12

"How's married life?" Penelope sat across the conference table from Anders, leafing through the packet of merger and acquisition papers for a meeting that was due to start in less than fifteen minutes.

"It's fine," he said automatically, because how else was he supposed to respond?

Was he supposed to admit that he'd barely slept a wink in the week since he and Chloe had been married, because if he let his guard down for even a second he might give in to the impulse to toss the covers aside, crawl into bed with her and cover her exquisite body with his? Was he supposed to say that he woke up hard for her every day, but he hadn't laid a finger on her since their wedding night?

"The ceremony was beautiful." Penelope arched a brow. "Not at all what I expected, but certainly lovely."

Anders looked up from the document in his hands. "What exactly did you expect?"

She shrugged. "I don't know, just something less..."

Less real? *Join the club.*

"...warm, I suppose. Celebratory." She angled her

head and studied him. "You've been awfully scarce around here lately. I'm beginning to think you found an actual bride after I turned you down."

Anders's jaw clenched. He was hoping they could forget the whole marriage contract thing had ever happened, and proceed with business as usual. He had enough relationship problems at the moment without adding Penelope to the mix.

Oh, so now you and Chloe are in a relationship?

"It's the holidays," he said with a shrug.

He'd spent a little more time out of the office than he usually did this time of year, but not enough to be noticeable. Or so he'd thought.

But things were different now. He had Lolly to think about. Plus, living with Chloe Wilde was like having one of Santa's helpers under his roof. The woman seriously loved Christmas. The first day he'd left her alone in the penthouse, he'd come home from work to find a Christmas tree in his living room. Not an elegant, professionally decorated artificial tree like the ones he usually had delivered, but a real tree. A noble fir, covered with strings of popcorn and ornaments Chloe and Lolly had made out of construction paper, glue and glitter.

The tree was a disaster, as was his apartment. He'd never get rid of all the glitter; it was everywhere. But Lolly was besotted with the scraggly tree that refused to remain fully upright in its metal stand, no matter how many times Anders crawled beneath its branches and tightened the screws holding it in place.

Likewise, she'd practically glowed the next night when Anders walked in the door and found Prancer darting around the apartment in a Santa costume, complete with a tiny white beard strapped to her chin. Once again, it had been Chloe's doing. The following day, he'd found himself coming up with an excuse to leave the office an hour earlier than usual. He'd been unable to concentrate as he sat at his desk wondering what he'd stumble upon next. A snowman on the terrace? A Christmas cookie bake-off in the kitchen?

Wrong on both counts. When he walked into the penthouse, Lolly and Chloe had been decked out in ugly Christmas sweaters, wrapping a package with his name on it. He was now the proud owner of an ugly Christmas sweater of his very own. It matched the one they'd bought the dog.

"Since when do you take any time off at Christmas?" Penelope rolled her eyes.

"What time off? I've been here until five every night this week."

"My point exactly. You're never out the door before seven." She studied him for a moment and then shook her head. "Oh my gosh, it's true, isn't it? Your marriage to Chloe isn't fake at all. It's real."

A pain flared in Anders's temple. "It's not. Can we get back to business, please? The client is going to be here any minute."

Penelope waved a dismissive hand. "No, he won't. Eric Johnson is never on time. He thinks it's a display of weakness. You've been working with him long enough to know that."

Indeed he had, but that still didn't mean he wanted to

discuss his marriage, fake or otherwise, with the woman he used to occasionally share a bed with.

Not that he'd given much thought to his ex. She didn't even qualify as an ex, really. What they'd shared had been convenient, and now it was over. He couldn't imagine picking things up with Penelope again, even after his marriage ended.

If it ended.

He swallowed. Of course it would end. They'd made a deal, and so far, nothing had changed. "It's a contract marriage. Everything will go back to normal after the guardianship hearing and Christmas have passed."

"Sure it will." Penelope resumed flipping through the pages of the merger acquisition.

Anders knew better than to push. He'd wanted the discussion to end, and it had. But he couldn't let it go. Not like that.

He sat back in his chair and crossed his arms, as serious as if they were putting together a stock offering. "What's that supposed to mean?"

"It means you're fooling yourself if you think the two of you will walk away from this brief holiday union unscathed. Marriage means something, whether you want it to or not. I tried to warn you, remember?" She shook her head. "Besides, I was there. I saw the way you looked at her on your wedding day. I saw the giant rock on her finger. You're not faking it, Anders. If you think you are, you're in for a rude awakening."

He opened his mouth to protest and then promptly closed it. They sat in silence while her words sank in and took root.

"You're wrong," he finally said quietly. Chloe had drawn a line in the sand, and he wasn't about to cross it again. His entire life had been turned upside down. He certainly didn't need to invite any more chaos into it by trying to throw their arrangement out the window and asking her to marry him for real.

Besides, that was not what he wanted at all. Sure, he might like the throaty sound of her laughter and the silly, high voice she used when she talked to Prancer. He might spend long minutes at his desk thinking about the softness of her skin or remembering how the scent of her hair on their wedding night mirrored the blooms in her bridal bouquet. But that didn't mean he wanted to love, honor and cherish Chloe for the rest of his life. Did it?

Hell no, it didn't. He wasn't thinking straight, that was all. He was still grieving the loss of his brother, and everyone knew grief made people crazy. That was why the experts in such matters always urged grieving people not to make any major life decisions. Getting married—or, in his case, *staying* married—definitely qualified.

Penelope held up her hands. "I stand corrected, then. After Christmas, you can stick to the terms of the contract the two of you signed and go your separate ways."

He looked away. He wasn't about to admit that he'd never drafted a contract. Penelope would have a field day psychoanalyzing that little tidbit.

"But I hope you don't, because I know one thing for a fact." She gave him a knowing smile. "You never once looked at me the way you look at Chloe."

"Penelope…"

She held up a hand to stop him. "If you're about to apologize, save your breath. I'm not jealous. I could have been Mrs. Anders Kent myself. I'm just saying you might want to consider the possibility that you've been given a precious gift, something that a lot of people spend a lifetime hoping for, before you throw it all away."

A precious gift, just like all the wrapped packages Chloe had been piling underneath their pitiful tree.

No. His teeth clenched, and he tightened his grip on his Mont Blanc. He and Chloe were pretending. She'd be gone and his life would be back to normal before that Christmas tree dropped its needles.

"You've got it all wrong," he said. Penelope's opinion on the matter didn't mean a thing to him, so he wasn't sure why he was trying to convince her she was wrong.

Maybe you're not. Maybe the person you're really trying to convince is yourself.

The unwelcome thought hit him like a ton of bricks as Mrs. Summers appeared in the doorway to the conference room.

"Mr. Kent." She smiled at him, and then her head swiveled to Penelope. "Ms. Reed."

"Yes?" he said, grateful for the interruption. Short of the entire firm crumbling into ruin, he would have been thankful for just about anything to get his mind off of the woman who'd been sleeping in his bed, *by herself,* for the past seven nights.

"Your client is here. Shall I send him in?"

He nodded. "Yes, thank you."

Thank God.

Work was precisely what he needed at the moment. He could handle work. He was good at it, unlike everything else in his life.

But as the day wore on and he guided Eric Johnson through the terms of his pending acquisition, his mind kept wandering. And when the meeting wrapped up shortly before four o'clock, he put away his things and strode past the receptionist's desk without bothering to tell her where he was headed.

He'd had enough commentary on his personal life for one day.

Chloe glanced at the time on her phone as she stepped off the elevator in the lobby of Anders's posh building and hastened her steps.

Emily wasn't expecting her at the studio until six o'clock, which meant she'd be nearly an hour early, even navigating the subway during rush hour. But Lolly wasn't home, and Chloe had been doing her absolute level best not to spend any time with Anders alone in the penthouse.

It was a desperate plan, made all the more desperate by the fact that, thus far, hanging out with both Anders and Lolly hadn't lessened her attraction to her temporary husband at all. Even the ugly Christmas sweater had backfired. She'd never seen a man look so insanely hot in garish plaid with tiny little stockings hanging from his chest.

Watching him interact with Lolly was even worse. He was so patient with her. So kind. It killed Chloe to think he could end up losing her. The thought of Lolly being taken away from him was the only thing keeping her from packing her bags and pulling the plug on their excruciating arrangement. Every night she spent in Anders's bed without Anders was another exercise in self-torture. But she couldn't bring herself to walk away, not if it meant leaving him high and dry on the date of the guardianship hearing.

One week down, one to go.

She could do this. She could definitely hold out another seven days now that she'd begun overhauling the Wilde School of Dance. Anders had wired half the money he owed her into her account on the day following the wedding, and she'd wasted no time lining up all the necessary improvements. The new lobby furniture wouldn't be delivered until after the holidays, but she'd managed to schedule the floor installation for the upcoming weekend. Come Christmas Eve, *Baby Nutcracker* would be performed on a gorgeous new dance surface. If that didn't increase enrollment in the New Year, nothing would.

An extra hour or so at the studio wouldn't kill her, especially if it meant she could avoid the ridiculous breathless feeling she always got when Anders walked in the penthouse door at the end of the day and scooped Lolly into his arms. Even Prancer had gotten in on the honey-I'm-home action, running circles around Anders and nipping at his designer shoes while Chloe stood there like a third wheel.

If she was really being honest with herself—brutally, painfully honest—she didn't feel like a third wheel.

When Anders would meet her gaze over the top of Lolly's little head, it took every ounce of her willpower not to join in on the affectionate display. They weren't a family and they never would be, but in those moments, they looked like one on the outside. And on the inside, they felt like one. No matter how very hard Chloe tried to deny it.

She had no idea what that domestic scene would feel like minus Lolly, and she was afraid to find out, hence her hasty exit from the penthouse a good half hour before Anders ever came home. But right after she waved goodbye to the doorman and bent her head against the afternoon snowfall, she plowed straight into the very man she'd been trying so desperately hard to avoid. Her husband.

"Whoa."

His voice was as deep and gravelly as ever, and the only thought running through her head as she collided face-first into his solid wall of a chest was that she needed to back away. Far, far away. Because he smelled so good, so manly, like warm cedar and pine, and his cashmere coat was so impossibly soft against her cheek that she was on the verge of purring like a kitten.

What on earth was wrong with her?

She must be in some kind of withdrawal. There'd been no physical contact between them whatsoever since the morning after they'd slept together. The last time he'd touched her had been over brunch at Bennington 8, and that generous dose of PDA had been for the benefit of her family. It had all been for show.

And whose fault is that?

Hers. Anders had done exactly as she'd asked and kept his hands to himself.

And it was driving her crazy.

"Sorry." She jerked backward before she made a complete idiot out of herself. She needed space. Loads of space—several feet, if possible.

But it was too late, because Anders's hands were already planted on her shoulders, steadying her, even as her legs went wobbly. She'd actually gone weak in the knees, like the world's biggest cliché.

He let out a little laugh. "Where's the fire?"

Everywhere. She nearly said it out loud, but stopped herself in the nick of time. The air was thick with a wintry mix of snow and frozen drizzle, and still she'd gone molten from his touch.

"Nowhere. I just…" She wiggled out of his grasp so she could form a coherent thought. "What are you doing home so early?"

His arms hung there for a second, as if they didn't know what to do now that his hands were no longer resting on her shoulders. Then he cleared his throat and shoved his hands in his pockets. "It's not that early."

"Yes, it is." She was keenly aware of what time Anders came home from work. Her self-preservation depended on it. So long as she knew when to expect him, she could put up her invisible shield, perfectly designed to keep him at arm's length.

Chloe wasn't good at surprises, particularly when those surprises included her charming pretend husband. Since their night together at the Bennington, it seemed like the biggest charade in her life wasn't their marriage at all, but instead the daily pretense that everything between them was still just platonic. When she was prepared, she could put on a decent act, in the same way that hours of rehearsal and time in front of the lit makeup mirror backstage used to prepare her for a performance. Everyone at Radio City knew what time the heavy red velvet curtain rose. Showtime was calculated down to the second. If the curtain had ever gone up a minute or two early, there would have been chaos.

And now the chaos was inside her heart, beating wildly at the sight of Anders on the busy snowy sidewalk, with a cozy Burberry scarf wrapped around his neck and his hair just windblown enough to remind her what he looked like when he climbed out of bed in the morning.

She swallowed. What *was* he doing home so early?

"Things were slow at the office." He was lying. Chloe had seen his calendar, and his phone chimed day in and day out with messages from his assistant, Mrs. Summers. Things were never slow at Anders's office.

He glanced up, toward the penthouse. "I thought I'd see what you and Lolly were up to this afternoon."

Lolly. Of course. He'd come home to spend time with his niece, which was sweet. Really, really sweet. Chloe wasn't sure why the shrinking feeling in her chest felt so much like disappointment.

"Lolly isn't here. She's still at the studio. Allegra let her stay for tap class and beginning ballet because she wasn't ready to go home after our recital rehearsal." The little girl was becoming more besotted by the day. It made Chloe even more determined to not only save the dance school, but help make it thrive again. "I think you might have a future dancer on your hands."

"Just like you." Something in his gaze softened, and it made the breath hitch in Chloe's throat. "That wouldn't be the worst thing in the world."

Their eyes locked, and for a dizzying second, everything around them faded away. The city streets, always humming with the blur of taxis and siren wails, faded into the background, until all she could see was the unexpected softness in his gaze and all she could hear was her pulse roaring like a wildfire in her ears.

Her family still didn't know she'd been fired. Only Anders knew the truth, and here he was, telling her he'd be happy if Lolly grew up to be just like her.

She shook her head. "I'm not a dancer anymore. Remember?"

"You'll always be a dancer," he said simply, and with enough conviction that she almost believed it.

She took a deep breath. "I should go. I need to get back to the studio."

"Isn't the nanny with Lolly? She can bring her home."

The nanny. Right. He still didn't know.

"I gave the nanny a week off. I hope it's okay. I just figured since it was Christmas she might want to spend some time with her own family, and I'm here now." *It's only temporary, remember?* As if she could forget. "But don't worry—she'll be back the day after Christmas."

He nodded as a cold understanding passed through his gaze. He'd need the nanny again once the expiration date on their makeshift family had passed. "I see. And of course it's okay."

"I should go." She couldn't keep standing there chatting about the nanny and Lolly's schedule, as if they were a real couple. A real family. "I need to get back to the studio."

"Aren't you finished teaching for the day?" he asked, before she could take a step.

"I am." She couldn't help but smile, despite her very real, very pressing urge to flee. *Baby Nutcracker* was one thing that seemed to be going right in her life. "Class was great today. You should have seen the kids working on the dance of the snowflakes choreography. It was adorable."

"I'm looking forward to seeing it Christmas Eve."

"Of course." Her smile faded, as it always did when someone mentioned Christmas Eve. It had always been her favorite day on the calendar, but not anymore. Not this year. "Anyway, I'm going back to do a little painting after hours."

"Painting?" He angled his head, and peering into his blue eyes was so like lifting her face to a crystal-clear sky that she had to look away.

She aimed her focus across the street, where a group of tourists was gathered around a Salvation Army volunteer ringing a bell and lip-synching to Mariah Carey Christmas songs. "I'm making a few improvements at the school. You know, so we can put our best foot forward at the recital."

"And you're painting the walls yourself?" He seemed puzzled, but then again, Chloe supposed billionaires typically didn't spend their off-hours doing manual labor.

"Yes." She lifted a brow. "It's really not that difficult. You should try it sometime."

He shrugged and his mouth curved in a half smile. "Okay."

And then, before she could wrap her mind around what he was doing, he moved past her toward the curb with his arm raised. A black town car materialized out of nowhere, because of course Anders Kent was the sort of man who got what he wanted, exactly when he wanted it.

It was beyond annoying, especially when he looked at Chloe as if the thing he wanted most of all was her.

One more week. That's all.

"What are you doing?" She made no move toward the curb, where he stood holding the door of the sleek black car open for her. And she tried her best not to look at the leather interior of the back seat or think about how much warmer and comfortable it would be than the subway.

"I'm going with you to help you paint. You said I should try it sometime." He leaned against the car and crossed his feet at the ankles, clearly prepared to wait things out while she tried to come up with an excuse to turn him down.

"But you're wearing a suit. You can't paint dressed like that."

"Watch me." He held out his hand, reaching for hers, and all she had to do was walk away, toward the subway station. Or make some kind of excuse to go back upstairs, and then she could leave in a little while, once he was busy with a work call or something.

She didn't do either of those things, though. Instead, she placed her hand in his and let him help her into the car, telling herself all the while that it would be fine. They'd be painting the walls, not slow dancing. Besides, no one fell into bed doing manual labor together.

But nestled beside her husband in the warm car, while twilight descended on the city and Manhattan shimmered in the golden glow of twinkle lights, looking as radiant as it could only at this time of year, she had to fight the urge to rest her head on his shoulder. To press her thigh against his just to feel the solid warmth of his presence before she lost it. To climb into his lap and kiss the winter chill from his lips.

And then she began to realize that falling into bed shouldn't be her biggest worry.

After all, she was a dancer, and as every ballerina knew, there were far more dangerous ways to fall.

An hour later, when there was a brush in Anders's hand and paint splatters covering his oxford shirt and bespoke wool dress pants, he was willing to admit that he probably should have changed clothes before heading to the studio.

All the same, he had no regrets. If he'd paused long enough to go upstairs and change, he would've given Chloe the opportunity to leave without him. And he couldn't bear the thought of being stuck in the empty penthouse all evening.

He'd lived alone his entire adult life, so he should have felt perfectly content in an empty apartment. But he'd grown accustomed to the happy chatter that had filled the space for the past seven days. He liked the pitter-patter of Lolly's tiny feet as she chased Prancer around the Christmas tree. He liked listening to Chloe's voice—as silvery and lovely as tinsel. He liked falling asleep at night knowing that she was in the same room, even though the small amount of feet that separated them felt like miles.

She was *there*.

A week from now, she wouldn't be.

He wanted to hoard what time he had left with her as if it were gold, and if that meant that one of his best suits suddenly looked like something straight out of the Museum of Modern Art, then so be it.

"You're surprisingly good at this." Chloe watched as he covered the last bare patch of wall with color in the main classroom.

They'd been alone for hours, sometimes painting in comfortable silence, sometimes talking about all the time Chloe had spent here as a child. He liked hearing new details about her life, filling in the blanks of her past and getting to know her better. He'd seen the tiny flare of panic in her eyes when Emily and Allegra had left for the evening, taking Lolly with them for another cozy Wilde sleepover.

He also knew what that look meant—his wife was trying her best not to be alone with him. But they'd needed this. He was tired of pretending their night together had been a mistake. It hadn't been a mistake at all.

It had been perfect.

And the way he kept catching her looking at him tonight when she thought he wasn't paying attention told him she thought so, too.

She glanced at him again, her gaze flitting from his hands to his mouth to his eyes before she flushed and looked away. "Seriously, is there anything you can't do? I would have never expected a legendary bachelor businessman to be handy with a paintbrush."

"I'm not a bachelor anymore, remember?" He arched a brow at her and carefully placed his brush in the drip tray. "And there are plenty of things I can't do."

She rolled her eyes. "Like what?"

"Like dance. I'm a hopeless disaster on the dance floor."

Her mouth dropped open, giving him a tantalizing glimpse of her perfect, pink tongue. "I don't believe you."

He held up his hands. "Would I lie to a dancer about my having two left feet?"

"Be honest." Her gaze narrowed. "Is this outrageous falsehood just an attempt at getting me to slow dance with you?"

He reached behind her and gave her ponytail a playful tug, eliciting a wholly satisfying gasp. "There's only one way to find out, isn't there?"

"Well." He could see the wheels turning in her pretty little head. She had the same little furrow between her brows that she always got when he undressed for bed. Temptation. "I suppose I owe you a dance lesson, since you just spent your evening painting with me and ruined your suit."

"One dance, then we'll call it even. Deal?" He offered his hand for a shake.

She took it in her own, and the simple, innocent contact of her fingertips brushing against his was enough to make him hard. He didn't just want her. He *craved* her. He'd been craving her for a week straight.

"Deal." She smiled. "Do you think we'll ever have a normal, spontaneous interaction or will everything we do together be part of some kind of prenegotiated arrangement?"

He waited to answer until she slid an album out of its cardboard sleeve, situated it on the record player, and strains of something sultry and French filled the air.

"Well?" she asked, after she'd walked back toward him and stood close enough for him to see the tiny gold flecks in the depths of her beautiful brown eyes. "Do you?"

"I really don't care one way or another, so long as I get to touch you…" He slid a hand around her to the small of her back. "…here."

She bit back a smile.

"And here," he said, taking her hand in his so that they were in a traditional dance hold.

"Well played, husband," she murmured, as they swayed to the music.

"Thank you, wife," he whispered into her hair.

They stayed like that, hand in hand, thigh to thigh, reveling in the familiar heat of one another…waltzing… wanting…until long after the music ended and their only accompaniment was the sound of their hearts, beating as one.

"Just as I suspected," Chloe said, lips moving softly against his neck. "You lied. You're a fantastic dancer."

He let out a low aching laugh. "We have to stop, or we're going to have to renegotiate another one of our key terms."

She pulled away just enough to meet his gaze. "I thought you'd never ask."

Then she rose up on tiptoe and kissed him as if she had every intention of welcoming him into her bed again, which she did.

Every single night until Christmas Eve.

Chapter 13

"All rise. The Family Court of the City of New York is now in session, the Honorable Judge Patricia Norton presiding." The bailiff stood in the corner of the room with his hands folded neatly in front of him as a robed woman entered the paneled room.

This is it, Anders thought as he rose to his feet. This was the moment that had been hanging over him since he'd learned about the special provisions in Grant's and Olivia's wills. Had it really been less than a month ago? It felt like years since he'd last seen his brother's face. So much had changed. He wondered what Grant would think if he could see him now, standing alongside Chloe.

Would he be proud?

Shocked?

Probably some combination of both, at least until he realized the marriage wasn't real. The fact that Anders had been desperate enough to hire a wife wouldn't have come as a shock to his brother at all. A disappointment, sure. But not a surprise. Everyone knew Anders Kent wasn't a family man.

Strangely enough, he felt like one now. Something about finally being face-to-face with the person who would decide whether or not he would be Lolly's father figure brought out a fiercely protective instinct that had him gripping the wooden railing separating the bench from the courtroom's front row, where he, Chloe and Lolly had been waiting with Anders's attorney. He glanced at them—at Lolly's dainty, innocent face and Chloe's exquisite, feminine features—and a familiar sense of panic seized his chest.

For weeks, the three of them had been living under the same roof. They'd eaten meals together, shared secrets and hung stockings from the mantel with their names spelled out in glitter. For six nights running, he and Chloe had spent their nights in the same bed, touching, kissing, loving. What had started out as a charade no longer felt like one. And as he looked at them now, he realized why the hollow feeling he'd felt right after Grant's accident was beginning to gnaw at him again… to consume him.

It was because some way, somehow, while they were pretending to be a family, they'd actually become one. Lolly and Chloe were his. No matter what happened here today, they would both be etched on his heart forever.

And now he might lose them both.

"You may be seated," Judge Norton said, peering down at a stack of papers on her desk after giving the people in her courtroom a cursory once-over.

Anders bit down hard, clenching his teeth. He clasped his hands in his lap to keep them from shaking.

Not now. Don't fall apart now.

He'd been handling things so well. Granted, he still couldn't bring himself to open the door to Grant's office and walk inside, but their argument was no longer the first thing his mind snagged on when he woke up in the morning or his final thought before he closed his eyes at night. He hadn't forgiven himself, because how could he? But he'd managed to push those feelings aside and get on with things. He was functioning again. He was in control, just like always.

Or so he'd thought.

"Our first order of business will be the matter of the guardianship of Lolly Kent." The judge looked up from her papers. "Is Mr. Anders Kent present?"

"Yes, Your Honor," Anders said, with a tremor in his voice that he'd never heard before—not even when he'd had to tell Lolly her parents were gone and they were never coming back.

Chloe reached for his hand and squeezed it tightly. He didn't dare look at her. To his horror, he realized that if he did, tears might well in his eyes. He hadn't shed a tear since his parents died. Even then, at seventeen, he'd cried only once—at the funeral, and never again.

"Hello, Mr. Kent." Judge Norton nodded in his direction. "I assume you have an attorney here representing you, as well?"

Anders's attorney stood, introduced himself and asked to approach the bench. He passed Lolly's birth certificate to the judge, along with copies of Grant's and Olivia's wills and the crisp new marriage license signed at the bottom by Anders and Chloe.

It was all happening so fast. Too fast. The judge

barely looked at the stack of documents before she motioned for Lolly to come forward. Lolly's little head swiveled toward Anders, her eyes wide.

"It's okay, sweetheart. She just wants to ask you a few questions." He gave his niece the most reassuring smile he could manage.

They'd known this was coming. The attorney had warned Anders and Chloe that the judge would want to talk to Lolly and ask her what living with Anders had been like. But he'd failed to tell Anders that his heart would feel like it was being ripped right out of his chest when he watched her walk toward the front of the courtroom.

"This will all be over soon," Chloe whispered. "It's going to be fine."

He dropped his gaze to his lap, where her hand still rested on top of his—covering, protecting. The diamond on her finger glittered, reflecting a kaleidoscope of light in all directions. And when he finally looked at her, it was with the knowledge that she'd done the same. She'd been a stranger who'd come into his life during its darkest moment, and she'd been more than just a convenient wife. She'd infused the darkness with goodness and light.

"Will it?" he asked. "Will it really be fine?"

Because suddenly, he didn't see how it could. The impending sense of doom in the pit of his gut wasn't about Lolly. Not entirely.

"Of course it will. Watch and see." She smiled.

I don't want to lose her. She turned away, toward

the bench where the judge was speaking in whispered tones with Lolly. *I can't* lose her.

Neither of them had said a word about what might happen after today. As far as he knew, they'd part ways on the steps of city hall the minute all this was over. They'd had a deal, and they'd both done their part.

But deals could be renegotiated. He handled mergers and contracts on a daily basis. He excelled at it. He'd simply talk to her after the hearing and suggest an extension of their arrangement. They could postpone their separation, and maybe even date like two normal people.

It would all work out. It had to. Right now he just needed to think about it rationally, like a business deal, so he could get through the rest of the guardianship proceedings.

"Thank you, Lolly." Judge Norton leaned forward and handed the little girl a candy cane. "You may sit down now. I'll make the rest of this quick since it's Christmas Eve. I'm sure you're anxious to get home. We all are."

Lolly thanked the judge in a bubbly, animated voice, prompting a titter of laughter through the courtroom. Even Anders managed a chuckle. Now that he had a plan, he could breathe again.

"All right, everything seems to be in order. It looks as though all the provisions of the guardianship have been met, and Lolly is clearly thriving under the care of Mr. Kent. I see no reason why custody can't be granted at this time." Judge Norton reached for her gavel. "I hereby appoint Anders Kent as the permanent guardian for Lolly Kent."

The gavel came down hard on the bench, marking an end to so many weeks of worry and speculation.

"Merry Christmas, Mr. and Mrs. Kent. You, too, Lolly." The judge winked. "You're a family now."

You're a family now.

The judge's words resonated in Chloe's mind with the utmost seriousness as she, Anders and Lolly made their way out of the courtroom.

As relieved as she felt that Anders had been granted permanent custody of Lolly, Chloe had never felt like more of an impostor. Of all the lies she'd told in recent weeks, her wedding to Anders had been the biggest. She'd known that going in, obviously. But it hadn't really sunk in until moments ago.

She'd been so worried about getting her heart broken that she hadn't thought long and hard enough about all the other things that could have gone wrong. What if they'd been found out? What if Anders had lost Lolly?

The devastating potential had hit her like a blow while they'd been sitting inside the courtroom. She'd held Anders's hand, and she'd done and said all the right things. But inside, she'd been terrified. Now she was almost too shaken to be relieved.

It's okay now. She concentrated on breathing in and out as Anders exchanged parting words with his lawyer. *It's all over.*

But the finality of the matter was little comfort. What, exactly, was over? Just the worry about Lolly's custody?

Or her relationship with Anders?

She swallowed and did her best to smile as Anders embraced them both in a group hug. Chloe's father used to do the same thing when she'd been a little girl. He would wrap his big arms around Emily, and then Chloe and her siblings would pile in. Her dad called it a *family* hug, and it had felt so much like this one that she couldn't quite breathe all of a sudden.

Are we a family?

Are we really?

She stepped out of the embrace and crossed her arms, steadying herself.

They should have talked about what would happen today. She had no idea whether she'd be sleeping beside Anders again tonight, whispering his name as he made love to her, or whether he expected her to pack up her things and leave.

She almost wished they'd stuck to their original agreement. At least then she would have known where she stood.

"Are you all right?" Anders studied Chloe as Lolly busied herself unwrapping her candy cane. "You've gone pale."

She nodded, blinking rapidly. "I'm fine. I just..."

I just don't know where we go from here.

I just think I might be in love with you.

She shook her head, trying to force the thought right out of it. Falling in love had never been part of the bargain. Sex was one thing, but love was another matter entirely. She didn't want to be in love. She couldn't... not with someone who might not love her back.

Been there, done that. Never again.

"Sorry. I promise I'm really fine." She cleared her throat and nodded toward the courtroom. "That was just more intense than I expected."

He curved an arm around her waist and pulled her close. "But it's over now."

There was that word again: *over.*

She stiffened against him, and something that looked suspiciously like hurt flashed in his sapphire eyes.

Chloe's cell phone rang from the depths of her purse, and she bent to search for it so she wouldn't have to see that terrible look on his face. "I should probably get this. It might be my mom or Allegra calling about the recital tonight."

Anders nodded and crossed his arms, and for a quiet, confusing moment, he looked exactly as he had the first time she'd ever laid eyes on him—all hard lines and chiseled resistance. It made her heart beat hard in her chest, and when she finally located her phone, her hands shook as she dragged it out of her bag.

"Oh," she said, frowning down at the device's small screen.

"Is it about the recital?" Anders asked.

"No." Chloe swallowed. "It's the Rockettes."

The contact information for Susan Morgan, the dance troupe's general manager, flashed on her phone's display. Chloe hadn't spoken directly to Susan since the day she'd been removed from the performance schedule. Her reindeer shifts were supervised by someone much further down the chain of command.

"Answer it." Anders arched a brow. "It could be good news, right?"

It could.

Or it could be bad news, but either way, knowing would be better than uncertainty. *Nothing* in her life was certain at the moment, especially her relationship status. Facebook needed to invent a whole new description for this scenario.

She fixed her gaze with Anders's and pressed the button to accept the call. "Hello?"

"Hello, this is Susan Morgan from the Rockettes. Is this Chloe?"

"Yes, it is. Hi, Ms. Morgan." She gave Anders a slight smile. Susan sounded cheerful, not at all like a person who was about to fire somebody on Christmas Eve.

"Excellent. Listen, Chloe. I know this is last minute, but I also know you're anxious to start performing again. I've heard you've been working really hard on the promotional end of things, and I assure you that your time spent on flyer duty hasn't gone unnoticed."

"That's good to hear." Chloe began to pace in front of the low bench where Lolly sat swinging her legs to and fro.

This was it. She was getting her job back, and her life was finally going to return to normal. Chloe had been waiting for this moment for a long time—since Thanksgiving Day.

She wasn't sure why it didn't seem as exciting as she'd thought it would.

"One of the girls in the touring company just sprained her ankle, and we need a replacement. If you're able to leave for Branson tomorrow, the spot is yours."

Susan's voice brimmed with enthusiasm, as if she was Santa Claus granting Chloe's biggest Christmas wish.

"Branson?" Chloe's feet stilled, and Anders's eyes locked with hers. "I don't understand."

The Rockettes had a smaller group of dancers that toured the country, performing in various venues, from coast to coast. The touring company traveled by bus, and they were on the road for up to nine months of the year. Chloe had never performed with the touring group, nor did she know any of its members.

"If you want to get back onstage, this is your chance. The bus leaves tomorrow afternoon," Susan said.

"But tomorrow is Christmas."

Now it was Anders's face that went pale.

"I'm emailing you the details. Think it over and let me know as soon as possible." Chloe could hear Susan's fingers tapping on her computer keyboard. "But I'm going to be honest with you, Chloe. This is a onetime chance. It's this or nothing. Understood?"

"Yes," Chloe said. "I do."

I do.

Wedding words.

She ended the call and glanced up at the puzzled expression on her husband's face.

"Good news?" he asked, and there was an edge to his voice that rubbed her entirely the wrong way.

He didn't know the facts, and besides, she wasn't sure she even wanted to go on tour. Shouldn't they talk about what was happening between them?

Was there anything happening between them, or had she simply been fooling herself all this time?

"Yes," she said woodenly. "They want me to join the touring company."

"I see." He cleared his throat. "Congratulations."

Seriously? That was all he had to say? *Congratulations?*

She still hadn't said she was actually going anywhere. And she didn't know what she expected him to say, but she definitely thought it would be something more than a single word.

Her chest grew tight, and a flare of panic hit her somewhere behind her breastbone.

Actually, a single word would have been fine. She just thought it would be a different one. The word she most wanted to hear wasn't *congratulations*; it was *stay*.

Oh God, he wasn't going to say it, was he? Their deal was over, and he was perfectly fine with her turning around and walking away.

"The tour leaves tomorrow." What was she doing? She was acting as though she wanted to be on a bus to Branson tomorrow when that was not what she wanted at all.

She bit her lip and blinked up at him.

Please ask me. Please just say it.

Stay.

"I heard." He took a deep breath, and for a moment he looked at her in a way that reminded her so much of the way he had on their wedding day that her panic ebbed. Maybe she really did love him, and maybe—just maybe—he loved her, too.

But then his gaze shifted until he was no longer looking her in the eyes, but instead at a blank space slightly over her head. "A clean break is probably for the best."

He didn't mean it.

He couldn't.

She waited for a good three seconds, giving him as much of a chance as she could for him to take it back, to somehow make those terrible words go away.

But he didn't. He let them settle into her bones, into her soul, until the only thing she could do was turn around and walk away, with her heart breaking cleanly in two.

"But I don't understand." Emily Wilde's coffee sat untouched on the table in the cozy kitchen of the brownstone as she stared blankly at Chloe.

Breaking the news to her mom about the Rockettes tour wasn't going nearly as well as Chloe had expected, and she hadn't even gotten to the part about her marriage being a big fat fake. She'd hoped the pair of gingerbread lattes she'd picked up en route from the courthouse would soften the blow, but clearly it was going to take more than a Christmas-flavored beverage to worm her way out of the mess she'd created.

"Why would you leave to go on tour? It doesn't make any sense." Emily picked up the coffee and put it back down without taking a sip. Not a good sign.

Chloe took a deep breath. "Because if I don't go, I won't be a Rockette anymore."

It was time to tell the truth…about everything. "I lied about why I haven't been performing the past few weeks. I wasn't injured. I was fired."

She winced, waiting for the dressing-down that was surely coming. She definitely deserved it.

But instead of rebuking her, Emily just shook her

head and smiled. "I wondered when you were going to get around to telling me the truth."

Chloe blinked. "You mean you knew?"

"Yes, dear. Of course I knew. I've been a ballet teacher long enough to know when a dancer is too hurt to perform and when she's faking it." She lifted a brow. "I'm also your mother, so I know when you're going through something. I didn't want to push. I figured you'd tell me when the time was right."

Her mother had known the entire time. Chloe wasn't sure whether that made her feel better or worse. Then again, she was about as low as she could possibly get at the moment. There was no *worse*. This was it. This was heartbreak.

She took a shuddering inhalation and blinked hard against the tears that she'd been holding back all afternoon. If she cried now, she'd never stop. All she had to do was get through the rest of the day and the recital later tonight. Once she was on a bus headed away from Manhattan, she could cry all she wanted.

"I guess now's the time." She gave her mom a watery smile. "I didn't want to tell you. I was ashamed because I'd put my career first for so long, and when it all came crashing down, I realized how much I'd missed my family. I wanted to make it up to you..."

"Oh honey. Is that what working at the school and the new floors and the rest of the improvements have been about?"

Chloe nodded. "Yes."

But that wasn't quite the truth, was it? Not all of it, anyway. And she didn't want to lie anymore. It was too exhausting. Lies had led her to where she was right now, and she'd never felt more lost. "It started out that way, but spending so much time there made me remember how much I love it. I don't want to see the school close, Mom. It can't."

Emily's lips curved into a bittersweet smile. "The school won't be there forever, but that's okay. If and when it closes, I'll be okay. So will you. In the end, it's just a building. The heart of the studio is our family, and family is forever. You don't need to ask my forgiveness or make up for anything. I love you unconditionally, sweetheart. I'm just glad you've finally come home, no matter what brought you back."

And now she was leaving again.

Chloe stared down at her coffee. She couldn't bring herself to meet her mother's gaze anymore. She knew what going on tour would look like. It would seem like she was running out on Anders and Lolly, like she was making her same old mistakes. Which was precisely why she didn't want to go.

She had to, though. Her pretend marriage had turned into a very real disaster. Anders had point-blank told her she should leave.

Perfect timing...a clean break.

The words kept spinning in her mind, over and over again. She couldn't make them stop.

"Stay," Emily whispered. Then she said it again, louder this time. "Stay, Chloe. Don't go on tour."

They were the words she'd longed to hear, the only words that mattered. But they were coming from the wrong person. "Mom, I can't..."

"I'm not asking you to stay for me or for the school. Stay for Anders and Lolly. They need you, but more than that, you need them."

Truer words had never been spoken.

She closed her eyes, and the judge's words came back to her.

Merry Christmas, Mr. and Mrs. Anders. You're a family now.

But they weren't. And she couldn't need Lolly and Anders. She had no right.

"There's something else." She pushed her coffee cup away. The gingerbread scent was making her sick. It reminded her too much of reading Christmas stories to Lolly, decorating the tree in Anders's penthouse and the way she'd looked out his bedroom window and watched the skaters spinning round and round on the frozen pond below while he'd wrapped his arms around from behind and pressed tender kisses to her shoulder.

"I suspected as much," Emily said calmly. Too calmly, as if she knew exactly what Chloe was about to say.

Was her mother some kind of mind reader? Or was Chloe just *that* transparent?

The latter, probably. She felt as delicate as tissue paper right now. "The only reason Anders and I got married was so he could be appointed as Lolly's guardian. The hearing was earlier today."

There. She'd said it. She'd confessed all.

She'd been holding so much inside that she should have felt unburdened, but she didn't. It still felt as if there was a ten-pound weight attached to her heart.

"And?" Emily prompted.

Chloe swallowed. "He won. It's over."

"Are you sure those two things go hand in hand?" her mother asked quietly.

"Yes." She was tired of fooling herself. She couldn't do it anymore. Since the night Anders had helped her paint the studio, she'd let herself pretend their marriage bargain was in the past. Technically, there'd never been a formal contract. Maybe on some level, Anders hadn't wanted one. Maybe she'd been different. Special.

Now she knew the truth. She wasn't. She could have been anyone.

"I'm not going to pretend that I didn't have doubts about you and Anders. It all came about very suddenly, but I supported you—as did the rest of your family— because you assured us it was what you wanted. Biting my tongue was hard, but not for long." Emily reached forward and cupped Chloe's cheek, forcing her to meet her gaze. "Look at me, sweetheart. Listen to what I'm saying. That man loves you. Maybe he can't articulate it, or maybe he hasn't realized it yet, but he does. It's been written all over his face since the morning after your wedding. He's been through a lot. He lost his brother, and from what you've said, he nearly lost Lolly. If you love him, too, you owe it to him to give him more time."

"He could have asked me to stay, but he didn't." Chloe choked on a sob. "It's too late."

"Oh honey, it's never too late. Not while you're still wearing his ring."

Chapter 14

Chloe toyed with the diamond on her finger as the elevator carried her to the top floor of Anders's office building.

How could she have forgotten to return the ring?

She hadn't even realized she'd still been wearing it until her mother pointed it out. It had become part of her in the same way that a dancer's choreography became rote after enough repetition. Muscle memory, they called it. A body remembered what it was supposed to do—feet moved in time to music without the dancer having to give it conscious thought. Most people thought that memories lived only in the mind, but they were wrong.

And now the ring felt as if it belonged on her finger. The day Anders had given it to her, it felt so foreign, so strange. She couldn't stop looking at it, even though she knew it didn't mean anything. It was just a symbol, part of the charade.

Somewhere along the way, she'd forgotten that significant fact. It had become more than a ring. More than a diamond. It was a sparkling part of her heart, a memory belonging to the body's hardest-working muscle of all.

She slipped it off and tucked it into her coat pocket as the elevator slowed to a stop. Keeping it was out of the question. It had to be worth a fortune. But she definitely didn't want to return it to him at the recital later. She was planning on staying as far away from him as she possibly could. It was her only hope of getting through the night and doing her job without breaking down.

Nor did she want to go to the penthouse. If a clean break was what he wanted, she'd give him one. He was supposed to be out of the office all day, so she'd simply put it in an envelope and leave it in his desk drawer. She'd send him a text, so it wouldn't come as a surprise. It was the polite thing to do.

She shook her head. Good grief, their parting was all so civilized and businesslike, the complete opposite of a normal breakup. It was ending in the same way it had begun. Maybe that was fitting.

Or maybe you're still fooling yourself.

The elevator doors slid open, and there was nothing businesslike about the way her heart pounded when she pushed through the paneled entry of Anders's investment banking firm, or the way the diamond felt like it was burning a hole in her pocket—all light and heat, out of sight but not out of mind.

"Mrs. Kent." Anders's assistant, Mrs. Summers, knitted her brow as Chloe approached. "I'm afraid Mr. Kent isn't in right now. He took the afternoon off."

"Yes, I know." Her gaze darted toward the closed

door to Anders's office. "I just need to drop something off. Is it okay if I go inside?"

"Of course. We're closing in just a few minutes, though, so everyone can run last-minute Christmas errands."

"It won't take long. Thanks so much." She wished Mrs. Summers a merry Christmas and then stepped inside the office, clicking the door shut behind her.

Chloe flipped the lights on and then paused, feeling like an intruder. The space was so quintessentially Anders, with the same sleek, classic decor as the penthouse. It even smelled like him, warm and woodsy.

She hadn't set foot in this building since the day she'd turned up in her reindeer costume to insist that Lolly keep the puppy, and instead had ended up engaged to be married. Something about the space seemed different, but she couldn't put her finger on it.

It didn't matter, though, did it? She just needed to leave the ring somewhere safe and get to the Wilde School of Dance so she could prepare for the recital. She had plenty to keep her busy until the touring company left town. If she just kept moving, maybe she'd get through the next twenty hours in one piece.

It wasn't until she crossed the room that she realized what was different about the office. A collection of shiny new picture frames decorated the bookshelves to the right of the desk. Her breath caught in her throat when she saw that each and every one of the photographs were of either her or Lolly. But then she turned her back on the frames and reminded herself that they were only props, just like her. All for show.

She moved behind Anders's desk, searching for an envelope. There weren't any—not anywhere on the desk and not in any of the neatly organized trays on the credenza. She should probably ask Mrs. Summers for one, but that might lead to questions that Chloe was in no way prepared to answer.

She was going to have to open one of the drawers and pray that no one walked through the door and thought she was snooping.

Just do it and get it over with.

Chloe slid open Anders's top center drawer as quickly as possible, but as soon as she saw what was inside, she froze.

It was a file folder labeled *Premarital Agreement*, and the sight of it caught her so completely off guard that she couldn't seem to move. Or breathe. Or even blink.

Was this the contract that Anders kept talking about in the beginning, but that never seemed to materialize? It had to be, right?

There was only one way to find out. And even though looking at it would be painful, maybe she needed to see it. Maybe it would remind her what she'd signed up for in the first place. Not a real relationship, and definitely not love.

Love.

Was she in love with Anders? She couldn't be, could she? People didn't fall in love in a matter of weeks. She was just suffering from an intense case of Christmas infatuation.

She flipped open the file folder, fully prepared for the words on the contract to reinforce her theory. If there was one way to convince herself she wasn't in love, seeing the details of their marriage spelled out in black and white would surely do the trick.

But the name at the top of the contract wasn't hers; it was Penelope's. The only contract in the folder was the very same one she'd spotted on Anders's desk weeks ago. She flipped through the entire stack of papers just to be sure, but her name wasn't on any of them. Only Penelope Reed's.

Chloe's name wasn't the only notable omission, either. None of the numbered pages included a single mention of an engagement ring.

But that didn't make sense. She'd specifically asked Anders if the sparkling diamond was part of the contract and he'd said yes. It was all part of the package— the package he'd first offered to Penelope.

Unless it wasn't.

For the first time since their tense exchange in the courthouse hallway, Chloe's heart felt as if it were expanding instead of shrinking into nothingness. Could it be true? Could the ring have been meant for her all along?

If so, maybe she'd never been just an interchangeable, convenient bride. Maybe what she and Anders had really meant something. Maybe it had all along.

Maybe it really *was* love.

She pressed a hand to her breastbone to try to calm the frantic beating of her heart. She wanted to believe Anders loved her. She wanted to believe she'd been different from the very beginning. She hadn't realized how very much she wanted to believe until right that second.

She squeezed her eyes closed tight and let herself imagine, just for a moment, that everything had been real. And a feeling so pure, so sweet wrapped itself around her heart that it was like Christmas Past, Christmas Present and Christmas Future all rolled into one. Timeless.

When her eyes fluttered open, the first thing her gaze landed on was a picture frame at the head of Anders's desk. Inside was a photograph of Chloe on their wedding day, and it wasn't facing outward like all the other newly framed pictures in the office. The photo faced Anders's chair, where only he could see it.

Her eyes swam with tears.

What had she done?

Her mother was right. She'd been so ready to believe Anders didn't love her that she'd acted as if she really wanted to go on tour, when all the while he'd been sitting at this desk every day looking at her picture. And now it was too late—too late to tell him she wanted more, too late to stay.

Or was it? Emily's words from earlier echoed in her consciousness, as sharp and clear as if her mother was whispering them in her ear. *Oh honey, it's never too late. Not while you're still wearing his ring.*

Chloe picked up the diamond, and with tears streaming down her face, she gingerly slid it onto her finger.

Back where it belonged.

Anders moved in a daze after he left city hall.

He remembered holding Lolly's tiny hand in his, but he couldn't quite recall walking down the build-

ing's wide marble steps or sliding into the town car
that waited for them at the curb. It was as if one minute
he'd been standing in that awful, institutional hallway
watching Chloe walk away, and the next, he was sitting inside the car, staring blankly at his driver's face
in the rearview mirror, unable to answer the question
that had been posed to him.

"Sir," the driver repeated, more slowly this time.
"Shall we wait for Mrs. Kent?"

Anders blinked. Hard. "Ah, no. She won't be joining us."

The driver's gaze flitted briefly to the columned
building, and his brow furrowed. Mercifully, he didn't
press for an explanation. "Yes, sir."

Then the car was winding its way through the holiday traffic, and once again Anders felt as if he were in a
dream—a garish nightmare in which everything around
him was too loud and too bright. The tree in Rockefeller
Center loomed over the block, dark and terrible, and the
animated store windows on Fifth Avenue seemed to be
moving in double time. Snow flurries whirled dizzily
past the car window, making him sick to his stomach,
so he closed his eyes and leaned against the headrest.

Anders loved Manhattan. He loved that he could
walk down the street and hear multiple languages spoken all at the same time. He loved the way the subway
was like a spool of Christmas ribbon, tying all the different parts of the city together, making it feel like he
could be anywhere in a matter of minutes. He loved the
way the lights of the surrounding skyscrapers made
the East River shimmer at nighttime, like liquid gold.

Most of all, though, he loved the way the sidewalks and the streets pulsed with life at all hours of the day and night. All the hustle and bustle, all the noise—they made it easier to forget that sometimes his chest felt hollow and empty. Even the loneliest person in the world could feel a little less isolated in Manhattan.

But now the city he loved so much was betraying him. His life had come to a screeching halt, and everywhere he looked, people kept moving. Throngs of last-minute shoppers filled the streets, and the decorations that transformed the gray, urban grit into an enchanted wonderland—the giant stack of oversize red ornaments on Sixth Avenue and the neat rows of trumpeting angels that towered over Rockefeller Center—seemed more surreal than beautiful.

What the hell had just happened?

Lolly was safe. She was *his*. The judge had called the three of them a family, and immediately afterward, he'd somehow let Chloe walk away.

No, that wasn't quite right. He'd pushed her away.

A clean break is probably best.

He'd actually said those words, as if a clean break from Chloe was what he wanted, when it wasn't at all. He didn't want any kind of a break.

He tried to take a deep breath, but his throat closed up.

You did the right thing.

He'd done it for her. Chloe deserved better than what he'd offered her, better than a fake marriage to a man who'd made a mess of every personal relationship he'd ever had. She deserved the world.

He knew she wanted to dance again. She'd told him so herself at Soho House. If performing again hadn't meant so much to her, she wouldn't have kept turning up in Times Square in that crazy, blinking reindeer suit.

A smile came to his lips at the memory of the day they'd first met, at the animal shelter. He would never look at a reindeer the same way again. Or Christmas, for that matter.

Lolly tugged at the sleeve of his coat and he turned to face her. He needed to keep it together. But, damn it, how was he going to explain Chloe's sudden absence from the penthouse? On Christmas, no less. "Hey, sweetie."

"Your phone is ringing," Lolly said. "Don't you hear it?"

He hadn't heard it, probably because it was just part of the sensory overload that was bombarding him at the moment. So much noise, so many feelings…all pressing in around him.

"Thanks. I'll get it." He ruffled her hair and managed a smile. She grinned back up at him and then went back to sucking on her candy cane and looking out the window at the snowfall.

Anders pulled his ringing cell phone from his pocket, and for a brief moment of pure optimism, he thought perhaps it was Chloe. But it was the office, of course—at two in the afternoon on Christmas Eve.

Mrs. Summers's familiar contact information flashed on the display, and as if by rote, his thumb hovered over the accept-call button, but he stopped just shy of pressing it.

The old Anders would have answered the call in a heartbeat, but he didn't want to be that person anymore. He was Lolly's father figure now, the only family she had. He wanted to be better. He *needed* to be better. Whatever was happening at the firm could wait.

So he did something he'd never done before in his entire professional career. He let a call from his assistant roll to voice mail. And he had no qualms about it, until the phone started ringing again almost immediately afterward. Mrs. Summers never bombarded him with repeat calls. Then again, he usually picked up the first time.

Something was wrong. He could feel it. He wasn't sure what it could possibly be on Christmas Eve, but it had to be important.

He glanced at Lolly again, but her gaze was still glued on the scene out the window, so he finally took the call. "Hello?"

"I'm sorry to bother you, Mr. Kent. I know it's Christmas Eve, and the office is about to close." Mrs. Summers's voice lowered to a murmur. "But Mrs. Kent is here, and she seems rather…sad…so I thought I should call."

Anders's heart hammered hard in his chest. "Chloe is there?"

"Yes. She's in your office. I hope it's okay that I let her go inside."

"It's fine." Chloe didn't want to see him. That much was obvious, since she knew he wouldn't be at the office. "I'm glad you called."

It's clearly over. Let it go.

"I was just on my way out, but I can stay if you like."

She cleared her throat. "You know, in case you'd like me to keep her company and give you time to get here."

Subtlety had never been his assistant's strong suit. She'd obviously picked up on the fact that there was trouble in paradise.

Mrs. Summers knew the marriage was only temporary. So did Penelope. Why was he the only one who seemed to remember that significant detail?

Chloe remembers.

He ground his teeth. "Thank you, but that won't be necessary. You have a merry Christmas."

As soon as he ended the call, the driver met his gaze in the rearview mirror. "Mr. Kent, has there been a change in plans or are we still headed to the penthouse?"

"No, I…" Anders looked up and realized the car was sitting in traffic, gridlocked in the familiar landscape of the West Village. As usual, a crowd was lined up at Magnolia Bakery, just to his right. Right around the corner was the Wilde School of Dance.

Allegra would be there. So would Emily. If he stopped there now, they might be willing to watch Lolly for him if he wanted to get to the office and see Chloe… in private…for a proper goodbye. She deserved that much, didn't she?

By now, though, her family probably knew the truth. They'd probably despise him on sight.

Was he really that desperate?

A final goodbye. One last kiss.

Yes…yes, he was. "Actually, there's been a change of plans."

Chapter 15

By the time Anders dropped off Lolly and made his way to the financial district in the Christmas Eve traffic, he was too late.

Allegra had greeted Lolly with open arms and treated him in the same easy, lovable manner she always did. Emily had been quiet and there'd been a bittersweet, knowing smile on her lips when he'd told her he needed to find Chloe so they could talk. She knew. He was certain of it. But she'd been nice enough not to mention that he hadn't exactly been the husband her daughter deserved, and said simply, "Go find Chloe. Lolly can stay here, and we'll see you later tonight at the recital."

There'd been such hope in his heart on the way, but now here he was, and his office was empty, as quiet as a tomb. There was no sign Chloe had even been there. If he hadn't gotten the call from Mrs. Summers, he would have never known.

He ran into the hallway, darting from room to room, searching for her—searching for some kind of hint as to why she'd shown up. It didn't make sense. Nor did his frantic hunt through the office, but he didn't know what else to do. He just knew he needed to keep moving, because if he dared stand still, the reality of her absence would be too much. Too real.

He stopped short of the door at the end of the hall—the room he'd been avoiding for weeks. His brow broke into a cold sweat and his hands clenched and unclenched at his sides, as if he was preparing for a fight.

But he was tired of fighting. So very, very tired. He'd been fighting for weeks—fighting his grief, fighting his feelings for Chloe, fighting anything and everything trying to make its way into his cold, dead heart.

He stared at the closed door, letting his gaze linger on the familiar name embossed on the wood paneling.

Grant Kent.

He reached a shaky hand toward the doorknob.

Now's not the time. Walk away.

When was the time, though? Was he going to avoid entering this room for the rest of his life? Was he just going to keep walking away every time he began to come face-to-face with what he'd lost…?

Just like he was doing now.

Just like what you did with Chloe.

His hand clamped down on the knob and turned. Then he pushed the door open as he'd done a thousand times before, only this time it wasn't to crunch some numbers or argue over an IPO or a contract or a million other things that Anders had always thought were so important but never really mattered.

This time, he was here to say goodbye.

He walked inside, marveling at how normal everything seemed. Papers were still strewn all over Grant's desk, and if his laptop hadn't been closed, it would have looked as if he'd just stepped out for a minute and would be right back. It smelled the same, too, like the aftershave Grant used after his lunchtime gym sessions, with just a hint of the Cuban cigars he brought out whenever one of them pulled off a significant business deal. Light streamed in the windows through a lacy veil of frost and snow, making it seem as if the office had been frozen in time.

Anders knew better.

Time kept spinning forward. People moved on.

Only if you let them.

The words came to him, as clear and distinct as if Grant had spoken them out loud.

"What are you trying to tell me, brother?" Anders whispered.

Great. He was talking to ghosts now.

Except there were no ghosts here. Anders knew that. If Grant's spirit lingered anywhere, it wouldn't be in this room. He'd be somewhere else, someplace more meaningful. Someplace where he could see his daughter or the spot where he'd first kissed Olivia or even Yankee Stadium for an afternoon of beer and baseball. His brother worked to live, not the other way around. How many times had he tried to explain that to Anders?

He still hadn't learned. Today was Christmas Eve, and look where he was standing. What was he doing?

Searching for her.

Searching for a life like the one his brother had lived. Searching for love.

He *loved* Chloe.

How could he have thought otherwise, even for a second?

If she wanted to go on tour, that was fine. He'd support her in whatever she chose to do, but she needed to know that when she came home, he'd be right there waiting for her. So would Lolly. And even Prancer, too.

Because they were a family.

He'd made a vow, and he intended to keep it—not because of some stupid agreement or because he needed a wife, but because he wanted one. He wanted *her*, and it was time he let her know. He'd gotten here too late and she wasn't here, but he knew where to find her.

Anders took one last look around, remembering all the time he'd spent in this office. Times when he and Grant had laughed, times when they'd argued. Somehow he'd forgotten that the former far outweighed the latter. Echoes of that laughter rolled over him now, and he realized that no matter what Grant's intentions had been when he'd signed his will, the marriage provision on Lolly's guardianship had ended up being a gift—a fateful, final Christmas present from one brother to another, the gift Anders needed most of all.

Thank you, brother.

"Where's Uncle Anders?" Lolly peered through the classroom window as Chloe wound a pink satin ribbon around the little girl's high ponytail.

Baby Nutcracker was set to start in just ten minutes. Lolly was all dressed up in her Clara costume—a long ruffled nightgown with a fluffy petticoat that swished around her slender legs when she twirled. Her face had lit up like a Christmas tree when she'd first put it on, and ever since she'd taken that initial glimpse of herself in the mirrored walls of the studio, she'd been asking for Anders.

"He'll be here. I know he will. He wouldn't miss this for the world," Chloe whispered and gave the little girl a kiss on the cheek. "It's probably good that he hasn't seen you yet. Won't he be surprised when you chassé onto the stage?"

Lolly nodded and giggled, appeased for the time being, and Chloe guided her to the spot off to the side of the classroom where the other kids were seated and waiting for the performance to start. They had six mice, six snowflakes, three sugarplums and a few fairies and snow queens. But as Lolly pointed out with pride, only one Clara. She was the star of the show.

And her uncle was nowhere in sight.

"Mom," Chloe whispered, pulling Emily behind the Christmas tree in the lobby—the closest thing to privacy they could get, since the school was filled with wall-to-wall parents, grandparents and siblings, all waiting to watch the adorable holiday spectacle. "Anders still isn't here. What *exactly* did he say when he dropped Lolly off earlier?"

"He said you were at his office and he needed to talk to you about something." Emily took a deep breath. "Something important."

They'd missed one another, which wasn't surprising, considering the streets were filled with last-minute shoppers and people on their way to Christmas Eve services at church or other holiday celebrations…like the one she was in charge of, starring his niece. Which was supposed to start in less than five minutes.

She tried her hardest not to think about what he'd wanted to say to her, but possibilities kept pirouetting through her head, each one worse than the next.

He'd had goodbyes in his eyes back at city hall, and he probably wanted to get the ring back. Or the key to his penthouse. Things he couldn't have said in front of Lolly.

Of course Mrs. Summers had called and told him Chloe was there. She didn't know why she hadn't anticipated it, other than she hadn't been thinking clearly. She'd been moving on autopilot, doing her best to survive until she went on tour the following day.

There would be no tour now. No more sequined reindeer costumes, no more passing out flyers in Times Square. Not for Chloe. She'd already called and officially resigned from the Rockettes roster. She wanted to teach full-time at the Wilde School of Dance. She wanted to stay right where she was, and if Anders still wanted a clean break, she'd give him one. She'd move into the Wilde family brownstone if she had to, but she wasn't leaving New York. She was home to stay.

"Lolly will be crushed if he doesn't get here in time," she said, just as the overhead lights dimmed. She waved her arms at Allegra, standing on the other side of the room, trying to signal for her to slow down. To wait just a few more minutes. But her sister-in-law was already placing the needle of the record player on the smooth, rotating surface of the Tchaikovsky album.

The opening bars of the beloved *Nutcracker* score filled the air, and Chloe couldn't wait any longer. It was time for her to lead the children onto the center of the new Marley floor for the beginning party scene.

"Look, dear." Her mother gave her arm a squeeze. "He's here."

Her heart gave a not-so-little pang, and beyond the fragrant boughs of the evergreen tree, she saw Anders push through the front door of the studio and rush into the classroom.

He stood in the very back, against the wall, where, as usual, his presence seemed to fill up the space and steal the breath from Chloe's lungs.

She stared at him for a beat, frozen, until Emily cleared her throat. "Are the children going to hit their cue, or are we going to have to start the music over again from the beginning?"

Right. There was a recital happening, and she was the person in charge of it.

"I'm on it!" Chloe slipped as discreetly as possible to where the kids sat, waiting to go on.

Chloe's mom had always believed in holding recitals for the very young children here in the school rather than in a stuffy auditorium. Her theory was that the familiar, intimate setting made it less scary for the kids, which definitely seemed to be the case. Three-year-olds, four-year-olds and five-year-olds needed encouragement, not an intimidating introduction to performing that could lead to debilitating stage fright.

She crouched down and gave them a last-minute pep talk as the prelude started to wind down. "Remember, guys, this is just like class. Only this time you're all dressed up, and tonight is Christmas Eve."

Miraculously, they all glided to the center of the floor, hand in hand, just as Chloe had taught them. She considered it a minor victory that none of the little ones cried, although one of the mice stood, holding the tail of her costume for a full minute or two, instead of doing the simple somersault combination they'd been practicing every day for a week. But about a third of the way into the program, she finally started moving her feet.

Chloe stood off to the side, marking the choreography with subtle movements so her students could follow along in case they got confused. Her position so close to the mirror allowed her to steal a glance every so often at Anders, still positioned at the back of the room.

His attention was trained on Lolly, who floated across the floor with a wide smile and a wave for her uncle. He waved back at her, and then, so quick that Chloe almost thought she'd imagined it, his gaze locked with hers in the mirror. He winked.

Then, in a flash, he was watching the performance again, and she was left to wonder if it had really happened. Had her temporary husband just shot her a flirty little wink just hours after they'd agreed to a clean break? If so, this might not be such a blue Christmas, after all. It could possibly be the best she'd ever had.

It took every ounce of concentration she could muster to keep miming the footwork for the kids, but the half-hour program passed quickly, punctuated by hearty applause and several bursts of laughter from the parents. In the end, even the children were surprised when the wind machine Chloe had secretly rented from a Broadway theater company blew tiny bits of fake snow all over the makeshift stage.

The audience rose to its feet as the classroom was transformed into a winter wonderland. And for some silly reason, Chloe's eyes filled with tears.

She'd received a standing ovation more times than she could count at Radio City Music Hall, one of the oldest and most storied theaters in the country. Never had it meant as much as this one did, though. Because this time, she wasn't made up to look exactly like the other thirty-five dancers onstage. She was simply herself, Chloe Wilde.

But that wasn't quite true, was it? Her name was Chloe Wilde Kent, and as her students danced and twirled in the swirling bits of snow, her husband was walking straight toward her through the parted crowd with two bouquets of red roses in his arms.

She froze, unable to move, unable to breathe. If this was some kind of wonderful Christmas daydream, she didn't want to know. She wanted to stay in this perfect, private snow globe forever, where she was surrounded by her family—and where that family included a little girl dressed in a nightgown and ballet slippers, and a man who never failed to take her breath away.

Anders bent to give one of the bouquets to Lolly. Then Chloe took her attention away from him long enough to lock eyes with Emily through the dizzying snow flurries, and her mother simply mouthed the words *I love you*, followed by *Merry Christmas*.

"I love you, too," Chloe whispered.

Merry Christmas, indeed.

Then Anders was right there, just inches away, with snow in his hair and a look in his eyes that was so reverent, so pure that her tears spilled over and streamed down her face.

He handed her the bouquet in his arms and said, "Don't cry, love," so softly that she could barely hear his lovely baritone above the strains of Tchaikovsky, mixed with the happy sounds of children, parents and grandparents. Of family.

And then Anders cupped her face, brushing her tears away with the pads of his thumbs. His hands smelled of winter and roses—so good and familiar that it was like being wrapped in a blanket. Then his face grew serious as he said, "I lied, Chloe. I don't want a clean break. Not now, not ever. I'm in love with you. There's nothing in this world more real than the feelings I have for you."

"I love you, too," she breathed.

There was so much to say, so many promises to make, but before she could utter another word, he dropped down on one knee and smiled up at her from the floor, now completely covered in white, like an up-turned bowl of sugar.

He took her hand and kissed the diamond ring on her finger—the one she'd never take off again. "Will you stay married to me, Chloe? I know the proposal is a little late, but I never asked you properly the first time."

All around them, tiny ballerinas sprawled on the ground, waving their arms and legs, giggling and making snow angels. It didn't matter to them that the snow wasn't real or that they were in a ballet studio dressed in recital costumes instead of bundled up in frosty Central Park.

They believed.

Sometimes pretending was better than the real thing. Sometimes it was a precious, perfect gift.

"Yes." Chloe nodded. "I will absolutely stay married to you."

Anders rose to his feet to kiss her, and as her eyes drifted closed and his mouth came down on hers, warm and sweet, she was conscious of only one, overriding thought.

I believe, too.

She believed in love. She believed in Anders. She believed in *them*.

And for the first Christmas in a very long time, she believed in the magic of make-believe.

* * * * *

**IF YOU ENJOYED THIS BOOK
WE THINK YOU WILL ALSO LOVE**

HARLEQUIN
SPECIAL
EDITION

Believe in love. Overcome obstacles. Find happiness.

Relate to finding comfort and strength in the
support of loved ones and enjoy the journey
no matter what life throws your way.

6 NEW BOOKS AVAILABLE EVERY MONTH!

HSEXSERIES2020

SPECIAL EXCERPT FROM

(H) HARLEQUIN
SPECIAL EDITION

When Grace Williams topples from the balcony at the new Hotel Fortune, the last thing she expects is to find love with her new bosses' brother. Wiley Fortune has looks, money and charm to spare. But Grace's past makes her wary of investing her heart. This time, she is holding out for the real deal...

Read on for a sneak peek at
Her Texas New Year's Wish
by Michelle Major, the first book in
The Fortunes of Texas: The Hotel Fortune!

"I didn't fall," she announced with a wide smile as he returned the crutches.

"You did great." He looked at her with a huge smile.

"That was silly," she said as they started down the walk toward his car. "Maneuvering down a few steps isn't a big deal, but this is the farthest I've gone on my own since the accident. If my parents had their way, they'd encase me in Bubble Wrap for the rest of my life to make sure I stayed safe."

"It's an understandable sentiment from people who care about you."

"But not what I want."

He opened the car door for her, and she gave him the crutches to stow in the back seat. The whole process was slow and awkward. By the time Grace was buckled in next to Wiley, sweat dripped between her shoulder blades, and she felt like she'd run a marathon. How could less than a week of inactivity make her feel like such an invalid?

As if sensing her frustration, Wiley placed a gentle hand on her arm. "You've been through a lot, Grace. Your ankle and the cast are the biggest outward signs of the accident, but you fell from the second story."

She offered a wan smile. "I have the bruises to prove it."

"Give yourself a bit of…well, grace."

"I never thought of attorneys as naturally comforting people," she admitted. "But you're good at giving support."

"It's a hidden skill." He released her hand and pulled away from the curb. "We lawyers don't like to let anyone know about our human side. It ruins the reputation of being coldhearted, and then people aren't afraid of us."

"You're the opposite of scary."

"Where are we headed?" he asked when he got to the stop sign at the end of the block.

"The highway," she said without hesitation. "As much as I love Rambling Rose, I need a break. Let's get out of this town, Wiley."

Don't miss
Her Texas New Year's Wish *by Michelle Major,*
available January 2021 wherever
Harlequin Special Edition books and ebooks are sold.

Harlequin.com

Copyright © 2020 by Michelle Major

HSEEXP1220

*Heartfelt or suspenseful,
inspiring or passionate, Harlequin
has your happily-ever-after.*

With new books published
every month, you are sure to find the
satisfying escape you know you deserve.

SIGN UP FOR THE HARLEQUIN NEWSLETTER

Be the first to hear about great new
reads and exciting offers!

Harlequin.com/newsletters

HNEWS2020

Love Harlequin romance?

DISCOVER.

Be the first to find out about promotions,
news and exclusive content!

Facebook.com/HarlequinBooks

Twitter.com/HarlequinBooks

Instagram.com/HarlequinBooks

Pinterest.com/HarlequinBooks

ReaderService.com

EXPLORE.

Sign up for the Harlequin e-newsletter and
download a free book from any series at
TryHarlequin.com

CONNECT.

Join our Harlequin community to
share your thoughts and connect
with other romance readers!
Facebook.com/groups/HarlequinConnection

HSOCIAL2020